RETURN TO MOURA

F

RETURN TO MOURA

VIRGINIA COFFMAN

G.K. Hall & Co. • **Chivers Press**
Thorndike, Maine USA   Bath, England

This Large Print edition is published by G.K. Hall & Co., USA and by Chivers Press, England.

Published in 2000 in the U.S. by arrangement with Chivers Press Limited.

Published in 2000 in the U.K. by arrangement with Severn House Ltd.

U.S. Hardcover 0-7838-8838-4 (Romance Series Edition)
U.K. Hardcover 0-7540-1384-7 (Windsor Large Print)

The text of this Large Print edition is unabridged.
Other aspects of the book may vary from the original edition.

Set in 16 pt. Plantin by Minnie B. Raven.

Printed in the United States on permanent paper.

British Library Cataloguing-in-Publication Data available

Library of Congress Cataloging-in-Publication Data

Coffman, Virginia.
   Return to Moura / Virginia Coffman.
     p. cm.
   ISBN 0-7838-8838-4 (lg. print : hc : alk. paper)
   1. Large type books. I. Title.
PS3553.O415 R48 2000
  813′.54—dc21
                                                      99-048478

RETURN TO MOURA

I

For me, the fear began on one of those nights some years ago, in the late 1820s, with the rain pelting across the narrow, cobbled London streets, and sodden tendrils of ivy outside my window twisted in a thousand eery shapes, while each splashing raindrop was a footstep creeping nearer.

It seemed no different from any other stormy night, except in one particular: those phantom footsteps did not dissolve into commonplace sounds at my door, but brought into my life such sensations as even in my hectic twenty-four years I had not yet dreamed of; and their penultimate gift was to be stark, anguished terror.

The footsteps led me far afield, but always and inevitably back to the desolate, unhallowed corner of a village churchyard, which was the burial place of the one they called "The Devil-Vicar." In the end, when I came again to that churchyard I had so often contemplated, at first with curiosity and finally with torture, I understood why the villagers were awed by the long twilight common to the north country.

For it was in these hours of the great undark that they saw the Devil-Vicar. But on the rainy November night when one life quietly ended for me and another began, my knowledge of devils and phantasms was confined to the book I read.

It was past ten o'clock and I was busy at my recently inherited home on Berkeley Square, copying the more illegible pages of a manuscript for the publishing firm of Sackerby, Perth, Ltd. Old Mr. Osmund Perth desired to read the manuscript at his breakfast table on the morrow. He had arrived nearly at dusk, which may have persuaded him that an apology for such haste was in order.

"It's extraordinary to me, Miss Wicklow, as I have heard your late benefactors — Mr. and Mrs. Varney — often say, how a person may have the talent to put one word before the other, and yet write like a heathen in the jungle scratching on a drumhead. However, make of it the best you can, and try not to let its contents alarm you into fancying ghosts in the night; for it is all fustian, you know."

His wrinkled, pink, babyish countenance relaxed into its more congenial shape, and his mouth took an upward curve. His elbow jogged my ribs with that irritating familiarity that "old friends of the family" so often seem to adopt with young women. "North country clods, you know, sometimes produce prodigies, for all their talk of ghosts and goblins. One of these days we hope to strike fire with another *Frankenstein*. Excellent story if you like hobgoblins, by that wild-eyed Shelley's wife. Not published by us, worst luck. . . . So, do your best, m'dear. Pity you must. A young miss barely twenty —"

"Twenty-four," I said.

"Yes. Just so. Barely twenty-four, as I say, should have better things to do at night than to ruin those lovely eyes over copywork. But these are hard times, Miss Anne."

Doubtless he made that last remark, as though it were being observed for the first time, to dampen any hope I should have for ha-pense more the page.

My pecuniary difficulties having accumulated in part because Sackerby, Perth paid my benefactor more in praise than coin for his monumental histories — *An Emigré Views the Career of Napoleon* and *Recollections of a Child of the Ancien Regime* — I felt that no comment on "hard times" was necessary. Little did Mr. Perth suspect, however, that I intended to broach the subject tomorrow when I returned the manuscript.

Poor Mr. Varney was a frightfully incompetent man of business. That had been one of his boasts, an extraordinary quality in a Frenchman, but fortunately, I showed his sharp-eyed wife's instinct for an honest sou. I was determined never, never to sing again to the genteel poverty of the bookish man who saw his wife and copyist support him during the major part of his life.

At the end of Mr. Perth's visit, I showed him out into the street where puddles of rain between the cobbles already reflected the stormy evening sky, then hurried to my work in the little corner room on the ground floor of the house which had been my mother's dowry.

I would have preferred to work upstairs on the

9

first floor, which I let to a colonel's widow, for the noise of criers and sellers by day, and coach wheels almost at our doorstep in early evening, was disturbing enough; but on such nights as this in early November, when the first storms of winter swept through our little square, I did not like the irritating and inexplicable noises I was apt to hear at my window, which opened directly upon the street. I was not precisely frightened, but I did feel a distinct distress.

Once in a while I even fancied that such scratchings might be my mother or my father calling me. It was absurd, but it was all part of living alone after many years of happiness with first two and then one person, whom I adored.

On that November night I hurried through the manuscript Mr. Perth had left with me, paying little heed to the sense of it and skipping the more legible pages, so that I might concentrate upon the production of a neat, flowing hand for which I was being paid. I was more in haste than usual. I had another manuscript that I had promised to have ready for a rival publishing house within a day or two, and this manuscript was even more impossible to read. I glanced at it now and then as it lay on my desk with its wrappings half off, where I had left it when interrupted by my portly friend, Mr. Perth. Well, it would have to wait.

It was not until all identifiable human noise in the square ceased that I noted, as on other stormy nights, the dozen peculiar sounds now vying for my attention. The ancient ivy that curled upward around and above my window was certainly responsible for the curious flutterings against the shutters. And the stealthy footsteps approaching that same window were nothing more than the untidy spatter of rain. But why should I hear those odd little stirrings in the dark passage beyond my study door? The street door was bolted, and Mrs. Colonel Fothergay was long since tucked into the great canopied bed that had been my father's. Our little cleaning maid went home to Cheapside before dark, and my tenant on the second floor, an actress of some distinction, was at present touring on the American continent.

I returned to my copywork, only to find this edifying paragraph in the manuscript:

The furtive rustlings of unsuspected life on the moors during the long un-dark can take on monstrous importance when one lives alone among these becks and dells.

The twisted and mangled body of the unhappy Mr. Abernethy had been found in just such a haunted place, and the inhabitants of the scattered moorland villages were appalled by the savagery. . . .

That was enough of that.

I stopped reading, looked up and listened again. Really, one would think I was up in darkest Yorkshire, alone in some haunted dell with "the unhappy Mr. Abernethy." The sounds in the house had definitely increased. Even the staircase outside my study door squeaked monotonously, as though one of my lodgers were tiptoeing up to the first floor.

Absurd. I was being influenced by this ridiculous story. To take my mind off it for the moment I carefully rewrapped the manuscript I was to work on tomorrow. But I could not forever put aside *The Corpses on the Moor*. They must be piled up in neat and bloodless order on Mr. Perth's desk by tomorrow morning.

I riffled the pages of the manuscript, discovered that "Mr. Abernethy" had been selected by the author as the first in what promised to be a gory series of victims of some monster called a "Gytrash," who preyed on the moorland people.

Thinking of the author, I began to consider the handwriting. It was curious — entirely written in a backhand slant so that one could not guess the sex of the writer, or indeed, any especial character. I searched in my throw-away sewing basket for the cover and read the superscription to Sackerby, Perth on a heavy type of wrapping paper upon which a shopkeeper had figured, in heavy charcoal, certain items down to the last shilling and ha-penny. The author had tried to scratch this out, but I thought I could make out on the list a man's starched white cravat and then — to throw me off the scent — a lady's bonnet. The sender's name appeared as secretive as the handwriting, for the return address was "Care of the Postmistress, Upshed, West Riding, Yorks."

Yet I could see upon close examination the almost obliterated name of the shopkeeper, no doubt: "H. Peysworth, Maidenmoor, Teignford, Yorks."

I wondered why the author had shopped in Maidenmoor, yet chose the postmistress of Upshed to receive his or her mail. I knew I was reaching for a mystery where none existed. But at least it had taken my mind off the cracks and creaks and prowlings outside my study door. I bent over my work again.

The storm beating through the square rushed to a crescendo, as though jealous of my inattention. The front door shook and rattled in an angry grip. I paid it no heed.

Because the idiotic plot, full of sound and fury, signified nothing, I found it a growing source of amusement, especially the Gytrash, which, as nearly as I could gather, was a huge ghostly animal with a human intellect. Was it possible that such an unlikely — no — impossible tale, could be printed and bound and actually bought by gullible readers? I'd dare swear there wasn't a Gytrash in the whole of England, with Scotland thrown in, and as for dozens of strong, sturdy Yorkshiremen being obliterated by this fantasy with its gleaming red eyes and teeth long as a young elephant's tusks . . . well, what was the reading public coming to?

Curiously enough, for all my mental reservations, I could not stop reading the abominable thing.

I had just reached the page upon which the monstrous Gytrash leaps to devour the helpless heroine when the storm set up such a clatter at the front door that I dropped the book and lost my place in the carefully laced manuscript.

Taking up the lamp, I decided that I had had enough. Whether it was the storm making such havoc or not, I would have to satisfy myself on the matter. I did not like the notion; for I was not the bravest woman in the world. But when even my study door shook, and I began to imagine all sorts of hobgoblins in the dark little reception hall beyond, there was but one thing to do, and I did it, if reluctantly.

I threw open the study door, found nothing in front of me except the newel post of the staircase leading to Mrs. Fothergay's apartments, and, of course, the long mirror at which every woman, even our cleaning maid, must smooth her hair before opening the front door. I glanced at the front door which still shook under the gusts of wind, but, perhaps it was my imagination, it did not seem as noisy as it had sounded from my study. Beside the door was a long narrow strip of carefully bevelled glass which had been my mother's pride and joy; for by this, she and the maid could see who our callers might be, and thus avoid tradesmen and revenue collectors.

Outside that strip of glass which was the length of a man, I could see the rain beating slantwise across the square, causing the little trees in the center of the square to commit all sorts of acrobatics in their effort to escape the pressure. From the corner of my eye I saw my lamp catch its reflection in the mirror on the wall facing the front door, and although I had just looked at the mirror a moment before and knew perfectly well it was there, the sudden glowing image surprised me. I turned my back to the door and glanced at my reflection and that of the lamp in the mirror.

I was more startled the next second; for what looked back at me was not only my own face and the lamp, but one like a shadowy image of my face, seen through a watery, uneven surface, behind me. My heart thundering in my bosom, I turned and stared at the door and at the long glass beside it.

Something was peering in at me through the bevel-glass, in the midst of all that rain and wind outside. The night was so black and gloomy I could make out nothing but the muffled figure, a little taller than I, and the dark eyes, the windblown black hair and upper face which closely resembled one I had seen before, but I could not place it.

I gave a yelp that sounded in my own ears like a dog whose tail had been trod upon, and stood there shaking while I tried to think what to do. I knew there was no help from Mrs. Fothergay upstairs; for she would only fuss and produce more confusion, interspersed with shrill demands that

I send someone to fetch the police — At Once! Since there was no one but myself to send, I should get nowhere there.

The face was close to the glass, the eyes peering in. Then a hand came up and gestured at me, and to the door. The rain slackened a little, and in that short time I saw the creature was a man, quite young, shrouded in one of those heavy traveling cloaks that we see occasionally in London, and which mark the wearer as what Mr. Perth would call "a wealthy clod from up Yorkshire and the North" . . . where the climate was reputedly fearsome.

Whether this insolent creature peering in at me was from the North I did not know, but I doubted very much if his own wretched climate was much worse than we offered him tonight. Seeing that the man was human and apparently absurd enough to want me to open the door to him at this hour, I shook my head and in the lamplight made gestures for him to go away.

He must have guessed my panic for after a moment or two I saw him smile, not an unhandsome smile, but the sight of those white teeth flashing out of the stormy night put me in mind of my friend the Gytrash, and I waved him away indignantly. He threw both hands up in the air, shrugged, and gave up.

I was very much relieved when I saw nothing but the stormy out-of-doors through the long glass.

After I had given him time to be gone, I set

down the lamp on the newel post and very quietly went to the door. I listened. Not a sound. Breathing quickly, I shot back the bolt and opened the door just an inch or two, to see where he had gone.

A pair of cold, wet fingers closed around the door. I had not opened the door far enough to see the face of the creature out there, and now I slammed the door so fast it caught those two fingers and just missed crushing them completely, before they were snatched away. I heard a masculine voice swear very humanly, and then the wind and rain washed away whatever other sounds were uttered. I leaned against the bolted door and shook at my narrow escape.

Meanwhile, my scream when I caught sight of those pale fingers had roused my lodger. Mrs. Fothergay came shuffling along to the top of the stairs and looked down at me over the stair-rail. She was a sight to conquer all my fears; for nothing more ridiculous could be imagined. Greying tufts of her blonde hair were squeezed into strange little papers of assorted colors, obviously having been crimped hours before. Her stout, flabby figure was wrapped in a blanket that must have come off the bed when she did. Her face, mottled by the hot suns of the India Service, was as fiery as a sunset.

"Good heavens, child! What is it? What is happening?"

I took a deep breath, recovered myself.

"It was nothing, Mrs. Fothergay. Some fellow

hanging about, peering in at windows. I think he was trying to find a way to break it. I can't imagine what we have that he wanted. But I got the door bolted in time."

"Are you going to fetch the police?"

I wanted to reply that she might go out in that dark and stormy night if she chose, but as for me, I should certainly wait until morning to inform them.

However, I managed to quiet her down, and we said good night as Mrs. Fothergay went back to bed, making sounds like "tsk-tsk" all the time. Her last words to me were, "I shall certainly lock my door, Miss Wicklow. Had I known that this neighborhood would come to have house-breakers and thieves prowling about, I should never have moved here. Who knows? One of the creatures might peer in at *me*. I always seem to attract so many ineligible, though I will say at-tractive, young men. Ah, well. . . ."

I made a face at her retreating back and took my lamp into the study. However, it soon oc-curred to me that I was at the mercy of any housebreaker who felt up to breaking in a window and some ancient shutters so, after one or two more attempts to work on *The Corpses on the Moor*, I gave up and went to bed.

It is not surprising that I dreamed all night of pursuit by a gigantic Gytrash with the head of a man — a young man with burning dark eyes and slim, cold fingers that gleamed with a ghostly light. I could have uttered a few curses myself, at

18

Mr. Perth, for handing me such nonsense to dwell upon on a stormy night.

It was odd, though, about the housebreaker. I could not recall where we had ever been troubled in such a way before. And then too, the cloak he wore, which, for some reason — doubtless the manuscript — made me suspect the housebreaker was from the north, from the country of my Gytrash friend.

II

By well timed good fortune, for myself, not for Osmund Perth, the publisher was unable to reach his offices the next morning, having been confined to his lodgings with a bad case of the gout. When the boy who ran errands for the publishing house arrived for the Yorkshire manuscript, I was still unfinished, and sent him off with some excuse while I worked on the Gytrash, his victims, and the fiendish human monster back of the whole business. To my surprise, the human monster turned out to be a nice and a rather charming way of playing down the heroine at moments when she became too bumptious. It appeared that when the moon was high the flippant young man turned into a Gytrash, reverting to his charming self upon satisfying his desire to kill. Somewhat disappointed at this preposterous solution, I finished the manuscript of *The Corpses on the Moor*, surprised at how ineffectual it seemed by daylight, with the storm gone and a watery sunlight trickling into the study.

Seeing me at work, Mrs. Fothergay stuck her head in to inquire whether I was going to speak to the police about these prowlers who swarmed all over the place to get a look at her at night.

"For if you won't go, I shall, my dear. I'm sure it isn't anything I do, but somehow I have the most irresistable attraction for young men. In Calcutta they were forever peeping, watching me with those big grins on their faces. Hoping to catch me in my boudoir, I daresay."

"I daresay," I said drily, but could not put off the matter any longer. On the little tabouret beside my easy chair I laid the wrapped manuscript on Red Indians that I had put aside when I took the assignment for Mr. Perth and his Gytrash. I would begin to read it when I returned home, although I did not expect it to be so diverting as the Gytrash tale. I fetched my street cloak and bonnet and went off to inquire just where the Metropolitan police were stationed.

Before doing so, I paid a few visits to shops, examined carpeting for the upstairs corridor, belatedly delivered *The Corpses on the Moor* to the offices of Sackerby, Perth in Cornhill, and returned home just on tea time, in the company of the gigantic, mutton-chop whiskered gentleman from the Metropolitan Police. He wore no uniform and was dressed like a newly-prosperous greengrocer in garments a shade too snug for

20

him, which made him look even bigger. In size, at least, I thought him a much more terrifying proposition than my intruder of the night before, but perhaps that was all to the good.

In the reception hall I pointed out to Constable Whacker just where the housebreaker had peered in, and where he had seized the door with two fingers. He examined the premises closely. I wondered what conclusions he could come to with so little to go on, but he seemed satisfied with himself, muttering several times as he pulled on tufts of his whiskers.

"Hmmmm. . . . Just so. just as I thought. . . . just . . . so."

Good. Then he recognized the technique. Doubtless, he knew the housebreaker.

"You have come to some conclusion?" I asked, puzzled at his assurance.

"No doubt. No doubt of it at all, little lady. Fellow wanted to get in. Plain as a pikestaff."

While I was trying to frame a polite answer to this astounding observation, we were both startled by the trill of Mrs. Fothergay's gurgling laughter. It came from my study, of all places, and the door was closed.

"My dear Mr. Branshaw —" my lodger was saying to someone within. A little pause and then the coy return, "— well . . . *Marc,* if you insist . . . you do flatter me. Just a teensy bit."

"Relation of yours, mum?" asked the constable.

"No. My lodger. But I don't understand why

21

she should be entertaining in my study. She has a very fine, large study and a ballroom on her own floor."

I went to the study door and opened it. I was about to remove my mantle and bonnet but stopped abruptly, astonished to see Mrs. Fothergay seated at my desk, one pudgy hand with its many rings only just escaping my inkstand and pen. She had flung her other arm over the back of my chair in a stiff, unwieldy pose that only an idiot would have assumed, in normal concorse.

But all was explained by the sight of her companion. Mrs. Fothergay was being sketched. The man she addressed as Marc Branshaw, astride a pantry work stool across the room, was the artist, and as soon as I saw what his profession must be, I realized that I recognized the name as distinguished in the field of portraiture. His back was to the room, and I could see only a slight man, rather disreputably dressed in shirt and trousers. A frock coat which I took to be his was thrown over the little tabouret beside my easy chair. His shirt sleeves were pushed up to his elbows, the collar of his shirt turned up at the nape of his neck until it met his black hair, which he wore rather longer than the fashion dictated in London. He was a provincial then. But I was sure I would know the lecherous, dissipated face that I should see when he turned around. I had met artists before.

"Dear Miss Wicklow," my lodger gushed upon seeing me, "do forgive us. Marc — Mr.

Branshaw — insisted that he must 'do' me at a workaday desk. The contrast would be the better. With my hair and my manner, he insists I am too flamboyant in my own little world. Like a peacock, didn't you say, my dear Mar— Mr. Branshaw? My background must be subdued. Isn't that absurd?"

I would like to have agreed, but said instead that the picture would undoubtedly do her justice, and tried to get only the most complimentary meaning into the remark. Mrs. Fothergay accepted it as her due, and Constable Whacker was too busy studying the room to care, but the artist, who had stood up a moment before, raised his head suddenly and I caught a glimpse of dark eyes and black eyebrows that took a sardonic curve at my words. He understood my meaning, and although he refrained from smiling, there was a mischievous look on his face. He appeared younger than I supposed "dissipated artists" usually were, hardly older than myself, but from his free and easy attitude, I suspected he had seen a good deal more of the world than I.

"Good heavens, what am I thinking of? Miss Anne Wicklow, Mr. Marc Branshaw," said my lodger. "Such a delightful surprise! To have the great Marc Branshaw sketch one! Really more than one deserves."

My curiosity getting the better of me, I crossed the room and looked over the artist's shoulder at the sketch in his hands. It was cruelly overdone in every way, but there was skill in the caricature.

I had a suspicion Mrs. Fothergay would be pleased at this comedy fishwife decked out in great puffs of hair, with eyelashes patently exaggerated and mouth widly overripe; for he had managed to make her look twenty years younger with all the exaggerations.

"Don't you agree with me? Surely, Mrs. Fothergay deserves no less," said the artist in a low voice. This impertinent remark eluded the artist's subject and certainly did not interest the constable, who was staring at the beautiful white paneling of the walls as though he expected our housekeeper to crawl out of them.

"I'm sure it is worthy of you," I said, with an edge to the words, but his own quick grin was so infectious that I caught myself smiling back at him.

For the first time I looked at Marc Branshaw directly. I think it was the sight of his teeth, perfectly normal and white though they were, that gave me my first sensation of alarm.

I knew that smile. I had seen it last night through the bevel-glass as the dark-eyed prowler had peered in at me. How could I find out if it really was so? I glanced at his hands, thin, not very large, with prominent bones. I could not see whether the fingers had any bruises on them, at least not this far away; so I put on a fine show of enthusiasm and said loudly:

"But where are my manners, Mr. Branshaw? It is an honor to take the hand of so celebrated an artist."

I think I put him off guard, for he stared at me in surprise, but offered his hand as I curtseyed. He understood immediately after. Instead of putting my hand in his in the accepted fashion, I seized his and squeezed as hard as I could across his knuckles. He winced and there was a whiteness about his mouth. It must have been an effort to conceal the shock of pain. His hand jerked out of mine, and he gave me a swift, furious look. I was aware that in this second he could have struck me. He was the prowler, and no mistake.

"What a pity!" I said sweetly. "Have you hurt your hand?"

Before he could reply, I untied my bonnet strings and started to turn away from him. It was only a play for time, as I hoped that there would be some way to broach the matter to the constable without seeing him snatch up the young artist and put the handcuffs on him, or whatever one did with criminals, but I was startled by Mrs. Fothergay's shrill voice:

"Well, I never! The two of you have a certain resemblance. Fancy!" She tittered at her little joke. "Could you be brother and sister, by chance?"

I don't know whether Marc Branshaw was as amazed as I was. By the time I looked at him, having not a word to say for myself, he was already the practiced flirt again.

"I shouldn't like that at all," he said, with a meaning which even I, in my inexperience, could not mistake. I flushed a little, because it was going to be difficult to arrest someone who behaved so annoyingly well.

I said, "Nonsense. If Mr. Branshaw were my brother, I'd see that he was put to bed without his supper, for I imagine he needs a setdown."

"On the contrary, I would turn you over my knee for your sauciness, Miss Wicklow. Thanks for your permission, Bedelia. I think I shall make it my business."

Upon this embarrassing observation, I decided that Marc Branshaw might just as well be occupied with defending himself as poking fun at me.

"Constable," I said, "I don't think you have further to look for your housebreaker. Mr. Branshaw is the man I saw last night." And then, as everyone in the room, except Mr. Branshaw, tensed awaiting an explosion, I added pleasantly, "I'm sure he has some defense. It is possible I was mistaken about his . . . intentions."

Marc Branshaw put his hands on my shoulders and moved me aside, murmuring as he did so, "Thank you, little sister. That should help me." His irony did not escape me, but he seemed more amused than angry. I was only relieved that when he touched me he did not carry out his first threat.

He went across the room to the constable, but managed to rest his uninjured hand lightly on Mrs. Fothergay's frilled pink morning dress, just where the sleeves joined the shoulder. She purred under his touch and looked up winningly at the constable.

"I think — er . . . Constable . . . that Mr. Branshaw may have been paying a rather late call upon me, naughty boy! And Miss Wicklow did not perfectly understand his motives. Mr. Branshaw explained to me today that he had called once before to ask my permission to sketch me."

"At eleven o'clock at night?" I asked indignantly.

"I do my best work at night," explained the artist, looking as though he were silently laughing at me. I ignored him and demanded of the constable,

"Aren't you going to do anything?"

"Well, mum, it does seem like the gentleman ain't like to be the kind that breaks in of nights." He saw how well Mrs. Fothergay and the artist were getting on, and added, "Don't hardly seem like he needs to break in, excuse me for mentioning."

I waved my hands in exasperation and gave up.

"Very well then. If people can come round breaking in at all hours and be let off, then I've nothing more to say. Now, if you will all excuse me, I have work to do, and I would appreciate having my room back."

The constable tipped his hat, plunked it back on his head and after one more tug at his whiskers, departed, having proved to his own satisfaction that my house was just the sort of rendezvous for the disgusting goings-on between

Marc Branshaw and this woman old enough to be his mother.

By the time I had seen the constable out, Mr. Branshaw was approaching the door, with his coat thrown over his arm. I opened the door for him and just as I curtseyed with frigid politeness, he said, "You hurt me damnably last night, you know."

"Good," I said. "I'm glad to hear it. And it's not very nice of you to make that poor woman think you care for her, just to get into the house and steal the silver. Why, she might have been your mother!"

"Not mine. Mine was a dark-eyed pert baggage, very like you, my dear sister!" He reached for a lock of my hair and pulled it hard. I was aware suddenly of the coldness of his fingers as they brushed my cheek. What an extraordinary chill! I don't know what he would have done if I hadn't pushed him out the door and slammed it behind him. I looked out the bevel-glass to watch him cross the square with a jaunty, light stride. Although the weather was a bit nippy and storm clouds hovered on the horizon, he still hadn't put on his coat.

Mrs. Fothergay came up behind me, murmuring softly over her sketch.

"How charming of the dear boy! You see, he plainly thinks me younger than I actually . . . What a charmer! Don't you agree, Miss Wicklow?"

"No, I don't. He's a thief. He took manuscript paper from my desk for that sketch of you. I think he is a housebreaker, and I strongly suspect you will find your best silver plate missing tonight."

For some reason, my disapproval of the artist pleased Mrs. Fothergay and she smiled at some dream of her own. She was still standing there when I started to my study. I passed the hall mirror and saw my reflection. No wonder Marc Branshaw's face had looked familiar last night. It did resemble mine slightly, especially now, with my hair smoothed back from my ears. I did not know whether to be flattered or not, for he was much handsomer than I was. But it irritated me to be called his sister, and that was something I could not understand.

What I saw at once, or did not see in my study, was an absence so loud it fairly screamed at me.

The manuscript which I had laid aside in order to do Mr. Perth's story, and which I had re-wrapped last night, was missing from the tabouret. Since Marc Branshaw had laid his coat over it, I looked all around the room, thinking he might have put the manuscript somewhere else. It was nowhere to be seen.

I rushed into the hall to catch Mrs. Fothergay as she was going upstairs to her own lodgings.

"Did you see that artist fellow take a brown package when he left?"

"How should I know, dear? He had his coat over his arm. I didn't see what was in his hand."

"My manuscript!" I shouted. "I told you he was a thief. He's stolen my manuscript. What will I say to Hubbard and Wilson when they call for it?"

"Now, why should he do a thing like that? A gentleman of Mr. Branshaw's breeding! I don't believe you know his reputation, Miss Wicklow. When his paintings were first exhibited in Paris he was a sensation! My dear, the nudes he painted, the most exquisite tonal quality! Everyone in France knew of him. Three years ago they were even wearing Yorkshire cloaks and bonnets, and the ladies were painting their eyelids what they called "Noir de Marc" in imitation of his eyes. I never dreamed he would seek me out for a sketch."

"Yorkshire . . ." I repeated, thinking over the problem.

The manuscript he had stolen was about Red Indians in North America. Yet, the wrappings of the two manuscripts had been the same. Even the writing was similar to that on the Yorkshire manuscript of *The Corpses on the Moor*. Had he intended to take the Yorkshire manuscript? But why not ask me straight out? Of course, I would have refused. Was it possible he had actually come to my house to sketch Mrs. Fothergay and taken the manuscript as some joke of his own?

"Do you know Mr. Branshaw well?" I asked her.

She simpered. "Not as well as I should like to. Most mysterious young man. A mutual friend suggested he do a sketch of me but he won't tell me the name. I imagine it's someone I knew in Paris."

"Then you met this artist in Paris?"

"Oh, heavens, no. I've never seen him before. But he was arguing with that wretched little cleaning maid of yours — wanted to get in and wait for you; at least that's how your maid understood him. It turned out that he had no such intention. But you know how stupid the help is today. As soon as I saw him, I recognized him, of course. I had seen his miniature on one or two charming throats in Paris. In diamond frames, my dear, let me tell you. And I remember a rather large portrait of him done by the distinguished Vicomte de Gris and hung at one time, I believe, in the Louvre or some such place."

It was growing more ridiculous all the time. It was obvious to me now that Marc Branshaw had come here to get that manuscript and merely used Mrs. Fothergay's fawning attentions as a ruse. What a devil he was!

But what possible interest could he have in the Red Indians of North America?

No. He had mistaken the wrapping. He wanted *The Corpses on the Moor*. I wondered if he had written the novel and then changed his mind about its publication. Now that I thought of it, the charming young monster in the story was startlingly like him in appearance and manner. The idea was singular, even a little chilling. He had looked so very harmless. Except, I remembered suddenly, during one brief moment when he had given me that murderous glance.

III

The thought of reporting the loss of the stolen manuscript to Hubbard and Wilson severely tried my nerves. Aside from the unfortunate author, I could imagine what it would mean to my own good name, my credit as an honest copyist, and perhaps lawsuits which I should lose since I was clearly culpable.

Oh, that wretched, thieving artist!

Without even waiting for tea, I hurried out again, hired a horse and cab, with mental reservations to collect the fare from Master Branshaw, and had myself driven to Osmund Perth's lodgings to ask his advice. Much good it did me; for he was sleeping off the effects of laudanum taken to ease his discomfort, and his housekeeper refused me admission to him.

I called upon several of the leading hotels in the City and the Straund, but none of them had any record of a guest named Marc Branshaw. Perhaps he did not sleep of nights. Then it occurred to me that when he discovered his mistake, the artist would return the manuscript, hoping to substitute the right one.

I hurried home, barely got through a late bread-and-butter-and-tea, and waited the interminable evening through, but no artist appeared. When Mrs. Fothergay knocked on my study door with the intention of discussing her insufferable Marc Branshaw, I very nearly ran her out of the room and myself out of a paying lodger.

I slept ill again that night. I would have welcomed my thieving "brother" in any guise, even as a Gytrash. It was far better to be chewed by a monster than to lose one's credit.

Desperate now to forestall what I clearly saw as personal ruin, I dressed quickly the following morning and was about to visit the offices of Hubbard and Wilson to discover how soon the manuscript must be returned, when Sackerby, Perth's young errand boy came by and asked me to accompany him to Mr. Perth's house. It seemed the old gentleman wished to speak to me about a manuscript.

I devoutly hoped this would be the missing manuscript about the Red Indians. Rejoicing in this rescue of my credit, not to mention the poor author, I took a cab with the errand boy and was presently ushered into Mr. Perth's Green Room, which was in every respect a most descriptive term for that glassed-in chamber. It was a jungle of growth, pervaded by a strong smell of rich soil and what Mr. Perth often referred to as his "interesting" fertilizers. It always seemed to me that I also smelled the decaying leaves and some rather overpowering scents of flowers that would have better graced the ladies of Cheapside.

The Green Room was so full of potted plants and wild Sandwich Island growths that I nearly had to grope my way to Mr. Perth, who was seated with his leg propped up on a settee halfway down the long conservatory. Behind him was a huge green-leaved plant so tall that it bent over him in a way he doubtless found protective. I shouldn't have been surprised to find that it had tentacles as well. I stayed away from it.

"My dear Miss Anne, good of you to come. So obliging."

I got to the point at once.

"It's about a manuscript that was stolen from my home. Do you have it, sir? It is extremely important. I shall be in disgrace if it's lost."

Mr. Perth scratched at the bandages of his swollen leg thoughtfully.

"No, I'm afraid I cannot help you there. But something may be arranged. Perhaps compensation to the author. At any rate, to get to the point —"

"What?" I demanded, raising my hand quickly for emphasis and nearly knocking off my bonnet. "You mean you didn't call me here to talk about the stolen manuscript! Then I'm afraid I cannot stay. That — that horrid man whose manuscript you sent me about Yorkshire is the man who —"

He coughed, cleared his throat and generally behaved most unlike his suave self, even putting one hand out to stop me.

"Please, my dear — may I —"

"He is a thief. You apparently deal in thieves,

34

Mr. Perth. And I strongly suggest you take action. As detestable and sly a creature as I have ever —"

"I couldn't agree with you more. A detestable creature!" said a voice behind that accursed potted palm, and out came the Detestable Creature himself, as jaunty as though he had just been picking roses, which, as a matter of fact, he had. He offered me the thorny, heavy-headed flowers and when I refused them indignantly, he agreed.

"Quite right, dear sister. White roses are not for you. Only small roses the color of a deep blush will do you justice. I shall remember that."

"Pray do not trouble. Where is my manuscript?"

"Oh, that. I sent it up to my home by the post. How fortunate!" He turned to Mr. Perth, who agreed sagely.

"Most fortunate. Most opportune."

"I don't see how. I must have that manuscript back immediately." Nevertheless, it was difficult to remain angry, for the artist did look silly, standing there with those roses drooping over his fingers, and trying his best to soothe my ruffled feathers.

"Just so. And you shall have it. You have but to accept my offer."

"We are to bargain for it now? What is the ransom he demands, sir? I told you he was a pirate, Mr. Perth."

"Oh, tut-tut," said Mr. Perth, his pink jowls

joggling as he chided me. "Mr. Branshaw wishes to revise certain chapters of the manuscript that has been submitted to us. It was originally written by a friend of his. It seems that in his small village there is no one familiar enough with the script to copy as he makes the oral changes, and he suggested that since I could vouch for your good character, you might be the very person."

"Vouch for my good character!"

"But of course," Mr. Branshaw agreed with the smuggest hypocrisy. "I cannot afford to introduce any but persons of the highest character to the people of my village. You will appreciate my delicacy."

"I trust the members of your village have more character than you have!"

He smiled. "On the contrary," he said, looking directly at me with those black eyes as though we were alone in some secluded place. But his words, the last I expected in the circumstances, were puzzling.

"He often speaks like this, my dear," Mr. Perth said hastily. "It is merely his habit. Mr. Branshaw is a man of sterling reputation, above reproach. And he has offered you twenty pounds for the task before you. I explained to him the situation in which your dear friends left you. Such a fine man, but improvident."

"We will leave my friends out of this."

"I think we are going rather far afield," Marc Branshaw put in. "Possibly you had better ex-

36

plain to Miss Wicklow that I didn't regard my taking of the manuscript as a theft, since it belonged to someone in my — acquaintance. I had no idea, at first, that I had actually sent home another person's manuscript."

I was too confused to ask how he discovered it was the wrong manuscript if he had already sent it home, or any of the dozen questions I thought about much later in the day.

"Mr. Branshaw even mentioned a desire to sketch you. A compliment, my dear."

Mr. Perth gave us both a paternal smile and pointed to a large, unframed oil painting which rested temporarily against the further wall.

"The crowning touch to my collection. Mr. Branshaw has been kind enough to sell it to me, and at a very moderate price, I assure you. Just look at those tonal colors." He glanced over his shoulder at the painting, then abruptly changed his mind. "No. I never thought! I believe, Miss Anne, it is not the sort of painting that should be graced by a maiden's eyes."

This, naturally, made me all the more curious to see it. I took a few steps toward the painting while Marc Branshaw, with a mischievous look, obligingly stood aside.

The background of the picture was a glade of gigantic greenery, and very much in the foreground, coyly rising from a huge clam shell, was a young woman. A trifle overfed, I thought, but obviously and inexorably nude.

Although I daresay I was the color of a fresh-boiled lobster, I remarked as coolly as I might, "You say, Mr. Perth, that I may be invited to pose for the gentleman? One never knows when one will receive so pretty a compliment. And this early in the morning, too."

The artist laughed aloud, but Mr. Perth was embarrassed and made a somewhat confused statement that there had been no intention of sketching me in anything but my street garments, or any other way I chose.

"However," put in the artist, "you may, of course, pose as Venus if you insist. I have no unalterable objection."

I should have slapped his face, but I said instead, "You will kindly send back my manuscript as soon as you reach your home. I say nothing of the cab fare and other expenses you have put me to. Good day, gentlemen."

Mr. Perth called to me but I ignored him. I half expected the artist to run after me to make his peace but the disgusting creature made no move whatever, except to call after me, "I'll wager I see you in Yorkshire, all the same."

Barely missing a prickly desert plant and one or two African thickets, I left the Green Room in a huff.

The most important matter now was to find out how long I had before Hubbard and Wilson expected the return of their manuscript. I went directly to their offices and received encouraging news. Both gentlemen were away from London,

Mr. Hubbard visiting his wife's relations in Cornwall and Mr. Wilson taking the waters at Vevey on the Continent. They were not expected back until a fortnight before the Christmas holiday. This gave me more than a month in which to see that Marc Branshaw returned the manuscript, and if he did not I should certainly set the constables on him. In fact, if I had been acquainted with any local Gytrash, I would have set that useful animal to work as well.

Trusting souls that they were, Hubbard and Wilson's company had sent over another manuscript in my absence, and I kept a close watch on this one, all the while that I prepared my lunch.

I turned back to the pantry only for a moment, to fetch the vinegar cruet, yet when I returned to my tray in the parlor, this manuscript too had been moved mysteriously from the loveseat. I was ready to scream when Mrs. Fothergay interceded.

"Your manuscript, my dear. Here it is, safe and sound. And you were such a naughty girl to accuse Mr. Branshaw, when you had it in your parlor all the time."

"I did not do your dear Mr. Branshaw an injustice, I assure you. This is another manuscript."

"Oh. Well. . . . However! Come, Miss Anne, do sit here and I'll sit on this side. So comfy. I have something of excruciating importance to tell you."

She was suffing and puffing pretty badly, from

which I took it that she was wearing her best cor-
sets. She always bought them a size too small; so
in charity I could hardly refuse to let her sit
down. But I never had liked the loveseat, partly
because it was the favorite seat of Mr. Sackerby's
overgrown son when he came to call, and he
began each of his proposals of marriage by archly
calling my attention to his choice of the loveseat.

"Now, dear Anne . . . I may call you Anne,
since we shall presently be seeing a good deal
more of each other —"

I wondered what this betokened.

"Yes, you must look upon me as your moth—
your elder sister; for you simply must accompany
me. All is lost if you do not."

"What on earth can you mean, ma'am? Where
are you going?"

Could it be possible she was inviting me to accompany her to Paris? What a dream! My dream
home. The city of the Varney family. I must be
very kind and polite to Mrs. Fothergay. I could
not afford to lose such a chance.

"I cannot tell you of my delight," she went on,
"I don't believe I have ever been so flattered. In
short, about half an hour ago I had a caller. You
will never guess."

I did not try.

"Yes. just as you surmise. Dear Marc came
calling. He wants me to come to Yorkshire for a
visit. He has decided he must do me in oils."

I was speechless.

Mrs. Fothergay giggled. "That surprises you,

doesn't it? To think I should consent when he has done so many of those — well, there is no other word for it — nudes, you know. In deference to my position, however, he wishes me to pose in a boudoir gown. Quite proper, my dear; for we shall have a chaperone."

"Not —"

"Exactly so. Yourself. Oh yes. Marc thinks of everything, the dear. He tells me that he cannot risk any scandal attached to my name. I must bring a chaperone. Isn't that touching, from such a sophisticated young man?"

"Touching is not the word for it."

"No, of course not. But then, there really is no word for his kindness to me, and his admiration; for I am just a teensy bit older than he, you know. However —" She shrugged her thick shoulders. "It was always so. Something about me appeals to young men, ever since the Colonel died. I am always being told I am too feminine to have all the worries of the Colonel's estate. Charming thought. You will come with me, there's a dear."

"I couldn't possibly. I have too much work to do. I am a business woman, you know, ma'am. I must keep busy."

"How stupid of me! I neglected to tell you the best part. He is so anxious for me to arrive safely that he offers you twenty pounds for the journey. He says you may be handy also to copy some manuscript or other. Now, that takes care of your little scruple about money."

That dastardly villain, Marc Branshaw! Get-

41

ting around me in this underhanded manner. I did wonder what on earth he wanted of me up in his Godforsaken country. I was not quite so beglamored by my own charm as Mrs. Fothergay by hers, and seriously doubted if he went to this trouble to get me up there just to seduce me, or even to paint me in the nude. What then was his purpose?

"I'm sorry. I can't leave London at this time. I'm sure there will be no problem. After all, you are a grown woman, a widow. You may surely conduct yourself as you like without duennas and chaperones. He's only teasing you. He cannot possibly need me."

"So I told him," she admitted ingenuously, "but he would not have it so. For my own reputation, I absolutely must bring you. I imagine, though he did not say so, that it may have something to do with the murder. Perhaps he fears something may happen to me."

"How exciting! I always suspected that fellow was up to no good. Whom has he murdered?"

Mrs. Fothergay wanted to evade the subject, but seeing that she had interested me, she finally got up from the loveseat, brushed out the feathered wrapper she had apparently been wearing when she entertained Marc Branshaw, and went to fetch one of the papers to which she subscribed. She returned with the newspaper and also a wide vase of white cabbage roses that looked a trifle blowsy and exceedingly familiar.

"From Marc. Wasn't that dear of him? A bit

wilted, perhaps, but he said he picked them just for me, because I reminded him of white roses."

I became suddenly very busy and did not look at the flowers. After all, they were technically mine. What right had he to give them to her?

The murder Mrs. Fothergay had spoken of was in the oversheet of the *Yorkshire Post*, dated several days ago. She read the date, fumbled through some engrossing advertisements on cures for sheep disease, restoratives to manhood, and applications for posts as governess by needy young women.

"Ah, here it is:

"MONSTER ANIMAL SLAYS SHEEPMAN.
"William Grimlett, a sheep farmer resident on Maidenmoor heath, in the West Riding, was savaged to death Saturday evening last while combing the moors for stray sheep. It is believed that the brutal and bloody attack which tore out the unfortunate man's throat and worried his features until they were virtually unrecognizable, was made by some savage animal of the cat or lion breed, perhaps escaped from a carnival or a wandering gypsy caravan.

"Upon the same night that sounded the death knell for Grimlett, a child, wandering the moor in pursuit of his pet sheep, was frightened by a savage animal which leaped into a tuft of heather at sight of the child, but which the young witness later described as

43

being much too large for a dog, and of a dun color popularly associated with the leonine family. 'He had fur,' said the lad. 'Like ye sees at the fair down to Bradford. Happen he was a lion-like.' "

I snatched the paper from Mrs. Fothergay, who went rattling on happily.

"My dear, it's simple. Marc wishes me to have an escort because he's afraid for my safety. Since that farmer was murdered just outside Marc's own village, Marc feels, and rightly, that I should be protected."

The newspaper was dated exactly a week ago. A horrifying idea occurred to me. If the manuscript about the silly Gytrash had been written after the death of the farmer Grimlett, then the explanation was simple, a mere re-telling of the unfortunate man's death, with dramatic license. But the novel was written before the man's death, and described several murders just in the manner of Grimlett's death. Was it possible that the animal which killed the farmer was known to the author of *The Corpses on the Moor*? Small wonder Marc Branshaw had gone to such lengths to get the manuscript back.

Possibly the novel was a coincidence, an accidental foreshadowing of the real crime. Was it a foreshadowing also of the real animal that had committed the murder? Too much coincidence. In any case, this horror was no inducement to me to visit Yorkshire and a man who knew about

44

savage killings before they occurred.

"I'm sorry, Mrs. Fothergay, but I don't think Maidenmoor is a place for either of us to visit at this time."

"I see." Mrs. Fothergay took back her paper, folded it several times, as though pleating a skirt, and then stood up ponderously. "In that case, my dear Anne, I think you had better advertise for a new lodger."

Mrs. Fothergay was not the only one who "saw." I had planned to buy carpeting with the next quarter's rental. I wanted to repair the shutters, and get twenty yards of a bewitching striped *barège* which would give me nineteen yards for one of the new full skirts that flared out with style.

"Perhaps you are right," I gave in ungracefully. "I will leave the arrangements to you, ma'am."

She brightened at once. "I knew you were a sensible girl. We will stay at the inn in the village, of course. Mr. Branshaw will meet us at the Teignford rail stop and take us on to Maidenmoor." She went on making all sorts of plans about schedules, prices, wondering about the virtues of the new fast schedule mail coach versus the old and infrequent stagecoach route, and finally came to what she considered the most important instruction.

"You will call me Bedelia, my dear, and I shall call you Anne. That will make us truly sisters." She went off, happily carrying her vase full of my roses.

I stared after her. She had not evinced one flicker of fear or nervousness about the doings on those mysterious, impenetrable moors which, as I understood from the manuscript, completely engulfed the little village.

But then, I knew something of which she had no knowledge. Somewhere in that village, and undoubtedly known to our host, was a man or a woman who, weeks before it happened, knew that a savage animal was going to kill a man, and in just such a manner, almost at the very spot pointed out in the manuscript.

I was selfish enough to turn to a question even closer to me. It was obvious that this whole stratagem of "Painting Mrs. Fothergay" was an effort to get me up to Yorkshire. What did I have to offer Maidenmoor and Mr. Branshaw that required such elaborate staging to get me there?

IV

I was alone, as solitary as a wanderer on the face of the moon, and the realization was unnerving.

I stood on the hilltop, catching my breath, and stared at a vast green world all around me, in which I could not make out one sign of human habitation. Yet there was a curious life of sorts in this emptiness of the rock-studded moors; for the thick, deep green turf, wet with late rains, seemed to throb somnolently, like a great serpent curled around me in many humps and twists, waiting . . . faintly breathing, but not yet aroused. The moors were not flat and brown as I had thought, but endless, bleak rolling hills separated by tangled folds of still deeper green that carried pretty little becks whose trickle of water, hardly wider than a human finger, made their crisscross way over and under the back of that great green monster.

It was my fault that I was alone. I had come this far along the road from Teignford toward the isolated village of Maidenmoor entirely on my own initiative, paying no heed to the innkeeper in the town who tried to dissuade me.

An hour before, it had been just as I might have predicted. Mrs. Fothergay and I arrived on the Leeds and Bradford stage from London only to find that our host, Mr. Branshaw, was nowhere in sight, had not been expected, and undoubtedly had forgotten all about us — or else was playing this trick for some humorous reason of his own. Worse than all, every bedchamber in the Teignford Inn and the other two hotels was let to visitors for the Woolens Market Day.

It was past sunset and we could not wait here indefinitely. I inquired of the innkeeper the distance to the village of Maidenmoor.

Like one or two other Yorkshiremen we had encountered on the mail coach, he had an over-the-border burr in his speech that did not make his broad Yorkshire accent any clearer.

"Ay, mum, a wee step, but up a stout hill or two, then down in the bottoms, crossing a beck

47

here and there, and nothing around ye but the moors. Then up another hill, and ye be there. Bide the night, mum, and happen y'll find some'ut here with the gig or yet a nag."

As the innkeeper could make no adequate provision for sleeping quarters during the night, it seemed to me that his advice was not very sound.

"Is it safe to walk to Maidenmoor at this hour? Is it often done?"

He looked surprised.

"Ay, mum. Done it myself times out of mind. But then, I'm born to it. The moors is no surprise to me. It's different-like with an outcomer."

Rightfully applying the "outcomer" to myself, I asked, "Why?"

I didn't really want to go. In the first place, I am not an inveterate walker and in the second place, the world outside the inn had began to look passing dour, as did the whole town. A glorious sunset, feathered with many hues of orange, red and pink, as seen through the pall of smoke from the Teignford Woolen Mills, was now gone and we were apparently in for the long, gloomy dusk of the North Country, that time of night referred to in the manuscript of the *Corpses on the Moor* as the un-dark. To compound the unpleasantness, there was rain in the air. Even within doors, before the cosy comfort of an open fire, I could smell the acrid, wet odor of the great unconquered heaths that surrounded these Yorkshire towns, often encroaching on the villages themselves. But I was determined not to satisfy the detestable Marc Branshaw by sleeping on a hard, cushionless settle in the Public Room, or some other grisly method devised by our goodnatured host. Besides, he would be sure to charge us dearly for any little "comforts" of this sort that he added to our reckoning.

No, indeed. Master Branshaw had promised me twenty pounds for this journey, and to provide shelter at the Maidenmoor Inn which was, if the innkeeper told the truth, "only a wee step." I was determined that the artist should be made to pay. I could see him now, smirking at our discomfort, never dreaming we would have courage enough to come after him and face him in his lair.

Mrs. Fothergay fanned herself with her handkerchief, and occasionally stopped to rub her poor swollen toes, which were encased in town boots much too narrow for the short, squat shape of her feet.

"Dear Anne, what can be keeping him? Frankly, I don't understand this at all. Could he be ill? I do believe that must be the case."

"Oh, nonsense," I said. "He is about as ill as — as our host here."

Our host looked from one to the other of us. He was an enormous man, like most of the men I had seen in this part of the country, except Mrs. Fothergay's Gay Romantic, Marc Branshaw, and the host's leathery countenance with its high, red cheeks and twinkling little blue eyes, looked eternal as the moors.

"Best be making yourselves do here, such as can be. It's no time for a lady like yourself on the moors. Now, mum, what'll be for supper? Boiled mutton and turnips. Ay. We'll fix ye all right and tight. See if we don't. Bessie!"

Whoever Bessie was, all this sounded expensive. He had obviously seen us coming and took us for green ones.

"Never you mind that," I said. "Just set me on the road to Maidenmoor and I'll fetch Master Branshaw or know the reason why."

A little thread of a frown crossed our host's leathery brow.

"Now, mum," he began soothingly, like a great mastiff licking one's face. " 'Tis a long way for such a little lady. Ay, and dark afore the hour's gone."

I looked out through the one open shutter.

"It won't be dark for two hours yet. I know a little something about this country." I didn't tell him that I had garnered my information from sundry books.

"Well then —" he shrugged and gave me up.

"Really, dear, are you sure you're doing the right thing?" Mrs. Fothergay asked me. I wondered if she was concerned with my welfare — an unusual quality in her. She soon disabused me on that point. "Do you think I shall be quite safe here . . . all alone?"

The innkeeper and I looked at each other almost without intending to, and I caught the faintest of smiles on his pleasant, homely countenance. I assured Mrs. Fothergay that she would be quite safe. No one had designs on her. I suspected that she wasn't too sure, and she proved this by whispering as I said good-bye, "When I prepare for dinner, I shall take care to make myself as plain and — er — unobtrusive, as nature will allow me. No need to encourage their pretensions; for I have already seen two of these rustics eying me in a certain way."

I assured her gravely that if she tried very hard to disguise the great endowments of nature, it was possible they would not find her irresistable. I left her by the fire, still uneasy that her fatal charm would crack a few local hearts.

The innkeeper walked with me to the cobbled street and pointed to the road which wound up over a hill and vanished. Along the upward slope of the hill, lining the road, were many gray York stone workmen's houses slap up against each other, like lean-faced, hard-working men, united in a huddle against the cold and misery of the world.

"Yon's the way."

I started off but he caught my cloak.

"Don't ye maunder to one side or t'other and ye'll get there afore ye knows it. Ye looks ahead and walks straight as a lance. Mind now. The moorland's a passing strange creetur. He don't pay no mind to his own, but them as is outcomers is not made t'home. Happen a man could die out in them moors, lost and feared of

51

such false creeturs as the Gytrash and all. Besides all else, there's the pot-holes. So ye best keep the road, mum. No matter what! For I tell ye here and now — if ye tries to cross the moorland without ye has a man of the countryside along of ye, there's many a thing can happen. Now, give ear t'that!"

With this cheerful piece of advice ringing in my ears, I left him.

I felt a drop of rain upon my head as I proceeded up the hill alone, but I was prepared for such weather in November, and was wearing a mantle and hood which were very nearly waterproof. I climbed the hill rapidly, from flagstone to flagstone, reaching the top almost before the innkeeper had gone back inside his warm taproom. But my haste was at some cost, for I was soon out of breath, and on descending this hill on the further side, I paid no attention to my surroundings but stepped onward until the gray, time-polished stones underfoot seemed slowly to dissolve into the stark earth of the wagon-rutted road. Once the house of Teignford ceased to line my route, I was not aware of any impediment to my view on either side of the road.

From the blue-gray light of the cloudy heavens that illuminated my way, I seemed surrounded by open spaces. I paid no heed until a little trickling beck crossed the road in front of me and vanished in the undergrowth of a gully on my left side. I had to pick up my skirts to cross the water. Even then the toes of my shoes got wet and I could feel the sogginess creep into my stockings.

The road wound around over the next hill and at its peak, already tired, I stopped to get my breath and study the surroundings. The intermittent sprinkles foretelling a shower turned gradually to a fine misty spray. The scent of the green moors and the blackened heather was pervasive.

It was then I knew that I had never been so alone in all my memory.

I tried to make out the countryside through the mist, but it was difficult, for a stiff breeze blew the spray across my face and made the whole scene appear blurred, as through a freshly washed window-glass. I thought I made out the topmost lines of a bell-tower across the narrow valley that dropped off from the right-hand side of the road. But the rest of the tower, and apparently the town, were tucked behind a hill even more steep than the one I stood on. By peering hard through the mist I saw the steep descent of my road probably half a mile beyond me, down into the valley on my right, and then climbing that impossible hill which I supposed must lead to, and conceal from my present sight, the village of Maidenmoor. My friend, the writer of the Gytrash tale, had not exaggerated when he described the location of the village in his story. Nothing could be further cut off from "civilization", unless it be a vessel at sea.

The walk from here to that formidable hill across the valley was certainly more than a "wee step" and I was greatly provoked with myself for having taken, the innkeeper's description at face — or foot — value. I should certainly not reach Maidenmoor before dark, upon my own feet.

After studying longer the wider expanse of moors around me, I began to see at last the faint signs that man had made some effort to conquer this green monster. At spaced intervals the bleak, empty scene was riven by low, black stone walls that rose and fell over the distant prospect and which I took to be the indications of private property. Still, it seemed to me that the blackened heath, blending into the green of the moorland itself, looked no more fit for human habitation than those sections on the far horizon that had no York stone boundaries. Man might fancy he had conquered nature, but I was inclined to agree with the innkeeper of Teignford that the moors were still no place to wander alone. If there were, as I had read aloud to my father in learned chronicles, certain dimensions beyond ours, certain places where Man was not yet the master but only a puny, poor little visitor, then I had come to one of these places. But if Man did not command here, then what intelligence, under God's, ruled these vast unconquered moors?

I suddenly remembered that preposterous Gytrash, and wished I hadn't.

At the same moment, it was almost as if my thoughts took form. Somewhere among the wet green verdure at a short distance on my right, below the road, I made out furtive movements and saw a bird fly upward, as though startled by a higher animalism in the heath. A fleck of dun color gleamed above the high vegetation, as a drop of rain glanced off the surface of some beast. The creature was hidden, for the most part, behind a curious formation of solid-packed turf and brush that at first I took to be a very large tuft of heather but which I realized must be a man-made shooting butt. From the careful movements I assumed the animal was one of the solitary and aloof breed which knows no allegiance to man. It could not be, then, as I had at first hoped, a large dog of the neighborhood.

I began to panic. If this thing mounting the moorland hill to the road was actually, as the Yorkshire papers had said, "of the leonine family", a rapid motion on my part would be fatal. But every second's delay made me tremble the more. I lost all caution and started to run, with all my skirts and petticoats flapping about my ankles. Then I looked back. The beast was coming into view. I gaped at it.

The dun-colored creature of the moors was nothing more terrifying than a dainty-footed mare, an animal not likely to be found in these parts where more serviceable breeds were needed. Behind the mare, taking long leggy strides with more force than the animal, was a very tall, well-built man in his middle years.

I felt more than a trifle foolish, for I had been so obviously running away that even a blind man could read my panic. Unlike myself, the gentleman, as his first words proved him to be, was not in the least surprised to see me.

"Ah, there. Delightful weather. I say, you must be devilish fond of capering about in the wet, madam. Carriage broken down?" Although the situation warranted curiosity on his part, I could not but feel that he spoke in a sardonic way, as though my plight was amusing to him. His blue eyes were a trifle weary, his face just a shade puffy beneath the ruddy complexion that he appeared to share with most Yorkshiremen, but I suspected from his voice that he was not a native of these parts. I could only sum up the general impression he made on me by a quote from my father who had a friend "with a pleasantly dissipated face." And so it was with Sir Gareth Owen, as he introduced himself.

I explained briefly that a lady and I were to have been met at Teignford, and finding there had been a mistake somewhere, I was now walking to Maidenmoor to discover what had gone amiss. I added acidly, "I had no notion just how far this wretched village would prove to be."

"Wretched indeed," he laughed, and I thought a little of his boredom was lifted as he looked me up and down. I had not traveled in Mrs. Fothergay's company for nothing. I was becoming quite a female coxcomb, yet I could not but be flattered, although I took him for a man who spent his life making himself agreeable to women, so practiced and yet with that aloof indifference which was always a challenge.

While I was beguiling myself with the notion that he found me attractive, he took the most peculiar interest in me. At last he said, "Would you oblige me, madam? Just raise your eyebrows and stare at me as though you could cut me down at twenty paces. Stand on tiptoe. No, no. Keep the hood of your cloak around your face, just so."

Utterly confounded, I did as I was bidden, feeling like a schoolgirl, while the mist swirled around us and this towering man, with his only half-concealed insolence, considered me.

He murmured after too long a time, "For a moment you put me a little in mind of. . . . May I ask the name of the person whom you were expecting at Teignford?"

"An impudent young artist named Marc Branshaw."

He was satisfied, but puzzled too. "Now, what the deuce is his object? Personal, of course. Hmm. No matter. Come madam. Let me make amends, for the sake of the family, as it were."

"Are you — ?"

"Gad, no. But it was a near thing. We were fortunate. My sister Catherine escaped his designs. In short, he jilted her. I knew his mother. Sort of thing she would do. Piquant charmer, was Moyna Branshaw. Broke many a heart, I daresay. And such a faithful, devoted mistress, so loyal to a tender memory! Touching, I'm sure. Don't know how she came to produce her revolting offspring. . . . Here. Here. What am I thinking of?

Your shoes are wet through. Come! Up on Jassy here. Won't hurt you in the least, ma'am."

I stood uncertainly in the muddy path, only to be swept into his arms and up onto the back of the quiet mare who gave me one look of mild interest before snorting in a gentle way. I was not sure that I approved of these masterful ways of Sir Gareth, but at the same time, I did not approve of walking another hour in wet feet either.

"How do you find young Branshaw, Miss Anne?"

"I find him odious."

"Ah! Always pleasant to have one's own judgment vindicated."

I thought I could plainly see why Sir Gareth and the young artist would always be in dispute. The peer seemed to me very like his blue eyes — bored and disillusioned, perhaps early indulged, and now despising the more commonplace virtues of humanity, such as Moyna Branshaw's fidelity to her husband, as I suppose he had meant to imply. Sir Gareth was surely a man whose character was easily read. On the other hand, I remembered Marc Branshaw's eyes with their dancing blackness against his sallow olive complexion. Those eyes, I thought, were as unfathomable as a deep pool at night. Sometimes, in my memory, they seemed ageless, as though they had absorbed and then concealed a whole lifetime of experience, at great variance with his look of youth.

Even in general configuration, Sir Gareth held

all the cards. He was so very big and ruddy, so very Anglo-Saxon. Everything Marc Branshaw was not. Why then should he interest me less than Marc?

As we jogged along down the road toward the valley and the beginnings of what appeared more and more to be an appalling ascent of the hill leading to the hidden village of Maidenmoor, I studied the man walking ahead of me, leading the patient Jassy.

Sir Gareth was dressed, like so many men of the district, in leather breeches and leather jerkin, as well as what appeared to be a home-spun shirt and an expensively cut but none too new jacket. Instead of wearing boots, as one might have expected of a sporting man, his limbs were encased nearly to his thighs in well-rubbed leather.

Either he had no taste for the expensive garments of the gentlemen, and this seemed unlikely, considering the cut of his clothing, or he had come upon bad times and was playing the gentleman without a gentleman's purse. I remembered the prosperous, if Bohemian, look of Marc Branshaw. It must have been painful for the aristocratic Owens to lose both a husband for his sister and the Branshaw money.

Why had Marc Branshaw jilted Sir Gareth's sister? It did not set him in a very pretty light. Probably there was no betrothal at all, merely an understanding. Anything else would be unforgivable in a gentleman.

As we approached the flagstones at the foot of the road that mounted to Maidenmoor, I became aware of the sudden snuffing of the last blue-gray streaks of light in the sky. How dark it was!

With the wild expanse of moors everywhere rising around us in even darker shadow I saw something dotting the distant hills like insects, with flaring, fiery wings.

"What are those odd lights?" I asked, pointing to those curious little flames that came and went, up and down, sometimes disappearing, then rising again on a further ridge, against the stormy night sky.

"Oh, that." Sir Gareth glanced at it in his supercilious way. "The lights of the searchers, I should imagine."

"Searchers! After what?"

"My dear madam, why do you suppose Branshaw did not meet you at Teignford? He is playing the hero, a party to the search. Not from choice, you may be sure, but because it would be worth his neck to commit a suspicious act at this time. Missing girl, you know — daughter of one of the sheep cotters. It seems she was out where she shouldn't be, on the trail to Marc's cottage across the moors. He paints. Women, you know. Doesn't live there all the time, but visits the place for his work. Desolate, Godforsaken. Roof falling in. Frightful inconveniences. His mother died there, though what she was doing in such a rat's nest I'll never know. Probably saving pennies."

"Yes, yes. But why are they searching for this girl?"

He looked at me in his bored way. I could not see his features too well but I guessed his manner from his voice.

"Because she is missing, naturally. Left her father's cottage before the rains yesterday and never returned. Marc Branshaw claims he wasn't expecting her. Cowardly little pup would claim that, in the circumstances. Still, only thing to do, I suppose. Girl's probably lying in some pot-hole with a broken limb. Pity. Beautiful limbs."

I was somewhat uneasy. Surely, a girl living on the moors would know her way well enough to avoid pot-holes. Was there foul play? Horrid thought.

"Then that is how you happened to be crossing the moors on Jassy, sir? In your search?"

"Gad, no. What do you take me for — a blasted hero? I was doing a little shooting."

Curious, that explanation for his only weapon was a large pistol carelessly stuck in Jassy's saddle, its barrel cold and wet even through my skirts. It was the kind of implement one associates less with field sports than with highway robbery, or perhaps self-defense. Was Sir Gareth afraid of something?

As Jassy put one dainty foot before the other, mounting this incredible hill paved in deeply scarred old flagstones, I reminded Sir Gareth that I must return to Teignford tonight with a horse and a gig, or at least be at the expense of hiring a trustworthy local tradesman to fetch Mrs. Fothergay in his conveyance. I will admit I was hoping that Sir Gareth would offer to furnish the gig himself. He did better than that.

"Don't give it a thought, ma'am," said my new friend. "Fetch her myself. Sounds just in my way."

Good Lord! I thought. Was Mrs. Fothergay about to be wooed in very earnest, and by a peer of the realm?

Although the first stone buildings of the village loomed up now ahead of us, I could make out very little of the particulars. I was surprised to discover that, although the two-story houses appeared austere and even forbidding, they were like guardian walls between the life within the town and the encroaching green monster that sprawled all about them, licking at every little vacant space where the stone walls and fences had worn away.

Another reassuring thing was the loud clap of bootheels ringing on the wet, shining cobbles of the street as the residents went about their business, probably home to supper. There seemed to be some sort of iron-clad rule that all should be dressed in black; for I never saw a man in the streets who did not wear a black jacket or coat, sometimes of leather, and those solid, noisy black boots, either ankle high or nearly to their thighs. The women, except for a few old ones with daringly scarlet cloaks, were for the most part swathed against the rising cold in black as

62

well. I was surprised to note that their footgear made even more noise than the boots of the men, and discovered that the older women were shod in furiously clanking iron-patched wooden shoes.

This was no deserted village, but an up-and-coming little town with a not undistinguished past, known in the North, as the inhabitants soon told me, long before the woolen mills of Bradford and Leeds robbed them of their skill at the hand looms by substituting machinery. Still, it was grim. When Sir Gareth lifted me off uncomplaining Jassy's back and set me on the stoop of the Yorkish Lion Inn, I glanced up the street, which glistened under the smokey glow cast by the outside lamp of the inn, and I thought how much more cheerful the village might be with pots of bright geraniums in some of those wide, empty-looking windows.

We stepped into a passage that held the warm glow of the fireplace we were approaching in the old-fashioned parlor with a taprail at one side. Several men, all in black, and calmly smoking smelly pipes between long draughts of spirits at the taprail, turned to eye me curiously. I noticed that although their glances at me were indifferent, they were not hostile. So much could not be said for their treatment of Sir Gareth, whom they plainly disliked. Nevertheless, they addressed him politely enough.

"Evenin', mon."

Sir Gareth was expansive but I fancied he

overdid the politeness, as though he found something amusing in these surly villagers.

"Jolly fine evening, Cutter. But I am surprised to find you here. Have they found your pretty playmate then?"

"My playmate?" thundered the man at the rail, turning red. "Now, what'll ye be meaning with that? I know'd Abbie Hinchley, as did a mort of others, not to be naming no names."

The other two men at the rail looked uneasily at each other, from which I reflected that the missing Abbie had a wide acquaintance. For some reason, I was relieved to know that Marc Branshaw, detestable as he might be, was not the only man concerned in her affairs.

"Manners, gentlemen," said the woman behind the taprail, and I saw a female of thirty-odd years, with delicate features and a manner as quiet and incisive as the tone of her voice.

Sir Gareth brushed aside the subject of Abbie Hinchley.

"Hallo there, Rose. I've been out beating up custom for you. The young lady is to stay the night. After that, I imagine our dashing young local celebrity will have other arrangements to make. I believe she is employed by him."

Apparently Miss Rose knew who the "local celebrity" was. I tried to enter into an explanation, but saw that it would only make matters worse. All three of the men looked at me, obviously thinking me another Abbie Hinchley, and as for that tiresome Sir Gareth, he looked at me as well, in his lascivious way which I was beginning to find irritating, and remarked that I must be lonely as he would return presently with my friend. He did not explain to those in the taproom that my friend was a female and I knew perfectly well what they thought, but I was tired and annoyed and the woman behind the taprail guessed as much, for she raised the bar and came around to me.

"Come, Miss, let me help you. The side chamber is not occupied. It should do for you tonight, at least."

I thanked her for her courtesy, but actually, I was thanking her for her quick acceptance of me without foolish questions. On the way up the newly painted white stairs behind the taproom, she explained to me that her name was Rose Keegan and that she and her nephew owned the Yorkish Lion in partnership.

"What? Both of you?" I asked, laughing a little.

She smiled. "You will find that Jamie is quite as responsible as I, though he is only eleven."

The upstairs hall creaked like a thing in pain as we crossed the ancient planks to the door of the side chamber, but I liked the atmosphere, for there was no mistaking the home touch of Miss Rose: a rose-tinted lamp on the flat newel post, a pretty little side-table against the wall, tiny touches of delicacy and charm in this grim village.

My room was small and bitter cold, but in other ways adequate, with a neat bed that I was happy to see had no moth-eaten tester and dingy curtains — merely a hand-loomed coverlet, spotless pillows and four well-carved sturdy posts. There was a commode beneath the cracked but clean mirror, and on the commode, a polished jar and basin, completely free of the soot or coal-dust I had observed everywhere in Yorkshire.

I was drawing back the starched yellow curtains in order to see what lay beyond my window when Miss Rose spoke up.

"The front bedroom is permanently let, miss. Else I shouldn't have put you here. The view is —"

But I had already opened the shutters. Marching right up to the very walls of the Yorkish Lion was the community graveyard. When I was able to take my eyes off the truly horrifying gravestones, some laid out flat, the exact size of a human corpse, some standing up like a ghostly army in the rainy night, I saw the outlines of the village church which formed the opposite boundary of the graveyard. The church itself was gothic, forbidding, and of course, formed by the omnipresent York stone. A kind of diseased, grasping ivy crawled up the stone walls to the bell tower. Fearing the contagion of that ivy, I looked straight down at the sides of the Keegan inn, and found more of the same crawling up toward my window, its tendrils extended and swaying in the rain as if blindly seeking me.

I said "Good heavens!" and pulled the shutters

to and then the window.

Miss Rose made no apology beyond saying that if I did not think about it, I shouldn't be troubled. This was undeniably true, only the doing was harder than she apparently thought.

"Supper is served sharp at half after six," she said, and with a pleasant smile left me to my solitude and my companions in the graveyard.

I was combing my hair in a curlier style about my face and studying the result in the cracked mirror some minutes later when a voice spoke to me out of nowhere, it seemed. My scalp tingled. The voice was young, light, phantomlike — not the voice of anyone I had heard in the tavern.

"Happen you're one of them, be ye?"

I looked into the mirror. A small, sturdy boy of ten years or so was standing there watching me. He was a handsome boy, slightly resembling his attractive aunt, for I took him to be young Jamie Keegan, her partner in the ownership of the inn.

"I don't know," I replied, turning around and receiving his polite handshake with what I hoped was a matching grace. "Am I? I am from London."

"Ay, ye be. They're from York and Leeds and all over since it happened. Come to see if they can fetch out the Gytrash."

I smiled, thinking he spoke in fancy, but then covered the smile, for I saw that his smooth young face looked troubled. His blue eyes, studying me, were as grave as an abbot's. Childlike, he had apparently salted the broad tongue of the West Riding with half a dozen other brogues, so that I had to listen hard to unravel it all.

" 'Twas me saw it, love. Sir Gareth's sister, Miss Catherine, she give me a lamb, by name Gambol, and it maundered out on the moors. Can I sit on your bed? I been over far as Mister Marc's cottage 'cross the moors. We didn't find her though. Marc said for me to go home to supper. He's good, and he's thoughty-like."

I wondered if the boy and I could be thinking of the same Mister Marc.

"He's my best friend. He's a love, that he is. And so's Miss Catherine. Not like her brother, Sir Gareth. You don't catch him looking for poor Abbie. . . . Gytrash's got her in his lair."

I began to understand. "Then it was you the newspapers quoted. You saw the tawny-colored thing like a lion that attacked the sheepman. That was very brave of you."

"Ye might call me 'love' if you're a mind to. You're a dancey lady, with dancey eyes. I like that."

"Thank you. But don't you think it's possible what you saw was a lion escaped from a fair in some village or other? Or perhaps a large dog that belonged to wandering gypsies?"

He had seated himself comfortably on my bed and was getting his bottom settled after a good deal of sliding back and forth, while he looked at me in the style of a very mature man trying to teach an untractable pupil.

"Now you're talking like Sir Gareth. Come, mum, you didn't see the Gytrash. He's a great flaysome brute, with a mane, I think. And great, long claws that's curled up — like this —"

He made the requisite gestures, which caused me to back off precipitously.

"I understand. I see it, vividly!"

"— and he jumps into the heather and away. He's half man, half beast. That's what he is. Some's said he walks like a man when he chooses. . . . I fancy I seen him t'other night out yon in the graveyard where the Devil-Vicar's bones is buried, but I can't be sure. I'd had a Shandy Gaff after supper and I might a been a wee bit dipped in the nob. Besides, there's a heap a live ones to eat. For why should he be hanging about the gravestones? But if ye sees him out there tonight, ye must let me know. Promise, now."

Jamie leaped off the bed, jarring the uneasy floor as he landed in his iron-tipped boots. "Come. It's suppertime. I'm to take you to supper. Ay, and time, too. I be that starved."

Wondering who the Devil-Vicar might be, I thought of the graveyard outside, the ivy climbing up to my window, and Master Jamie's friend, the Gytrash, lurking about in the wet darkness among the gravestones, and I asked myself if I could ever eat again.

Clearly, Jamie had no such doubts. He took my hand, once more my very correct host.

"You're a tiny thing, for a fact. Not much

bigger'n me. Well, ye come along a me, love. Mark me, though. The Gytrash was feared a me; so ye see, you're safe with ol' Jamie Keegan."

He was so convincing, I very nearly believed I was.

V

Through the early portions of my meal I was the solitary diner in the little back parlor which had been newly whitewashed and the shutters firmly bolted behind freshly dusted drapes. The flagstones were so cold they seemed to carry ice clear through my morocco shoes. There were three tables in the small room which barely accommodated them, and although the tables were covered by charming old clothes freshly laundered, stiff and clean, the tables themselves were unpolished deal tables — practical, functional, and enduring, like the Yorkshiremen themselves.

Young Jamie kept me company for a few minutes, but then he saw someone of greater interest in the taproom and scampered out to where the excitement was, the searchers having begun to straggle in for their "pint" to give them sustinance for the long, bitter cold night of searching still ahead.

I was joined briefly by one of the searchers, the Reverend Frederick Niles, curate of the local church, who proved to be a quiet, attractive, blond young man.

"Are you visiting us for long, Miss Wicklow?" he inquired as he ate a quick meal standing up, ready to rejoin the search at any moment.

I explained that I expected to be gone the next day, if not sooner, and when he looked surprised, I did not bother to explain further. He said after a slight pause, "A pity you were not able to visit us earlier in the season. I cannot recall when the heather looked lovelier."

"Are people often lost on the moors hereabouts?" I asked, discourteously avoiding pleasant topics.

He flushed a little at my changing the subject and replied with a sincerity that almost made me smile, "Believe me, ma'am, Miss Hinchley's mysterious accident, if accident it was, has us all baffled. It is much out of the common way, believe me."

What a pedantic young man! But oddly touching in his sincerity.

Presently Miss Rose Keegan came in with my second course, which proved to be a slice of well-turned roast of beef, and as she set my tray down she indicated the two persons entering the little dining parlor. At the sight of them, for some odd reason, the young curate gulped down the last of his tea, bowed briefly to the newcomers and departed in haste. Rose Keegan smiled at his swift exit and nodded to me significantly, so that I could only conclude the young curate was not on the best of terms with the man and woman who entered now.

"The Reverend MacDonnachie and Mrs.

Emily," said Rose Keegan. "We have let the front parlor rooms to the vicar since there is no parsonage, and the Reverend's grown used to those rooms. He has had them now for well on sixteen years."

I wondered what circumstance it was that left the local vicar without a vicarage, but soon I felt my curiosity on that matter as well as the obvious coolness between him and his young curate would be satisfied in short order, for the Reverend MacDonnachie proved to be a huge, red-bearded, talkative man who insisted that, "if the lady would do him and his good wife the honor" he would share my table.

"Please, by all means," I said, and began to push the dishes and teapot about to get them out of the Reverend's great hands. When he moved things you could almost hear them crunch under his prodigious paws. His wife was the very opposite — a frail, wistful, breeze-blown creature with a faraway look, a sweet, absent smile, and extraordinarily pink hair whose texture, if not its color, reminded me of cat fur.

She looked toward the door. "Poor young man," she murmured, meaning the curate, Frederick Niles. "Always a little in awe of my dear husband. They are so very different."

I believed that. Nothing could be more ludicrous than the contrast between the esthetic-looking young Reverend Niles and his superior, the stout vicar, who was obviously a good trencherman.

"Ah, there, Miss Rose. Food for the gods, I see. Be quick! Be quick! Or I shall eat this pretty thing you have served me."

Mrs. Emily leaned over me, saying in her far-away voice, "My dear, he means you."

I thanked her with a smile and abruptly went to another topic. He was rather overwhelming, like a gigantic cliff overhanging one.

"I am given to understand that we are fellow boarders here at the inn, sir."

"Yes, yet. Fortunate, eh? By George, that beef does look good. What say I slice off just a wee . . . wee . . . morsel. . . . Ah! Um! Good! By thunder, that's good!" I looked down ruefully at my denuded plate. What a pity! And it had looked delicious, too, swimming in its own juice. Mrs. MacDonnachie patted my hand.

"Never mind, dear. Think how good it is for the figure. And poor Cadmon, he does require more food than the ordinary man." She smiled at him fondly. "Of course, that's because he is not an ordinary man. Dear me, no. Not like that tiresome young Reverend Niles, always preaching continence and abstinence as though we were in eternal Lent." I suspected she was quoting from her husband. She looked like one of those dreary women whose opinions shifted like weathercocks, to suit whatever man was present.

Getting back to the non-existent vicarage, which these Yorkshire people persisted in referring to as a parsonage, I said, "But I don't understand. Surely, with such an imposing church, you have a vicarage."

The red-bearded gentleman threw back his great head and roared with laughter. "Had a parsonage once, you know. Yes. But they burnt it down. Twenty years ago, must have been. . . ."

"Nearer fifteen, love," put in Mrs. Mac-Donnachie faintly, but he ignored this interpolation.

"Since then, the vicars have lived wherever the townspeople could find room for them."

"Yes, but how did it happen that the original parsonage burned?"

"Had a wee dispute concerning Holy Writ. Occupant of the parsonage disagreed with the congregation. Taught them all that the Devil could appear among them as a dog or a cat or in any form. Preferably, as himself. Had them so terrified they wouldn't venture out of doors after dark. Some of the congregation disapproved. Riots. Clubs. Blood. . . ."

"Please, dear, not at the table," murmured his wife.

"Ah, just so. Now you put me in mind of it, delicious juice to this meat."

Let us not get off the subject again, I thought, and ventured, "In short, the vicar preached that the Devil could appear in the form of a . . . Gytrash."

"Precisely." He beamed at me approvingly, while mopping up the dribble of sauce on his healthy red lips. "All nonsense, of course. I do believe the fellow was mad. I was one of his curates in my beardless days, you know. At any rate, he planted the idea. Gradually, it occurred to his congregation that if he knew so much about devils, and about men who could take the form of an animal, he must be the Devil himself. It was just after a time of great strife, you understand. The Dissenters had crept in everywhere. Every second preacher was a Methodist. Church of England fighting for its very existence in these parts. So — when they thought our handsome Devil-Vicar was elsewhere, some of the good folk burnt the parsonage — like the purging of an animal's lair, you understand. Then they tore down the foundations, stone from stone. After that, it was quite some time before anyone dared mention a Gytrash again. Matter of fact, even the Devil is not as welcome in church as he once was."

"And the Vicar — and his family?"

"Oh, them. Emily, would you call his . . . er . . . connections . . . a family?"

Thus questioned pointblank, the lady looked up in panic, her watery eyes wavering helplessly from object to object in the little dining parlor.

"I — I believe not, love. Such a painful subject. They found what was left of the . . . the body of the Reverend Morgan, you remember."

"Yes, Yes. Quite cooked, I assure you. Nothing but the bones remained. Poor devil never got out of the house. Everyone had thought he was gone, you see. But it wasn't so. Probably knocked unconscious beforehand by some idiot. Let us

75

hope so, at any rate. Which explains the talk about monsters. One always hears that after a murder."

"They do say, dear, there was talk when the Owens moved into this district, about five years after the fire. From Wales, you know, Miss Wicklow. Very odd people, the Welsh."

"Emily, I put it to you. Could anyone in his right mind mistake Gareth Owen for the Devil-Vicar, or even a Gytrash, when it comes to that? Why, the man's too dashed lazy. Almost the antithesis of our Devil-Vicar in looks. It's all balderdash. The Devil-Vicar's bones are snugly buried in the ashes where the parsonage stood, at the southwest end of the graveyard behind the inn here."

I said, "Is it not a little odd that the very villagers who must have been present at the burning of the parsonage should once more fancy they see men in the form of animals?"

Miss Rose came in before the Vicar could answer, and, apparently familiar with the Vicar's ways, she brought me a fresh plate, this time with a potato and a turnip as well as a slice of beef in its own juice.

"You must pay no mind to the Reverend," she told me, before the Vicar himself, who grinned widely. "A legend began this business on the moors, and now children and mischief-makers are carrying it on. Believe me, Miss, they enjoy talking about Gytrashes and the like."

"But your nephew saw it first," I said.

Miss Rose smiled, although I could see that she was not too pleased.

"My nephew is only a lad. He tells what people want him to tell. We've had people lost on the moors before. In summer we are always setting out to find them. Outcomers, for the most part."

"Will Grimlett was no outcomer," put in the Reverend.

"Will Grimlett drank," said Miss Rose succinctly. "My own tapster has tried to persuade Will to give it up on many a night — and taken him home safe to bed as well. No. I shouldn't use Will Grimlett as an example."

She swung the door to behind her.

Reverend MacDonnachie chuckled.

"What a pity! She'll spoil every fine tale we conjure up to frighten the natives."

In spite of his horrid stories, I could not help being amused by him. I said with a smile, "I suspect, sir, that you have a little of your martyred predecessor's love of deviltry."

"Oh, more than a little. I confess it. A delightful rogue he was. I have tried to spread the rumor, to no avail I am afraid, that I am actually a rebirth of my friend, the Devil-Vicar."

"My love," his wife chided softly. "How foolishly modest of you! Everyone knows the Devil-Vicar was the veriest dab of a creature. Dark foreigner from Wales, you know, Miss Wicklow — moody and mysterious like all the Welshmen. Handsome enough in his way perhaps. We were all very struck by him, I do confess. But he was nothing compared to Cadmon. Cadmon would make two of him."

"What a pity!" sighed the Reverend Mac-Donnachie, taking out a huge handkerchief and blowing his nose like a trumpet. "I've always suspected the Devil-Vicar was burned, not for his religion, but for his success with other men's wives, and one lovely widow in particular. Rather fancied her myself."

"Really, dear," his wife protested feebly.

Miss Rose came in with the MacDonnachie supper and a word for me.

"Marc Branshaw's come, Miss. He would like to see you, when convenient."

I went on eating indifferently, but I noticed after a few movements of my hand that I was unusually nervous. That rogue managed to get the better of me every time we met. I was resolved it should not occur this time.

"How curious!" said Mrs. MacDonnachie. "We were just talking of the Devil-Vicar, and now, out of nowhere, Marc Branshaw's name is mentioned. One's heart goes out to the dear boy. He's not precisely well, my dear. I have often felt that I could be of some service to —"

The Reverend burst into this plaint, "She wants to mother the fellow every time he has a headache. Thinks to take Moyna Branshaw's place."

"Now Cadmon, you know the Keegan lad saw him quite ill once, and I saw him recovering another time."

"That's as may be. But since he refuses to let a

doctor touch him, you can be sure it's nothing more than artistic indulgence. We are dealing with a painter from Paris, m'dear."

I did not doubt that. "Was he so fond of his mother then?"

"How could he be? He never saw her after he was six or seven. Reared on the continent. But you see, Moyna was a beauty, and most of the women hereabouts were jealous of her because she attached the Devil-Vicar."

"Cadmon! Your language, my love!"

"How did she die? Mrs. Branshaw, that is," I asked.

"Fell into a pot-hole, just about a year ago. Sort of thing that happens to the merest visitor to these parts."

"My love, you will give Miss Wicklow an entirely false picture of Moyna Branshaw. I assure you, ma'am, the lady in question was a faithful and honorable widow. Her husband died a year before the Reverend Morgan — that is, the Devil-Vicar — came here to St. Anthony's in Maidenmoor. She'd only just returned from taking her son, Marc, to the continent for the cure of some ailment — lungs, I believe. At any rate, she'd intended to sell out her property, the Branshaw mills and Branshaw Hall, and rejoin the boy. But after she met the Devil-Vicar, she never went back to France, even when he was burned to death. So there was her son, reared alone, in foreign parts, and behaving in such a fashion, never returning until she's under the sod, not but what he is a love, in many ways."

"Which brings us back to your beginning, m'dear. You'd like to take Moyna's place. You're long of wind, as usual."

"You aren't interested in Marc because you just don't like the lad," Mrs. MacDonnachie reminded him, in the first tone I had heard her use that held a faint edge to it.

"You are partially mistaken, m'dear. 'The lad,' as you call our very sophisticated artist, interests me profoundly. I am curious concerning . . . or, many things about him. But to get back to our Devil-Vicar —"

I could not but feel that the two were somehow connected in the Vicar's mind.

"Why? Are they related?"

The Reverend MacDonnachie guffawed into his food, but Mrs. MacDonnachie flushed rosily.

"My dear, what an idea! Marc was born in Maidenmoor and duly enrolled in St. Anthony's Register here as the first-born son of Josiah Branshaw."

"Wouldn't be the first time an old gaffer's been cuckolded by a pretty young wife," put in the vicar, who appeared to know a great deal about such worldly matters.

"How can you say so? The Devil-Vicar arrived in Maidenmoor some seven or eight years after Marc's birth, and as I recall, the Devil-Vicar seemed too young and too serious to have sired anyone eight years before — dear me — what am I saying?"

The Reverend MacDonnachie was overjoyed at having trapped his wife into an indelicacy.

"They mature fast, those Welsh males."

"You say he was serious," I remarked. "I think he must have been nonsensical to play such tricks about devils and Gytrashes and all."

The vicar looked at me with his big head cocked on one side.

"There is nothing more serious, I assure you, than a trick played by a very gloomy and romantic young man whom all the world thinks incapable of displaying a sense of humor. As to his having been rather young eight years before he arrived in Maidenmoor — well, that is not a problem. We have no real notion how old he was when he arrived here, only the hair-brained ideas of a pack of gossiping women half in love with him."

"Yes, but where could they have met before he came to Maidenmoor?" murmured his wife. "I'd swear they met here for the first time. It was I who introduced them in the chancel of St. Anthony's one Sunday night at service. And Marc was seven years old at that time."

"Ah-ha! But what of Moyna's summer outing eight years before — in fact, the year before the boy's birth? Miss Wicklow, about three years ago, the villagers caught a look at a miniature Moyna's son sent her from Paris, and when they saw that miniature, how the busy tongues of the village ladies wagged. Such delving into old records you have never seen, lassy! It seems that our dear Moyna spent the summer before Marc was born in Wales, of all places, where the Devil-Vicar came from. His name was Ewen Morgan, by the way."

I said, "And he waited seven or eight years after . . . conceiving the boy, before returning to the village of his lady-love? It doesn't sound very passionate to me. And a vicar of the church, at that."

Mrs. MacDonnachie coughed delicately.

"My dear, even a servant of the church may sometimes fall into temptation — especially when he is extraordinarily attractive. I could tell you of the temptations Cadmon has been forced to resist! As for the boy, Marc, let us not forget Josiah Branshaw had accepted the child as his own. I am convinced Marc is Josiah's son, no matter what they say about idyllic summers in Wales and the like."

"And wouldn't you say," put in the vicar, "that seven years later, when Josiah conveniently died, the Reverend Ewen Morgan arrived on the scene more coincidentally?"

"But Cadmon, there is no proof whatever that Moyna had ever met the Devil-Vicar before, in Wales, or anywhere else."

"None except Marc's own extraordinary appearance."

Mrs. MacDonnachie lowered her voice to what was almost a titter. "Dear Miss Wicklow, they say even worse about poor Marc. Some people wonder if he is the Reverend Morgan come back to life, and that would make Marc a being returned from the dead. Absurd, is it not? Only if he really were a devil could he manage such a trick."

I did not know what to say. Her words made me shiver — her words and the memory of Marc Branshaw's chill fingers.

The Vicar waved his fork at me. "When you've the time, you might visit my office in the church. If you've any interest in our Devil-Vicar, there's a striking portrait of him I resurrected from Moyna Branshaw's property. Hangs over my desk . . . as an inspiration to deviltry, you know."

"Sir Gareth Owen had ambitions to marry Moyna last summer before her death," Mrs. MacDonnachie added as I got up to go and meet Marc Branshaw. "But she wouldn't have him. Not Moyna. Loyal to her memories."

"I wonder if she died for that refusal," her husband remarked and was hastily hushed by his wife.

What? I thought. Two jilts from one family? Small wonder Sir Gareth had no use for the Branshaws.

As I went to the taproom I tried to imagine what connection there could be between the young man in his early twenties, as I took Marc Branshaw to be, and a murdered vicar who died in agony almost twenty years ago.

I supposed Mr. Branshaw would meet me in the taproom but there were only Jamie Keegan and a close-packed crowd of men in black, all talking and blowing pipe smoke and drinking at the same time. I wondered if, among them, were the men who had years ago accidentally burned to death the vicar of their church.

Jamie pushed out of the crowd and joined me on the lowest stair, eager to escort me to my room. Somewhere upstairs the night elements were worrying a loose shutter. It made me aware of the great darkness outside.

I said sternly, "You'll not tell me he's the impudence to be in my room!"

"Come, mum," said Jamie, holding out his hand. We went up the stairs together, and the boy left me at the door to my room.

When I walked in, I saw Marc Branshaw blowing on his cold hands, and clapping them together to restore the warmth. He was in the grass-stained garments common to the countryside, his boots badly scuffed, his jacket collar pulled up around his throat as though he were still cold. He seemed very tired, with sallow smudges of weariness under his eyes and below his cheekbones, across the thin lower half of his face. I found my anger evaporating, and could not suppress a kind of protective instinct at sight of him. Surely, he could not have slept for several nights. Under the bright fire of the lamp on the commode, he appeared somewhat older than I had remembered. His slender build, his easy, impudent charm, were deceptive.

Forestalling what I felt sure would be a lie, I said, "I daresay you wouldn't be in the least sorry if your guest were out on the road now, being eaten by Gytrashes."

Outside my graveyard window a shutter banged to and fro. It disturbed me but seemed to have no effect on my uninvited guest.

Marc Branshaw was nonchalant.

"But you aren't out on the road, being eaten by Gytrashes, I am happy to say."

"Your guest, Mr. Branshaw, is a lady named Bedelia Fothergay. And she is, at this moment, on that very road, somewhere between here and Teignford."

"Dear old Bedelia. I had forgotten her entirely. How tiresome of her to be so prompt!"

He moved away from the bedpost and came toward me. I did not know what he was about to do, and suddenly shifted. I saw that his aim was for the center of my bed, where he settled himself comfortably.

"Now come and sit down beside me."

I backed away.

"Don't be tiresome. If I wanted to make love to you, as I suppose you are thinking, I should do so. But I don't."

I approached the bed in a gingerly way and, seeing that he apparently meant what he said, I sat down tentatively, ready for instant flight. He began to take off his jacket. I started to rise and was stopped, not by the quick motion of his hand, which knocked my hair loose from its pins, but by the sight of the nasty deep scratch across his throat, and another, crisscrossing that, upward toward his chin. Both had bled but the blood was now dried, and he must have forgotten them. He had certainly been in some wild country today. I began to perceive how rough the search for Abbie Hinchley was.

"Jamie says Gareth Owen has gone to fetch the delectable Bedelia. How did you happen to meet Owen?"

I explained and he grinned.

"What a happy couple! Gareth and Bedelia! How divinely suited by providence!" He added after a moment, with an insistence that puzzled me, "You saw Owen first on Teignford Brow; did you not? Do you recall the exact time?"

"Now how should I do that? But never mind. Tell me what you want with me," I demanded, while my mouth was full of hairpins and I was torn between this, the banging shutter, and the necessity to keep one eye on my companion.

"I want you to come to my house, properly chaperoned by Gareth's sister, Catherine, and take down what she tells you. In short, to collaborate in the revision of a manuscript she has written."

So it was his jilted betrothed who wrote *The Corpses on the Moor*! No wonder she had chosen Marc for her villain. I did not begin to understand it, for if she had chosen him for her villain, why were they now friends again?

"Will you give me back my manuscript about Red Indians of North America?"

"Solemn promise," he said, looking anything but solemn.

"And Mrs. Fothergay?"

"Ah, the ubiquitous Fothergay. That presents a problem. Well, we must see that Owen makes himself useful. Catherine shall tell him the lady is fabulously wealthy. Her late lamented husband was an India Nabob."

"Yes, but — there must be many ladies in London, or in York or Leeds, who might do what you require of me."

I was hardly thinking of what I said; for my mind was upon those long, ugly scratches on his face and neck. Surely they were painful. I longed to apply an excellent salve which had been my mother's recipe, and was most efficacious in such matters.

He frowned when he saw the direction of my glance and changed the subject in the rudest way. "There's no use in looking like that. I'm not going to, you know. Haven't time."

I committed the shocking blunder of understanding him. "I never asked you to, and wouldn't permit you to touch me if you did!"

That put him in a good humor again, and he stretched and yawned. I thought for one horrifying moment, during which my heart beat very rapidly, that he would stretch out on the bed behind me, as comfortable as you please. He did not, however.

"Leave your hair alone, you foolish girl. Wear it long while you are here in the village." It was puzzling, the inordinate interest he took in my hair.

He got into his jacket as he talked, but managed to reach over and knock my netted hair down again. I could have slapped him. "Wear it down, I said!" This time he saw that I had my hands full and basely took advantage of me. He leaned over me, saying, "Well . . . if you insist!" though I hadn't uttered a word.

I was used to being asked for a kiss, followed by a rather inept aim at my lips. There was nothing inept about Marc Branshaw, who had all too evidently mapped out his destination while we talked. I put up a pushing resistance but the bastions soon crumbled. He wasn't nearly so tired as I had thought him. I felt excited, light in the pit of my stomach. I remember the look in his eyes and then the dark lashes very close to me, and me closing my own eyes and thinking, "How odd! I feel all prickles."

I wondered why he did not kiss me. Then I heard his laugh and felt myself pushed away like an importunate child. I opened my eyes, outraged. He reminded me, "You said you wouldn't, but I think you would."

The man was a cad. No two ways about it. I did what I should have done much earlier. I slapped his detestable face.

I am happy to say that he winced, but in spite of the hard little glitter that had come into his eyes, he smiled and got up as if nothing had happened.

"As I was saying, Catherine Owen will come for you tomorrow. Now, be a good girl and go off to bed before you go about getting into more trouble. Next time you may find yourself teasing the Gytrash and not a gentleman."

The "gentleman" in question crossed the room with his light, almost noiseless step, and went out the door to the accompaniment of the banging shutter across the room. He left only just in time. I was feeling around for something to throw at him. He had done it again, got the better of me.

Of course, I would not visit him tomorrow, or any other day. His conduct had made that quite out of the question.

I was, however, curious to meet Catherine Owen. It appeared now that in writing *The Corpses on the Moor* it was she who had written a guidebook for a bloody crime, but the association of ideas was ridiculous, even as I considered it. The animal that killed Will Grimlett certainly could not read.

I wondered about Catherine Owen. How could she be so complacent about her jilting lover? I should have died of shame and humiliation, if not sheer rage. Perhaps she considered it revenge enough when she made Marc the villain of her manuscript. But knowing the hold the scoundrel could take on one's emotions, I thought Catherine Owen must have extraordinary self-control, for I should have been undone by his behavior.

Eventually, I located all my hairpins and having decided after due thought that my hair did look better down, I rolled it as best I could, and went over to fasten the shutter. This entailed looking out over the graveyard, and I was sure, after the Reverend MacDonnachie's tale at supper, I should see at once the corner where the martyred Devil-Vicar's bones lay buried — if, of course, he wasn't out prowling the countryside in the shape of a Gytrash.

What did a Gytrash look like? In spite of Miss Owen's graphic description in her novel, I still couldn't consider the notion without laughing. Preposterous, the superstitions of these northern people.

The window opened stiffly, thanks to the rain which had warped the casement. I reached around the corner of the window to take hold of the shutter and after I had felt the latch, I realized that it had not been broken, but simply locked improperly, and come unfastened under the pressure of the weather. It was impossible for me to reach the entire shutter, so I took hold of the bottom of it and began to pull it toward me.

In spite of my resolutions, my eyes wandered out over the patch of graveyard just to the left of my window, which marked the burning of the old parsonage, and the bones of the unfortunate young vicar. How cold and dreary it looked, with the white mist rising from the sodden ground! Not at all the sort of bed for the romantic trickster and charmer that I pictured the Devil-Vicar to be. I forced myself to look away from that ground and carelessly glanced beyond at the gray tombstones crowding the yard like witches huddled in the misty night.

Come, Anne, I told myself; *you will dream of this for sure.*

I pulled the shutter toward me, reaching far out to do so. The act was difficult and forced me to look downward at the vines under my window, and the muddy ground below that. I was chilled and shocked to see a woman huddling on her knees there against the wall of the inn, a little to this side of the bare place which marked all that remained of the Devil-Vicar, and the parsonage. The woman was huddling just as my witch-tombstones had seemed to huddle a few seconds before. Her youthful face was staring up at the heavens, her eyes wide open, though the mist swirled around her. She must have been sunk several inches in mud, and wretchedly uncomfortable.

I called to her, "What is it? What are you doing there?"

She continued to stare at the sky in that motionless way until a sudden gust of wind flung me against the side of the window and wrested the shutter out of my hand so that it started banging again. The same gust of wind struck the woman below my window and, to my horror, she toppled stiffly over on her back, still staring up at the heavens, ghastly white and unmoving.

She lay now upon what I took to be the Devil-

Vicar's unmarked grave.

I knew then what my senses would not credit before. Either she had been dragged there, or she had crawled to that place, kneeling in that horrid suppliant position for death to encircle her.

Did *he* know, there in the unhallowed ground beneath her? Did the Devil-Vicar know that she lay there, like a human sacrifice to his corrupt and tragic spirit?

My throat closed and what I had meant for a scream came out a mere whisper of itself. But at last I got the sound out, and kept on screaming until the room was full of people. Live people.

VI

Bedelia Fothergay could not have timed her arrival more opportunely to suit her tastes. For at least an hour that night I kept thinking she would run out of breath, which is clear proof that I was not acquainted with her enormous reserves. Despite the horrifying discovery of Abbie Hinchley's body on the barren ground traditionally assigned to the Devil-Vicar, Mrs. Fothergay surprised me by showing no fear, but only a highly developed sense of her own dramatic role in the tragedy.

"To think, my dear Anne, only to think that poor creature should have been discovered precisely as Sir Gareth and I arrived! And attacked by the same creature that killed the sheepman!

Why, had we arrived an hour earlier, I myself might have been the victim."

"I doubt that," I put in drily, when I could get in a word. "You are not sufficiently acquainted with the Gytrash. I understand it was he — or it — who killed Miss Hinchley."

"Dear me, dear me! Nor do I wish a closer acquaintance. Truly now, haven't you noticed that women of that sort usually have some prior . . . er . . . dealings with their murderers?"

"Murderers? How can you call an animal a murderer?"

Mrs. Fothergay put one pink finger to her lips and looked coy.

"Never you mind. But someone — some charming person who shall be nameless — told me, on the way to Maidenmoor, that he suspects a human intelligence behind the death of that dreary little sheep farmer and the disappearance of Miss Hinchley."

"And did this nameless person say whom he suspected of going about in a lion's skin, murdering sheep farmers and the like?" I wondered what would have been her reaction if Sir Gareth, in his natural antipathy to Marc Branshaw, had named Mrs. Fothergay's beloved artist as the Gytrash.

"No, but it should be obvious. The Hinchley creature was murdered by some man with whom she had played the jilt."

"And the sheep farmer?"

"Oh, well," she shrugged, "I can't be expected

to furnish the answers to all the questions that disturb this heathen place." She had begun to divest herself of numerous and expensive cloaks, pelisses, jackets, and I was hoping she would proceed to her traveling gown and so to bed, but she stopped at this crucial point and sat down on my own bed instead of retiring to her room. Indeed, my bed had become the rendezvous for half of Yorkshire tonight.

"Fate, my dear Anne, that's what it was! Fate! I do have that effect upon events. Some sort of cataclysmic aura. I no sooner arrive at my destination than strange things occur. I cannot begin to explain it."

She did, however, at length, while I alternately huddled in a corner of my bed with my eyes closed, trying not to think of what was occurring beneath my window, and then sat up and rubbed my hands and feet, wondering if it were my imagination or if there actually was a thin coat of ice congealing my room. There was no carpet on the floor; probably these sturdy north people found it superfluous, a mark of the effete Londoner. But for me the damp cold seemed to ooze out of the floorboards when I set my stockinged feet down, and when my elbow accidentally struck the whitewashed wall, the chill of it froze me to the marrow. Perhaps it was because only that wall separated me from the witch-tombstones out there, and from that other place, untended, unhallowed, where the Devil-Vicar slept.

At one moment during Mrs. Fothergay's endless discourse, I wondered what the Reverend Ewen Morgan had been like and, in spite of the denials of both the Reverend MacDonnachie and his wife, I subscribed to the theory that he was humorous, quick and satiric, with a highly developed sense of the ridiculous. He must have been so, to have told such tales about devils and Gytrashes. The truth is, his tragic history and his doomed romance captured my fancy, and I gave him rather more of my thoughts than one customarily devotes to an uncharacteristically bad servant of the church who has been under the sod these fifteen or twenty years.

If he was not a humorist and actually believed in the horrid things he preached, then the mere thought of him lying out there under the muddy ground, no doubt directing the acts of this killer-animal who roamed at large, was too dreadful to contemplate; for in that case, he must have directed his Gytrash (or was he himself the Gytrash?) to lead poor Abbie Hinchley to his grave for her own demise. We torture ourselves with such fearful imaginings by night, where the same impetus by day would merely make us smile at the preposterous thought. But it was now close on midnight and I was no more immune than the next person to the influence of that witching hour.

I shuddered and tried to concentrate on Mrs. Fothergay's ramblings.

"Well, I know you are frightened here alone,

Anne," she said at last, yawning delicately, "but I really do need my sleep. I'm afraid I must leave you. I am a person who manages with very little rest, in spite of a fragile constitution. But . . . there comes a time! Good heavens above! What is that?"

"That" was a stiff knock on the door. A moment later I heard Miss Rose's quiet, confident voice.

"I thought some hot tea might not be amiss, ma'am, seeing that the whole village is congregating beneath your window."

I welcomed her gratefully.

"Yes. Do come in. Thank you so very much."

How good it looked, the steaming teapot, and the sturdy, shining blue cup and saucer! There were also two thin, delicate slices of buttered bread. As for Miss Rose herself, one might have thought she discovered dead bodies beside her inn almost any day, for she was so unruffled as to give the whole room a glow of warmth and peace.

Mrs. Fothergay made some ado over the tray, but Miss Rose carefully set it near me and told my companion, "You will find a tray in your room, ma'am."

Mrs. Fothergay looked flustered, appeared as though she might take this as an insult, but then decided aloud:

"Of course. You must have known I crave solitude after this ghastly experience. How kind of you, I'm sure! For you must know, I only escaped your savage beast by the matter of minutes."

Miss Rose looked at us with justifiable surprise and I explained. She did not look amused, but her eyes might be said to have smiled. Mrs. Fothergay bade me good night, with one last apology for leaving me, which she would never have done except for the delicacy of her constitution. Miss Rose was about to follow when I asked her to stay.

"I thought perhaps you were tired, ma'am."

"Nervous, yes. But I doubt if I could sleep yet. I keep thinking of what they are doing out there."

"Oh, that." Miss Rose waved her hand. "They'll be removing the girl presently. Most of them are out there now smoking and recounting, each of them, the exact location at which they stood in the village when the word of the girl's discovery reached them."

"Why," I asked her suddenly, "hasn't the community ever built another parsonage for the Vicar?"

"We are not a rich village, ma'am," she reminded me.

"Yes, but you have a very old church which does you credit, and it would seem to me that —"

"It is, perhaps, a superstition," she explained after a little pause. "Since there has never been enough money, and since the Vicar seems quite happy in his own apartments here at the inn, the years have gone by with no action in regard to a new parsonage. But I think, also, the village feels its guilt in the matter of the fire, and in some way

97

this is a punishment it has brought down upon itself." Then she smiled. "However, when all is said, money is probably at the root of it. It usually is."

I listened, hearing telltale sounds outside the window.

"I should have thought they would be pursuing the creature instead of standing out there gossiping."

She looked at me rather oddly, I thought.

"The Gytrash, or whatever it is," I explained.

"They are doing that too. But, miss, I did not think you believed such a witches' tale. Of course the thing was done by a human being. Perhaps the girl was savaged by a dog, as Grimlett was. But the deaths were certainly inspired by human agency. You must have guessed that."

I sat with my mouth open, staring at her.

"Who?"

She raised her eyebrows, and gave no other reply.

"I can see why a man might kill Abbie Hinchley," I went on. "For . . . well . . . for the usual reasons. But what have they to do with the sheep farmer?"

She watched me pour the tea and drink it, scalding hot as it was. The tea brewed here in the north was much stronger than the London tea I was used to, and stimulated me almost like strong spirits. At the moment I welcomed its effect.

We both heard the Vicar's booming voice below my window.

"No question but that she was dead some hours before we saw her. Wouldn't ye say now, Billy-boy?"

"Ay, sor. Stone dead. Likely was dragged here. They's marks in the wet, mostly smeared."

One of the men gave a yelp that unnerved Miss Rose and me. She went to the window and thrust it open. Neither of us had closed the shutter yet. I did not want to linger there long enough to do so. She called down to the men:

"What is it? Have you found something?"

The young curate, Frederick Niles, answered her in his calm way.

"We were discussing the curious nature of the wounds. The hands and limbs had been badly savaged, as though she were defending herself against a creature that clawed at her."

"Mebe so," said another voice, "but no dog done all o' this. Crushin' blow to the head here."

"Big dog perhaps," went on the Reverend Niles. "Tooth-marks here. But it may have been a large cat."

"Ay, but what a the nasty bit a work on the back o' the skull? What o' that nasty work, I'm askin'?"

There was muttering among the men and stout Vicar MacDonnachie called up to Miss Rose:

"It's the same as Will Grimlett. Remember, Miss Rose? Lost on the moors, you said. What do you think now?"

"Ay, mon," said another voice, "but what o' the bit a business on the back o' the head-like?"

Miss Rose closed the shutters and the window. She turned back to me.

"You mentioned Abbie's sex, Miss Wicklow. But it had nothing to do with these crimes. They'd do better to concentrate on that bruise or whatever it is that they've found on the back of her head. In my opinion, these crimes are all part of something that happened here years ago. You recall the story the Reverend MacDonnachie told you at supper?"

"Yes, yes. The Devil-Vicar's love affair with Mr. Branshaw's young widowed mother, and all the suspicion that came of that. But Abbie Hinchley is too young to have been involved; isn't she?"

"Abbie used to hint that, as a child, she peeped in the parsonage window and saw the person who struck down Ewen Morgan. The story made her important. But she would tell none of us who the murderer was. It was Abbie's secret, and considering the blood guilt of the village, no one wanted to press her for the name. I say 'murder' since it was this attack Abbie witnessed which prevented the Reverend Morgan from escaping when Will Grimlett and the others set fire to the parsonage."

"Will Grimlett set fire —"

"And Will Grimlett had been killed by the Gytrash."

There was a little silence in the room. Outside, the voices of the men grew fainter. I hoped they were through with their conjectures and going about their business.

I said finally, "Why should the murderer wait so many years to kill Abbie? And who is the murderer?"

"I have no notion, in either case."

"Could it be —" I hesitated, feeling foolish, but I had to have her denial in good, plain terms. "Could it be that the Devil-Vicar himself has somehow succeeded in avenging himself? Perhaps he felt that Abbie was guilty too and must die."

"And the Devil-Vicar's theories were true then? He could return after death? In short, he could turn himself into a Gytrash because — he *was* the Devil? Is that what you mean?"

How ridiculous it sounded, brought out into the light by her matter-of-fact voice! I blushed for my fears. I had never felt more nonsensical.

"No. Of course not. I don't know what I meant, really."

"Because, Miss Wicklow, that is what the village ponders. In my opinion, it is what the murderer wants the village to think. And so long as they believe that, they are not going to find the real demon. I'll say only one thing for our people: at least they do not believe the obvious, the efforts to make Marc Branshaw look suspicious."

I drank the rest of my tea in silence and chewed the thin, delicious slice of bread. One moment I was reassured, the next I was uneasy again. I wished she had not said that. I almost

101

preferred to believe in the Gytrash.

She saw my indecision and left me shortly after.

I did not sleep well that night, which is understandable, but I managed to dream inordinately, and always of the Devil-Vicar. There was no sense to my dreams — no beginning, no end. But I was aware that I dreamed. It was curious, for I had only the vaguest idea of what the Devil-Vicar looked like, and yet I was sure it was he whose pale and shadowed face haunted me. I promised myself that as soon as the opportunity afforded, I should go to look at that portrait of Ewen Morgan in St. Anthony's church across the graveyard.

I detest being watched by some people as I sleep, and it was in no very pleasant mood that I awoke the following morning, to find Bedelia Fothergay's mottled, pink-powder face gazing down at me while I lay in bed.

"What the devil?" I cried and sat straight up in bed, furious.

Mrs. Fothergay was a good deal astonished, not so much at my conduct as at my use of that naughty word.

"Up-up-up, my dear. Time for tea. Your tray was left before your door, whole ages ago. I took the liberty of bringing it in. Then, breakfast and away we go."

"Away we go where?" I asked, not thinking very clearly. When I awaken suddenly everything has cobwebs on it, and for the first hour or two I do nothing but ask people to repeat things.

"To visit that handsome artist who took such a fancy to me in London, my dear Anne. Why else are we in Yorkshire, after all is said? He insisted on doing me in oils."

"I'm not going," I said firmly, drawing my cold feet up in the blanket almost under my chin.

"Now, don't be tiresome. Of course, you are. That is what you are being paid for. Besides, you cannot disappoint Sir Gareth and his charming sister. The poor thing. And so in love. So — hopelessly in love." From her tone, I imagined that she regarded herself as the chief obstacle to "poor" Miss Catherine Owen's love for Marc. With less self-confidence, *much* less since my scuffle with the artist on the bed the previous night, I also felt that Miss Owen held very little place in his mercurial affections. However, I was not ready to sympathize with her just yet. She may have been deeply in love with Marc, but even if she were as charming as Mrs. Fothergay said, and as extremely forgiving as Marc implied by his present relationship with her, this bird of so much perfection was not altogether without malice. I had read *The Corpses on the Moor* and her portrait of her villain, while charming and likeable, turned pretty savage before the end.

I knew all along that I would have to see her. My curiosity was too strong for me.

In the little back dining parlor I met Frederick Niles, who was finishing breakfast as I entered. He arose and bowed to me politely and looked as though he might be conversable if given a chance.

I asked if I might join him and upon being accepted with flattering promptness, I inquired if any new discoveries had been made in connection with the recent deaths.

"Nothing of consequence, ma'am. We are in hourly hopes of tracking the beast, however."

"You think it was a beast, and not a man?"

He looked at me, his blue eyes for the first time a little disconcerting in their direct gaze.

"Why do you say that, Miss Wicklow? You cannot think a man made those horrible wounds."

"What if a man used the beast to — to finish the task?"

He gave my idea an unwilling smile.

"Such theories require a savage imagination, and, I am afraid, not a very Christian view of mankind."

"Still, it would not be the first crime committed in this village. If these people suspect their murdered Devil-Vicar has come back for revenge, why don't they admit it?"

He said stiffly, "It is true these people murdered a man once, inadvertently. They feel that they owe it to themselves, if not to their fellow men, to go warily this time. If you mean to suggest some blood tie between the dead vicar and Marc Branshaw, I must tell you, most of the villagers like young Branshaw. He has a way with him, as you may have noticed." He added, seeing my surprised look, "You must not believe the misguided humor of — persons in high places."

"Like your own vicar, sir?" I asked maliciously.

He looked uncomfortable, but whether from indignation or embarrassment, I could not tell.

"The Reverend MacDonnachie had the advantage of a personal acquaintance with the late so-called Devil-Vicar. I don't doubt that with his peculiar sense of fun, he amused himself in teasing you about the Reverend Morgan's conduct. But I am sure the Reverend MacDonnachie does not condone it. Just prior to the Devil-Vicar's death, there was a movement afoot to remove him." He finished his ham and eggs and arose from the table, saying with a gentler look, "The fact that Ewen Morgan boasted he could change into a Gytrash or a devil, has nothing to do with young Marc Branshaw. It would mean another disaster here if such a line of thinking were pursued, and whatever may be the policy of the Reverend MacDonnachie, I assure you that I for one would make a strong protest if such a threat were made."

I respected him for this defense of Marc.

"Then you like Mr. Branshaw? He is an odd man, but very clever and talented, I believe."

"I dislike him profoundly," said the young curate, not mincing words. "I am not a humorous man, and can see nothing admirable about a propensity for paganism. He is supercilious, irreligious, and amoral. I have not seen him at one service in St. Anthony's since his return last year."

I was somewhat crushed by this severe observation and could find no defense, but he finished less sharply: "Nonetheless, I doubt if he is a re-birth of the Devil-Vicar, as some persons hint. And I shall continue to say so, in spite of all humorous efforts to the contrary."

The Reverend Niles was fairminded, I had to admit, after he was gone. I wondered, however, if his dislike of Marc was based solely on moral grounds.

I had barely finished breakfast, eaten rapidly because my mind was on so many things, when Jamie Keegan came clomping in to announce:

"Miss Catherine and that old Sir Gareth's out with Miss Catherine's horse and gig. They'd be obliged was you to join them, love."

Mrs. Fothergay, who was standing over my table by this time, urging me to hurry, assumed at once that Jamie's term of endearment was addressed to her, and replied as she patted his head, "Dear boy! He's a love, too. Yes, he is, calling his dear Bedelia a love! Children are always so fond of me."

Under her ample arm Jamie made a face at me and grinned. I could not but grin back. I appreciated his feelings. As we passed Jamie on our way down the passage to the taproom and the street, however, the boy clasped my hand and squeezed in beside me.

"Watch yourself, will ye now?" His seriousness was not like him and I stared at him, upon realizing the change in his voice. Even his little-boy face with its endearing nose was troubled.

"Why must I watch myself?"

He said nothing, just looked at me. I did not like it, not half. Jamie was too wise, too intelligent, for all his talk of Gytrashes and other demons. He meant something or someone in particular by his warning, and I couldn't fathom exactly what it was.

Certainly not too much damage could be done to me or anyone else, when five persons were included in today's outing. I did not know what Marc Branshaw would do when Bedelia Fothergay arrived on the scene, but I thought it might be well worth the expedition just to see how he contrived to divide his charm among three women of assorted sizes, ages and temperaments.

Harnessed to a black gig, and nervously pawing the wet cobblestones in front of the inn, was a small, long-haired horse little larger than a pony, yet with those hard prominent bones that made the other citizens of Yorkshire so durable and formidable. He tossed his head at sight of me, or perhaps it was at sight of Mrs. Fothergay, elaborately bedecked in her frills, and crowning all by a huge hat like a catherine-wheel, tied with a large, gauzy bow under her chins. Small wonder the horse was upset.

I was glad, for the sake of the hat, if nothing else, that the weather had cleared to a certain extent. When I say cleared, I mean that the mizzly climate of last night was now more or less obscured by a thick gray overcast that shrouded the houses on the steep main street of the village, but only made the distant prospect the more green and desolate by contrast.

Outside the confines of the village I could see no sign of human habitation. The villagers under direction of the vicar and the curate Niles, looking for the killer, whether man or beast, of Abbie Hinchley, had been absorbed on the moors as if swallowed in a thick green quicksand.

It was with relief that I turned to the very human face of Miss Catherine Owen, who sat in the gig. Her brother, Sir Gareth, was waiting to greet us, looking not quite so bored as yesterday. Behind those pale blue eyes he appeared alert. I had been expecting his sister to be big-boned, husky, ruddy haired as he, with the look of arrogance that Sir Gareth never troubled to hide. Catherine Owen was unlike her brother in almost every detail. Her hair was dark, thick, worn in a style that was some fifteen or twenty years out of the present mode — puffed too much on the sides, and with a knot in the back, so that it accentuated the broadness of her cheeks. Her eyes were hazel, large and honest. I suspected they could light up with laughter, given the right impetus, but that laughter would not be pointed and cruel. She was solidly built, with a becomingly small waist, but I felt that her dull, dark paisley-print gown and short pelisse might have been more wisely chosen. In short, she endeared herself to women by being friendly, modest, a trifle dowdy, and with an inclination to submissiveness. Her voice when she spoke was young, sweet and girlish, and it suited the sweet, broad-cheeked, childish look of her face, although she must have been in her late twenties, if not older. It was not that, like Mrs. Fothergay, she strove for a semblance of youth, but rather, I thought, that her face had never quite caught up with her intellect.

"How very nice to meet you, Miss Wicklow!" She held out one hand in a neatly darned black mitt. Her clasp was strong and almost as firm as a man's. I was surprised but could not help liking her.

"I do trust you will forgive me. I am afraid there's only room for one other in the gig. If you don't mind walking with my brother as escort —"

"My pleasure, I'm sure," put in her brother gallantly.

Miss Catherine glanced downward at the thick folds of the hem of her gown. She brushed aside the folds. I saw nothing unusual in her two neat, motionless feet, carefully shod in low kid boots, until she added, "I do not walk. An accident on the moor last year. Mrs. Fothergay, would you oblige me by riding with me?"

Mrs. Fothergay was whispering to me behind her hand, "No wonder he jilted her. Good heavens! What a dowd!" but I turned my head away, pretending not to hear her. Sir Gareth had bowed first over Mrs. Fothergay's hand and then mine, languidly acknowledging my curtsey, but now he said with firmness:

"I don't like it. Damned if I do, Catherine.

Why the deuce should that little whelp have any business with you? After what you've been through. However —"

Mrs. Fothergay nudged me. Annoyed, I stepped away from her and crossed the cobblestones to the other side of the gig while Sir Gareth lifted her into it, amid her flutters and little cries of panic. She was soon safe beside Catherine Owen, who looked across her imposing form and gave me a warm smile before taking up the reins in her capable-looking, hands.

"Did you read my manuscript, Miss Wicklow?"

I was thinking that it was a curious kind of manuscript for a woman of Catherine Owen's temperament to write. I should have thought a high-spirited person with a vivid imagination had written all that nonsense, and here was this calm, quiet, strong-handed young woman, crippled yet capable, acknowledging she was the author.

"A little, here and there," I replied. "I recopied certain pages. I'm afraid I don't have time to read entire manuscripts," I explained as Sir Gareth began to walk beside me. I found it difficult to keep to his great stride. When I lagged a moment, his heavy arm came under mine to lift me along, and it seemed to me that his fingers pried more than necessary along the underside of my arm as he did so.

"Yes," said Miss Owen. "I noticed you had not

rewritten the last sixty pages. But perhaps you did not have time to read them. It must be tedious, copying badly written manuscripts."

I shrugged and she sat back comfortably. I saw now that she was relaxed and realized what I had thought to be a firm control of the reins a few minutes ago was actually a severe spasm of the nerves. One would never have guessed that her kind, phlegmatic constitution was so susceptible.

Sir Gareth said to me, "I hope you do not expect to do much business with Branshaw, Miss Wicklow. He is extremely unreliable and I shouldn't be surprised to find that he has forgotten you entirely. . . . You must then let me show you around our countryside. I'll show you a time you won't forget, will she, Catherine?"

I did not doubt it for a minute. Already he had made an impression upon me, particularly upon my arm and now and then my waist when he conceived the road too difficult for me.

But I said innocently, "He would indeed be forgetful then. He was very set upon our coming when he spoke to me last night."

I saw something shadowy out of the corner of my eye and knew that either Catherine Owen or Mrs. Fothergay had looked at me quickly, but I could not tell which.

"Oh, well then, if you had had a *tête-à-tête* with Branshaw already —" He lowered his voice romantically. "I shall see that there are no more between you. I'm your man for that, Miss Anne.

111

You want a man for good company, not a frippery fellow who's lived among the French all his life."

I sensed that the two women in the gig were waiting for my indignant denial of the *"tête-à-tête"* so I said nothing, only raised my skirts to keep from dragging them in the dirt of the lane, for we were now on top of Maidenmoor Rise and had lost the security of the cobblestones.

Mrs. Fothergay twitched around on her seat, muttering, and then squealed.

"Ah! What am I sitting on? Good heavens! I have crushed the box. What can it be?"

By this time the sheets of Catherine's manuscript were scattered over the seat and her dress, and several fluttered across my vision, into the blackened heather at one side of the lane. I ran to pick them up, feeling the thick carpet of wild vegetation underfoot, and with Sir Gareth's help we finally located all the scattered pages.

"Gad! What drivel, Catherine!" Sir Gareth bellowed, studying the loose sheets as we approached the two in the gig. "How's this, ladies, to frighten you into a fit of the fidgets?" He began to read from the top pages in his hand, in the manner most calculated to drive the author out of her mind:

" 'She shrieked at him in a fury, and indeed she was a fury! Well-made and tiny-waisted. Seeming human, but a cruel enchantress. Her Irish eyes snapping. . . . And then he saw her hands, held to him like claws, and she made as though to tear at his face. . . . She was no longer his little Monanne, his precious Irish enchantress, but a demon. Possessed —' "

Here Sir Gareth gave out in the trumpetry of a bad actor:

" 'He had known all along, and yet, fool that he was, he loved her. She it was; who had worn the habit of the Gytrash. No! Said he so? She *was* the Gytrash!' "

Sir Gareth shook his head. "Oh, come now, Cathie, surely this will never reach the printed page."

"Well!" said Mrs. Fothergay. "I never! It's enough to give one the shivers. And out in this lonely country, too."

Miss Catherine smiled at her criticism as she had smiled at her brother's.

"What do you think of it, Miss Wicklow? Do you agree that it is pretty poor stuff? Or perhaps — ?" she ventured with a waver of hope in her voice.

I started to say something and realized that my hand was at my throat. I felt dry as bone; for this page had never been in the manuscript that I read, and the description of the Gytrash, allowing for a bit of self-flattery, might have been myself. It is true that my name had not been used, but "Monanne" was near enough to "Anne" to be an-

113

noying if not downright alarming.

Where could she have gotten my description but from Marc Branshaw? It was like what I had suspected of him, too-cruel and wicked and perverse. He probably thought it a great jest. I had an appalling instant when I almost cried with the hurt of it, but then I looked up and, hating her and the rest of them, said calmly, "It is quite in keeping with the popular mode."

Mrs. Fothergay took the conversation from me at once.

"In keeping with this horrid countryside. Yes, indeed. If it were not for the keen disappointment to that dear boy, I should turn around instantly and take myself out of this dreadful place. One never knows when a blow will come, to wipe one out precisely like that unfortunate girl last night."

Catherine said, "Oh, no, ma'am. I hope you will not let my nonsense disturb you. It was only made up out of my head, you know."

"From living in this wilderness. I can well believe it."

With that lovely, childish voice, Catherine remarked to me, "I know you will understand, Miss Wicklow. From what Marc tells me, you appreciate the things I appreciate. You can see the beauty in this landscape. Can you not?"

I smiled at her.

"I should think we might share many of the same tastes, ma'am. And you mustn't underestimate your ability with a pen. One can do a great deal with such an instrument. I do a little work of

114

my own. However, I am afraid I have no brother to keep my pens sharpened. I sharpen them myself."

My animosity seemed to surprise her. I could not get her to reveal her true nature. There she was, bewildered, behaving as though she did not understand any more than her brother and Mrs. Fothergay were meant to understand.

"Now you can see it on the Brow yonder, the Hall. Moyna Branshaw's house," Sir Gareth announced as the horse and gig jogged across the rutted lane and entered on a path even narrower.

I did not at first hear him. I was still puzzling about Catherine Owen.

"What an actress she must be!" I thought; for I could have sworn that her innocence over the manuscript was not assumed.

VII

Mrs. Fothergay and I looked with interest across the high, rolling plateau with its color like the heart of an emerald, and made out the rectangular two-story gray stone building set attractively on a slight eminence above even the plateau on which we stood. Settled around the main house were various small outbuildings housing poultry and appurtenances to a house of the prosperous merchant class, neither too grand nor too gothic for the old Yorkshire family it had housed these two centuries.

It was about ten minutes' walk from us and I liked its look of a gentleman's house — solid, respectable, with the gracious air that so many homes built in the seventeenth century seemed to acquire. I think Mrs. Fothergay and I half expected a ghost-ridden haunted castle, that being more appropriate to the desolation around us. We were very much relieved.

"Why," said she, "It's quite — quite unexceptionable."

"All of that," Sir Gareth agreed drily. He had given his sister her manuscript and was reaching for my arm, but I had other things to think about and made the fatal mistake of crossing a gurgling little stream without relying on his outstretched hand. I had a suspicion, from the way he seemed torn between fixing his interests with me and with Mrs. Fothergay, that he was weighing our respective charms in his mind. Whatever else we might have offered the roving eye of a bachelor, certainly Mrs. Fothergay's comfortable little fortune should have been taken into account, and I think it was.

"How very odd," said Mrs. Fothergay suddenly. "There is no smoke coming out of the chimneys, and on such a day."

"Not odd at all, ma'am, for that fellow," said Sir Gareth. "The miserly beggar has a positive aversion to wasting fuel on the firegate. Never saw such a penurious dog. And if one wants a fire, one must provide it, and light it oneself. Isn't that true, Catherine?"

"Well, yes, but he likes it a bit . . . cool."

"Cool! He always has the place cold as ice. And what's more, when you touch him, he's cold as a tomb himself. If he's that cold, why doesn't he light a fire?" He broke off suddenly to tighten his grip on my arm. "Come now, Miss Anne, why should you tremble? Don't tell me you're frightened of that puppy."

"Heavens, no!" I said quickly, attempting a laugh that was more nervous than convincing. "It's just that I really am cold."

I may have been cold but I was also nervous over how I should behave without doing bodily harm to that horrid Marc Branshaw. Yet, from the first moment when he peered in at me in London like some resurrected ghost, to a moment ago when I began to suspect he gave my description to Catherine for such a mean, malicious joke, he had made it all seem reasonable. If there were some deep motive, I might understand, but from what I now knew of him, he had a naturally cruel sense of humor. Small wonder that I was nervous.

We came to a hollow outlined by several heavy chestnut trees, one of which overhung the lane, twisted precariously by the years and the harsh winters, until Catherine Owen's gig barely crept past the hungry black branches without being entangled. As we mounted to Branshaw Hall beside a low stone wall in good repair, I saw the slender figure of a man standing on the wall at the top of the hill, feet apart, motionless, but in

117

the oddly graceful position of a schoolboy about to leap off into space. He saw us and waved, then actually did leap off the wall and come down to meet us. I was walking close beside Catherine Owen and saw her hands tremble noticeably upon the reins. Without having the right to, I pitied her. But then, I was very nearly as nervous as she — and I had less excuse, for I was the merest acquaintance of our fickle young man.

"Insolent pup!" Sir Gareth exclaimed. "Catherine, the fault is yours. Why do you permit him these familiarities, as though he might run to you like a lad to his lass, whenever he may choose?"

"Please, Gareth, be quiet," said the lady, without, so far as I could see, losing her temper. I stepped back and she leaned out of the gig to call to Marc Branshaw. "Good morning, Marc. How are you?"

The gentleman, in excellent humor, took her hand. "I needn't ask how you are, Cathie. Sweet as always." His glance flicked over her brother with a brief, malicious, "Ah! Ever the attentive escort, eh, Gareth," and his glance at me was just as indifferent except for a little crooked smile at the corner of his mouth. I wondered what he found amusing about me. "Good. The lady from Sackerby, Perth. We need that fine Italian hand of yours." He reserved his effusive greeting for Mrs. Fothergay. I could not understand his motive, although I knew there must be one.

"Bedelia, ma'am, radiant flower! How kind of

you to come! Did you have a pleasant journey, ma'am?"

He walked on up the hill on Mrs. Fothergay's side of the gig and as we passed the carriage block, and reached the walled garden gates of Branshaw Hall, it was he and not Sir Gareth who lifted her to the ground. A groom from the Hall came to take the horse in charge. Sir Gareth, angrily chewing his lip, picked up his sister and carried her into the entrance hall, which was pleasantly carpeted in worn but rich green and gold drugget. All the time that Sir Gareth was muttering his disapproval to his sister, Marc Branshaw was chatting animatedly to Mrs. Fothergay. Once only, when we entered a large main room on the right and saw at the far end of the room a great Jacobean fireplace, unlighted, but stacked as though ready for burning, our host spoke to me. I was by this time inured to the indifference of all concerned, and thought at first there was a mistake. He spoke almost in my ear, very low.

"Come, don't look so cross. I'll be rid of them. Bide a moment." He must be mad. I, of course, said nothing to such effrontery.

Catherine was seated comfortably in a heavy chair decorated with Jacobean carvings like all the furniture in the room — solid, very old and worn, but of excellent workmanship. The windows opened out upon a delightful view of the little garden, where a thorn tree was surrounded by rose bushes and some green foliage with red berries still dripping from the morning dew. Beyond was the garden wall and then the lane back down past the ravine of the ancient chestnuts and up to Maidenmoor Rise.

"Whole thing's preposterous," Sir Gareth was saying. "My sister's manuscripts are no concern of yours, Branshaw, and as for Mrs. Fothergay —" The more attention his host paid to that lady, the more attached the baronet became to her. He had obviously made his choice between her and me.

Marc looked from one of them to the other.

"But — I had no notion. Are you acquainted with Mrs. Fothergay?"

The lady fluttered.

"Oh, indeed, yes. We are old friends, are we not?"

"But not such friends as the lady and I." Marc argued in that tone of sweet conviction most calculated to irritate Sir Gareth.

"Rubbish! The lady and I journeyed from Teignford together."

"Good Lord! But that was only yesterday. I have known her this age; have I not, dear ma'am?"

Mrs. Fothergay protested laughingly but I saw how it would be in the end.

Sir Gareth grew more cutting and determined, until there was only one thing for it. Marc retired gracefully from his position, yielded his prior claim on Mrs. Fothergay and ended by propelling them both out to the garden. He suggested

120

that it was a pity Miss Catherine's gig could not be used by Sir Gareth to show his charming companion the countryside —

"— while we three get on with such dull stuff as musty manuscripts."

"Certainly I may have the use of my sister's gig!" cried Sir Gareth, rising instantly to the bait. "One would think I have nothing to say in my own household. Catherine, I am driving Mrs. Fothergay to — to —"

"Why not try Upshed?" suggested his sister.

Sir Gareth favored us all with an indifferent glance from his cold, blue eyes, and a few minutes later we could see him out beyond the garden gates, taking the reins from the hands of the groom and turning the gig while Mrs. Fothergay chattered happily at his side.

Catherine laughed.

"And if you had asked Gareth to leave with that woman, he would not have budged from this spot! You are quite incorrigible, Marc. You are determined to make that poor woman believe she's broken your heart. Must you pretend with everyone?"

After giving me a sheaf of paper, during which brief contact I realized his hands were excessively cold, and seating me beside an inkstand on the great dining table in the center of the room, Marc sat down on the table's edge.

"Not everyone, Catherine. Perhaps she merely leaped to a conclusion, as women often do. They have the invariable habit of believing everything

121

that is said of them in their praise. It's a dangerous habit."

She blushed and looked discomfited.

"You are right," she admitted reasonably.

He seemed more annoyed than pleased at her sweet disposition.

"Well!" he said after a pause. "Let's have a go at the manuscript. Have you made the changes I suggested?" He began to rifle through the pages, now and then looking down at me, although he addressed no words my way. I was wondering how I could reproach him for the wicked description of me, since he here confessed that the changes were of his own devising. Once, when I caught him looking at me, he smiled in such a way that it was painfully difficult to resist smiling back, so I ended by catching myself in a ridiculous grimace which had begun as a smile.

After an hour had passed and we were all tired, he skipped through and glanced over the climactic pages. He frowned.

"What is all this, Cathie? What the deuce made you change your villain?"

Catherine said faintly, "I — I thought people might take you in dislike if he were as much like you as you said."

"I said change the details about the Gytrash nonsense, so that it shouldn't be traced to what's going on here, or we shall have mobs taking matters into their own hands as they once did. I didn't say it was necessary for you to shield *me*. That is not, and never was, your job, Cathie."

She was frightfully hurt. I knew that. I wished I might vanish for it was painful to witness this scene. I had no business here. I looked down at the sheaf of paper on which I had jotted certain changes as he dictated, and began to draw meaningless little checks and figures.

As he read on, he was less and less pleased. He laughed shortly. It was an ugly laugh.

". . . Irish-eyed Monanne. . . . Now I wonder who that might be."

I kept my gaze fastened on the sheaf in my lap, but my cheeks, I am sure, had bright red spots in them. True, I had eyes almost too dark to be called green, but the implication and the further description, were there. He went on in that cuttingly polite way.

"You have outdone yourself, Catherine. Half the good citizens of Yorkshire will recognize Moyna, my mother. You conceive that to be an improvement, I take it."

She quailed in embarrassment.

"No — no. I made up that description. I scarcely remember Moyna's eyes. Were her eyes Irish?"

Marc moved off the table and walked across the room. When still some distance from the great fireplace, he stopped and studied a portrait over the mantel. I did not know how he could see it so clearly, and wondered that he did not move closer, for it was dim in the November daylight. He said, with his back to us:

"Pale green, I seem to recall. I am surprised

123

you did not mention her height — she was quite tall for a woman — and the red hair as well." He turned suddenly, looking at Catherine Owen in the way of a black cat about to spring. His voice was silken and made me shiver. "But then, you must remember her eyes. You were with her two hours while she lay dying. Did you never look in her eyes during those hours, my dear Cathie?"

Catherine's answer was a pained outcry.

"Marc! I could not walk. You know that. It was the shock of seeing her fall like that, I think. Or perhaps when it took so long to save her. You know I was injured as well, in trying to rescue her."

"Moyna was familiar with every pot-hole on the moors. She knew every bog, every fallen place. She would never have taken that last step herself."

"You don't know! She was willful. She went where she chose. She — she said the place had old memories. She had been on that trail so many times with the Devil— with Ewen Morgan."

"And she wanted to take you?" he asked ironically. "It was not like her to share her memories."

"I wanted to write about her and the Devil-Vicar. She knew the silly passion I had about the memory of him. I knew him when I was a girl in Wales. He scarcely knew I lived, but I remember him. Moyna was amused. She said it would avenge her upon the village if I wrote about him. She agreed that I might accompany her when she walked up to the cottage. She even mentioned that I would be amused at the contents of those journals she kept. We were speaking of them when she —"

It seemed to me that Marc was suddenly very much interested, but I could not be sure. It was natural that he should have an interest in his mother's journals. Miss Catherine went on.

"And then she fell. The earth seemed to give way. It was very boggy there. I tried to get her out ... but I discovered I couldn't walk either. I think I'd got my legs caught in those horrid submerged tree limbs where the ground and turf collapsed when I tried to help her. My legs were numb ..."

I could not contain myself longer. This was a terrible scene with which to tax Miss Owen.

"Please, Mr. Branshaw, surely the lady has suffered enough for the accident. Can't we talk of something else?"

I don't believe Miss Owen really thanked me for the interference. She gave me a quick, straight look from her large hazel eyes and then smiled apologetically.

"I do not often discuss my infirmity. I hope you will believe that, ma'am. As for Marc, we know each other so well, we can make allowances. Marc, my dear friend, can't we have tea? That should cut the gloomy atmosphere."

I could see that her kindly defense of him and her assumption of the hostess role annoyed him but he shrugged and reached behind him to pull a worn bell-cord. When a pert young woman with an Irish face appeared in answer to the summons, Catherine spoke before Marc could do so.

"Tea, Dilys, and, if we may, a few slices of that delicious parkin that Cook makes."

"Ye'll be meanin' the moogin, mum?"

"Muggin or parkin, or gingerbread!" her employer cut in sharply. "What does it matter? Go along, Dilys." But the girl did not take Marc's tone amiss. She merely looked from him to me, grinned and said, "Ay, sor. It's parfectly clear. Tea an' moogin for the lady . . ." She glanced briefly, insolently at Catherine. "Ladies, what I mean to say," and left.

I was surprised at her apparent animosity to Miss Owen, whose forbearing nature under her affliction should have commended her to everyone. Everyone, it would appear, except Marc Branshaw and his servants.

What a queer-tempered creature he was! In the clouds one minute, chattering and casting a spell with his smooth tongue, the next minute down in the depths and cross as a cat.

When the tea and gingerbread came, Dilys set the tray on the table near me. I was dumbfounded and pushed it toward Catherine, not knowing what else to do, but Marc interfered.

"For heaven's sake, will someone pour!"

I poured.

Catherine's cheeks were flushed, but she managed to look pleasanter than she felt, I daresay.

No one said anything for a time, and Marc, trapped between one woman who was looking injured and noble, and another who was scowling at his shocking display of bad manners, finally broke down.

"All right, Catherine. I'm sorry."

True, he did not have to be so excessively sorry. He stepped over to her chair and, leaning over her, kissed her lightly upon the cheek. It was so quickly and carelessly done that I hardly thought it warranted such rosy confusion on her part. In fact, I thought the whole episode a little overdone. I doubt if Marc did, though, for he went back to the plate of "parkin" or "muggin" and began to eat.

As for me, I felt clearly now the chill of this great room which, with a fire burning in the grate, would have been an ideal place. I reached for my cloak, forgetting that it had been removed when we came into this room. Catherine saw my gesture and seemed to be thinking busily. She was looking directly at me, yet she did not appear to see me at all. She said, after she had reached her decision:

"Marc, our — your guest is chilled. Don't you think we might have a small fire? I see there's one laid."

He did not glance at the grate, or the huge fireplace itself. To my surprise, although he had been happily eating gingerbread a moment ago, he was now very much occupied with Catherine's manuscript.

She began again. "Marc. . . ."

"Yes, yes. I hear you. Miss Wicklow, if you will

do this page over, I think it will save us all from wearing spectacles."

I took the page he handed to me, and we looked into each other's eyes. His dark brows curved in a puzzled frown.

"Do you really want a fire? I feel quite comfortable."

Nevertheless, his fingers, when they touched mine, were colder than my own. I stared at his hand. There was nothing in the least odd about it, but he snatched it back and looked at it. I don't know what he expected to find on it. Apparently he realized that it was its unnatural coldness which had interested me. He smiled.

"I suppose you think I am cold-blooded; is that what you would like to say?"

"That goes without saying," I remarked tartly.

He laughed and went over and summoned Dilys. I had turned my attention to the manuscript pages when I noticed Catherine's arrested pose. She was watching the Irish girl and Marc Branshaw with an attention that the act of lighting the fire certainly did not merit. The moment Dilys came back with a lighted spill from the kitchen Marc turned his back to her and to the fireplace and went to the great baronial table at which I sat. He leaned forward over a page of manuscript, with two fingers of either hand tightly clutching the carved table edge. Behind him, across the room, Dilys started a sputtering light in the grate and left us. Catherine looked up at me. As I watched her, she deliberately extended her arm as far as she could reach, and pushed the burning newspaper off the coals. The fiery paper went on burning but, of course, it would not catch on the coals. I gaped at her, ready to say something, too amazed to know what to say. She put her finger to her lips.

Marc, sensing our abnormal stillness, raised his head, but he did not look around to see what we were up to.

Catherine exclaimed suddenly, "Oh! What a pity! The flame's fallen off the coals. . . . Marc!"

He did not turn around, but his head was still raised. He was tense as though there had been a gunshot. He put out one hand without looking around at me.

"Miss Wicklow, would you be so good as to —"

I think the thing that almost unnerved me was his hand. Just for an instant, it trembled. Then he seemed to recover himself and took up the manuscript pages again.

Astonished at what I could only suppose was a humiliating display of cowardice, I went to the fireplace and kicked some of the coals into the little blaze so that they eventually caught. As I rose from the fireplace I exchanged a look with Catherine. Her eyes were all sympathy. She touched her temple significantly and nodded in Marc's direction, as one would say: "It is a madness."

If the scandalmongers were right and Marc Branshaw was the natural son of the dead Devil-Vicar, then his abhorrence of fire was more understandable, for he must often think of that agonizing death his father suffered.

I ignored Catherine's expressions and said calmly, "Shall we resume the reading, Mr. Branshaw?"

His stiffened form relaxed. When I came and sat down facing him, his eyes had such an expression of anguish and shame in them as was almost heartbreaking to see, and I could have cheerfully slapped Miss Catherine for putting him to this ordeal. His face was damp with the cold sweat of his effort to conceal his panic from us. Then he got hold of himself and managed to say, as though nothing had happened:

"You haven't seen house yet, have you? Suppose I show it to you while Catherine makes the changes. It's rather an interesting old relic, fortunately built in a day when the architecture wasn't quite so monstrous as these presentday horrors. Can you get on alone, Catherine? You will probably welcome the peace and quiet in which to work."

She hesitated just a moment before saying in her pleased way, "Thank you. I shall be quite content. There's so much to do on this silly manuscript. Just so that the bell-cord is within reach."

"Will you come?" he asked me, holding out his hand. I was put in mind of Jamie Keegan using the same gesture. I took Marc's hand. It was warmer after we had gone a few steps. I thought, with the conceit of all womankind, that if Marc

Branshaw saw very much of me, I might thaw out that appalling physical chill of his flesh; for there was nothing chilling about his look or his manner to me. I was sure that, despite his taste for cold rooms, his lips were not cold, as I very nearly knew from experience, and his eyes, in my company, were not always haunted and suffering.

I remained with my illusion for some time that day.

VIII

Neither of us said anything for the first few minutes. He cast sidelong glances at me now and then to see how I reacted to his curious display in the drawing room. When I did not speak, he said defensively:

"I don't always behave like such a complete and utter fool, you know."

I said, "Don't talk about it. We all have things that annoy us."

His fingers tightened their grip on mine. I had a notion the gesture was to reassure himself that there was someone near.

"Frightfully oppressive place," he went on, referring to the walls around us. "I always feel like a very small intruder who may be booted out if he's caught."

We were walking up the great carpeted staircase, which I found pleasantly grand, but it was

131

only afterward that I remembered anything about the interior of the house. I was too much absorbed in my companion. Perhaps he felt the inadequacy of his excuse about the fire. When he spoke again, he was back at the thing that really troubled us both. He was still fearfully nervous when he mentioned it. I could sense the tension in his body, and for that reason, I tried not to let him suspect I considered his behavior to be an act of sheer cowardice.

"It was because you were watching — that made her fire trick a little more ghastly than usual. I knew you were watching. Even so, I — I couldn't. You won't believe it, but I tried. I really tried."

Attempting to cover the little break that came with his last words, he cleared his throat, but that naked, betraying emotion lay between us in the silence. I was conscious of a twist at my heart which was more than sympathy, though less than understanding.

"It doesn't matter in the least. Don't talk about it unless you wish."

"Why does she do it? *Why?*" He paused, took a deep breath. I tried not to notice the strain in his voice and his face.

"Miss Owen?" But that's nonsense."

"She's done it before, but always when we were alone. . . . This time —" His eyes opened wide. He struck the polished oaken balustrade with a ringing slap. "Of course. It had to be so. That you might spread the story."

I did not agree with him aloud, although I suspected he was right. But I recalled that she had grounds for her behavior. While I was wondering how I should venture onto the boggy ground between him and the girl he had jilted, he pointed out to me several portraits of severe-looking Branshaws, or the handsome Rivercombs who were, he explained to me, Moyna's people. There were no pictures of his legitimate father, Josiah, and I supposed that if there had been, Moyna must have removed them in the long years she lived here alone.

The bedchambers were on this floor and Marc pointed them out, showing me one or two which were nicely kept, dust-free and clean, but somehow rather sad for it was impossible to prevent them from giving off a curious, unused odor, like the musky scent of costumes in an old trunk.

He did not show me his room, except to point it out, which was not surprising, for from my observation he seemed never to sleep. We came presently to his mother's room, and he showed me around it, watching my reactions I suppose, because he was proud of the room. It was indeed attractive — all white, with low, whitewashed cross-beams, dimity curtains, a lovely canopy over the bed, and carefully chosen furniture, done in elegant *petit point*.

My eyes went back to the bed. I don't know what I would have thought eventually in connection with it, but at the moment I was innocently considering what type of material had been used in that tester which was still kept so clean and neat.

Marc's mind obviously did not run along the same path.

"I imagine that bed could answer a number of questions that still puzzle the villagers. My mother used to say 'My bedposts could tell many a story that the gossips would like to hear.' "

I was embarrassed at his bringing up such a thing, but in order to save face, I pretended to be as sophisticated as my French ancestors would have been.

"Do you think she and the Devil-Vicar met here, in her husband's house?"

He started to answer me, stopped suddenly, then shrugged and called my attention to the portrait on the near wall, which was of an exciting red-haired beauty with green eyes. I knew that it must be Moyna Branshaw herself, yet it puzzled me. Something in the face, or the eyes, made me recall an idea I had formerly held. Why did I think that Marc Branshaw's mother was Irish, brown-haired and dark-eyed? Where had I heard that other description? And why should someone lie to me about Moyna Branshaw's appearance?

"She's beautiful," I remarked, unnecessarily. She was also selfish and charming and sparkling with sly humor, I guessed.

To my surprise, he studied the portrait thoughtfully, and then said, "I suppose she is.

When I was young, I thought so. An enchanting companion — I've been told. But . . . one's ideas change, as people change. So I cannot say now."

"Anyone that beautiful must have been a little selfish and she may not have given you the attention you thought you merited as a child." It was curious how little she resembled her son, except in her nature perhaps.

He was amused.

"How old you sound! But you needn't bother making excuses for her. She never expected them. That's one reason why she was always teasing and worrying Catherine Owen. She used to write to me of the girl with her sweet fawn's eyes. They troubled Moyna, who was more salty herself. But Moyna was Moyna. The village forgave her very rapidly. It was her wicked seducer — our Devil and Monster — they blamed."

I could not help reminding him. "They certainly treat him with deference today. No one has an unkind word for him. Everyone seems to think he was the pride of Maidenmoor's past."

"Pity he didn't know that, while he was burning," said Marc.

I felt a little sick at his words and changed the subject quickly.

"From the look of her, I wouldn't put it beyond her to have seduced the poor Devil-Vicar."

He laughed at my female wisdom. "I don't doubt you're right."

He took my hand and drew me out of the

room, whether I wanted to go or not.

When we came out upon the narrow side gallery, we stood there a few moments, staring at the vista of far, green rolling country that looked so harmless from this height.

"Do you ever feel smothered by all those moors?" I asked him.

"I loathe them!"

The furious passion in his voice startled me.

"You can't mean that. These people are human. They have tried to make amends to you and your mother for their crime. You must wish them well for that."

"Wish them well! I wish them at the bottom of a bog!"

"Not all of them, surely. I met the young curate, Frederick Niles, last night. He is a good man."

"Detestable creature!" exclaimed Marc, with one of his self-derisive smiles. "He is a constant reminder of the kind of man I should have been and am not. If only he were righteous, or even pompous and absurd, like MacDonnachie. But no. He must be kind and understanding, and intelligent . . . and," he ended on a laugh, "of course, I detest him for it."

I changed the subject. "But it is a beautiful country, in its way."

"And its citizens are beautiful, in their way," he mocked me. I stared up at his face. Now and then I seemed to glimpse another soul behind the lighthearted, gay, mocking young man I thought I had known in London. It was a bitter, hardened soul that had gone through fires of which I knew nothing. It was older, as old as his bitter world, and the gay, mocking young man was — at these times — devoured by that other creature lurking always behind the facade.

The curious thing was, I found myself drawn to that hardened soul fully as much as to the gay, mocking young man. Perhaps because I sensed he needed me the more.

"I can understand your feelings, because your mother had such an unhappy romance with that . . . that man. But even so, they are your people, and this is your own country."

"Much you know about it."

"Then why did you come back?"

"I wanted to discover if they had hounded my mother to her death as they hounded that poor idiot who was her lover. Now you know."

"And did they?"

He turned away.

"I can't say. If I could find her journals, I feel sure I would know. Catherine mentioned them, you remember."

I decided I might as well ask my question now as later. "May I ask a question you might not wish to answer?"

"Certainly. If I may give you an answer you may not wish to hear." When he smiled in that way, half his face looked different, so that his mouth and his eyebrow curving upward gave him a kind of cruel, mocking cynicism. I was learning to be uneasy when he looked like that. I wished I could dislike him at such times. I went on being uneasy, hoping the quick mood would pass.

"Did you jilt Catherine Owen?"

I don't think he expected that at all. He had the decency to redden a little.

"Not . . . technically."

"No. But literally?"

He sighed in a bored way. "Must we talk about that tiresome great creature?"

"She was crippled trying to save your mother."

"Still," he said, in the most cutting way, "she did not *quite* save her, did she? And she has played on that ever since. From the moment I reached Maidenmoor, I've been reminded by all and sundry of my debt to Catherine Owen. So I was friendly to her, hoping to discover what she really knew. But then, her creep-mouse ways, and her pawing! Good God! She makes me shudder sometimes at her sheer goodness!"

I began to be frightened. Was no one ever allowed to express any emotion over this curious man? What if one could not help it?

I said, "If you'd ever been in love, you could not feel this way. Think of your mother. She knew what love was. Can't you make allowances?" I began to wriggle my fingers in his grasp afraid he would think I was like Catherine, cloying and clinging to him.

"Good God!" he exclaimed. "Do you think I'm averse to love? But why doesn't she stand up to me? Those ways of hers. That grimy, sweets-filled paw of hers! No, I thank you! Not my sort, and never was!"

He felt my attempt at retreat and laughed.

"Oh, come now. Don't flatter yourself. You are neither sweet nor pawing. You're as prickly and as salty as Moyna was, I'm sure." I was wondering how to take this dubious compliment when he went on, firmly. "Catherine doesn't love me. She loves some idiotic conception of me. I feel as though I were a ghost; and she were looking through me at something — or someone — else. Besides, it's quite possible she did lead Moyna to her death. It was either Catherine or her brother. I am . . . I was convinced of it."

"But why?" He had let go of my hand and I decided that if I wanted to keep his good regard, I had better not make any "sweet" gestures.

"Why?" he repeated. "Because of Moyna's letters to me. She said she was amusing herself, playing a game with a person she suspected of attempting murder long ago. That would not likely be Catherine, of course, but suppose she had found out something about Catherine's brother?"

Moyna sounded as devilish as her Great Love, I thought.

He took a deep breath. "How glad I'll be when this thing is done and then it's back to France again, to work! I don't belong here. I hate them all too much."

"Not quite all, surely."

139

He smiled. I'm sure he thought I was making an exception of myself. But he did not answer. I went on.

"Jamie Keegan worships you."

Frowning, he stared at the countryside that lay all around us. He had probably caught sight of several men in the distance, moving quickly through the blackened heather, crossing the Branshaw grounds to the north. They all carried weapons — clubs for the most part — and I thought I made out one or two hunting rifles.

"Jamie," he repeated thoughtfully. "That lad knows something."

"Naturally. He saw the Gytrash. He is a witness."

"My dear girl." He turned around and took me by the shoulders, shaking me for my stupidity. "My girl, there is no Gytrash. There is no animal, unless it be some wretched hound or other. There's a human intelligence behind all this, and Jamie knows it. He told the Gytrash story to conceal something . . ." He stopped rocking me back and forth, for which I was only half grateful; I liked the sensation of his hands upon me. He added in a whisper, "something . . . worse."

He let go of me, behaving almost as if he were alone. "Now, what can be worse to a boy like Jamie, than a Gytrash?"

"Why don't you ask Miss Catherine?" I said, remembering suddenly. "She invented the Gytrash for her novel. Probably that's where young Jamie got his idea."

"Ah, yes. We return to the delectable Catherine. . . . I had to post to London once, to snatch up that stupid manuscript. She was so obliging as to tell me about it — after she had sent it. Heaven knows what made her change her mind. Conscience, perhaps. All apologies, she was. She wanted to know if it might do me any harm — as though I cared for that! But the Gytrash, that had to be changed. I think she was writing about someone she knew. That's why she asked me to get the book back . . . not to protect myself, but to protect someone else."

Behind him I could see the men in the distance, crossing to the north, where the country looked darker and more boggy. Two men had broken away from the main group and were hurrying toward Branshaw Hall.

Marc turned and leaned over the stone balustrade.

"What is it, Sam? What the deuce is all that running about?"

A big Yorkshireman looked up and waved to us from the garden gates before opening them and coming around to the side of the building. Behind him, trotting along as fast as his girth would permit, was Reverend Cadmon MacDonnachie.

"I say, Marc, old chap, we need you. We've treed him."

Sam, the other one, made motions.

"Hugh great sheep dog, Mister Marc, like we all said. He belonged to an old weaver from Upshed — old Danbery — died some weeks ago.

141

The poor beast been lone an' lorn-like ever since. Half-starved, poor creetur. Must've been what young Jamie Keegan saw. We got the beast treed over past the Brow, in the Wind-Rock."

"I'll join you. Go on."

The Vicar called up to us: "Is that a lady with you? Ah, just so — Miss Wicklow. Can you spare us a bit of your time, ma'am? We've got the boy, Jamie, to identify the beast, and it's too far to go back and fetch his aunt. He's a bit skittish. Seems he needs a female to give him countenance."

Marc went back to the balcony. "Don't be ridiculous, Cadmon. I'll not have Miss Wicklow caught up in this thing. There may be danger up there. My housekeeper is over in Maidenmoor, but I'll get Cook to go with Jamie. She'd frighten any self-respecting beast."

"No, no. Ma'am!" trumped the Vicar. "Ma'am, the boy knows and likes you. There'll be no harm to you. We've got twenty men with us. Will you come?"

I looked at Marc. He shrugged and we left the balcony togther.

"Don't blame me if the damned thing chews you up," was his consoling remark as we returned to the upstairs hall.

I must say. I would have preferred that they send Marc's cook or someone else, but after privately thinking of Marc himself as a coward, I could not commit the same folly. Marc found some of his housekeeper's heavy walking shoes for me and, after stuffing one of Marc's handkerchiefs into each shoe to fill up the hollows, I felt ready for the moors.

I did not know too much about the quirks of the human brain, but it seemed odd to me that he should not be afraid of searching the moors for wild beasts, as he had done now for several nights, and yet be terrified of lighting a simple fire in his own grate, merely because of the fate that had befallen his supposed father. Perhaps a man could be only half a coward. I supposed some women would shun him for his half-cowardice; I despised it, but it did not have any effect on my feelings toward him. Rather, it seemed to augment them, since it was obvious that he needed someone, if only to light his accursed fires for him.

He considered me.

"Will you be warm enough? No. Of course not." He asked Dilys to fetch one of his own short hunting coats and then helped me into it in Moyna Branshaw's bedchamber, pushing my arms into each sleeve with the usual male carelessness for such things as linings and fingernails. I liked being bundled into his coat, especially when he smoothed the shoulders, turned up the cuffs, and raised the collar around my neck, then stood me there while he inspected me. When Dilys had left the room, he moved me about as though I were some toy.

We were both standing in front of Moyna's exquisite long mirror. He turned me around, pushing me this way and that, and then unfastened my hair. He swept it straight back above my ears in a fashion almost boyish, pulling the long strands so tight I was flat as flat can be. As to the other features, I winced.

"Hold it there!" he commanded me. I reached around, under considerable strain, and did so while he played with the tendrils of hair over my brow, trying to make it stand up, but it was too soft, and he gave it up, taking my hair out of my hands and loosening his grip a little. I still saw nothing in my looks to excite either of us. If he thought my hair might resemble his for some practical jest, he was mistaken, for it was lighter than his. His, being perhaps not so fine, was inclined to wave, and his hair curved naturally upward from his brow while mine saw not the slightest similarity. It must have been only a quick — very quick — impression that had made Mrs. Fothergay, and later, Sir Gareth, see something of a resemblance.

This matter of my hair occupied him a great deal more than it occupied me. I wondered if he had forgotten about the savage beast the villagers were going off to capture. But I was quite willing that he continue his playing forever.

Standing immediately behind me, with one hand holding my hair and one on my shoulder, he studied both our reflections and, although he frowned, he seemed satisfied. Then he turned me with my back to the mirror, and again looked at my reflection. I could not imagine what was so interesting about my back, unless it was his coat, which fit me surprisingly well except in the shoulders, and the sleeve length.

His own coat was very old, almost threadbare, and of a cheap plaid cloth such as the poorest man in the district might have worn. It did not have the quality and grace that most of his clothing suggested. I wondered at his ever having purchased it, and for what cause.

Finally, he gave me a little push, and said, "Now, do your hair up again. Ready to go?" He half-dragged me out into the hall and downstairs while I was still pinning up my hair, raining pins as we went.

I had had such tricks played on me before, but always for some ulterior purpose, such as the change to embrace me. But Marc Branshaw showed no signs of wanting to do so. I was just a tool to him. I could not conceive then what his purpose was.

IX

In the drawing room as we passed the open doors, we saw the red-bearded Vicar Mac-Donnachie leaning over Catherine Owen, apparently trying to persuade her of something. He stood up as he saw us.

"Marc, my lad. I can't get this charming lady to go with me. Thought Mrs. MacDonnachie might drive her home; she has her carriage and our wretched nag out on the road. But Miss Catherine is faithful to her vows. Said she's promised you she'd finish the manuscript."

Marc had been about to pass the doors without going in, but he stopped long enough to say indifferently, "By all means, Cadmon. Persuade her. We shan't be back until quite late, I've no doubt. Come!" he said to me.

We were arrested by the Vicar's voice.

"No use. Stubborn child." He pinched Catherine's full, childlike cheek and she smiled at him, but gave Marc a little glance to see how he took this. The Vicar sighed, left her, passing me in the hall and going on out to speak with his wife, who was waiting in an ancient covered carriage.

Catherine called softly, "Marc! May I speak with you?"

He let go of my hand and crossed the room quickly.

"Marc . . . do you really think I should go? I mean — would you rather?"

"I think you'd be more comfortable in your own house, don't you?" He looked around at the handsome interior of the drawing room. "You can't possibly enjoy this lonely place, and we shall probably be very late."

"Well . . ." She sighed. "Perhaps you're right. Would you oblige me?" She put out her hands. For just an instant he hesitated. Then he picked her up in his arms and carried her past me in the doorway. Looking back over her shoulder, Catherine smiled at me and held out one hand.

"Dear Miss Wicklow, I am so glad to have talked with you. Please come and see me often, won't you?"

Looking impatient, Marc stopped while I shook the hand she extended to me. Again, I was impressed at the warm, solid strength of her hand. What a pity such a healthy young woman, with so much to live for, should be crippled in this way! I felt that Marc behaved badly to her. She let her arm drop around his neck, but a quick motion of his head, whether by accident or intention, threw off her touch. She looked straight ahead afterward.

He took her out, set her in the carriage beside Mrs. MacDonnachie, and waved them both goodbye, which they correctly took as a hint to be off.

Marc and I started across the thick, wet turf to meet the distant group of hunters. I could understand his cross behavior, but it did seem excessively rude by comparison with his sudden change of manner now. His scowl had disappeared and he was behaving in the friendliest way, like someone who has observed the proprieties and almost expects to be thanked. It was difficult to be cross with him, no matter how he deserved it.

The trail we followed after crossing the Branshaw fields was hardly more than a sheep track, twisting, winding and rising all the while between the dying heather and the bracken that grew more heavily on the slopes as we ascended.

More frequently now, giant slabs of naked rock masked an occasional cave but gave us no shelter from a biting wind. I huddled further in Marc's coat, thankful for its high collar.

"Ay, mum," said the big man called Sam, seeing me shiver. " 'Tis wutherin' this day," and he pointed into the face of the wind.

"I told you you shouldn't have come," Marc reminded me. He put his arm around me, which was not much protection against the wind, but I let him think so.

I soon found all this climbing hard on my breath and limbs. I was little used to walking in London, and not really constituted for the long country strides of these Yorkshiremen, and I would soon have turned back but for the knowledge that everyone except Marc Branshaw seemed to expect strenuous efforts of me.

He laughed when he helped me after I had stumbled a second time and said with mock severity, "You would play the heroine!" It was a relief when I perceived that he was not ashamed of me, for I had begun to realize the immensity of this task I'd set myself. Then we saw Jamie Keegan running down the sheep track toward us.

"Marc! Marc! You're come now. I'm that glad to see ye. They said it was a female I was wanting. But I said I must see you first. I'll say no word of the beast til ye tell me." He shook Marc's hand like an adult, winked at him, and then looked at me.

"He's half a mind to snatch you from them London men; he told me so. You've a mind to let him snatch you, mum?"

Any other man might have been either cross or embarrassed at this disclosure. But while I tried hard to look indifferent and ignore the question, Marc Branshaw ruffled Jamie's hair, thus completing the wild job already begun by the bitter wind.

"That's the chatterbox!" He laughed. "Now you've ruined any chance of my discovering whether Miss Anne would let herself be snatched."

"What a magnificent view! I had not thought we'd come so far," I cried suddenly, so that I should not be said to commit myself.

Jamie stopped on the brow of a hill in the lee side of a great, overhanging boulder, and pointed out what he claimed to be my own room in the Yorkish Lion Inn. Looking back over the glens and rolling landscape below us, broken by out-croppings of rock, nettle and black peat, I could see nothing beyond the distant spire of Maiden-moor church and decided Jamie's vision was fanciful.

"Where did you see the Gytrash?" I asked him, thinking of the relief to the countryside now that the starved and savage beast was cornered.

Jamie said not a word. When the silence became a little oppressive and I could hear only the wild roar of the wind whipping through the bracken and against the ageless rocks, I looked at him. He and Marc were staring at each other in a curious way, both alert, keenly pitched, as though they waited. For what?

Marc and I glanced at each other. I was remembering what Marc had said two hours ago — that the murders were not the work of an animal but a human intelligence. He had been proven wrong almost immediately. Yet he said now, gently, to the boy:

"That's what we must be sure of, Jamie. Don't you agree?"

Jamie's eyes looked a little wild, trapped. I had an inexplicable sensation that he was undecided which way to jump. "If — if there's no more killing . . . then, does it matter?"

I could not help saying, "It matters a great deal, Jamie. If a beast kills a man, the beast should be destroyed."

"Even if he never kills no one else?"

What ailed the boy?

"This is very silly, Jamie. I'm surprised at you. Your Aunt Rose wouldn't believe a murderous beast should be spared. He might kill again."

"But — if a beast don't know? What if somebody — something I mean to say — is punished and then . . . then it . . . ain't the one?"

Marc said pleasantly, "Do you mean there are two savage dogs loose in this Godforsaken wilderness? Come now, Jamie lad, you've already testified that you saw the beast." His voice was gentle but I sensed the dagger sharp attention he was giving to his words and to the boy's reaction.

150

Jamie did not say anything. He began to walk. We saw then that he was crying. He made no attempt to wipe away the tears. The wind whipped at his face and the tears dried in streaks. Marc and I followed him. He was facing some sort of a problem that came even before his devotion to Marc. I was afraid to interfere further between them.

On the north side of the great jutting boulder we received the full impact of the wind, and although it was unpleasant in its furious gusts, it carried the wild, half acrid, half sweet odor of the wilderness that lay now all around us. Where, in the heights and glens of the Maidenmoor country, there had been sheepcotes peppered about the landscape, almost but not quite hidden from view, here the country which led down to a noisy stream and over toward Moyna Branshaw's cottage on the opposite hill, was even more rugged. I could see no sign of habitation except the Branshaw cottage, which I now beheld somewhat dimly, as clouds came and went over the watery November sun. The path meandered around clumps of heather and bracken, now and then soggy, so that one's feet nearly bounced over the dark turf that was the remnant of ancient bogs.

The Reverend MacDonnachie came puffing back up the trail to meet us. He had with him a quiet, gentlemanlike man whom he introduced as Dr. Ralph Lowther from Upshed, the physician the old weaver had been visiting when he died of a heart seizure.

"Yes," said the doctor, upon Marc's questioning, "it's the old fellow's dog, right enough. I never thought him savage. But he was a one-man dog, as the saying goes. When he lost his master and wasn't fed, I daresay he took to savaging whatever he could lay teeth to. Must have met old Will Grimlett on his forays and Will tried to stop him robbing the sheepcote of the poultry yard — something of that sort. The beast is just down below the brow of the hill, in an old hollowed passage in those crags yonder. A couple of sheepmen trapped the creature there before dawn, and lost two dogs to the beast. Can't get him to come out."

The Vicar rubbed his red beard as though it itched, and said, "Damnable thing is, the creature's very liable to find another way out, and then it's the Devil to pay."

Half a dozen voices broke from the confused gathering at the mouth of what I took to be the passage worn into the rocks and perhaps leading far to the other side of the hill. The passage was directly below a trickle of water that must have been a gushing torrent in spring, sweeping across the bracken-covered brow of the rocks and then descending, to wind its way through the narrow passage and empty itself into the Maidenmoor country on the other side.

Many of the men and boys, with one or two warmly-dressed women, were strangers to me, and from their greetings to the group from

Maidenmoor, I took them to be from Upshed.

One or two boys had tried to wriggle their way into the narrow passage, hoping to get a shot at the animal, but hastily scrambled out when we all heard, inside the passage, the gutteral growl of the beast who had already murdered two people. Hearing the warning sound, the wounded dog began to whimper, and the Reverend Niles took a shawl offered by one of the women and spread it over the suffering animal.

"I couldna get a line to shoot on," complained one of the boys. "Yet I heard un."

"We all heard him," Dr. Lowther agreed. "The thing is to get near enough to shoot the creature."

The Vicar turned to Marc, who was studying the situation with what I could only hope was simple curiosity, not the careful eye of a man who intended to go into that horrid place.

"Ye'll have no trouble with the light. It's light as a lamp inside," explained one of the boys, encouragingly. "All the daylight comes in, like in a cave."

"A great help to the beast as well as to the man who must flush him," murmured the doctor.

The Vicar seemed to find Marc's progress interesting, for Marc had climbed the side of the boulder and was examining the higher, more open crevices some six feet above the ground.

The Vicar called up to him:

"Miss Moyna knew this passage, didn't she, laddy? She met my late predecessor here now and again, if legend serves me. Did she ever mention it to you?"

The crowd grew still. Everyone was staring up at Marc except Jamie, who knelt with his head down, picking wet bracken that grew on the outside slope of the path. I saw that his breath was suspended, however, and he was waiting for Marc's reply like the rest of them.

Marc called down to us, "I imagine she did. I have some vague recollection. . . . The beast is not in sight — I can see that much. He must be hidden in a recess behind the cave."

"Was there any other way out?" asked Dr. Lowther.

"Now, now, doctor," put in the Reverend MacDonnachie. "How would Marc know that? It's only Moyna and the Devil-Vicar who would know." He winked at me but his joke was in bad taste, I thought, and I looked stonily ahead.

"I believe there was another way out," Marc said, as he moved up further to the top of the boulder, getting a handhold rather precariously, I thought, from the tufts of dead ling and bracken. "It may have been sealed up by the bogslide on the Maidenmoor some years ago."

"But you can't be sure," said the Vicar.

"Have a care, Branshaw," murmured Frederick Niles.

The others began to buzz about the danger. Someone said, "He's got to be got out; that much we know. If we can't see to shoot the bugger from here, we got to go in and do it proper. Who's to flush him?"

The Vicar examined the opening in the rock, which was certainly not large enough for a man of his girth to penetrate, although I thought perhaps either Frederick Niles or Dr. Lowther might make it. But the young curate appeared a trifle clumsy and I doubted if Dr. Lowther would be a match for a beast that had killed a rugged sheep farmer. Holding tight to his hunting gun, the Vicar fingered the crevice with his free hand, attempting with ludicrous results to force an entry which would give room to his great stomach and hips, as well as his weapon. What he attempted was so impossible that I almost suspected the good Vicar of merely making a brave show.

I was surprised at the laughter among these rugged men, even in the face of this danger. Some tried to push and crowd the Vicar into the aperture, and, failing, joked about his size and how he would have to starve and come back another day, with less belly to handicap him. But the women murmured, as I would like to have done, at the notion of any man going through that ghastly crevice, at the mercy of a savage killer-dog. I would have voted to camp here until the dog became starved enough to come out, or, at the worst, to place some poison handy. But the men seemed determined to do things in their own way.

"You'd best give it up, sir," said the Reverend Niles to the Vicar, offering a handkerchief. The

Vicar wiped the sweat off his brow before the wind could chill him, then climbed back out, stamping his feet to restore circulation. "Thought I caught a glimpse of the beast's eyes blazing at me in there, but I may have been mistaken. It'll take the Devil's own spawn to squeeze in there — and then he might not be got out. Besides, he'll get but one shot."

As if by common consent, all heads moved slowly upward, upon the Vicar's careless words. I looked with them, yet hating the inclination that made me betray my thoughts when "Devil's spawn" was spoken. One of the villagers was not so careful.

"Ye've hit on it, Reverend-sor. They's none but the Devil's spawn can do it."

Marc looked down at us from the brow of the crags, and then descended easily to within a few yards of the Vicar's head. He said quietly:

"There's another way — just over the brow. Give me your weapon."

"Now, lad —" began the Vicar, but Frederick Niles pulled at his sleeve.

"Someone must go. I believe Mr. Branshaw is the logical one. He is fast on his feet. Do you think you can manage it, sir?"

Marc did not reply. He moved back up the brow of the crags and down the other side. Several of the men climbed up after him, and Jamie suddenly ran up the trail, retracing his steps, with me hot behind him, in a tempest of anger and concern to keep him, at least, from running into Marc's danger. Jamie came to a stop not far from where the men stood, watching Marc as he tore away great handfuls of dead nettle and tufts of bracken, to uncover a hole the size of a wagon wheel in the rocks. This hole, apparently torn away by erosion of water and wind through the ages, opened straight down into a section of the rock passage some six or seven feet below. Marc swung his legs over the side, and dropped through that repulsive hole. His feet touched the earth below so silently that we could not hear the sound. The men looked down through the hole, breathing fast, but keeping absolute silence for fear of disaster to Marc. I glanced in, between two villagers, and saw Marc move through what was, as he had predicted, an extension of the cave-like room we had glimpsed from the aperture, where the Vicar and the others now stood ready, should the animal be driven out. I saw an item even more odd — a ring set in the wall of the passage, and, beneath it, the frayed end of a coil of rope. Had the dog been kept prisoner here and had he worried his way free of the rope? But how would that explain the fact that the villagers had treed him in this spot? Probably, upon their giving chase, he had returned to the place which was at the same time his prison and his haven.

Suddenly Marc stopped, backed up stealthily, and we could see him raise the gun to his shoulder.

The angry snarl of the beast before him in the passage reached us on top of the crags and we shuddered. Marc took aim, fired. The sound reverberated underground but our own shock was covered by the Vicar's voice on the other side of the crags.

"Got him, by George! Good shot!"

Jamie pushed me aside and peered in so that I could not see. "No, Marc! He'll leap! They don't die sudden-like. . . ." He broke off to scream.

Jamie's cries mingled with the shouts of the Vicar and Dr. Lowther, trying idiotically to advise Marc.

I was only just able to see Marc raise the gun as a club before the maddened, dying beast sprang at him. While I closed my eyes, too horrified even to pray, I heard the sudden gasp of astonishment around me, and looked again. The paw of the beast — a large black and white, long-coated dog, of a kind seen commonly around the sheepcotes — had torn a great gash across the breast and shoulder of Marc's coat, but then, either because he was dying or for some other obscure reason, the dog dropped before Marc and, in his last struggles, managed to crawl to Marc's boots and crouch there, sniffing at Marc as at a friend.

One of the men behind me raised up after watching this eery sight. He traded glances with the others.

"Quite a power over beasts, has our Mister Branshaw."

Marc looked up at us.

"Over and done, or just beginning?" whispered a male voice behind me. "Remember that Other One? He said he had power over savage beasts. Ay, but Mister Marc proved it."

"Like father, like son," said another voice.

Unsteadily, Jamie clutched my arm, but I looked at him with as much stern resolution as I could summon.

Frederick Niles had joined the group and was briskly scoffing at their suspicions, but I saw him cast an occasional puzzled glance down into the Wind-Rock passage.

Marc called, "Jamie! Fetch someone to get the carcass. One of you, give me your hand up."

Three or four of the biggest among the men hesitated, but when Niles and I reached for Marc's hands, the others were finally shamed into helping the man who had, alone, destroyed their murderous Gytrash. Marc pulled himself up before we could help him, and by the time the Vicar came lumbering over to give a hand, Niles had retreated, and Jamie and I were dusting off our hero. Marc grinned at Jamie, pulling the boy's hair and behaving as though the curious incident of the dog crawling to his feet had never happened.

Niles stared at Marc, especially at his jacket, and presently I glimpsed a smile on his sober features. He must have found an answer to the mystery of the dog's behavior that escaped the rest of us.

I was thrust aside by the well-wishers who did not share the view of the superstitious, that Marc

Branshaw had revealed some of his supposed father's Devilish powers over the dog. It was only when the Vicar smacked Marc hard on the back and shouted that he was the "preserver of Yorkshire" that I noticed the slight signs of strain in Marc's face, and his occasional circular exercise of his shoulder, as though it bothered him. I wondered how deeply the dog's paw had gashed through his clothing, whether, in fact, it had touched his flesh.

Meanwhile, as Marc received congratulations with an indifferent and almost sarcastic air, two of the boys in the crowd had brought up the dead dog and laid it on the bald crown of the rock. Marc looked at me as the others buzzed around it, studying the muzzle, the great canines, the paws, amazed that such an ordinary animal had done so much harm under the impetus of starvation.

He said, "You aren't dancing a farandole over the body, I see."

"No, nor am I like to do so. Did you notice how starved the dog was? It looked as though he'd been kept prisoner in that place. I found all the signs, including an iron ring in the rock. How could the dog be starved, since it has, presumably, been wandering about all these weeks?"

"Ah!" he smiled. "If we knew that, we should know . . . a great deal more than we know now."

At this unsatisfying answer I could not help making a face at him. He seemed in a humor to tease, but a flicker of pain crossed his features, and he massaged his shoulder mechanically.

"Are you hurt? Let me see. Perhaps I can oblige by —"

To my surprise, he drew back out of my reach, and then, apparently realizing that such modesty did not suit the stories about him, he said brusquely:

"No need to fuss. I'll attend to it later."

I was more puzzled than angry at his rebuff, and he could see this. He must have felt that some explanation was due, for he said after a moment, and with a look which promised all sorts of forbidden pleasures, "But if you insist you may come to Moyna's cottage with me. Who knows how you may oblige me there?"

"If you're going to be insulting —" I began, but Jamie cut me off sharp, saying quickly,

"You're to go to the cottage with Marc and me. It's a fine place. I learn to play chess there — ay, and to paint pictures like Marc. You'll come, love?"

I laughed. "Shall I come with Jamie, Mister Branshaw?"

"Certainly. And if you ask very prettily, I may even allow you to sit for us."

At this invitation I was prudently silent.

"See here, young Jamie," called the Vicar. "Come and identify your monster. . . . What do you say? Is he your Gytrash?"

The boy left Marc and me reluctantly, shuffling his feet along the nettle, as he walked up to the body of the dead dog. He licked his lips and squatted beside the animal, staring at it.

"Well, Jamie?" Dr. Lowther prompted him.

Jamie looked around helplessly.

"Must I?"

"Yes," said Marc quietly. "You must, Jamie."

"Ay." Jamie appeared to be thinking as he pretended to examine the dog, touching the long hairs, but he was gazing blankly into space. "No. It wasn't this dog at all. This un's got black on it. I said the Gytrash wasn't black at all. Not a bit black. It was — it was — like a lion. Not black."

Everyone began to look uncomfortable, casting exasperated glances at the boy, and Dr. Lowther said soothingly, "I think we may account for the boy's confusion by the frightful experience he underwent that night. Are we all agreed that this is our celebrated Gytrash?"

"But he was bigger," cried Jamie. "He was bigger and he was dun-color and not black or white."

They all seemed in agreement to disregard this, although one or two of the men, who had whispered about Marc, now gave him odd looks and nudged each other. I was surprised, however, when the Reverend Niles came strolling over to us, with a frown.

"It seems odd, to say the least. You would do well to train your young friend to be more observing. We have had enough of careless suspicions in this village."

Marc nodded. "I have thought so for some time. Jamie fancies he may have seen me as a

Gytrash, and doesn't like to say so. I'm afraid his loyalty is only making matters worse."

Reverend MacDonnachie and I, who heard this, were both startled. The Vicar said gruffly, clearing his throat, "Then I'd advise you not to be so free with such talk. Niles is right. Great Giliad, man! Do you want to arouse the village as they were aroused over your — over that Other One?"

"Later," said Marc soothingly. "He will know later that it was not me he saw. And now, if these good people will clear out to wherever they are going, I think I shall spend a quiet evening at Moyna's cottage, without all this disturbance."

The Vicar seemed half of a mind to challenge this.

"Do you think that's wise? If any harm should befall you as a result of the boy's careless talk, well. . . . You know what happened to my predecessor. And you alone in that forsaken cottage!"

Marc smiled in the way I had learned to mistrust. "But I thought your influence had civilized them."

I could not blame the Vicar when he puffed angrily to get breath, but as the young curate touched him warningly on the arm, he completely reversed himself.

"Now, see here, laddy — I like you, but it's not right to hold the whole village responsible for the actions of a few hotheads fifteen years ago. That business with the Devil-Vicar was started by some malcontents, ruffians. The villagers did more to put out the fire than start it."

"Shall we talk of something else?" asked Marc idly.

The Reverend MacDonnachie, still upset at these unkind reflections on his Christian work, turned and stamped off.

As I started to go after Jamie, Marc took my hand.

I was surprised at his gentleness after the recent display.

"I don't want these people to know that I've asked you and Jamie to come up to the cottage. Come as far as Upshed turning, and Jamie will pretend to lead you back to Maidenmoor. Instead, he will take you to me. Do you understand?"

He saw my dubious expression and added with some amusement, "It has nothing to do with 'obliging me' and the rest of it. Word of honor. But I do need you."

I assumed that his shoulder must be hurting him, and he needed me to apply bandages or something of that sort, and of course I agreed.

When Jamie came to us and Marc told him what he was to do, the boy looked glad, but there was still a hang-dog air about him. Marc slapped his cheek in a friendly way.

"Here, Jamie, what's this? You told them the truth. If they won't believe you, that's no concern of yours."

Jamie said nothing. His fingers idly twisted and untwisted the button at the throat of Marc's coat. Suddenly, he looked from the coat up into Marc's face, and to our consternation, his eyes grew enormous and he whispered, "I did right, didn't I? Please say I did right."

Marc brushed back the boy's windblown hair and said in a caressing voice, "Of course, you did; exactly right."

X

There was a good deal of milling about, relief expressed on all sides that the beast was dead, and one or two glances in Marc's direction, which hinted that news of his odd behavior had spread among those not fortunate enough to have witnessed it. I thought Marc might be upset by it all, but, on the contrary, it seemed to me that he almost welcomed their suspicions. I supposed he thought it funny, just as the man thought to be his natural ancestor, the Devil-Vicar, had gone to so many pains to present himself as a devil and weird phenomenon.

I would like to have mentioned the ring I saw in the Wind-Rock passage, the signs that the dog had been kept confined at one time, but I was afraid to interfere with Marc's plans. Obviously, he knew these people better than I.

Dr. Lowther and a number of the Upshed people walked on down across the lowlands, through what they referred to as Heaton Clough, treading on the thick, boggy surface of the ground as though it were firm paving stones. I found the peat first amusing for its bouncy qualities, and then slightly more sinister as I perceived that if the rains came heavily, this area would all be bogs and mud, with the ability to draw one down into its horrid depths. Here in the sheltered glen where great trees grew thick in clumps and long processions, Jamie pointed out to me that the place where Moyna Branshaw had lost her footing and stepped off the turf into a bog-hole, was very like the uncertain ground we traversed. It was at the junction with a sheep trail winding upward toward the wind-swept moorland where her cottage stood in the direct path of the rushing storms.

"Up there it was," said Jamie, pointing to the green hillside above us. "Rare boggy it is, too."

"Mind that shoulder, Mister Branshaw," the doctor warned him at parting. "You'll be bandaging it, I trust."

Marc did not look at his shoulder but I could see that fringes of blood had seeped through the shirt and the torn coat, and it made me nervous to see him neglect the scratches. Heaven knows, it must have been painful. I was about to suggest that he stop and apply a cloth to it, when Jamie suddenly pointed out a horse and gig in the distance, rattling along from Upshed. It was trouble of sorts, for Mrs. Fothergay was at the reins, and upon seeing Marc, she stood up, waving her enormous ruffled hat at us and calling in embarrassingly loud tones to Marc:

"My dear boy, how nice! Come to meet me, have you?" Her clumsiness on the reins naturally confused the little horse, who began to shuffle and start.

Under cover of the chuckles and laughter and rib-nudging of the Upshed people, Dr. Lowther came to her rescue so she could devote her full attention to Marc. Like the villagers from Upshed, I could not help laughing at his discomfiture, but Dr. Lowther did handsomely by him. He looked from Marc to the lady and shook his head sadly.

"Ma'am, Mr. Branshaw is taken ill. I fear all this exertion in such freshing air is too much for the gentleman. He is about to retire. Are you not, Mr. Branshaw?"

Marc, however, showed a sudden interest in the lady, or her absent suitor. He moved through the listening, sniggering crowd to take Mrs. Fothergay's hand. When he made a pretense of kissing the gloved fingers, his lips only just missing them, there were perceptible murmurs of amusement among the witnesses, which did not stir him in the least.

"My dear Bedelia! How do you come to be alone? I had no notion Owen would be so ungallant."

"Wretched, odious man! He left me in Upshed. Some local person told him he was needed to capture that great, awful beast, and off he went."

"Impossible," murmured Marc, "to leave you

with so little ceremony." He looked around at the moorland, as though seeking some trace of the missing knight.

"Bedelia, *cherie,* he was a fool. Did he go with others, or alone?"

"Alone, I think. But what is this, Marc? Am I being quizzed?" Then she observed the stains on his coat and fluttered maternally. "You're hurt, dear boy! You will be needing me. Here, one of you" — she looked around with an officious manner — "take the reins. Marc, it's clear you need a woman's hand."

Marc was melancholy, noble, but firm. He even staggered a little, and the busy, listening crowd responded with a quick buzz of sympathy. At least two dozen hands reached out to catch him.

"I couldn't permit it, Bedelia. . . ." He seemed to become aware for the first time that he was being overheard. "Ma'am, that is — you embarrass me. I cannot inflict myself upon you in this ridiculous condition. Imagine how it would be if you came with me up that stony sheep track, on those enchanting little feet of yours. You would stumble. You would be worn to a fret. And I should be the cause."

She looked uneasily up the forbidding trail.

"Well . . . perhaps . . . But are you quite sure you can get on without me?"

"I must," he assured her firmly, kissing the fingertips she uncovered to him. Dr. Lowther let this continue a few minutes but he was eying

Marc steadily. He broke up the crowd's fun after a suitable time.

"I think you'd best have those scratches attended to. And at once."

Marc grinned but said a little faintly, "Thanks, I shall," and, pushing his way through the crowd, said a loud and public goodbye to Jamie and me, before he started on the sheep trail up to Moyna's cottage.

Jamie took my hand and hustled me out of sight of the others. It was not difficult to find another sheep track that crossed the trail of Moyna's cottage, and almost immediately, we began to climb.

We joined Marc a few minutes later, without anyone being the wiser.

This trail was the most uncivilized we had come upon. We seemed to be in the very belly of the great, seething monster which was the moorland. Once again all was green in every direction, with occasional outcroppings of primeval gritstone and rock. One twisted fir tree stood guard before the low stone walls of the cottage, and we could now see the gaunt limbs, like fingers, groping for the mottled sky. I wondered if there could be any other human beings in all this desolation.

"Are you sure we shouldn't have gone on to Upshed?" I asked. "It seems so isolated here if we need any assistance."

"My dear girl," Marc told me sharply. "It's the merest scratch, if that was what you had in mind!" I saw that Jamie clung to his arm more in the effort to be of help than to seek support. I did not dare lend my own assistance, but had to be satisfied with finding the correct path among several that crisscrossed the boggy moorland at these points.

Jamie did not lower the sinister atmosphere when he said, as he stopped suddenly, "Here it was Miss Moyna took sick. Fell into that bog there, behind the nettles."

I could see how it might have happened, for a sheep track crossed directly over the dark, swampy place which was masked, as Jamie said, by nettles and decaying foliage. It was not quite on our trail, but I supposed that Moyna Branshaw, being in a hurry, and perhaps thinking she knew the boggy moorland better than she did, stepped into that stinking black ooze, and her companion, Catherine Owen, found it impossible to get her out.

"I might have walked into it myself," I said, and tried not to look at the dreadful place.

"Ay," said Jamie, " 'twas a mucky day, with clouds hanging that low ye could fair touch un."

Marc stared at the place deliberately, and we stopped, hoping it would not revive other old memories. He said harshly:

"Yes. It was a gloomy day. If it had not been, she would have seen that the cover of rock and board had been removed."

"Removed!" I looked back at the place, realizing that there must have been something of the sort there originally; for the alternate trail, now grown over, cut directly across the boggy place.

"And Moyna's back was broken, and Catherine — so she says — was paralyzed."

Jamie and I started to speak almost together, hoping to drive off these vindictive thoughts, but they must have been embedded even before Moyna's death; for he answered us coldly.

"These people haven't changed. You saw them today."

"But the Owens an't our people," Jamie put in hopefully.

"I wonder," said Marc, "where Gareth is now. That I should like to know. Someone in this village is wearing a disguise, perhaps only mental. If I could rip off that bloody damned mask! Which of them is it? Which one is pretending he never saw me before? Well, lad" — he cuffed Jamie lightly across the cheek — "when we know that, we'll be a trifle less popular, I fancy."

Jamie peered around at me. He looked scared and I did not quite blame him. But then, I could scarcely blame Marc either, in the circumstances. He was looking tired, his features drawn and pale, older and somehow distant. The change may have been due to his troublesome injury, yet I wondered if the other man had always been there, unobserved because of his surface charm. I was nearly afraid to speak up, but remembering Jamie's young face, so loyal and so deeply concerned for his friend, I said:

"I hope you won't confuse Jamie and me with

the people you hate. We . . . we like you."

"You know nothing whatever about me," he countered deliberately. "You may fancy you like Marc Branshaw, perhaps, but you can't possibly like *me*. You don't know the first thing about *me*."

I tried to explain, with a lightness that was out of place, "We don't think you control savage dogs, or turn into a devil at night. We don't think you made that dog kill the girl and the old farmer."

"No!" He favored us both with a grim smile. "But I wonder if your precious loyalty would go further — would cover *me* — myself!"

Jamie shivered but kept tight hold on his friend's arm. I felt much the same. Marc's senseless protest did not touch us, for we didn't understand it. We saw one man, the one we both loved in different ways. His words about "me" and "myself" were so much nonsense. He might even be off his head, but we certainly knew he was Marc Branshaw, whatever crimes he might fancy set him apart.

We reached the great fir tree outside the low, broken wall of the farmhouse garden. Marc stopped a moment, pressed his hand against the torn place on his coat, and relieved Jamie and me by saying more softly:

"I'm sorry. I'm grateful to you both — I really am. Don't know what I should do without you." Grimacing a little, he made a flourish with his free hand. "Miss Wicklow, welcome to the cot-

172

tage — Moyna's haven. It isn't very respectable, but then its guests have not always been respectable either. One of them was said to be a devil."

The iron gates in the crumbling stone wall stood open, swinging back and forth and creaking as the wind circled the barren hilltop. All around the two-story farmhouse, the perpetual wind had shaped every growing thing to its own ends. Even the seedlings of the ancient fir twisted frantically away from the wind. Although the afternoon had not gone, the sullen sky made a kind of early dusk over the scene, and I wondered how we would find our way back to Maidenmoor tonight. Jamie boasted of knowing the moors as well as any man. But so had Moyna Branshaw.

There was no porch. When Marc unlocked the solid oak-studded door, we stepped from the moist ground into the living quarters of the house. The main room had a huge, comfortable fireplace, apparently used for cooking as well as heating, and the usual pieces of furniture of mixed age, period and worth, that are accumulated from the more fashionable "home residence." The floor was of stone, covered here and there by worn drugget, miserably cold to me even through the housekeeper's stout walking shoes. On the left of the heavily timbered room was a narrow staircase leading up to what I supposed must be the bedchambers.

Jamie volunteered quickly, "I'll light the fires, if you please, Marc. And maybe a smidgeon of tea for Miss?"

"Ay, love," Marc agreed in broadest Yorkshire, apparently determined to improve his disposition for us. "Do that, and I'll oblige Miss Anne by changing this sad coat. Hardly the proper attire for entertaining a lady, eh, Jamie?"

Jamie went through a small door at the further end of the room and then I could hear him rustling about, in what must have been the peat room, as he loaded fuel for the fireplace. Marc was looking at me, smiling in a half-melancholy, half-humorous way.

"Are you sorry I stole your precious Red Indian manuscript? You little thought you'd be tramping over the countryside a week later in a housekeeper's boots and a coat belonging to a bad-tempered chap so ill-natured he nearly forgot to say how much he needs you."

"I'm sure you need me for those scratches of —" I began.

He said without a change in his whimsical manner, "But not for those scratches of mine." He started up the stairs. "Don't go away. Jamie will find some fresh baked bread, I expect. At least it was fresh yesterday, when Cook baked it."

"But why won't you let me help you?" I asked him, perplexed.

He leaned over the stair-rail and explained, "Hadn't you guessed? I am a very shy fellow when it comes to my own flesh."

I laughed, because he doubtless expected me to, and besides, I was happy that he was in a good mood. A minute later I heard the creak of boards, as his footsteps passed overhead. Looking around for little signs that would give me a clue to Marc's true nature, I examined the room in which I stood, and more especially the good-sized window at one side of the room. Outside the window was a fairly clear view of enormous branches of an old lilac bush. It was impressive, that view, but cold.

Closer to reality were several female portraits and one or two male sketches of local faces. These works of art were stacked idly, against a leg of the old deal table in the center of the room, or lying on an over-sized bed or sofa under the window. On the sofa, still attached to a heavy board I took to be his easel, was one of the best and most revealing portraits, of a yellow-haired young girl with a common, but I should imagine, enticing face. The creamy throat and breasts were bare. I should have resented the portrait more if I hadn't detected the same cynical artist's hand as appeared in the London sketch of Mrs. Fothergay. It was inconceivable that Marc could care for a woman whose sly appeal he caught so mercilessly.

Engrossed in my thoughts, I was startled unpleasantly by someone who was sneaking up behind me, and I turned, breathing fast, not knowing what to expect. It was only Jamie. I had not thought he could walk so silently.

"That'll be Abbie Hinchley, that there picture," Jamie told me as he started a smoldering fire among the peat, the dead tree limbs, and a bundle of ancient *Yorkshire Post*s. He used an outmoded little firemaker and managed so well it was obvious he had much experience in that line.

"Ye must pay no mind of Marc," he told me wisely. "Once he fair broke his arm catching me when I slipped off Heaton Bridge, but he wouldn't let me nor nobody put him to mends."

Jamie and I were pouring tea when Marc came down to join us, and I was forced to admit privately he had changed his blood-stained clothing, and taken care of a painful bandaging job, more rapidly than I should have been able to manage. Marc had much better color now and seemed quite fit. Taking up one of the ugly ale mugs we used for tea, he sat down on the sofa and gestured with his forefinger for me to join him. I wasn't sure what he had in mind by that gesture, which was accompanied by a look that had more influence over me than I cared to own.

"Me too?" suggested Jamie, trying to worm his way onto the side of Marc.

" 'You too' over on the hearth, my lad."

Jamie raised his tawny eyebrows, but did as he was ordered. He sat there, however, watching us as we drank our tea.

"Ain't you going to kiss Miss Anne?" Jamie asked, somewhat puzzled by the extraordinary behavior of his idol.

I said quickly, "How nonsensical you are! I haven't said I'd kiss anyone. Do be serious, both of you. Why did you say I could assist you in some way, Marc?"

He shook his head and spoke to Jamie as though I were invisible.

"Such a head for business! One shudders for her dismal future. She will become the richest old unkissed lady in London."

"Well," said Jamie, joggling the tea grounds around in his mug. "I'd at least give it a try, that I would now."

As Marc appeared to think this reasonable and turned to me, I stiffened with apprehension. However, Marc removed the tea mug from my nervous fingers and brushed a kiss on my cheek. Then he calmly replaced my tea mug in my hand.

"Oh, poor stuff, that!" cried our audience disdainfully. "I'd do better if I was of a mind to do such mulling things."

"When your saucer-eyes are occupied with things more fitting to your age, I'll see to Miss Anne properly. Now, you've both had my tea and my bread, and Jamie, I see, has spice cakes which he's not had the politeness to offer us —"

"They're that hard, you'd break a tooth on un," Jamie excused himself, with his mouth full.

"— so you must pay me now," Marc finished. "I want it to be thought that I'm still inside the cottage, when in point of fact, I shall be outside, observing the nocturnal habits of the local fauna."

So this was why he had gone to such lengths to make everyone believe he was alone here! I did not like the idea of being used.

"Ay, let's play at it!" cried Jamie, clapping his hands, one of which held a buttered piece of bread. "We'll make out you're here. . . . But how, Marc?"

"You, my boy, will not be seen at all. You must contrive to hide yourself in here. It will serve very well — if there are no lamps to give you away. Just the distant glow on the hearth to suggest my presence inside — in outline, one might say."

"And I —" I guessed without enthusiasm — "am to be the outline of Marc Branshaw. Impossible." And insulting, too, I thought, to be suggested for a male role.

"Do you remember what I was doing to your hair earlier today? Can you sweep it back and somehow let the ends be covered by the collar of one of my hunting jackets?"

I said I supposed I could, but I felt little enthusiasm for the scheme.

"Because," he explained, "someone wishes it to appear that I'm capable of several brutal murders. When I'm alone in that chair across the room, at night, busy daubing, I am often watched. You will notice the window behind the chair. Sometimes I've heard sounds but have never been quick enough to catch my visitor. It's precisely upon these occasions that the Devil-Vicar is seen about the neighborhood — an hour or two later. And since I bear some resemblance to our late Clergyman, I know it is meant to appear that I am committing these crimes."

I glanced at Jamie, who was listening now in a perplexed way. I had a feeling that he still doubted, but was willing to accept any reasonable explanation.

"How could anyone be so fiendish?" I demanded, only half believing that Marc's view of the world was the correct one.

"How else explain that the murders and these mysterious appearances of the Devil-Vicar have always occurred on the nights when I was alone here, so that I could never prove my innocence, should it be necessary? After all, there are many times when I have not been alone in this cottage." (He need not have mentioned that!) "Yet no apparitions are seen, no murders occur, when I have someone who can testify to my presence here. Consider! Every night that some sheep farmer, some frightened farm girl, reports having seen the Devil-Vicar floating about the moors, *I have been here alone.* It took me some time to read the signs and to decide that the mysterious sounds I have heard on those nights were not my imagination, but deliberate spying, to make sure I should not have a witness afterward."

I said hurriedly, "I think you're wrong in imagining that the people suspect you. If so, they would have had you up on charges before this."

"Oh no." His mouth twisted in sardonic humor. "You forget. They think I'm the Devil-Vicar's son. They murdered him upon flimsy evidence and they're not going to chance it with me.

They do have consciences, of a sort. One day, of course, if I cannot find out the identity of my mysterious spy, they will have enough evidence. . . . That's why I asked you to help me. I thought of it that day in London when dear Bedelia mentioned that we might be brother and sister."

"And you want me to sit here and be spied upon while you are out — heaven knows where — and up to no good, I daresay."

There were times when I strongly suspected he did not hear me because he did not wish to.

"Come. Let's see. You aren't tall enough. No matter. I think if we raise your height somewhat —"

"Sit her on cushions," Jamie put in helpfully.

"Yes. I think, providing Jamie stays out of sight, near you in that dark corner beyond the window, we might satisfy a passerby that I was here as usual, sketching or painting."

I looked at the window. It was just high enough from the ground to accommodate a spying face. The notion of turning my back to it was exceedingly unwelcome to me.

"Why wouldn't your spy kill me, fancying I am you?"

"Because that's not his — or her — plan. I'm to be the culprit, not the victim."

"Oh, rubbish," Jamie said quickly. "Marc wouldn't let no one hurt you."

Marc had gotten up and begun to arrange an old, heavily upholstered chair, whose insides were already spilled upon the floor. He placed it just far enough into the room so that a man peering into the large window might see the outlines of the person in the chair. I liked it less and less.

"Jamie, you sit on a pillow in the corner. See to it that the fire is kept low so that it doesn't illuminate you. In that position, you may make out anything at the window without being seen. It's not at all certain that the spy will come tonight. Still, it's well to make our plans."

"I foresee that I shall spend an exciting evening," I prophesied. "Either nothing will happen, and I'll have sat a whole evening in a dark room, or — even more charming — I will have been the target for some monster because he fancies I'm you. Delightful entertainment you offer your guests, Mr. Branshaw."

Marc laughed at that. "Good work. You're in a pleasant humor again."

"Stuff and nonsense!" I said stiffly.

During our banter Jamie had grown thoughtful. He tugged at his friend's hand finally.

"It wasn't you but t'Other One I seen on the heath the night of the Gytrash?"

Marc looked at the boy and raised his chin with one hand.

"I am not the Gytrash, Jamie. Is that what you were thinking?"

Jamie swallowed convulsively.

"I — I never thought so. Only that ye was maybe — worse."

"Good heavens!" I demanded crossly. "What

could be worse?" I had begun to rearrange my hair, because I felt I should be a shabby thing indeed if I failed to cooperate, but I was nervous of the whole stratagem.

"Well . . ." Jamie murmured, avoiding his eyes. "Only — t'Other One's dead."

"What does he mean?" I asked, fearing the worst.

"He's talking nonsense, aren't you, boy?"

Jamie bit his lip and appeared to consider. When he looked up at me, he was fairly reassured. "Ay, mum. It's nonsense. Aunt Rose says so too. Only, I saw . . ."

"Yes, Jamie?" his mentor prompted him very softly.

"Nothing." The boy finished his tea in a great gulp, which appeared to revive his flagging spirits, and he became eager to go at fooling whatever it was they expected to come prowling about the cottage.

By the time they had arranged me absurdly in the chair, with my back to the window, they seemed as pleased with themselves as two children. I said stonily, "You realize, of course, Mr. Branshaw, that this gives you considerable more freedom yourself, for you are the only one who can be said to have been in two places at once."

"Very profound. Lean a little forward. There's the girl — just so." He had made me change to another one of his hunting coats, and now turned the collar still farther up to disguise the nape of my neck.

When he had finished re-arranging my clothing, he knelt before my chair to view the results. Then he covered my hands in my lap with his own and looked up into my eyes. Whatever influence he had over Jamie, I could feel now in his effect upon me. He was desperately sincere. What his motives were, I could not perceive, but I did believe him when he grasped my hands in his anxiety to make me understand.

"Anne, no one knows better than I that you're being treated abominably. But you must do this thing for me. *You must.*"

"Did you bring me clear up to Yorkshire for this?"

"I did, and stole your manuscript as well. I swear to you there's no danger, as long as you stay indoors. You don't think I'd risk your life and Jamie's do you? Do you?"

I did think so, for I was half afraid my confidence in him was bolstered only by his presence. He let go of my hands and took my face between his palms. Before I knew what he was about to do, he kissed me, and in a way Jamie could not possibly have improved upon. Behind Marc I heard Jamie catch his breath, but the warm, pulsing effect of Marc's lips on mine, and my own response, drowned out any further thoughts of Jamie for a minute or two.

He looked into my eyes then and murmured a little huskily, "I knew it would be so."

This curious remark left me with nothing to say, even if I had the strength to say it, but Jamie was prepared for anything.

"Is she better to kiss than the ladies in your paintings?"

Marc's fingers moved gently along the line of my cheek. He did not look at Jamie as he spoke.

"She's not like ladies in paintings, Jamie. My Irish love has a soul. And Anne," he added simply, "it was not only to get you up here for this purpose that I wanted you. I'm sorry I've teased you, but you are such a happy subject."

I studied my hands in embarrassment, and Marc slapped them in parting, before he left us by the low-hung door to the peat room. He said in the doorway:

"Remember, keep the door bolted and don't venture out, whatever you see or think you see. Ten to one it'll be imaginary. And in any case, I shall be close by. Jamie, you'll watch over Miss Anne. And Jamie, when I've gone, remember to make sure every door is bolted, including the laithe and the mistal. Then take out the gun we used for the grouse. Just be quite sure it's not me you're aiming at."

I said lightly, "Now, that would be a fitting end to this nonsense."

He laughed, and a moment later was gone.

A pity I hadn't asked him what Jamie should do if the spy he did *not* expect should shoot me through that accursed window! I decided that he would only have talked me out of my fears as he convinced Mrs. Fothergay and so many others. Was he no more sincere with me than with them?

184

Still, I had a warm memory that I felt instinctively Mrs. Fothergay and the others had not known. I could forgive him much for those few moments.

"Ah," cried Jamie mysteriously, "we're waiting — Spies and All Such! Come now and face your match."

"I'll thank you not to encourage All Such," I said, only half joking.

Jamie scoffed. "Don't be cow-hearted, mum."

Alas! To borrow Jamie's elegant phrase, that is precisely what I was — cow-hearted — for I could not rid myself of the notion that already there were eyes peering at my exposed back.

XI

Jamie busied himself bolting doors throughout the house and outbuildings, creating such a furor that I should not have been surprised if we would find it more difficult to get out than intruders to get in. With tremendous energy he ran upstairs and rattled around with the dormer window and one or two other places unknown to me.

He came down presently, waving something in the air which could only be a female's white cotton stocking, worked with peculiar pink clocks. "Belong 'a' Abbie Hinchley," he informed me with airy indifference. "Marc's going to be that cross! He told her not to take off her things here."

185

"Not to!" I repeated in surprise. "I thought . . . that is . . ."

"Oh no. Not Marc. Sir Gareth in town, he does them things now and again, and I hear Miss Catherine saying 'tis wicked, but Marc — he laughs at them and says when he's through with putting them on the canvas, they're no more use to him." He cocked his head to one side and regarded the stocking with interest. "They get mad as fire, but though Marc kisses them, it's not like he kissed you. Not with me about."

"Very obliging of him, I'm sure." Nevertheless, I could have kissed Jamie himself for the news.

"Now I think on't, I best be burning the thing. Marc'll be cross if he knew you saw it."

"More like him to flaunt it in my face, thinking it a very funny joke."

"May be. But he told me, he'd met *the* girl when he was down London way. You don't think he could maybe mean the old lady, with the big hat, do you? For he laughs at her. Marc does."

"Very likely. . . . What else did he say about meeting *the* girl in London?"

Jamie scratched his head with the stocking.

"Very odd-sounding it was. Said he was like Nar-Narcis . . . them posies . . . that he'd feel like them if he fell in love with this girl, but he didn't care a farthing for that. You make a sense a that?"

I hoped I read it right, but explaining it to Jamie was something else. I was feeling a little more confident of Marc's behavior to me, and blessed Jamie for it.

"Narcissus was a . . . well . . . call him a Greek. He fell in love with his own reflection in a pool."

"Oh." Jamie's mouth made a big circle and he tossed the stocking into the fire in the most careless way, but I don't think he quite understood me yet, and I had no mind to explain further. I thought it rather delicate and charming of Marc to put his interest in me, if he was sincere, in the form of such a mythological parable.

"Coming on dark, mum. I'll sit here like Marc said. No. Don't you move. You're to sit still. What a shabby thing if there be no spy at all!"

I did not agree, but I could see that nothing would convince a boy of Jamie's age that peace and quiet were preferable to weird eyes peering in at one's undefended back.

Having attended to his chores, Jamie sat down in the corner, facing me so that he might keep one eye on that horrendous window behind me. I had a brief glimpse of it when I turned, Jamie not having his warder's eye on me at that moment, and one glimpse was really all I needed. Outside, the dusk had become black as peat, and I remembered too well the great open space there, the hint of another, unhuman, world that lay behind us in every direction. The darker it grew, the more I sensed that world was pressing in upon us, and what more natural entrance could it gain than the window behind me?

Jamie settled comfortably, rubbing his bottom,

which had apparently received the full impact of the snapping fire.

"I'm that pleased Marc likes you," he said. "He laughs, but I don't think he likes many folk. He said there was one he liked once, but then they were only friends after. He said he'd learned ever after not to give himself, but only what they wanted."

"And what did he think they wanted?"

"Well now . . . that I don't rightly know. He said I was never to give my soul away, but to give them what they wants, he said. I asked him what that was, but he said when the time come I'd know."

I refrained from expressing my disapproval of Jamie's education at the hands of a *roué* like Marc Branshaw.

He read something in my face that I hadn't intended to show.

"You've no call to look so, Miss Anne. He says you've a soul . . . he thinks. He must find it out, he said. Do you now?"

"Yes, I have a soul," I said crossly. "But whether I shall reveal it to Marc Branshaw, I haven't the least notion."

"Ay. Sometimes you talk and act just like Marc. No wonder you're good friends. I thought maybe Miss Catherine might have a soul, but Marc says she's a silly one, loving what don't be real. Howsomever, he was kind to Miss Catheerine till I told him what I'd heard."

"What you'd heard?"

"Her walking, I mean to say. Aunt Rose says to hush up, that the doctor says it ain't so. But I heard 'em say it was Miss Catherine — ever trying to walk when no one was about. The servants say she tried it now and again. And crying over a stupid handkerchief she found. It was the Devil-Vicar's, Marc says."

I was chilled to the marrow.

"You mean — someone saw Miss Catherine walking?"

"Well . . . Aunt Rose says it's the same as me seeing the Gytrash. I didn't see that, of course. But I said I did. I knew it'd be better'n truth."

"Wait. One thing at a time. You say *someone* saw Miss Catherine walking. And you did *not* see a Gytrash?"

"Well now, not like that, mum. Myself, I never seen Miss Catherine walking. It's only the talk. And the Gytrash was no beast but on a sudden become some-ut like them robes that's worn in the church. Like maybe it was . . . t'Other One."

"What other one?"

His big blue yes looked up at me, round and innocent. "But the Devil-Vicar, mum."

"Never mind that. You saw Miss Catherine walking?"

"Well now, as to that, it's not certain. It's whispered. She's trying to walk so's to meet the Devil-Vicar — that's the tale the lads tell, because they never knew a lady that couldn't walk after such a little thing as tugging another out of a bog-hole. . . . Watch, mum, when you sit back.

The spy, he can see in and see you're not Marc."

In panic, I glanced over my shoulder, but Jamie leaned forward and grabbed my shoulder.

"You'll drive it away! Marc wants it to come."

I tried to restrain my mingled terror and anger that Marc should expose this child and me to such preposterous horrors.

"Listen to me, Jamie. The Devil-Vicar has been dead for twenty years."

"Sixteen," he cut in politely.

"All right. Sixteen. What is left of him is buried in the rubble of the old parsonage. Dead people do not walk at night. Or any other time!"

"Then what's Miss Catherine in love with?"

"With Marc Branshaw, that's what."

Jamie considered, but shook his head.

"It weren't no Gytrash I saw on the heath that night. It was — like I said. The robes and all."

"And you called it a Gytrash because you were afraid someone you liked, Marc, or Miss Catherine, might be implicated in the death of the old sheep farmer. That's the whole story, isn't it?"

"Ay."

"Then why were you afraid of that dog today?"

"But mum, I wasn't afeered of poor old Chaffer. I used to run with that old dog. Only he was sick now, and savage. When he crawled to Marc, it was like the days of the Devil-Vicar they tell of. And just there for a little, I thought maybe Marc had the soul of the Devil-Vicar. Or maybe the other way round. For Marc is cross with me at times. One time he's Marc, my friend; another time he's like somebody else — like t'Other One."

"Some people are very moody. Marc is like that."

The boy's pointed concentration on the window behind me was frightfully unnerving. I found myself watching his face for a telltale expression of sudden interest or fear, but it remained its eager young self. I considered what he had told me, especially the appalling notion that Miss Catherine's injury might be the cover under which she committed crimes.

"Jamie, what precisely did you see the night you were looking for your stray sheep?"

"Just at first it was dun-colored, like I said. It leaped fast-like into the bracken. I caught a glimpse of fur — red or dun-color. But then, when I hid behind a rock and looked again, and it was far off, I saw a great, floating white sleeve, like the Devil-Vicar's in the painting at the church. And it moved away. But you're not to think it was a real beast. It was a thing that turns from a beast to a man — or a lady. It turned after I saw it first and lost it. When I saw it later, far off, it was t'Other One."

"Really, Jamie, I do think you have the most extraordinary imagination. Miss Catherine cannot walk — both your aunt and the doctor say so. And as for what you saw that night, you must make up your mind to one thing or the other. Either you saw a beast or you saw a person. You didn't see one change into the other."

He paid no heed to me. His jaw had fallen and he was staring hard over my head. I felt myself beginning to tense again, and wondered what I should do if he actually did see something at that window.

"What is it?" I whispered.

"Hush."

We were as silent as in the tomb.

Presently he relaxed. The most annoying thing was his quick giggle at his own precautions.

" 'Twas the lilac bush. No more'n that. And here's me thinking it was maybe the Devil-Vicar."

I felt like booting him for the scare he had given me, but it was by no means his last such mistake of the evening.

It must have been near nine or ten o'clock when Jamie, looking up from the chessboard he was studying in the corner, to some point I had learned to ignore above my head, lowered his glance quickly and was silent. This time he had seen more than just a lilac bush at the window. Full realization stunned me. Damn that Marc Branshaw! I thought. What shall we do now?

"What is it out there?" I whispered nervously.

He said, "It was there and then gone. Kind of a face. Not too close. I can't make it out."

"Is it still there?"

"I think so, but back. Not too close. Trying to look in, I daresay."

"I daresay. What are we to do now?"

His eyes sparkled. "Better than the circus in

192

Bradford! Wait till Marc finds we've seen the thing."

"He'll find our bodies alongside it, I don't doubt."

"Oh, Miss Anne, you're poor spirited! It's adventure, like the storybooks."

"I know. I'm cow-hearted."

He grinned and whispered a little louder, "That's it. Make out you've no notion it's out there."

"Is it still there?"

He shifted his glance above my head, then looked casually around the room.

"Just the hand. The fingers, pressing against the window."

"Good God!" I said. "How long must we sit here?"

I felt so jumpy that I did not know if I should be able to remain in this position without screaming or turning around, or doing something else rash and foolish. I tried, with faint success, to recover. "What — what kind of hands? Are they big or small? A man's or a woman's?"

"Can't say. Oh. They're gone. But he's there. Back away, I'm thinking."

I did not know whether to rejoice that our caller might be departing, or begin to worry about the various locks and bolts in this isolated farmhouse.

"Is it still there?"

"Wait. I can see its shadow. Now I can't. Oh, it's gone!" He seemed terribly put out at this news, which I could only greet with relief. "I wonder now, does Marc know it's been and gone? Maybe we should let Marc —"

This sort of thing was precisely what our night caller would like, no doubt, and the very thing Marc had taken pains to warn us of.

"It can't be Marc himself we hear?"

Jamie shook his head. "Listen. I know Marc's footsteps, and they're lighter than this. Ay, and quicker too." He listened with his ear against the door. "It's going away. I can hear the steps."

"Good!" I said with gusto. "Now let Marc follow the creature and we're rid of both of them."

"I do think we ought to tell Marc. Maybe he don't know."

"Have you taken leave of your senses? You'll stay snug in this room or know the reason why!"

He grinned, not the least frightened of me.

"You talk like Aunt Rose. But Marc's got to know, so he can track un." He gave this some thought while I was edging back into the shadows under the window to see if I could satisfy myself that no gleaming eyes or groping hands remained there to haunt me. At that angle, of course, I still saw nothing. Our visitor should have been halfway down to the glen by this time.

Jamie said thoughtfully, "Marc must be about. If I could get track of the spy and show un to Marc . . ."

"Well, you can't, so sit down and mind your elders!"

"Miss Anne, don't you care if we lose the track?"

"Not if it means going out in the night when we were expressly forbidden to do so."

He looked at me with admiration.

"I'd no notion you're so biddable to what Marc says. You'll make him a good wife, that you will."

Already, he was edging across the room to the door of the peat stores. Suddenly, he stopped. For the first time this evening it was he who was petrified, stiff with apprehension. It must have been the strange bird-call I too heard in the near distance.

"Gorm! Hear that!"

Across the desolate emptiness of the moors enclosing us, the sound came to us once more, plaintive now, almost like a human cry.

"It's one of those moor birds, isn't it?" I ventured hopefully. "Those curlews, or whatever they are."

"No, no, mum. They're earlier in the season. And they're nothing the sound of that. That's a man."

I stood up in one panic-stricken motion.

"What can be happening to him?"

"The bogs, mum. He's trapped in the bogs. When they're trapped so, they make sounds — different — you know it in a minute!"

The sound came again, a hideous, wailing, dying away on the immense open spaces.

"But we must do something!"

"Suppose . . ." He turned to me, his eyes wide. "Suppose he's the one was at the window."

That gave me pause.

"Well, can it be false? Can he be making that sound to lure us out for some reason?"

"Oh, no. It's the sound of a trapped man. I know it well, mum. We had a man from Scarborough over, searching for queer bones and such, from days afore our own. He went down like that, with just such a sound."

"Did you save him?"

"Ay. But he was dead, poor soul. . . . There it is again, mum."

I did not know what to do. I was absolutely sure that in any other circumstances we should remain locked indoors. But I knew too that neither Marc nor I had counted on this kind of life-and-death disturbance. I should never forgive myself if we let a human being die in such horrible plight, without putting forth the effort to save him.

"Why must they fall into bogs in the middle of the night?" I demanded of Jamie, who hadn't the least notion. "Why can't it be in bright daylight? At noon!"

Jamie took this for assent to the rescue and ran for his coat and a hunting rifle belonging to Marc. Being an exceptionally provident boy, he also arrived on the scene a minute later with a coil of rope and a storm lantern of no mean proportions.

"Best I go through the laithe," he suggested in a low voice. "If the Thing is about the cottage, it's best I know afore it sees me."

I could not have agreed with him more. Even now I was ready to hold him back, for I had been listening and heard nothing more. I could not help telling myself that the first cries had been a bird of some sort, or even an animal unfamiliar to Jamie. I wanted to believe that with all my heart.

At the last, I volunteered to go with Jamie but was voted down. Jamie seemed bound to act in place of Marc Branshaw and I was amused at his orders, and his assurance that "Marc wouldn't never forgive me if any harm was to come to you, mum."

"I suppose it's quite all right if you should be swallowed up in some evil bog?"

"Who? Me?" Jamie scoffed at the idea.

I decided, however, that he might be right about checking the bolts, and followed him through the dark peat stores, which smelled of plant decay and fresh earth. Beyond, we passed through a barn of sorts. This had a door broken and open to the elements. Upon Jamie's advice, I retreated to the peat room, shot the bolt, and returned to the "houseroom" of the main building, dropping the bolt on the peat room door and checking the one at the front.

Then I sat down to wait. I suppose I was intimidated by Marc's instructions for I sat exactly as he had told me and, having nothing better to do, I picked up Marc's canvas of Abbie Hinchley and studied it. I could hardly be jealous of the shabby, overblown charms of the girl, but beyond that it seemed to me there was a calculating, cruel quality in those small, protuberant, pale eyes.

I stopped now and again to listen, but heard nothing more except the roar of the wind as it whipped the lilac bush against the window. I started to throw down the portrait of Abbie and, in doing so, saw a sheet of paper fall from the frame where it had been stuck, either for safe-keeping or to get it out of the way.

It was a torn half-page of letter and, since it was open and lying before my eyes, I saw no reason why I should not read it.

— boy's description, I should say, you have been subject to an attack of some severity. My dear Branshaw, these things are not to be shrugged off. One day, such an attack may well be your death, for others may not know the symptoms, nor how to treat them. Permit me to say that your fear of personal examination is beyond my comprehension. I can only call it fear — and a cowardly one — that you should shun a doctor who is as much a part of this countryside as your family were. Trust me, Branshaw. I may be able to help you, more than you guess.

You fancy that it is strength that gives you this energy. Believe me, it is more likely to be a kind of nervous compulsion and will inevitably lead to one attack too many.

Your obedient servant,
James Lowther.

I wondered at this warning, hoping that Marc had taken it seriously, but before I could think too much about it, I saw the charcoal sketch on the back of the letter. I should say *sketches;* for, to my overwhelming surprise and delight, I saw my own face down over a half dozen ways, with as many expressions, and as I examined all these little sketches, I was touched to see that his stick of charcoal had been much gentler than my mirror. One of the sketches nearly made me laugh aloud. It was my face as seen by Marc through the long, narrow window of my London house — frowning, frightened, but with something wistful and young in its expression which I am quite sure only Marc would have observed, for I had felt neither young nor tender at the moment. Another sketch was almost insulting, if one had no sense of humor. There I was, looking exactly as though waiting to be kissed, as I sat on my bed the previous night and he so rudely disappointed me. Even in this, though, he had put into my features a kind of endearing quality which only he saw, and I was more touched than I had been, even by Jamie's comment that Marc had liked me as long ago as the London encounter. This was clearer proof than mere word. I could have kissed the sketches for what they revealed of his feelings about me.

I thought of something then. Had Marc gone directly from the inn last night, and his encounter with me, to spend the night in this out-of-the-way place, instead of at home in Branshaw Hall? Did he never sleep? And if he hated the moors as much as he pretended, why was he always to be found, like one of the moorland creatures, alone in its great silences?

The world about me had been still for several minutes. Now the wind, dying down, made me aware of many sounds outside that I had not previously noticed. I wondered how the lilac bush could make those scuffling noises, like boots on gravel. Keeping my head forward, as though I were studying the painting of Abbie Hinchley, I listened. Behind me, outside that window, were sounds other than the lilac bush trembling in the now somnolent wind. There was no mistake this time. A body, perhaps that of an animal, had jarred against the wall of the cottage.

There it was again. Something approaching the window — cautious, but making mistakes in the darkness. My heart thudded, and to calm myself, I kept thinking.

"It must be Marc. Or Jamie. Yes. Of course. Jamie might do something like this — a boy, thinking it very funny to frighten me. . . ."

But I could not quite convince myself.

I raised the big portrait of Abbie and turned just a fraction, with the portrait concealing my face, as though I sought to study the portrait from a different angle. I was just able to see the vague outlines of something at the window. The face was not pressed against the glass as I had expected, but it was far off — a kind of floating thing that I could not identify — yet I knew it had not been there before. It was watching me.

Casually, I kept the portrait before my face and moved back into my original position, frantic with fear for my exposed back. What was it out there? If I had not known better, I should have said it was dun-color, as Jamie claimed when he saw the Gytrash change into the Devil-Vicar. But that was nonsense. This was no animal staring in at me. What animal was so large that it could peer in at that high window?

There were no fingers this time, nothing telltale. Only that floating, curious thing that might be a face, far back from the window. I sat stiff and silent, waiting.

Marc! I thought . . . Why don't you come and catch this thing? Where are you? Take it away!

It was too horrid. Suppose it vanished and Marc did not discover what it was? Suppose Marc was not looking in this direction now and missed it altogether? Using the portrait as a shield, I stole another glance.

The thing was gone now — swallowed up in the immense dark outside. Then I heard it again, pressing close against the house, moving around through the overgrown nettles toward the front of the cottage.

No. It must be Marc. The other thing I heard, the screams from the bog, they were the creature we feared. After all, hadn't Jamie seen it at the window? What was I thinking of? I opened my mouth to call Marc, and stopped myself just in time. Heavens! I must be growing hysterical.

What harm could come to me in here? Why, the doors were all bolted and a stout poker would do considerable harm to anyone who broke in through the window.

The thing outside brushed sharply against the wall, so close to me that it seemed almost in the room. Without being able to control the sound, I cried out, then hushed, with my hand over my mouth, waiting. Had my involuntary cry given me away as a woman? I could hardly imagine Marc crying out like that.

While I watched, with every emotion suspended within me, the latch on the door moved up and down, and again, gently. Then a push, testing the strength of the bolt. This time I screamed, very loud. Surely, Marc would come. Where in the name of heaven was he!

After my scream, the thing outside no longer feared to make a noise, and the door rattled furiously. Then there was a pause.

I thought with a twisted humor: I must tell Jamie. Gytrashes rarely try the latch of a door. It takes human beings for such refinements.

I rushed to the fire and was about to pick up the poker when I saw the long barrel of a shotgun behind the sofa. I took it out, not knowing what to do with it, but assuming that its mere presence and size would be enough to give an intruder pause. Behind me, there was a terrific crash against the door — a crash, I thought, that could not have been made by a human being.

Silence followed, and I stood still with terror.

The creature was moving along the house to the shed, the barn, the storeroom — any of which was less sturdy than the front door. I listened. Yes. Already he had gotten into the peat room. The door beside the fireplace was being tried, stealthily. It would not take long to come through that frail and ancient barrier.

I called out, shrill as a harpy, "What do you want? I have a gun. I shall fire." And then, in a voice that broke with my terror, *"Who are you?"*

The peat room door, which had trembled under an onslaught, was suddenly still.

I did not wait longer. Somewhere outside were Marc and Jamie. They were my only hope. Frantic to put space between myself and this monster, I shot back the bolt of the front door and then, with the gun in my trembling hands, stepped out onto the moors.

XII

Never in my life had I been so keenly aware of the hostile and unknown space around me. The stars were under fleecy clouds and the entire firmament was momentarily shrouded in Stygian darkness.

I sped over the ground, careful to step where the nettles tugged at my skirts rather than where the ground seemed easier on my feet but was more treacherous. I was aware of being, for the first time, a part of the infinite world of the moors where, for miles in every direction, there might be no human being except myself and the thing that had driven me out.

I seemed to be beyond the sound of the blows at the peat room door, or perhaps they had stopped. I found myself on the worn sheep trail we had taken up to the cottage so long ago this afternoon. There was no shelter ahead of me for several minutes, until I should reach the beginnings of the bog where Moyna Branshaw had received her mortal injuries. This made me completely visible as I ran, for there were no trees in sight.

I had run for several minutes, keeping close watch on the narrow sheep track, when I heard, from the direction of Moyna's cottage, a fierce and savage growl. It sounded like one of those enormous moor dogs, so useful with sheep. The barking was interrupted by several peculiar, piercing yelps. I tried to run faster. Then I fancied I heard winging sounds of pursuit behind me. In the great dark of the night, I was sure I heard the sounds of the Devil-Vicar — the great sleeves like wings on the wind, the skirts of a robe flying out as the thing hurried after me. I knew I should never outrun it. Faster, and faster came the sounds behind me.

The particular sounds at last parted from the roar of the wind, and they became the even tread of a four-footed beast. I could not believe this. Even the intruder at Moyna's cottage had had human sound, had displayed human characteristics. I cast a terrified glance over my shoulder and paused, involuntarily, dead-tired, and almost frozen with horror. It was a four-footed beast, and no mistake — a great, dark beast whose rough, thick-coated silhouette loomed up behind me on the horizon, rushing ever closer and closer. I began to run again but, in my mounting panic, tripped over a root in my path and fell headlong into the black heather. I covered my face with my hands, the long-barrelled shotgun wavering overhead. I had some feeble notion of using it to ward off the beast — the Gytrash, I reminded myself, still half-unbelieving.

I could hear the awful thump of its paws upon the ground, skimming along, until at last it shook the earth under me and the great creature came to a pause. Fearing the worst, my hands clutched the shotgun and I waited. I was prepared for a sudden leap and the tearing of my flesh by the fangs of the beast. But what I received was quite a different sensation. The beast came close upon me, halted, and sniffed around my face and head curiously. I made no move. The animal, which I now perceived to be a large, red-haired dog, satisfied his curiosity and was about to proceed upon its way when it paused again, standing almost at point, listening. Cautiously, I raised my head and watched it. The dog's dark eyes were focussed upon the darkness out of which it had raced. The beast, I understood at last, was as frightened as I of something in the direction of Moyna's cottage.

Apparently hearing what was silent to my own ears, it took off again on a tearing run down the slope, and headed to what I imagined must be its home among the sheep farmers on the moors. I only wished I might take such speed myself, for if this big beast were frightened, I saw no reason to be brave.

I got to my feet and ran straight down the long, steep bill, hoping against hope that somewhere in the night I should meet Marc Branshaw, or Jamie at the least. Since the earlier sounds of the man caught in the bog had come from this direction, it was my only chance.

The bogs, with their wonderful cover of foliage, presented also my greatest danger. I paused to get my breath and to see if I could hear any sounds of pursuit, but the wind managed to conceal any hint of the thing which had been separated from me only by the wall of Moyna's cottage.

I took the sheep track again, for I could make out the faint light from the window of a sheep-farmer's cottage, not far up the trail. As I hurried by, keeping to the center track so that nothing hidden in those boggy depths should snatch at me, I saw the signs of a recent struggle.

The mudbank had given way, its cohesiveness thinned by the late rains, so that the unfortunate traveler, whoever he might be, had slipped. His struggles to free himself from the entangling bushes, water-soaked foliage, and the filth of centuries, must have served but to draw him further into the slime. Great chunks of the mudbank had broken off afresh. But I was not so concerned with this evidence as I was over the problem of Jamie's disappearance. It was plain, whatever the discomfort of the traveler who had fallen into the bog, that he had been dragged out and was doubtless safe. I wanted to know what had become of his rescuer, as I took Jamie to be.

Close by in the thickness of the trees I heard the bubbling, gurgling noise of the bog, and paused, wondering what caused that unpleasant sound. Then I heard faint squeals, telltale sounds of a tiny moor animal in distress. I winced, wishing I might be of help, but when I took a step into the darkness and felt the yielding turf underfoot, I realized I would have to leave the poor creature to its hideous fate.

There was a choice of several sheep-tracks now. I took the one that appeared most heavily trodden. When I made my way beyond the bogs, it was faster going and, although I could now be seen by a pursuer, I could also see behind me. Nothing moved except the nettle and bracken, drifting with the wind. The sounds of the tiny moorland animal died away. In a few minutes I was at the door of the low, one-and-a-half-story cottage somewhat off the main track up to Wind-Rock. I was just about to knock when, to my amazement, Jamie appeared beside me, coming around from the barn. He looked me up and down.

"You shouldn't have left the cottage, mum.

Marc'll be that cross. Sir Gareth fell in a bog and near drowned, he did. It was him we heard calling. But Marc saved him. I followed the trail him and Marc made coming up here to the cottage. Marc said I was to stay by Sir Gareth, just in case he needed me."

"Oh, he did! Naturally, Sir Gareth would need you more than I, besieged by monsters and Devil-Vicars and I don't know what all! And is Mr. Branshaw here too, by chance?" I went on angrily.

Behind us, the cottage door had opened and a farmer stood in the doorway, trying to discover what was all this noise at his front step.

"Come in, come in," he said, more crossly than enthusiastically. He proved to be a lean, grizzled specimen of rugged manhood, with piercing gray eyes. His wife, from what I could see through the slit of light revealed by the half-open door, was a strong-armed, sturdy woman who looked formidable even in her present state of undress.

"May as well," she muttered, adding her gracious invitation to that of her husband.

I found myself in a low-roofed cozy room, where Sir Gareth was fastening a coat that fitted narrowly in the shoulders while the farmer's breeches, which were homespun and home-cut, did not suit the airs of the baronet at all, and I was hard put not to smile at the sight.

"Damnable impertinence," he was muttering. "I could have gone on with Branshaw. But no, he had to leave me here — to dry out, he said. Dry out, indeed. What's the man up to? Where was he off to in such a hurry that he could not await me?"

"He saved your life," Jamie put in loyally. "I'd never have reached you in time. It was great sport, Miss Anne. Marc saw Sir Gareth a-peeking in the windows of the cottage and followed him. Then he heard Sir Gareth scream when he fell in the bog."

"I was not 'Peeking in' as you put it," the baronet said sharply. "I thought, if he weren't in the cottage, I might stop in and borrow a glass of something to heat me on my way. I'd come all the way over from Upshed to help them tree that savage mongrel, but I lost my way. And I was in no good mood when I reached Moyna's cottage, I can tell you. Especially finding Branshaw at home."

"Why didn't you stop?" I asked, remembering how he had frightened us earlier in the evening.

"What? And pass the time of day with that rascal? Thanks. I prefer to have as little to do with the pup as I can. I saw him in there and — but pardon, ma'am. He was wearing the jacket you have on. Is it possible it was you I saw? Then how was it he came so quickly when I slipped into that accursed bog?"

"Because," Jamie told him in triumph, before I could shake my head at him, "Marc was watching the cottage. And when he saw you hanging about, he followed you. He thinks you're the

Devil-Vicar, the Gytrash. Are you?"

"Oh, Gad, no! I've better things to do, I can tell you, than go about in sheets, frightening women and curly-headed tots."

I was studying the faces of the people before me, wondering if I should mention the creature who had visited Moyna's cottage after Jamie left. It seemed to me now that if I told them of my encounter they would connect it at once with Marc Branshaw, who had delivered Sir Gareth to the farmer's house and then vanished. Sometime shortly after that, I heard the unknown and monstrous intruder around Moyna's cottage. The creature was going softly, perhaps only spying, until I made the mistake of crying out, thus informing it that I was not Marc Branshaw. I reasoned that the creature, discovering I was not Marc, feared I had seen it at the window or guessed its identity — and that I must be destroyed like Abbie Hinchley and Will Grimlett. But then, the pounding on the doors mysteriously stopped when I asked the question which I now believed had saved my life: "Who are you?"

This was all conjecture. Only one coherent thought leaped out of the terrors of tonight. Either Marc was lying from the beginning, or the creature had done as Marc predicted: it had tried to commit its crimes at precisely the time and place which left Marc with no defense. It was better to say nothing of all this to people whose minds would undoubtedly behave as Marc had predicted they would upon hearing fresh coincidences that bound him with the terror of the countryside.

While the farmer's wife brewed us some hot tea, Sir Gareth announced that, come what may, he was going past Wind-Rock and back to Maidenmoor tonight. I admitted I should prefer that, without explaining that I felt we might all be terrorized if we returned to Moyna's cottage. That was a story I would tell Marc alone so that we could make his defenses against accusation.

We set out, Jamie carrying Marc's rifle, Sir Gareth the shotgun which had proved so useless to me, and I, at my own insistence, carrying Jamie's lantern. I wanted to be absolutely sure of where we were going.

It was a trifle lighter, with more stars out, when we reached Wind-Rock and I paused to get my breath. Even Sir Gareth found the slippery, twisting journey more than he had bargained for. While Jamie waited a little impatiently, scuffing at the growth of dead heather in the path, the baronet heaved a sigh and propped his tall body against the Wind-Rock entrance.

"What a curious thing, sir," I remarked to him, "that your accident should occur so near that which led to Mrs. Branshaw's death, and your sister's misfortune."

"Well, don't be saying it's divine retribution!" said Sir Gareth acidly, "for I'd nothing to do with that, I assure you. Although I might have been tempted, sometimes. Moyna did have a way of making one think she might yield, and then when one expected her to — At any rate, she could turn from devil to nun in a moment. But I daresay she lost the one love of her life and just wanted to torment the rest of us. Gad! She told Catherine just the day before she died that she had one particular heart on a string, and had just discovered she'd kept it for fifteen years. Thought it extremely funny. Or so Cathie says."

"What did she mean by 'just discovered?' "

"Who shall say? Queer girl, Moyna." He added after a moment, "Don't imagine she was talking of me, pray, Miss Wicklow. As I told Cathie, the cream of the jest was that, in a sense, it might have been a female's heart she kept on a string. Perhaps she knew a secret that would hurt some female who . . . well, an enterprising man might make something profitable of that. We'll never know now."

I was heartily glad when we reached the gray cobbles of Maidenmoor, but on the fog-washed stoop of the Owen house we were met by the Owen maid servant. She was a prim, humorless woman in night curlers and a shapeless flannel robe, who beckoned to us with one hand while the other clutched the high neck of her robe. She said sourly:

"Miss Catherine's been askin' after ye. She's been up since all hours, poor lamb, worrit sick for fear ye'd fallen in a bog or the like, Mister Gareth."

"Good Lord!" Gareth exclaimed. "Well, we're for it now." He glanced down at his borrowed finery. "No explaining away that wretched farmer's raiment."

Behind the maid, in the narrow, dour hall of the old stone house, I made out the shape of Catherine Owen in a wheelchair. She waved to us. I wanted very much to get home to my icy bed in the Yorkish Lion, but there is no denying my curiosity about this woman had been piqued by the gossip of Jamie's friends, that she was trying to walk. Catherine took my hand in her familiar, pleasant way, remarking that I must be dreadfully chilled and then asking her brother what he meant by keeping me out until all hours.

"What a buzz the village will be in, Garrie! How could you be so thoughtless? I suppose you lost your way again."

"It was all the fault of that Branshaw pup," he told her. "If I'd known he wasn't indoors, I'd have stopped. How was I to know he'd follow me? As though I were a damned sharper!"

"He did save your life, sir," I pointed out, but Catherine was looking from one to the other of us in a puzzled way. "Sir Gareth fell in a bog," I explained, "and Mr. Branshaw rescued him."

"I'm afraid I must be frightfully dense. I don't understand how Marc could have been in Moyna's cottage, and still be here in Maidenmoor tonight." If the roof had fallen upon me, I could not have been more astonished. That is to say, astonishment was my first reaction. The burning fury came afterward.

Sir Gareth contradicted her, but without

213

my cause for emotion.

"Come now, Cathie, what's this? I saw the man myself. Saved my life, I'm bound to admit — but he did it in no friendly tone, I can tell you. Acted as though he thought I were a murderer or something equally nasty. He almost threw me back in."

"Then why isn't he with you now?" asked his sister patiently.

"Why he — he said there was something he must attend to, and off he went. Good Lord!"

"Just as I say," Catherine went on. "He returned to the village."

Leaving Jamie with a man he suspected of being a murderer, and me in Moyna's desolate cottage, the prey of all sorts of wandering intruders!

"Where did you see him exactly, Miss Owen?" I asked, trying to reflect on this thing calmly.

"He was in the mistal over at Branshaw Hall. He appeared to be searching for something. It was quite dark and Nettie only saw him in fits and starts from her lantern. She thought she was seeing the Devil-Vicar and set up a cry for me that must have sent the neighborhood into the shivers . . . unless, of course — Oh, no!"

We were all startled at her change of expression. She put her hand to her mouth. "But could it have been the Devil-Vicar after all?"

"Are we off again on the trail of two Marcs — twin brothers, or father and son?" Sir Gareth asked in a bored way.

Catherine nodded thoughtfully.

"But the truth is, one has a fairly clear view of the Hall from the back of our house. And Nettie and I did see someone over there who was dressed much more in the manner of the Devil-Vicar than in one of Marc's familiar jackets. The Other One is alive, as I've always believed. This proves it. But have we been dealing with Marc, or the Devil-Vicar? His fear of fire should tell us. Sooner or later it will break him down to an admission of his identity. Don't you agree?" She looked at me hopefully.

This preposterous theory did not wash with me any more than with the baronet. If Catherine had seen a figure like the Devil-Vicar among the outbuildings of Branshaw Hall, then it was Marc, and no nonsense about that.

"Miss Wicklow," Catherine called to me as I turned toward the Yorkish Lion. "Abbie Hinchley's funeral is for this afternoon. Then will come the Arvills before nightfall. Will you be so good as to attend the funeral with me? I would appreciate it."

I did not know who or what "arvills" were, but I was still curious about Catherine Owen's ability to move about, and I thought it would do no harm to see more of her, and perhaps discover her secret, if there was one.

"Very well, if you wish it. You know where to find me, ma'am. Come, Jamie."

I was snappish all the way home through the village, for I seethed at the thought that Marc

Branshaw was over prowling about, searching for heaven knows what, while Jamie and I risked our lives to give a false impression to all who passed. Marc's entire campaign to get me up to Yorkshire must have been waged for this purpose. It was very lowering. I had been led to believe that there was something personal in his interest, but I had only been used. Like Catherine. And I daresay, like many another of his females.

As Jamie left me at my room, he said hesitantly, "You mustn't think Marc lies. It's just that — he has reasons."

"On that we're both agreed!" I said with glacial politeness and added, "but it may interest you and Mr. Branshaw to know that Sir Gareth was not the spy he is trying to trap. There is another, who came to the cottage tonight after you had gone. A very dangerous Other!" With that I closed the door in Jamie's surprised face.

XIII

I did not undress for bed in the ordinary sense. I tore off the garments borrowed from Marc Branshaw and hurled them into a corner. Then, too angry to shiver in the ice-cold room, I dressed in my London night clothing, which was scarcely warm enough for Yorkshire, but that was also of no consequence. I was perspiring with my own heat of fury when I climbed into bed and slid one naked foot and then the other down over the cold sheets.

I lay for a few minutes, quietly burning, annoyed with the ruffle of my nightgown around my neck, for it seemed suddenly too warm and too tight. But the cold bed finally soothed me, and I went into a restless sleep.

It must have just turned dawn, for I recall that the room was already light when the door from the hall opened, and with very little ceremony. In fact, the noise of its opening awakened me and I sat up to demand fiercely:

"You have the wrong room. Out of here at once! Do you hear me?"

I hadn't the faintest notion to whom I spoke until the door slammed behind my uninvited guest, and he crossed the room to draw aside the worn, clean drapes that closed out the sunrise. It was Marc Branshaw, looking muddy, dishevelled, unshaven, and rather the worse for wear. I was glad that I had used the correct tone when he entered my room.

He turned to me, quite as furious as I.

"Where have you been?"

There is nothing that reduces one to complete self-possession like the shouting and temper of one's opponent. I said insolently:

"As you see — in bed. But in my own bed. I do not ask others to pass themselves off as myself while I leave them in danger and go off and play my games elsewhere."

He came to the foot of the bed and leaned over

it, raising a hand with all the fingers out-stretched, as though he were about to choke me.

"In your bed. *In your bed!* Do you know that I have been into and out of every bog, every pot-hole, every cursed trap in the entire West Riding, searching for you? I left our prowler, the good Sir Gareth, drying out at some farm, and hurried back to see to your safety, and what did I find? The cottage door unbolted, and no sign of you. Do you know that I have spent the last few hours imagining every conceivable accident had be-fallen you? Didn't I tell you not to leave the cot-tage, under any circumstances?"

"Including my own murder?"

"I had already found the man who was spying on me. And neither he nor his sister is very likely the murderer."

"I beg to differ. The murderer, or spy — as you choose — was at your cottage, in your absence, very busy trying to get at me. That's why I ran out — to find you, who had deserted me."

"I know all that. Jamie told me. But even so, it might have been the very thing he wanted, to have you driven out into his hands. It was a stupid thing to do. I came back for you as soon as I could get rid of Owen."

"It's curious that you didn't see me as I ran down to the bogs, and then over to that farmer's cottage — if what you say is supposed to be true."

He said with cutting politeness, "May I point out that the moors are rather spacious and that it was night?"

I slid back under the covers with an attitude of nonchalance. To tell the truth, I did not believe him. I thought this was a tale he had concocted upon hearing of my danger from Jamie. If he had left Sir Gareth in order to hurry back and see to my safety, then who was the Devil-Vicar person seen searching the outbuildings at Branshaw Hall? I refused to believe Catherine's romantic theory that her precious ghost still lived. . . . Was it possible that the thing which had tried to get at me in Moyna's cottage had had time to return to Branshaw Hall for the search? I supposed it was possible, but hardly probable. What was probable was that Marc had made up this story to explain his negligence. I decided to try him on it, and said smugly:

"At least I cannot be accused of being in two places at once."

He dropped his hands upon the bedpost. His fingers tightened around it until they were white at the knuckles.

"What do you mean by that?"

"Oh," I said pleasantly, "I didn't mean to be obscure. I meant simply that I don't ask my friends to take my place at home so that I may be seen by romantic young ladies while I masquerade at the opposite end of the county."

He slapped the bedpost.

"Good God! So that's what this is all about! Dear Catherine has managed to trade off a few lies about seeing me tonight. Did she tell you that the Devil-Vicar was floating about, making mad love to her? If she hasn't, she undoubtedly will. And what has all this to do with your leaving the cottage? Everyone told you it was worth your life. The countryside itself is dangerous, and then Abbie's murder . . . Will Grimlett. . . . Don't you know there's a killer loose in this district?"

"I ought to know; he very nearly got to me in your house. So don't come blustering in here expecting to find him under my bed. And furthermore," I added, growing more and more upset at his blaming me for doing the most natural thing, "you are as cold and hateful and cruel as — as your precious Devil-Vicar. At least Sir Gareth loves and cares for his sister. So I'll thank you to get out of my room."

"Is that your last word to me? After what —"

"Don't tell me what you've gone through," I said haughtily. "Come back when your manners are better. And don't think you can sweep into my bedchamber as though it were your fine friend Catherine's, either." That was uncalled for but by now I could hear stirrings in the chamber next to mine, which was Mrs. Fothergay's, and, even worse, low voices in the hall, which could only be the Reverend MacDonnachie and his wife. It was frightfully embarrassing. And I did not like it any better when I heard Mrs. Fothergay's twittering comments as she joined the Vicar and his wife in the hall.

Marc paid no attention to them.

"Very well! Run to dear, good, kind Sir Gareth! He's just the sort for you — a weak, great slug of a creature, who —"

"Weak!" I cried, and managed a fair imitation of a nasty laugh. "I am sure, if the necessity arose, he could beat you within an inch of —"

"— who, for all I know, has murdered three people!" Marc went on, deaf to my interruption. "Go! By all means! I make you a present of him." He swung around the bedpost and stopped in front of me, his dark face livid with anger and the strain of what must have been a very difficult night. "Marry him! Do! But I advise you at least to pretend to some of Bedelia Fothergay's money, for that is all he wants of you!"

This was beyond contempt.

"Thank you! I shall certainly do so. And when I've married Gareth and you have married Catherine, then, think how cozy it will be! You and I, from having looked alike, will then be truly brother and sister. Nothing could be happier."

Why this should have provoked him beyond endurance, I don't know, but for an instant I thought he would slap me. Instead, however, he struck the bedpost so hard the whole bed shook.

"The Reverend Niles said you were selfish and irreligious and amoral. He might have added you are surly and have dreadful manners!"

He threw up his hands.

"This is all that was needed. That you should talk about me behind my back with that mealy-mouthed curate! I suppose you'll say he sets me an example. Everywhere I go, every move I make, there is Frederick Niles to remind me. The good, the noble Frederick! And there am I — all that is despicable."

This time I was amazed. What was there about the young curate's sincere good works in the village that should shake Marc like this? How could Marc be jealous, a man with all his abilities and attractions?

He went out and slammed the door so hard that it swung open again, and, of course, awakened those who might have slept through his previous tantrum. It must have been maddening to him when he was stopped in his furious progress by Mrs. MacDonnachie, who said in her sweet, die-away voice:

"Marc, my dear! What is it? You must calm yourself."

Even more annoying was Mrs. Fothergay's fussy twitter. "My dear Marc, what an hour to call upon one! What business had you — er — here?"

Marc's voice cut her off harshly.

"No business at all, ma'am. Now or in the future. I am too unworthy! It was all a very bad mistake. Good day to you!"

"Come now, lad. Don't go off in a huff," the Reverend called after him, with his fat man's breathy laughter. "These things pass over. . . . Ah, Jamie-boy, did our impetuous friend awaken you?"

Jamie's voice came sleepily. "Aunty wants to

know what's amiss."

"Nothing, lad. Just a lover's quarrel."

"Hardly, that," Mrs. Fothergay interposed. "Mr. Branshaw mistook the door, that is all — and Miss Wicklow was probably alarmed."

Jamie was endearingly quick to ask, "Is she all right? Miss Anne?"

The Reverend MacDonnachie sounded playful but fatherly.

"Yes, yes. Don't disturb her. And you need sleep, you young rascal. I heard you get back in the wee hours of the night. Been out looking for Gytrashes? See the ghost of the Devil-Vicar?" He gave out a loud and audible shiver. "Damn — pardon, ladies. But it's cold as a tomb out in this windy hall. Well, is it back to slumber? Busy day ahead, what with the funeral and then the arvills. I do hope someone has bespoke some decent liquor for the arvills. Can't have a real funeral without a little refreshment, you know."

"Special best!" Jamie put in proudly.

"Really!" said Mrs. Fothergay, echoing my own slight shock.

Mrs. MacDonnachie was apologetic. "Cadmon's little jest, ma'am. The arvills in a home or the local taproom are a tradition here after funerals. But we do not take funerals lightly. It's a method of making the whole painful business easier for the bereaved."

"In this case, Abbie's father, that drunken sot, Abel Hinchley," put in the Vicar. "How he'll look forward to it!"

I looked, out into the hall about this time and inquired severely: "Has that awful man gone?"

"Oh, come, my dear! Not 'awful.' " Mrs. Mac-Donnachie made vague gestures but was cut off by her husband, with whose views, I must say, I agreed.

"Gone, Miss Anne, and in a fine rage. You must have sent him packing, with a flea in his ear."

"I did."

"Exactly so, ma'am. And now, may we bid you good night."

He took his wife's arm to escort her down the hall. They were an absurd couple — she all wispy and waving ruffles, he in a robe of the most violent sunset hue below and above which peeped hems of his woolen nightgown.

Once back in bed, unnerved and yet excited by my battle with Marc, I realized that I still didn't know whether Catherine Owen was telling the truth or not. Had Marc been in two places at once last night? Or was it possible for both of us to have seen him within a few hours?

Of course, Catherine's other claim, that there must be two Marc Branshaws, was in the realm of fantasy. It did present some interesting, and rather frightening ideas to me, however.

It was nearly noon when I awoke to see Rose Keegan trying to close the portieres in silence so that the bright sunlight should not pour into my eyes. I smiled and told her that the sun was as welcome as it was unexpected.

"We shall have a pleasant day for the funeral and the arvills afterward," she said.

I asked her if the arvills were a kind of noisy wake. She was not offended but assured me that she had never known a person to die in this area — least of all one of Abbie's character — who wouldn't have approved the social gathering in the Yorkish Lion taproom in honor of the dead, and financed by the nearest living relation or his friends.

"To my knowledge," she went on, "only in the case of the Reverend Ewen Morgan's death, there were no arvills."

"Didn't they think it worth celebrating the Devil-Vicar's murder?" I asked ironically.

Miss Rose arranged the drapes and curtains, picked up Marc's jacket, which I had unceremoniously hurled to the floor, and came back to the bed. While I got up and into a robe, she said to me, with that quiet conviction of the truth that was so much a part of her:

"Believe me, ma'am, the villagers had no notion of murdering Ewen — the Reverend Morgan, I mean to say. An enemy, jealous of him, committed the crime. It was intended by the village that he should be driven out by the fire. Instead, from all we have learned since, he was struck down secretly and left to die. There could be no 'celebration,' as you call it, over what the whole village felt to be a monstrous crime. And although my brother, Jamie's father, was the first in the ruins to try and rescue Ewen Morgan — for he was against the burning in the first

225

place — we all knew that as the crime was committed by one of us, so were we all to blame." She hesitated, picked at a spot of mud on the coat, and then added, "I believe, for some reason, the murderer of the Reverend Morgan has returned — if, indeed, he or she ever left Maidenmoor — and is at work again."

"Then you're quite certain Ewen Morgan is dead?"

She looked at me in an odd, speculative way. "My brother found the bones. Surely, he cannot have lived through that inferno."

I went over to the window and looked out. A thought occurred to me when I saw that bare, desolate patch of ground. "Where is Mrs. Branshaw buried?"

She came to the window and pointed out the most elegant group of tombstones at the north end of the churchyard. One had only to glance at those great gray slabs, presided over by a modestly nude white marble statue of Eternal Life, roughly the height of a man, to recognize the pride of the Branshaws, and the family's place in Maidenmoor's social life, even after death.

"How dreadful!" I murmured. "He died partly for love of Mrs. Branshaw, yet they can't even be together now."

She surprised me by smiling, as if at a memory. "I doubt if they would wish to be. I suspect Moyna taught the young man a great deal. But beyond being instructress and pupil in certain — if I may call them — *arts,* I think, had the affair not been interrupted by his murder, they would have drifted apart."

I was startled. "But if they were not everything to each other, what of their — of Moyna's son?"

She seemed to be caught unawares but recovered quickly. "Ah! Moyna's son. He was always a sickly boy — all the Branshaws were. It used to trouble Moyna a great deal."

"Aside from being afraid of fire, which I can understand because of what happened to his supposed father, what *is* wrong with Marc Branshaw?" I asked.

"With Marc?" she repeated in a surprised voice, as though we'd been discussing occupants of the moon and suddenly returned to earth. "Why, nothing, indeed! He is a little nervous. I'm given to understand that most artists are. And Jamie saw him taken ill once, after a bad headache, I think it was. He told Jamie it was nothing, and laid the blame to a severe shock or injury of some sort in his earlier years. But it's certainly nothing fatal. Even I have been known to faint upon occasion."

"Was that what was the matter with him as a child?"

"I really couldn't say. Will you be going to the funeral?"

That reminded me of my obligations and I began to dress hurriedly. "Yes, I must. I promised to go with Catherine Owen."

Miss Rose stopped in the doorway. "There's an unhappy woman. Something troubles her deeply. She had best have a care."

"What on earth do you mean?"

"Miss Catherine has some extraordinary ideas — unhealthy ones. But it's more than that. It may be that she's had something of my own odd sensation, that somewhere in Maidenmoor I sense a mask on a familiar face, or rather, a familiar mask on a face that is . . . not one of us."

I remembered suddenly. "Good heavens! Marc said almost the same thing."

"Yes. I thought he would feel it. Has he said whom he suspects?"

"Not to me. Surely, you don't think Catherine . . ."

"If Miss Catherine is not guilty, then she certainly knows who is. Her entire conduct — that book she and various villagers have discussed up one street and down the next — yes," she mused thoughtfully, "Miss Catherine knows. And if she isn't guilty herself, then she may precipitate the very thing she fears most."

I laughed, more to reassure myself than because I saw anything humorous in the situation. "I know she fancies herself in love with a dead man. But you can scarcely call that guilt. It's no worse than young ladies in London who fancy themselves in love with some actor at Drury Lane."

Miss Rose said without emphasis, "But those actors have not committed two and perhaps three murders."

She went out. On the whole, her exit line was worthy of Drury Lane.

XIV

A short time later I met Catherine Owen outside the church of St. Anthony's, she having arrived here by her own efforts, in her wheelchair. She was justly proud of this accomplishment and, no matter what people said of her, I could not help joining in congratulations at her own initiative.

"I suppose I seem very foolish to you," she apologized, "but the truth is, I have prayed for strength, and am hoping that one day, not too long from now, I shall be able to stand without assistance."

I told her I thought she was very brave, and meant it with all my heart.

"For I freely admit," I said, "that I shouldn't like to spend any more time in this strange, murderous village than is strictly necessary to recover the manuscript Mr. Branshaw stole from me."

"Murderous?" She looked up at me as I wheeled her into the vestry of the church. "But they've killed the dog who did those things, haven't they?"

"Nonsense. It was a human being who did it," I said, not being at all sure, but anxious to see if Rose Keegan was right, if Catherine did know something about the crimes.

Her long fingers, dainty yet strong in their little knitted gloves, dug into the arms of her chair.

"No, no. I don't believe it. It was the dog." She peered up into my face with a pathetic hope in her wide, hazel eyes. "The horrid scratches . . . the . . . mangled flesh. . . . Well, everything indicates a dog."

She was certainly distressed.

"Yet a dog might be set on a human being who had been struck down by a cudgel let us say. However, that wasn't the way it happened in your book, was it, Miss Catherine?"

I expected her to grow angry, but she surprised me by covering her face with her shaking hands. "That accursed book. It was only done in revenge. And then, when I changed it, I thought he would be amused. I never meant it to be seriously taken for Moyna. You see . . ." She got hold of herself, aware that others in the church entry were looking our way. She lowered her voice and finished, ". . . he's so different from the way I imagine him. When I'm away from him, I think of him as the Other One — Ewen Morgan, whom they called the Devil-Vicar. But when we're together . . . well, you saw how he acted to me. But suppose it were not he but the Other. . . ."

"Do you honestly think he's two people?" I asked her, trying not to smile. "That's a very difficult feat, to be two people and still seem to be one."

"You didn't know the young Ewen Morgan as I did when I was a girl in Wales. I went to all the services he took. I adored him. I never believed

230

what they said when he came to Maidenmoor. His portrait is in the Vicar's offices. If no one is in there, perhaps you could manage to get me over there now. To the left."

So there was a connection between the Owens in Wales and the late Devil-Vicar before he came into Yorkshire.

"And was he in love with you in Wales?" I asked, burning with curiosity.

She smiled wanly. "Heavens, no! I was a child then. I doubt if he knew I existed."

Several villagers made way for us and I pushed her along the narrow, gloomy aisle behind the nave. Despite the presence of clear glass panes instead of stained glass windows, the interior of the church was dark, and as damp-cold as the tombs beyond its windows, but I was not surprised that as we approached the vicar's study the air grew appreciably warmer. I could well imagine the Reverend Cadmon MacDonnachie was no suffering saint. He enjoyed such comforts as a small enclosed stove would give him.

The vicar was no doubt elsewhere encouraging his flock, so that for a few moments we had his office to ourselves. It was as typical of him as his red beard. Scraps of paper were scattered over the floor, which had been covered by a cheap but serviceable carpeting, and, to contribute to the general untidiness, an inkstand had been overturned and dripped slowly into its own soggy stain in the carpet.

In spite of its slovenly look, the room apparently served as a vestry as well as the Vicar's office, for there were a number of benches scattered about.

All along, I had put off looking up at the portrait, about two feet square, above the Vicar's desk, but finally I steeled myself to see the image of the creature who had caused such havoc in the village that he had to be burned to death.

At first, it gave me a start to see the surface resemblance to Marc Branshaw; yet the spirit behind those surface similarities was so different that I was at the same time amazed that anyone should have mistaken the one man for the other. What looked down at me — and those eyes seemed to stare directly into my soul — was an extraordinarily bitter, humorless face, so handsome that one could well understand Catherine's penchant for it, but otherwise alarming in its intensity. The hair, worn long in the back and rather longer in front than the current style, was black and glossy, the eyes shadowed by heavy lids and lashes, but penetrating in their power. Wherever one stood in the room, there were those eyes peering down, watching. The mouth, which might have been full and even passionate, was twisted into a thin, bitter line, unnatural even to the lips themselves, which appeared capable of violent passions.

I tried to decide how old the face was. But for the bitter, humorless quality, I should have said it was exceedingly young; yet those qualities made it seem about Marc Branshaw's age. It lacked the look of strain and of maturity around the eyes which occasionally betrayed in Marc's face an age not first evident. But in place of that, and above all, by comparison with the humor, the quick, effervescent personality of Marc Branshaw, there was the brooding Celtic quality of a man at war with himself, a man who must have hated his life and everything in it. Small wonder that he took out his hatred of the universe in such ridiculous tales as that he could turn himself into a Gytrash, and that he was the Devil come back to earth.

I considered the proposition that this portrait of Ewen Morgan might serve for a portrait of the Devil. But it was not so. I was quite sure no devil would ever appear so unhappy. This was a man, and if he had no other future than the one that appeared to haunt him in this portrait, then he was better dead.

"As you see, it's not finished," said Catherine, noticing that I wasn't able to tear myself away from it. The surplice had been only sketched in below the face, its white purity a violent contrast with the subject's eyes and shadowy hair.

"Does anyone know who painted it?"

"I don't believe so. The Reverend Mac-Donnachie found it somewhere. He adores it. Probably has a suppressed desire to be taken for Ewen Morgan." She glanced at me, and giggled, a young, uninhibited giggle that was rather winning. "If you can imagine anything more preposterous than Cadmon MacDonnachie emulating that man in the portrait — in anything."

"I don't know," I said defensively, trying not to be aware of those magnificent eyes watching and watching. . . . "If I were in trouble, I should certainly prefer to come to the Vicar Mac-Donnachie."

She raised her eyebrows at what she felt was my absurd prejudice, but I don't think she was sorry to lose a rival.

"I was mistaken in thinking Marc was my Ewen Morgan returned from death."

"And he knew nothing of you in Wales?"

"Oh no. How could he know anything of me? I was thirteen when he left Beaumaris for Maidenmoor. He was twenty-two — a brilliant young man, but much too young and too serious for such a post."

"Too serious?" I repeated, remembering Marc's light touch in almost everything. Certainly, the two men might be said to have violently opposing souls. "And yet you loved him. How then could you love Marc? They are nothing alike."

She shrugged and smiled sadly.

"He was a figure of romance, the Reverend Morgan. There wasn't a girl in Beaumaris who didn't share my feelings. Only I never outgrew them. Years later, when Garrie's expenses outran our income and we had to sell out, I told Garrie that we had to move to Maidenmoor. I'd heard about the Devil-Vicar and his unhappy romance with Moyna Branshaw, and the rest of it. And I wanted to be where he had perished. When I saw the miniature of her son that Moyna proudly displayed to the town a year or two ago, I fell in love with it. I half convinced myself that Marc was either my Ewen Morgan reborn, or perhaps, through some strange quirk, he was Ewen Morgan himself. Of course, he wasn't." She studied the portrait. "Ewen is quite different and — I believe — alive as well. . . ."

She put her hands to her cheeks and closed her eyes. I daresay she was dreaming of this man in the portrait, alive, and her very own. But I told myself he was much too humorless for me. I should have been quite overpowered by all that demoniac grandeur. Nevertheless, I was finding it difficult to take my eyes off Catherine's great love.

Catherine finally tore her attention away from her oil and canvas lover.

"The service will be beginning. Shall we go?"

I had a sudden, stabbing memory of the unhallowed ground out at the end of the church graveyard. To think that all that remained of the creature in the portrait was a handful of bones! It was a searing realization, more searing because it should have meant nothing to me.

I willed myself not to look back at the portrait.

We were joined after the service had begun by Sir Gareth, who was forced to step over Catherine's chair to get into the pew. Although we tried to make no noise, our entry had been noticeable, and a buzz of attention went up around us.

Up in the pulpit the Vicar stopped, for he had

been in the process of extolling the virtues of the deceased girl, and there were several titters from the congregation. I stared at Reverend MacDonnachie's big, hairy face and tried not to think about the unfortunate girl lying to one side of his pulpit, in her simple wooden coffin. I felt the insincerity of the Vicar's words, his effort to enlarge upon certain qualities that the dead girl had not apparently possessed. Once more my thoughts returned to Abbie Hinchley.

Was Rose Keegan right? Had the girl died for some secret she possessed, the identity of the man who had struck down and murdered the Devil-Vicar sixteen years ago? If so then the girl was indeed to be pitied, and I understood the Reverend MacDonnachie's attempt to make her a virtuous heroine.

Meanwhile, something was happening beside me. Sir Gareth had slipped a folded and sealed paper into his sister's hand and I heard him say in his hoarse whisper, "Nettie tells me it was on the hall table with the cards this morning. Addressed to you, as you see."

Catherine took the note, quietly ripped the sealed place, and then, a moment after, dropped the note into her lap and put her hands to her cheeks in a quick, nervous gesture. Her brother started to pick up the note but she whispered sharply, very sharply for Catherine:

"No. It's mine. It's nothing."

Sir Gareth resumed his sleepy contemplation of the Vicar. Out of the corner of my eye I watched Catherine. She seemed in a stupor. Her hands trembled now and then, and she quieted them with an effort. Her dreamy eyes were upon the Vicar, but I do not believe she saw him, for every minute or two she closed her fingers on the note in her lap, and held it tight, as though reassuring herself that it existed.

I was relieved when the entire service was over. It was selfish to be so little concerned over the unhappy Abbie Hinchley, but I had not known her, and I reasoned that even if she had died for what she knew, she must have been exceedingly selfish or perhaps a blackmailer, not to have revealed the murderer of the Devil-Vicar.

When Sir Gareth arose with the congregation and Catherine picked up her old-fashioned reticule, to do likewise, she dropped the note from her shaking hands. I picked it up for her, nearly dying of curiosity to open it, but could not do so under her trusting eyes.

Outside the church, Sir Gareth bade us good day, saying he was going to look for that "old charmer," Mrs. Fothergay. Catherine looked at me apologetically.

"Garrie seems to have taken a sudden fancy to your friend."

I laughed and agreed. Perhaps, because I had been influenced by Marc's maligning comments, I was sure it was the inheritance left to Bedelia Fothergay by the late Colonel that attracted the penniless baronet.

Catherine said, "It's no matter. Come nearer."

I bent over her. To my surprise and faint discomfort, she reached up and hugged me. "Dear, dear Anne, I must tell you. It's come. He is really here in Maidenmoor. Read this."

Feeling the supreme hypocrite, I tried to refuse, but when the little note was pressed into my hand, I read the cryptic line:

Ten at Moyna's stone. Then the flourishing single initial *E*. The writing and the initial looked familiar.

"What is Moyna's stone and who is *E?*"

I was remembering Marc Branshaw's quick handwritten changes on Catherine's manuscript. No doubt of it. There was a similarity. She was evidently so enthralled with her notion of meeting the Devil-Vicar that she had not noticed the resemblance.

Catherine said softly, "Can't you guess? It's as I said. Why do you think people have taken to seeing Marc in two places at once, and all that nonsense? There are two of them. *He* has returned."

"Who? Not —"

"Ewen Morgan. Surely it must be he remembers me from the old days in Beaumaris."

I was genuinely anxious. Even if Marc was playing some trick on Catherine, I hoped, for his sake as well as hers, that she would not abet him.

The Devil-Vicar! My heavens, Catherine, even if it were true — and of course it's not — why, the man would be a demon! He is dead. You must remember that."

She shook her head. There was an obstinate sweetness about her that was as annoying as it was unnerving.

"No, dear. Whether he is dead, or was dead, I don't care. I've loved that man since I first knew him in Beaumaris. I talked with Moyna about him for hours at a time. The only reason I thought I loved Marc was the silly resemblance. I was always attempting to prove he was Ewen Morgan, who would well be afraid of fire, after what he'd undergone. But now, if I meet the Devil-Vicar himself, there will be no need for all those fire tricks. Marc's fear will have some other explanation."

"Ewen Morgan is dead," I repeated patiently.

She was just as patient. "I don't care. I shouldn't care if he were the Devil himself." She gave me a funny, pitifully flirtatious look. "I rather fancy this note puts that quite out of the question, though. You can see that it's real — as I'm sure the Devil-Vicar is."

People passing us on the street had begun to look at us oddly, I thought, and I rolled Catheerine's chair back up toward her house.

"You realize," I said, "that if he really is alive, he must be the murderer of these people. Out of revenge."

"Impossible. He can't be, because you see —"
She stopped suddenly.

I looked down at her, but her expression was unreadable.

"Well?" I prompted her.

She shook her head. "It doesn't matter.

Nothing matters but that he is alive and wants me to meet him."

Remembering Rose Keegan's warning, I ventured, "If you do know or suspect something, shouldn't you tell the Vicar, or the police in Teignford, or someone?"

She looked up at me, her great eyes dazzled by her love affair with an oil painting.

"Why should I know anything? I thought that dreadful dog did it. I still do."

"Suppose the murderer kills your precious Devil-Vicar — and this time really kills him!"

Her head snapped up. I thought for one breathless moment that she would tell me something. Then she smiled.

"Nonsense. It was the dog that did it, I tell you. There wasn't a sign of anything else."

We had reached the ugly stone exterior of her house now, and I left her with a parting reminder.

"On the other hand, your lover may decide to kill you instead. But that's entirely your problem."

"So it is," she answered me gaily. "So it is."

XV

As I passed the graveyard I very nearly walked into Mrs. Fothergay and Mrs. MacDonnachie, who were coming out the iron gate that opened upon the street.

"Anne, dear child!" bubbled Bedelia. "You have utterly missed the most enchanting excursion. Yes, indeed. The dear lady has been conducting me among the tombs. Edifying, edifying."

"But not — alas! — profitable," put in the Vicar's wife. "I so hoped to recover Cadmon's warmest woolen stock. I believe he must have lost it on the trail yesterday." She hesitated, looked around in a conspiratorial way and, just as I was prepared to be her confidante in a murder confession at the least, she said, "Could you possibly cast an eye over the heather and bracken just off the path around Wind-Rock Rise, next time you go to Moyna's cottage? Possibly you might catch a glimpse of —"

I was outraged.

"I? Go to Marc Branshaw's cottage? Indeed not. I'm afraid you must ask someone better acquainted with the gentleman." What gave her the idea that I visited young men's out-of-the-way cottages? No one knew I had been there. Ah, but good Sir Gareth! He would talk!

I don't know which lady was more astonished at my outburst, but Mrs. MacDonnachie was the first to recover. "Yes, yes, dear," she said soothingly, after which she whispered something in Bedelia's ear.

It was Bedelia Fothergay's turn to be short with the lady. "You forget, madam, it was all a mistake. The young man confused Anne's door with mine. He wishes to preserve me in oils, you know."

"Oh," said Mrs. MacDonnachie doubtfully, and changed the subject.

As for me, I went up to my room and stood a very long time staring down at the wretched, forsaken ground where the Devil-Vicar's bones presumably had fallen to their rest.

I agreed with Catherine on one matter: no ghostly vicar, dead sixteen years, had written that note of assignation. But if those were not the Devil-Vicar's bones lying under the sod . . .

But such speculation was profitless. I did not, for the life of me, know why I didn't simply pack up and hire some conveyance back to Teignford and London. I had no emotion other than common curiosity about the events here in the West Riding, no feeling for the people except a liking for young Jamie and a furious dislike for Marc Branshaw, who had used me abominably. The difficulty was that I couldn't very well ask Marc for my manuscript on the Red Indians until we were on speaking terms again, and that, of course, would be never.

The men of the village and neighboring hamlets were now gathering in the taproom downstairs for what I supposed must be the arvills of which I had heard so much mention. It was not that they were unseemly, but rather that the occasion seemed to them, to judge by all the greetings and chatter, a social moment of no mean importance. Since I did not want to pass these men when they were doubtless full of the best liquid refreshment from the Keegan cellars, I sat in my room, wrote letters to Mr. Perth and other friends in London, and pondered on the strange events of the past few days.

Some time later, Mrs. Fothergay knocked on my door and called to me, but I didn't feel that her irritating voice would help matters, so I pretended not to be in. She tried the door and for an instant I thought she might have the presumption to walk in. I held my breath and she went away.

Later in the afternoon I heard a man's boots on the creaking boards of the hall. Having knocked on Bedelia's door and received no response, he presently stopped by my door. When he called to me, I recognized the voice of Sir Gareth Owen.

"Miss Anne! Rose tells me you've been up here all afternoon. Come and join us below. No one's going to force you to drain a mug of Dog's Nose, you know."

Good heavens! I should hope not. Dog's Nose sounded most unpleasant. I was about to keep silence when the baronet added:

"Your friend Branshaw's below as well. Got his audience in the palm of his hand but I daresay you're not foolish enough to be taken in."

I pricked up my ears. I did more. I went to the door and, thanking Sir Gareth for his invitation, replied that I had better things to do than to watch Marc Branshaw make a drunken fool of himself.

"All of that, ma'am. He must be drunk; he's

giving imitations of the Devil-Vicar. Several ladies tiptoed in from the parlor to watch and he's been putting them into screaming fits."

That would be worth seeing. What did Marc Branshaw mean by laying himself open to further comparison between himself and the late unlamented Devil-Vicar?

I went down with Sir Gareth to see this amazing sight. At the foot of the stairs we found two old and bearded combatants rolling half on the stairs, half on the floor, kicking and gouging and otherwise behaving as though they had never heard of the laws of fisticuffs. I stepped carefully around them and then moved more slowly to the open taproom. I could hear Sir Gareth behind me, encouraging first one and then the other of the two men to "have a go at it" and "not to give up like a damned townsman" and other helpful advice.

In the taproom, behind the rail, and leaning on it as though it were a pulpit, was Marc Branshaw, with his hair dishevelled and his face rather pale instead of its usual olive color. Except for these trifling differences, I don't believe I would have guessed that he was drunk. Perhaps he wasn't. I watched him, almost ashamed that he should expose himself to people whom he despised. But the longer I watched, the more I understood that he was enjoying himself. The actor, the artist in him, was in full command. He liked the exhibition he was making, and I must confess, it was bloodcurdlingly good.

"Behold! Sinner all! The Devil turns himself into a Gytrash! But the turning . . . stay, ma'am . . . the turning is only in your eyes, not in myself." He pointed at an elderly woman who was retreating rapidly under his sardonic gaze, and now stood there, clutching her shawl and looking terrified. Indeed, there was something fearful in his ability to create a mood, with his burning eyes, his dark brows that were so eloquent in expressing disdain and sardonic humor, but above all, in his astounding resemblance to the face of the dead Devil-Vicar. "Says not the Book that the day of the Beast is at hand? For hear me!" He stretched out his arm dramatically. "The Beast is in Man, and Man in the Beast. As was always the way. How came the victim to die to whose memory we drink today? It was she who saw the Beast, and in seeing had to die. Isn't so, Jamie? Jamie saw a Beast turn into a Man, didn't you, Jamie?"

But the boy was huddling against the wall behind Marc, as though to avoid his touch as Marc swung around to confront him.

"No — no. Please, Marc. Not here. They'll think . . . Ye know what they'll think."

"Ay, mon!" cried a voice, only half coherent, from one corner of the taproom. A shoddily-dressed old man shuffled forward. Even I could see that he had already consumed his pint for the day. "What've ye done a my Abbie? Kilt her, ye did. Ye devil!"

Marc paid him no heed. He had chucked

Jamie under the chin and was taking another drink.

"Hush, man," said one of the other natives. "It's only a game. Ye know young Branshaw when ye sees him."

But Hinchley went on, with drunken persistence.

"Well an' good. But that's not what Abbie told me. 'He's the Devil-Vicar.' Them's her words, poor Abbie. 'He's come back from the dead, and if I play my game right, I'll have him, dead or no.' That's what my Abbie said. She loved him. And for that, she's got to die. Was it you done it, sor?"

The crowd in the taproom seemed to break into component parts, the men looking at each other, echoing the remark of the pitiful Hinchley.

"Ay, mon," said one of them suddenly. "Explain that business with the beast in the Wind-Rock. If that weren't the work of a devil."

Hinchley nodded with alcoholic wisdom.

Marc smiled at them all. He leaned forward over the taprail, and they receded from him as from a wave that might engulf them. I could not blame them. It was not a warming smile.

"That's my secret. It's so simple, too. I'll wager you the Devil-Vicar had just such secrets to explain his powers. And you never guessed. But then — you are simple men."

"And you, sir, are offensive," said Sir Gareth, coming from behind me and approaching the taprail. "Whatever else you may be, and I'm sure that's the least of it, I doubt very much if you could charm so much as a flea-blown mongrel, much less one of the feminine gender with whom you make so free."

Marc had taken up his mug of some dark, thick liquid that did not look appetizing to me, but as he put it to his mouth, he caught sight of me over the lip of the mug. He glanced from Gareth back to me as though he read something in our presence together. This stupid and wilful misunderstanding annoyed me. Then he set the mug down slowly and, still smiling, asked in a way that suggested the purr of a tiger:

"What might you mean by that?"

"You know what I mean. Playing fast and loose with my sister. You'll not bandy her so."

Marc laughed. "Good God! I thought you were insulting quite another — but of course. it was dear, saintly little Catherine all the time! I would never dream of — how did you put it in your delicate way — 'bandying' Catherine."

"Nor any other decent female, by God!" said Gareth, now losing all patience.

"Well," said Marc reasonably, while some of the men began to laugh, "you can't lay claim to the whole lot of them, can you? Be specific. What ladies do you not hold claim over? I shouldn't like to think I was disobliging that distinguished man of means, that noble patron of the poor!"

Several of the men to whom, I gathered, Sir Gareth owed money, clapped each other on the back, and dug a neighboring rib or two to indicate that this was a palpable hit. It naturally served to infuriate the baronet.

"You cur! You little whelp! You mongrel, degraded . . ."

"A pity," said Marc in his friendly way, "that my sex prevents you from adding 'bitch' to all the rest of the canine family you've dragged out of the kennel."

"Your sex!" Sir Gareth, who was by now apoplectic, managed a momentary triumph of calm over temper. He looked Marc up and down in that sneering way I did not like, and added, "My dear Marc, that would appear to be your most . . . impotent defense."

A woman gasped. All laughter stopped. The silence fell so suddenly that I heard my own pulsebeat in my ears. The next second it seemed that a lightning bolt must have struck the house. Marc vaulted the taprail and caught Sir Gareth a shocking blow that only just missed his cheekbone and struck him hard across the chin. The sound was horrid and made me shudder; I, along with the three or four other women who had been foolish enough to enter the room, retreated in disorder.

But not before I saw that Sir Gareth was temporarily incapacitated. As both men were equally to blame, I felt that I should have gone to the baronet's aid, but for some incomprehensible reason, I turned at once to see whether Marc was hurt. He was not, except for the damage to his knuckles; he was holding one hand in the palm of the other and still looking furious, as the men, who thought it great sport, congratulated him, added the rider that they hadn't thought he had it in him.

I moved into the passage, and glanced back. I saw that Marc was watching me. The hot color had come into his face. We stared at each other for a long moment. Neither of us would give a cubit, and my last view of him as I turned away was that uncompromising look which did not auger very much for the future.

I met Miss Rose who was on her way to find out what the pleasant arvills had come to, and I explained somewhat incoherently. Her reaction astonished me.

"Good! They've been meaning to have it out for some time. Now, perhaps, they'll be civil to each other." She, however, shared my relief when we saw the Reverend MacDonnachie come into the inn and make for the taproom. "Come, Miss Wicklow," she added, and took my arm. "You'll see. It means nothing. The Reverend will attend to matters."

"Well, lads," said the Vicar. "I'm challenging all comers to a match that says I'll thrash the both of you and any as cares to join in." As he spoke, he was helping Sir Gareth up from the floor, and by the time he had finished insisting that he could beat both men though he gave them ten to twenty years in age, he had Sir Gareth, at least, muttering like a civilized person again.

As for Marc, he finished the drink in his mug and then quietly made his way through the crowd toward the side door that opened near the graveyard gate. He had to pass Miss Rose and me in doing so. I looked at him but said nothing. He was about to leave, but stopped long enough to say to me:

"I wish you joy of your precious champion! Much good he may do you!"

"What a tiresome young man!" I remarked to Miss Rose, and heard behind me the slamming of the door.

Miss Rose smiled.

The Reverend MacDonnachie was laughing in his fatman way, so that others joined in from sheer contagion.

"Gytrashes! Devil-Vicars! Now, gentlemen, I put it to you! Does that bad-tempered young man strike terror into your hearts? Oh, come now. . . . is he the kind of creature who goes about changing into animals at night or seducing fair ladies in ghostly guise? Why, he wouldn't hurt a flea! Present company excepted, Gareth."

Everyone laughed. Even Gareth managed a watery, bruised grin.

Then one of the sheepmen who had come in shortly before the fight started, spoiled the scene.

"Ay, mon, but what if he *do* them things? He's a fair one for the ladies. They made to-do over him. And ye say he don't command the beasties. But what of yesterday in the Wind-Rock? What of that, ay?"

The Vicar scratched his beard.

"Well, there you have me, laddie. I must think on it. But at any rate," he added staunchly, "he's a well-meaning young man and when he's in a rare humor there's none you'd rather have to tea or stronger drink, for the matter of that."

"That's it, sor," said another of his parishioners. "But how does ye know when he's in a rare mood? It's a problem. That it is. Fair gives me the freezing marrow, he did just now, lookin' that like the Devil-Vicar when he was set on mischief."

"Not to mention what young Jamie saw," added Hinchley, with harsh emphasis. "My Abbie was murdered. I stand to say so now and in future. And it wouldn't surprise me none if it was a man behind the beast what done it. I'm mentionin' no names," he added fairly. "We done that before an' let a innercent man be burnt. No more a that, I say."

"No, indeed," the Vicar agreed jovially, and they all went to drinking again.

Exceedingly sorry I had allowed myself to be enticed out of my room in order to have that almost silent encounter with Marc, I started back up the stairs again, but Miss Rose asked me to join the ladies at supper in the back dining parlor. This seemed preferable to forging my way through a noisy group of men on the stair landing, so I joined Mrs. Fothergay and the Vicar's wife, and — somewhat to my surprise — Catherine Owen.

They were arguing over the possibility that a

251

man, and not a dog killed by Marc Branshaw, had committed the two recent murders. I must confess that Catherine was the staunch upholder of the dog theory. When I had heard most of the arguments which, womanlike, were based on personal encounters with dog and man which were supposed to prove conclusively the argument of the speaker, I could not help suggesting to Catherine:

"If a dog killed the Hinchley girl, then did he drag her all the way from his lair up around Wind-Rock to drop her on the Devil-Vicar's grave? It does seem rather more clever than I would take the old beast to be."

Catherine flushed a little.

"It was pure coincidence. Probably the girl dragged herself there."

"My dear!" murmured Bedelia Fothergay happily, "you forget that the poor girl was so badly bruised and — er — mangled — that if she had been wounded, say, at the back of the head, it would have been difficult to find at this stage."

Mrs. MacDonnachie made a polite little face into her dinner plate, obviously wishing we would all change the subject, but Mrs. Fothergay was in her element.

"If I have said once, I have said a hundred times, one cannot be too careful of men. No one knows better than I. Had difficulties with them all my life. The poor Colonel, my late husband, used to say that he married me over the corpses of my admirers."

For the first time, I saw a streak of malicious female in Catherine, who smiled at me as though we shared a secret, while she remarked, "Heavens, ma'am! Had you that effect upon them?"

Mrs. Fothergay giggled.

"Lord, child! I was referring to the figurative corpses which the late Colonel left in his wake, in order to win me."

The Vicar's wife took this opportunity to change the subject, and we did not get back on it until late in the evening, when I volunteered to push Catherine's rolling chair up to her house — since it was apparent Sir Gareth had joined the men for the night.

The air was cold and crisp. Catherine began to count the stars as we moved slowly past the church and up the cobbled street. She gave up soon, for they were too vast and overpowering in number.

"The moon will be up soon. What a night! What a glorious night!" She shivered pleasurably in her heavy coat and shawl.

I said, "I hope you've given some thought to that message today."

"I have, I have," she assured me, giving the wrong interpretation to my words.

I reminded her again, "It might be dangerous."

"Are we to go into that again? Really, Anne, one would think you were jealous."

"No," I said, trying to keep my voice low. "I'm not jealous of your Demon Lover. But I think you ought to show a little common caution. Bedelia is right in one respect. That poor beast that Marc killed yesterday would hardly drag Abbie Hinchley so far just to drop her conveniently on the one grave that would be most appropriate."

"What do you mean by that?"

I could hardly explain, but put it in the best words that presented themselves. "It's like an offering. A dead offering to the spirit of the murdered Vicar. It's the sort of thing the Devil-Vicar might conceive of doing, if he murdered the girl."

She objected crossly, "If he is dead, then how can he kill Abbie Hinchley?"

She did not reply.

"You say he is not dead."

After a pause, during which we had negotiated the long roughly-cobbled surface leading to her doorstep, she asked me finally, "Are you going to tell Gareth?"

"I suppose not. But I ought to."

She shrugged and laughed quickly, without the young, rather poignant gaiety I had noticed in her before.

"Oh well, I shan't do anything tonight, in any case."

I was surprised. "I thought the note was for tonight."

"No, no. For tomorrow. At ten. Under the bright sunlight. So what is there to fear?"

Although it should have been nothing to me, one way or the other, I was relieved. I could not help feeling that an encounter with the Devil-Vicar or any of his imitators, at this hour, would be unhealthy in the extreme, and if Marc were the culprit, this act might precipitate his unmasking. Anything would be preferable to that.

"Shall I ring for your servant?" I asked.

She hesitated. "No. It's such a lovely night. Don't disturb poor old Nettie. I think I'll just rest here a moment." She held out her hand to me. "Good night, dear, and thank you for being my friend."

I curtseyed, taking her hand, and feeling thoroughly ashamed of myself — of my jealousy earlier in the day, and of my suspicions about her condition — all the things she did not suspect when she called me her friend. I left her in the starlight, the fingers of her two hands now tightly laced together, as though she held in some powerful emotion.

Poor Catherine. To devote one's life to the adoration of a portrait! Why should it hold such a fascination for her? I had seen it once, with no earthshaking results. A very ordinary . . . well, not quite ordinary, portrait.

I was so sure the portrait held no fascination for me that when I passed the doors of the church, which were still ajar, I dared myself to peep inside, just to prove that I had no fears of its effect on me.

There was a lamp glowing in the Vicar's office and I remembered his invitation to me on the day we met, to come and look at his precious portrait of the man of whom he — to quote the Reverend MacDonnachie — "wished he might be the rebirth." Anything less like the Devil-Vicar of the portrait could hardly be conceived.

I stepped inside, feeling the dampness rise from the stones under my feet as I walked through the shadows toward the glowing lamp-light.

In spite of the lamp, no one was in the Vicar's office. It was just like his untidy habits, to leave the light burning like this. Then I realized that without the Reverend MacDonnachie to give me countenance, I was a trespasser. I started to leave but could not help glancing up at the portrait of the Devil-Vicar just once. Due to the flicker of the lamp, the highlights and shadows cast by its glow, it seemed to me that the dark, shadowed eyes of the portrait gleamed like coals when a breath of air disturbs them. I shuddered and turned away, feeling the terrible attraction, and resisting it with all my common sense.

At that moment a loud, grating noise from the front of the building informed me that the sexton had shut and locked the doors. In a panic — for I had no intention of spending the night with the Devil-Vicar, however attractive he might be — I scurried out behind the nave and tried the doors. The great, vaulted interior of the church was dark as a coal-pit and I very nearly called for help. It seemed to me each time I turned in the silent church, the Devil-Vicar must be some-where in those gloomy shadows, watching me.

He had preached here long ago. He had died so close by, and his ghost, if there were such things, might very well be lurking behind the damp, stone pillars that supported the main nave.

"Be calm," I told myself. "There are always side doors." In fact, Mrs. Fothergay and Mrs. MacDonnachie must have gone out a side door today, for I found them just leaving the church-yard after their instructive tour of the local tombstones. If I could find that side door locked from the inside, I might cross the graveyard and reach the gate behind the Yorkish Lion. Nothing would be more welcome than that inn.

I crossed behind the nave and passed the Vicar's office again, feeling my way, until I reached the south window of the church. Faint starlight entering the clear glass gave me light by which I made out the door. I tried the door but it was locked. I paused to consider the direction of the other doors and could recall having seen but one on this side. As I made out the outlines of the family pews before me, and decided to cross down by the chancel rail, to see if there was a door at the back of the altar somewhere, I heard a scraping sound, as of a footstep among the rushes near the chancel rail.

Remembering that the Vicar might not have gone home yet, and hoping nervously that it would be he, I spoke, in an ordinary tone, not wishing to call the attention of the sexton.

"Is it you, Reverend MacDonnachie? I was looking for you — to see the portrait."

No answer. I had not seriously believed the Vicar was locked in with me at this hour, not at least the familiar redbearded Vicar of the present day.

My voice, which had begun almost as a whisper, echoed in a hoarse and unidentifiable way through the vaulting space overhead. I could scarcely have recognized it as my own. But the echo was the only answer I received, and I began to hope it was the sexton whose footsteps I had surprised.

Well, if it was the sexton, there was no need to play the innocent now. I had to explain and get out. I moved away from the south wall, toward the back of the church, retracing my footsteps to the nave.

Then I heard it again, the grating of a shoe among the dry rushes. It was as though someone were playing a silly trick upon me, and I knew of no one with that sort of humor — except perhaps one person.

At the head of the main nave, I stood trying to focus upon the dim, almost impenetrable dark before me, straight down the aisle to the altar. My eyes gradually made out the objects — the great pillars, and even the cruciform altar cloth. I recalled suddenly that the altar cloth was not, in fact, cruciform, and did not have white among its colors. What I saw must be something, or someone, standing before the altar, silently facing me down the long nave, a figure shrouded in the black of his surroundings, with just that balance of color provided by the full white clergyman's surplice.

It was impossible to make out the bodily contours at this distance among those clergical robes. But as I stared through the hollow darkness, I remembered the note of assignation Catherine had received, and that the handwriting resembled Marc Branshaw's.

Who but Marc would play such a trick? Who but Marc had this sort of twisted humor? This must be the trysting place he had chosen in which to meet Catherine. It was nearing ten o'clock. Catherine had lied to me. Her assignation was for tonight, after all.

Forgetting our quarrel this morning, and the unpleasant scene in the taproom of the Yorkish Lion, I spoke into the darkness that separated us along the church aisle.

"Marc! How can you? I suppose you think you will fool Catherine. What are you doing?"

The figure at the altar moved restlessly, the white of the cloth shifting in the dark against its black background. Then came a whisper, a strong enough sound so that I made it out, but as indistinct as my own voice had been a moment ago.

"Anne! Come here."

I was beginning to remember now that we had parted very bad friends, and it was a relief to hear him at least call me by name. I hesitated, then moved down the aisle toward him, demanding to know what he was doing, and what he thought he should gain by posing as the Devil-Vicar to win poor Catherine's love. I did not think so at the time, but long afterward I was convinced that, although I talked much to myself about his deceiving Catherine, I was chiefly concerned that he had been about to deceive me. I could not call my emotions anything other than jealousy.

Behind me, on the street, I heard the old sexton's voice as he spoke to some late passerby. On the spur of the moment I hesitated, turned, and almost went to the door to summon him. I though my gesture would send Marc packing by whatever manner in which he had entered the church, and his little masquerade would be over. Instead, I wrestled with the thought, and my own jealousy, then turned back and proceeded toward the altar. He had stepped away from the altar now and was below the chancel, hidden by the shadows of the pews.

When I reached the chancel rail, I discovered that I could not make out his figure at all. He was playing tricks, dissolved in the darkness and watching me, a thing I particularly disliked.

I stopped at the chancel rail and said sternly, trying to pierce the darkness on both sides:

"This has gone far enough, Marc! Stop playing games or I shall call the sexton. Marc? Where in blazes are you?"

There was not a sound behind me. I do not know why I started to turn. Some instinct, I suppose. Then I saw his arm reach out around me, passing before my eyes. I recognized the white cambric over the black sleeve. From behind my body, his arm moved gently closer to my face, and I thought, for an instant, that he would take my chin in his hand and kiss me, as he had that other night. I was torn between my desire for that caress, and anger that he had tried to fool me with his stupid games. I raised one hand to touch his arm, perhaps to ward it off in some belated attempt at coquetry. Suddenly, his arm pulled tight across my throat in an embrace I was far from expecting.

I gasped and tied to cry out his name:

"Marc!"

My hands clawed vainly at the sleeves of his robe. Even then I didn't quite understand that this was not my Marc Branshaw, until his other arm came up, and I felt my throat released long enough for me to gasp for air before both his hands drew a knotted cord up tight against my throat and pulled back upon it, strangling me. In the most intense and shattering pain, I felt the blood coursing against my temples, and my breath escaping through that corded vise in tiny, gurgling sounds.

In the far, far distance there was a noise of grating doors, and the sexton's complaining voice. "What's about? Now, who left the lamp so?"

The cord that had been drawing the last breath of life out of me, slipped off my throat and my assailant moved away swiftly. As I fell, I could hear faintly the flutter of robes as he ran.

"It can't be my own Marc," my shattered senses told me. "There's a mistake. I've made a terrible mistake."

I lay on the rushes, struggling to make some sound besides a groan, until I heard boots upon the floor of the nave, and the sexton's voice over me. He was holding the lamp from the Vicar's study.

"What's this, mum? What ye doin' there? Ay, and like ye was bad-drunk?"

I sat up, no thanks to him, for he stood helpless, shocked that I should be found in these sacred precincts. I touched my throat and muttered hoarsely that I had come to see the Vicar and had been locked in and someone had tried to strangle me.

"Impossible, mum," said the sexton seriously. "Nobody'd strangle ye here in the church. Indeed, no. 'Twas the dark, I daresay. Confused ye."

"And my throat?" which I exhibited as proof of my claim. "I suppose that was confused too."

"Ay, it's red. Right enough. Musn't rub it like that. Makes it red, as ye can see. Well now, ye've had a bad time and no mistake. Can ye walk, mum?"

Oh, this incredibly stupid villager!

"Listen to me!! The person who tried to strangle me — and I daresay killed those other two people — is somewhere in this church now. Go and find him."

The sexton raised the lamp, gave a quick,

sweeping perusal of the surrounding darkness, and made out nothing more suspicious than the shadows of the pillars.

"Not a thing, mum. Must be ye mere thought there was some'ut in here with ye."

By this time, my assailant could have gotten out of the church in a dozen ways, for I had no doubt the scene was more familiar to him than to a stranger like myself. I was too tired, and too near being nauseated, to care. . . . Besides, what if the fiendish creature with the knotted cord were actually Marc Branshaw? Should I then testify to my suspicions?

I did not know. I had to think. Were there any signs that proved it might be Marc? Any peculiarity of touch?

At the open front doors of the church I saw Catherine Owen in her wheelchair. She had paused before the doors and looked perfectly astonished at sight of me.

"If you're coming to your appointment with the Devil-Vicar," I told her hoarsely, "you had best give up the notion. He's been rather busy for one night."

She was all solicitude.

"Anne! You look as though you've seen a ghost!"

"You were right," I agreed. "I saw your ghost. Whatever it was, I met it by accident, and it very nearly strangled me."

"I see." She looked down at her gloved hands, and her disappointment was so keen, I nearly felt like offering her my own experience with her beloved Devil-Vicar. "Then it's no use my waiting."

"Not unless you have a taste for a knotted cord applied to the throat," I told her.

She took my hand. "I'm sorry it happened to you, dear, but don't you think it possible that you startled him? That he was, perhaps, disappointed, and reacted violently when he saw that you were not —"

I rolled my eyes heavenward and brushed off the restraining hand of the sexton as well as Catherine's thick, sweet courtesy.

"Take him. I make you a gift of him, Miss Owen. And if you find that he is also Marc Branshaw, when he has nothing better to be, you may have that one too!"

"Who is giving me away so freely?" asked a voice on the starlit street. Catherine and I turned, aware suddenly that several persons had collected outside the church to discover what Catherine and I were talking about so heatedly, and the curate, Frederick Niles, was calming them.

Catherine smiled at the voice we heard, but I did not, as we beheld Marc Branshaw crossing the cobblestones and making his way through the crowd to us. Although he joked, I saw that he was in a hurry, and he pushed his way toward us without ceremony.

The sexton hastened to say severely, "Lady was locked in the church, that's all to it. Good night to ye, mum. Next time, rap at the door to be let out. I'll hear."

"Nonsense," said the Reverend Niles. "Miss Wicklow seems to be hurt. Perhaps you can get the story, Mr. Branshaw."

Marc came to me and I studied his features, wondering if it were possible he could have tried to murder me only minutes before. In the starlight his face looked so like the Devil-Vicar's, and yet there was his smile, and the way he drew me to him, forgetting that we had been furiously angry on our last encounter. I don't know why, but I was reassured by a small thing — the fact that the sleeve of his short jacket was so obviously not the black robe and covering surplice I had seen in front of my eyes just before the knotted cord was applied to my throat. He managed to move me away from the gawping bystanders, and we got as far as the graveyard wall before he asked me what had happened.

"I thought we were not on speaking terms," I challenged him, getting down to more essential matters.

He laughed.

"Still wish to be brother and sister?"

He reached around and took down the hand that I had pressed to my throat, where the pain was beginning to reassert itself in a nasty, throbbing way. He examined the aching red marks.

"Who did that?"

I said, "If you can tell me, you will do a great favor to the village. I stepped into the church to see the portrait of the Devil-Vicar and he paid a personal call upon me."

"Good God! That tiresome portrait!" he exclaimed. And then, as he fingers gently traced the bruises left by the strangling cord, he added, "Did you see this Devil-Vicar?"

"No. Furthermore, I have no wish to. If that is Catherine's idea of a lover, I can only say I pity her taste."

He smiled and then, when I was totally unprepared, leaned over and kissed me. I was almost too exhausted to respond, but I made a valiant effort. It was comforting to make myself believe in him, whether I had any proof or not. I felt that his very presence was essential to my nerves and my morale, and was perfectly ready to risk whatever danger was entailed in loving him. The moment I returned his kiss, I felt convinced of his innocence. Infallible intuition!

"I do think," he went on, when we were not so busy, "if we are going to spend our lives quarreling, we would do better to spend them elsewhere, in greater privacy. Don't you agree?"

"I wish you would explain," I said, "because as it is I don't know whether this is a proposal of marriage or an invitation to slap your face."

"I suggest you don't slap my face, or I might change my mind — since it is a proposal."

At this, the Reverend Niles began to clear everyone off the streets, with a smile at our doings.

But I did not feel capable of pursuing Marc's banter. I was trembling with the excitement of the night, my narrow escape, and the cold, sharp northern air, and Marc regarded me with concern.

"Great George and the Dragon!" cried a familiar voice. Stalking up the street from the inn was the Reverend MacDonnachie, followed by his wife. "What's all that noise at our Cathedral of the Almighty? Never heard such a babble!"

"My love," ventured his wife timidly, "I think you've interrupted a — a — well . . ."

"No, blast it!" shouted the Reverend. "Not this. Anybody can see what *this* is. I'm talking about all that babble at the church. What is it? Another wild dog they've treed and are wanting Branshaw to exorcize with his magic?"

It was nasty of him to bring up again the queer business of Marc and the killer-dog, but Niles explained to him, in his quiet way, what had happened. His voice was punctuated by loud, explosive and unbelieving ejaculations from the Vicar.

Marc had just picked me up in his arms when we saw Jamie Keegan looking down at us from an open window of the Yorkish Lion.

"Thought you was goin' home. What kept ye?" he demanded of Marc.

"Yes," said Marc, "but I was busy."

Jamie looked down at me. "Why must he carry you? Can't you walk, Miss Anne?"

Marc grinned. "Never mind. This is my affair."

"Well," said Jamie. "I always thought Miss Anne could walk right good for a female."

"True. But you see, I was proposing to Miss Anne."

"Oh, that. I thought it was something important."

"I'm afraid," Marc told me apologetically, "that our news isn't of importance to anyone but ourselves."

Well, I've done it, I thought. I've burnt my bridges, confessed I don't wish to live without him, and for all I know he may strangle me in my bed some night.

But if I had it to say over, I should still have said yes to him, I knew.

XVI

Rose Keegan came to my room the following day to tell me that Marc had arrived with Dr. Lowther, but I was a great disappointment to the doctor as well as to myself, for he announced that he could find no mementos of my encounter worth mentioning. Even the soreness was leaving my throat muscles. Tea, and more tea, was prescribed, along with some choice gruel. Poor substitute for the coddling I had dreamed of from Marc, and no consolation for my dreadful experience.

While Marc stood behind the doctor, making silent fun of my chagrin at not finding myself a heroine, the doctor spoiled his entire diagnosis by warning me of another attack.

"You understand, of course, ma'am, that two of our people have died violently, in the recent past."

I wished he would not remind me. It only made my throat ache in sympathy with my renewed fears. These had been lulled to sleep today, during the few hours since Marc asked me to marry him. Marc's presence did more than that. It lulled me out of any suspicion that my mysterious assailant might have been Marc himself. I had only to look at him, to see his smile, and the way he regarded me with an expression, at once tender and warm, to banish all my previous fears that the Devil-Vicar was Marc Branshaw.

I told Dr. Lowther that I knew of the other deaths.

"Well then, I need not warn you, Miss Wicklow, that the attack on you today — that is to say, last night — might prove fatal on its next dosage. I advise you to take care. Extreme care. Perhaps it would be best if you trusted none of us, until you are on your way back to London." He patted the bedclothing in a paternal way. "And now, may I wish you a pleasant rest? I will not say recovery, for you are quite recovered now, I believe. In any case, I must be off. Some typhus cases in Upshed. Very unfortunate."

He packed together the horrid instruments of his trade and, in doing so, studied Marc rather carefully. Marc was uneasily aware of his survey and yet I could see that he pretended not to be.

"As for you, my friend, hadn't you better see me one of these days? One never knows, eh? You can trust me, my boy. No? Well — so much the worse for you. Good day to you both. Remember, Miss Wicklow, I prescribe rest and quiet. That means no visitors, for the moment."

When the doctor had gone, I laughed. "What a cheerful note on which to leave me! Does he expect some giant Gytrash to leap into my bedchamber and devour me?"

"He's a fool. Pay no attention." Marc kissed me goodbye, then paused before leaving. "But let us say I'm a jealous dog. Don't find yourself alone with *any* man. Promise?"

"Females too?" I asked with mock-seriousness.

"Especially females. Forgot to say so. Even if they — don't walk."

He left me prey to a thousand fantasies, each worse than the other.

That evening, during my supper of nauseous gruel, Jamie Keegan presented me with a bundle which, when unwrapped, proved to be the manuscript Marc had stolen from me, the one about the Red Indians of North America. With it was a note:

Darling Anne, I used this to entice you up here. Let us hope I will have no need of such methods again.

I hardly care whether they ever find their monster of Maidenmoor if it means danger to my dearest. I am done with my quest for knowledge in that department.

So it is back to London or wherever, as soon as we can dispose of Moyna's property, which she so foolishly left to me. Let me know when you feel up to another heated quarrel. The "making it up" is the best of it.

Have I told you? . . . I love you.

He did not sign his name, or even his initial, but I suppose he assumed that I should recognize it on the grounds that at the very most, I received only one proposal a day.

Studying his handwriting and trying to recall the note to Catherine, I convinced myself that there was only the most superficial resemblance. But to be sure, I asked Jamie:

"How long was it last night between the time you said goodnight to Marc and then saw him again with me on the street?"

Jamie ruffled his hair in thought.

"Ten minutes. Maybe twenty. He might've stopped in the taproom."

"But no more than twenty minutes?"

"Ay. No more."

The horror of those minutes in the church with the Devil-Vicar had made them seem an eternity but I felt that twenty minutes was too short a time for the strangler to perform all that had been necessary. Thank God!

As for Marc, he was as good as his word. When I thought it would be the proper thing to see him the day following his proposal, I learned that he had gone into Teignford to arrange for the sale of Moyna's property.

Mrs. Fothergay took the news of our engagement surprisingly. She said to me at once:

"How like the dear boy! Well —" She paused to sigh. "It was not to be. As I told Marc myself only a day or two ago, 'You and I can never be,' I said. Now, Gareth, there is a dear man, just the sort to suit me best. He wants to take care of me. So protective, you know. He asks me innumerable questions about my affairs, anxious to be of any help that he may. Charming man . . . and then too, I shall be Lady Bedelia. It has a ring to it."

I confessed that it certainly did. We were up at the local stationer's, I to send the Red Indian manuscript back to its publishers in London, and Mrs. Fothergay to order a quire of writing paper for her voluminous correspondence.

Just when she was hesitating between the lavender and the green paper to express her personality — "which is so changeful, so illusive" — she explained to me, Jamie Keegan came hurrying into the post office side of the shop.

"Ay, it's like I said, Miss Anne. I know'd whether to find you. Miss Catherine sent me to ask you to come to a party tonight. Not a big one. Just a comfortable one, she says. You and Marc, and the Reverend and the Missus, and one or two others."

"Myself, of course," said Mrs. Fothergay familiarly. "I was the first to be told, you know."

272

She took the two packets of paper to the open door and stood there, considering the colors.

Jamie whispered to me, "Miss Catherine would be that pleased if ye'd accept, Miss Anne."

"Has Marc accepted?"

"He will if you will. He was busy goin' over some old things Miss Moyna's thrown out in the mistal. Never saw so much trash in all his life, he says."

"Yes, but what did he say about Miss Catherine's party?"

"Made a face, he did, like this." He wrinkled his nose. "But he's to come if you will. Says it's one last chance to take the size of them that might've killed Miss Moyna and the others."

"What a romantic reason!" I exclaimed, somewhat put out.

But it ended with Marc's fetching me that evening and telling me about our future as we walked up to the Owen house, so that when we arrived I was in a flush of good humor. I had never been in love before, although, upon several occasions I had fancied I was, and I supposed that treading-on-air feeling, with no worries, no problems, only the all-consuming question: Does he really love me?

We stopped at the door and, as he raised his hand to the knocker, he looked at me. I realized only then that all his charming banter on our way had concealed what he was really thinking. His face, by moonlight, appeared to me dark and brooding and sad.

I said, "What is it? Are you quite well?"

He laughed, but I sensed that it was forced.

"Of course. Why do you ask?"

"Nothing. I thought — it was almost as though you were a different man somehow." I wished his eyes did not look at me like that. They brought to my mind the wonderful, terrible eyes in that painting of the Devil-Vicar.

"I must tell you something."

I stepped back, away from the door and into the shadows again, oddly disturbed.

"Then tell me now. While there's still time."

"What made you say that?" he asked, still like a stranger, careful and polite.

"I — I don't know. I mean, before we go inside. . . . Tell me here." Then I believed I understood. I swallowed as hard as I could and made my voice sound level and dry. "You don't want to marry me. That's it. They are all going to congratulate us, but you wanted to tell me, beforehand."

His laughter was genuine this time.

"You are silly, aren't you? Do you think I go about proposing to women I don't wish to marry? I've never proposed to another woman in my life — and expected to be believed."

I was not sure if this meant that I was more gullible than his other women, but to my enormous relief, he kissed me, and I thought that anything else in the whole world he had to tell me could not be so important as this.

Nevertheless, I was rudely jolted when a dry

274

voice cut into our little moment from the open doorway, and the Owen maid said sourly, "Ye comin'? Do I wait the night now?"

"Let's let her wait," Marc whispered in my ear as he tried to kiss me again, but several people inside the house were now peering out and making low-voiced, amused comments, so I ducked away from his hands and stepped inside.

It was only then I realized we had gotten away from whatever it was he wanted to tell me. It did not matter. I would ask him at the end of the evening.

When we joined the rest of the party in the crowded front parlor, I saw that, thanks to the heavy maroon furniture and portieres with their fluttering ribbon trim, the room looked blood-red by the light of several elegant branches of candles. The parlor was small and over-furnished. Though I recognized everyone, they seemed like strangers in their best finery. Cath-eerine, in particular, looked better than I had ever seen her. She had a high coloring in her prominent child's cheeks, and was wearing a shade of rich, golden brown that set off her hazel eyes charmingly. She was not in her wheelchair tonight, but "arranged" in a large chair not far from the fireplace, where the low-burning peat seemed in momentary danger of dying out. The folds of her gown, shimmering in the light of many candles, made her the center of attention, and I wondered with some uneasiness why Marc had never seen in her this charm and even this beauty. In spite of her sturdy frame, there was a fragile, helpless quality about her, and I had always supposed such things attracted men.

The Reverend MacDonnachie was holding Catherine's hand and flattering her in his great, elephantine way, so that Mrs. Fothergay tittered behind her fan, and inquired archly:

"Are you not jealous, ma'am? Miss Catherine seems to have made a conquest."

Mrs. MacDonnachie smiled her watery smile.

"Dear Cadmon. He does love the ladies." She was utterly unruffled.

Catherine turned away from her admirer to greet Marc and me, and to tell us how happy she was at the news that had come to her. Curiously enough, I had a notion that she was sincere in this, as she probably thought this left the way clear for her with her phantom lover, should he prove to be as real as she claimed. But then, Catherine was one of those complex creatures with honest eyes, of whom every one says: "I read her character and her thoughts as I read a book. Clear as pure water." I was learning that if one studied a very deep stream, no matter how clear it might be on the surface, somewhere in the depths was obscurity.

Presently, the Vicar suggested that if Catherine would grace the evening with her inimitable playing of the pianoforte, he would volunteer to work the pedals, and otherwise oblige by turning pages, et cetera.

Marc was abstracted and, although he smiled

and behaved in every way to indicate that when he saw me his thoughts were upon me, I wondered what troubled him during the moments when his mind was elsewhere. I think, almost without being aware of it, I had watched to see his reaction to the fireplace and its small, neat fire. He never went near it and, even more curious, never looked that way once during the evening.

A good deal of fun was made out of the moving of furniture, and the rolling of carpets into a corner that laid bare the clean, smooth sandstone floor — an odd dancing surface, but it served. There were any number of challenges and boasts of strength between Sir Gareth and the Vicar, both of whom claimed the title for Maidenmoor. However, I noted that while these two sturdy members of the stronger sex battled verbally, Marc and one or two other male guests managed to do most of the heavy work. I suspected Marc only wanted to get it done and out of the way. He seemed impatient with the whole business.

Nonetheless, when we danced the waltz together, Marc's mood improved perceptibly. We talked of the Continent and the places I had wanted to visit all my life from hearing my parents talk of them, and, most of all, we talked of ourselves.

I discovered during the course of our dances that Catherine could play very well in spite of her handicap. Her brother had lifted her to the pianoforte, and it was the Vicar who good-naturedly turned pages and saw to the pedals. I could see why he did not dance. It would have been like a bear capering his tricks.

When refreshments were served, Catherine raised her hands to Marc and asked if he would carry her to her chair by the fire. He obliged without comment, and I noted a sudden silence from all parts of the room as everyone watched the two of them. He seated her carefully in her chair, and handed her the dainty little glass of mixed ices that the Vicar removed from a sparkling crystal tray which I took to be the remnant of more prosperous times in the Owen family.

A mill owner from Upshed and his wife made some to-do over the picture Catherine exhibited as Marc's shadow was removed from her, and she smiled.

"One would think you are in love," said the mill owner's wife brightly.

Before the rest of us could do more than look uncomfortable, Catherine smiled and agreed that, "perhaps I am."

Gareth cut in sharply, "Cathie! Gad's life, girl!"

But Catherine waved her hand at him teasingly.

"Oh, no Garrie. I must only make certain of whom I love. A small problem of identity." I saw then, as her fingers tightened over something in her lap, that she still held, wadded in a ball with her lace handkerchief, the note that Sir Gareth had handed her in church the other day. So she fancied herself in love with the oil painting! Whether he existed or not, it was unnerving to me and I wished the matter hadn't been mentioned at all.

There was a clatter of silver, and then a moment's silence as we removed our gloves and busied ourselves with the ices. Catherine broke the silence.

"How provoking! Marc, would you mind putting more coals on the fire? You are nearest the tongs there."

Marc, who had been holding one of my hands, and yet seemed miles away in thought, stiffened, and I felt the fingers of his hand close on mine so fiercely that I nearly cried out. However, I was as near to the fire as he was, and I said quickly, while everyone in the room stared at us:

"There." I kicked several coals over into the faint glow of the fire with my slipper toe. "Now, Marc, you see what a good housewife I shall be! Always at hand — or should I say — at foot?"

The Vicar's laughter boomed out, and the others joined in. Marc, who had stared at Catherine without once looking at the fire, turned to me, and kissed me on the ear. I raised his hand and touched his fingers with my lips to show him that he could count upon me.

Catherine sat exactly as she had before, looking lovely, with a trace of brighter red in her cheeks, and a little puzzled frown marring the smooth broadness of her forehead. Beside her, the fire crackled as the coals caught on the pile of dried bracken that had been laid for the earlier fire and never burned. A spark flew upward to land on the hem of her gown, and I was much relieved to see Marc brush it off before I could reach it. When Catherine thanked him, he ignored her and asked me if I cared to leave, for the others were rising under cover of Mrs. Fothergay's noisy flirtation with Sir Gareth.

"Now, dear Garrie," she was saying, "you must not go out in the horrid cold just to see me home. I am quite sure the Vicar and Mrs. Mac-Donnachie will be pleased to oblige. . . . Well, if you insist. Really! I am quite overcome by such solicitude! Catherine, my dear, it will be a lucky woman who snatches your big, strong brother."

Catherine said civilly, "I am sure she will be, ma'am. Garrie is the most perfect of brothers." She put out her hand to me and said in a lower tone, "Please, Anne, stay a moment. Let them go."

Although I could see that Marc was in no mood to remain, I did not know what else to do. I watched the crackling fire as the little flames leaped up and then retreated into the cavernous recesses of the chimney. Marc went to the table and seemed very much interested in the crystal tray which took all the flashing light from the branch of candles nearby. Catherine watched him.

"Marc, dear, would you mind bringing me that branch of candles? I want to show Anne this lovely carving of the mantel here."

Without looking at the candles, he took up the base and handed it to her. I could see by his scowl that he was growing angry at her, or at something else which troubled him. I wondered at her attempt to upset him in this fashion.

When she had showed me the carving, I could see nothing of importance about it. It was a most ordinary mantel, and I did not like the careless way she used that branch of candles, for the tallow dripped down upon the hem of her gown, and once upon the flying ribbons of the runner on the low table to her left. I felt sure she was doing this solely to bring Marc to some rash act, because of his well-known abhorrence of fire.

"We really must go," I said nervously. "It was a lovely party, and we had a delightful time." I dropped a curtsey to Catherine. All the time I was aware of the candles waving in her hand.

"The polite formalities, by all means," said Marc, turning to face us, as cuttingly sarcastic as possible. "Tell the lady how charming she looks, Anne. Tell her how she behaved with her customary good taste, and made them all adore her. Tell her that if she isn't careful she is going to burn the accursed house down just to drive me out of my mind! And she has succeeded, admirably, beyond her wildest dreams. I wouldn't care if she *did* burn the house down, and herself with it!"

He seized my hand and almost dragged me away from her.

Embarrassed at his shocking breach of manners, I went along with him, turning only, and against his tugging hand, to wish Catherine goodnight, and to say, "Please forgive us. I'm sure you understand."

She did not seem in the least surprised by this scene which was so horrid to me, for I had never seen a man display such manners to a lady, and it was doubly hurting that it should be a man I loved who did so.

In the doorway I looked back to see her sitting there in a frozen position, still puzzled, but also, I think, satisfied of some conclusion she had drawn.

From her look, which was certainly not love, I concluded she had given up the notion that Marc was the lover out of her favorite portrait. But still, she must be quite sure. Doubtless, she had hoped to prove it by these tricks with the fire. Marc was right. Her actions had been deliberate. As I looked at her, she reached over to set the branch of candles down on the little table. The candles, tilted by the imbalance of her position, threatened to slip off the table. Tallow dropped onto the hanging fringe on the table, and I pulled at Marc's sleeve.

"She shouldn't. It's so unsafe."

Shutting the parlor doors, he said impatiently, "Where the devil is that maid?"

Nettie finally brought us our wraps and Marc put mine around me.

The night was splendid, full of stars. Marc and

I started to walk, arm in arm. I could see that, although he was shaken by his duel with Catheerine, my own influence could not be negligible, for he was soon calm. He tightened his hold around my waist, and pulled me to him.

"What a long time I've needed you!" he murmured, and I could have cried in the happiness of hearing that. He added, still with half his mind on what we had left, "I wonder what she expected me to do? Run shrieking from the house at sight of her innumerable fires?"

"No," I said, thinking it over. "She expected to press you so hard with — with your dislike of fire that you would turn into the ghost of the Devil-Vicar before her eyes. And then you would be entirely her property."

"Grisly thought." He kissed my cheek and asked in a voice he tried to infuse with his familiar, teasing tone, "Do you know any young lady in market for property, slightly scarred and not precisely what the wrapping indicates, but still of the required species?"

I admitted in his own style that, if pressed, I might find a place for the property in question. For a few minutes it was the most beautiful night I had ever known. I almost forgot that in this village a murderer still walked free, although his savage canine weapon was silenced. I was rudely shocked by Nettie's screeching voice as she ran out onto the street after us.

Marc did not move. His face in the moonlight was the color of ashes. Then, as though ashamed of his own fear or whatever memory destroyed him, he covered his face with a hand that trembled.

"God! I knew it would happen. I've known it all along."

I started back.

"It must be those wretched candles. Or the bracken in the fireplace. They've caught. Come. . . . Marc?"

I had to call to him again, more urgently. This time, after a sickening pause, he returned with me the few steps to the Owen House. Nettie had pushed open the parlor doors and we saw Catherine across the room, trying to shift her chair out of reach of the little flame that had leaped to the runner of the table and from the runner to the flimsy ribbons on the portieres. The candles lay burning themselves out against the sandstone floor but a trail of fire scrambled up along the long window, the length of the portieres. Catherine saw us and cried out.

"It was an accident! Take me out of here. Marc!"

I was petrified. It seemed the natural thing to cross that room, to seize the burning materials and stamp them out; yet, with the ribbons of flame flaring out wider every moment, I could scarcely move. But worse, I felt the deep, terrible reluctance of the man who had come in behind me. I could almost hear his heartbeat in the anguish of the struggle with his own morbid revulsion. Then Marc ran past me into the room, stopped at the pianoforte and leaned over the corner of the instrument, commanding her, just out of reach of her arms.

"Walk, Catherine! Walk! You haven't fooled me. Walk — or you will die."

She made a terrible effort, her face a deep, blood-dark color, the cords in her throat vibrating with the pressure she exerted. She leaped forward from her chair, the chair toppled over and she lay stretched on the floor, only inches from the smoldering flames. She screamed, holding out both arms to Marc, clawing at the air between them.

"Marc! I know you're not the Other One. You can help me. Please . . . Marc!"

I was as frightened of his reaction as I was of the fire so close to the invalid girl. His eyes glittered black and terrible. I did not know whether it was his fear of the fire, or his determination to prove once and for all that she could walk, which led him to say again:

"Come, Catherine! Walk to me!"

He held out his hands to her. I knew then, even if he did not, that she would have moved by this time if she could, and I ran toward her. As I did so, the portieres caught, and began to shower her body with shreds of burning materials. Even Marc was not blind to this. Whatever cowardice or cruelty had held him back was finally dispelled. He reached for her, seized her arms, and dragged her away. Then, as I beat the curls of flame off her skirts, he pulled the portieres away from her so that they hung half off their heavy rod. I helped him drag her away, conscious of the maid, Nettie, screaming out on the street, her every sound grating horribly on my nerves.

Marc was just lifting Catherine into his arms when the rod of the portieres snapped from its corner fixture, and its full length hurtled down across his neck and shoulders. Stunned, he went down on his knees under the impact, his body shielding Catherine. Though I trembled for his safety, I took Catherine from him, dragged her across the floor to the door, and only then could look back to see Marc getting to his feet with an effort. The rod and the burning portieres lay in a smoldering heap beside him.

Catherine was muttering, "I'm all right. See to him."

I rushed to Marc, helping him to the door and noting with sick apprehension for him that his clothing was seared in places, his hair disheveled, but his eyes were the most revealing. They were deeply shadowed with a pain and horror whose depths I could not begin to fathom. He leaned back against the door, and I put my arms around him. We hugged each other, to be quite sure we were both safe.

He buried his face against my hair.

"I never thought I could face it. I couldn't, if you hadn't been here."

"It's all right now, darling," I whispered. "It's all right."

"Is it — is it still burning?" He would not look.

I glanced around and saw that two men had come running from the street and were stamping out what little remained of the fire, which had burnt itself out upon the stone floor. A good deal of smoke filled the room, but the crisis was over, or so I thought.

Catherine sat on the staircase, with her maid hovering solicitously over her. She looked almost her usual calm self. She had not been burned, although she was picking at a burnt hole in the heavy material of her skirt, and sighing over the damage. She looked up at me.

"I'm so dreadfully sorry. I know now that Marc couldn't have gone back into that room if he had been the Other One."

"He is Marc Branshaw," I said coldly, "and you had best make up your mind to that."

Marc stared at me. He was shaken and dazed. His eyes had a fixed expression, as though he could not quite see me.

"Marc?" I shook him and he winced. I had almost forgotten the jolt he had received from the rod and the burning portieres.

"Darling," I said, when there was no response. "Let us go. It's late, and . . . I'm very tired."

He nodded, moved away from the parlor doors, and followed me. His quiet obedience itself was ominous. I said to Catherine at the last, "I'll have someone fetch the doctor to you — after he's been to Marc."

Marc scowled at this and seemed, momentarily, to recover his obstinate will.

"I'm perfectly fit. Send the doctor to Catherine. I'll see no doctor. Come, I'll take you home."

This was pure nonsense, but I did not make matters worse by arguing. I saw Sir Gareth hurrying up the street in a panic, having gotten word that his sister was trapped by a fire, and I went to him.

"She's safe. May we borrow your gig and the mare?"

"Yes, yes. Anything. In the stables behind the house. Good God. Branshaw! You in this too? What were you doing? Running away?"

"He saved your sister's life," I said sharply, as Marc did not appear to notice him. When Gareth had hurried on, Marc murmured to himself in a puzzled way, "She cannot walk. She cannot — possibly — walk. It's all wrong. If not Catherine, who then?"

"Don't think of it now," I told him. He was in no condition to solve in one night the mystery that had terrorized the whole of Maidenmoor for months, perhaps years.

With the help of a husky millhand we managed to get the mare and the gig into harness. Before I could stop him, Marc lifted me into the gig, and then got in. He could not control the trembling of his fingers as he took the reins, and when I insisted on his driving to Branshaw Hall instead of the inn, he made no objection. The night was bitter cold, and I hoped it would revive him, but I was now aware that his hands were burned across the palms and that there were searing marks across his throat and the nape of his neck. I was concerned for him, for many reasons, but most of all because he seemed so distant, and did not say a word on the entire journey.

When we reached the Hall on the green brow of the hill, I jumped out of the gig without assistance, and called to the groom. Marc followed me, moving with a quick, easy step, and yet I could see that the effort at normal behavior took a heavy toll on his strength.

In the pleasant reception hall of the house Marc looked up the long flight of stairs. I read in his eyes his terrible weariness. In alarm, I reached out to him, but before I could touch him, he took one step, stumbled and collapsed at the foot of the stairs. Panic-stricken, I knelt by him and called for help. He opened his eyes, whispered something faintly.

"Don't — let them touch me."

Here again was his strange, abnormal fear of personal contact, and I tried to be matter-of-fact.

"Of course not, darling. Why ever should they?"

He seemed reassured.

When I called his name a moment later, he did not hear me. He had lapsed into unconsciousness. I turned down the collar of his coat and his shirt and gently examined the back of his head and his neck to see where he was hurt. The rod of the portieres had struck just above the nape of the neck and his hair was singed there. Probably it was this blow which had done the most damage, although I could see no abrasions. But as I slipped his collar away, I saw a sign that made me shudder:

Below the fresh, searing scorch on his neck made by the portieres, were the deeper scars of a terrible burning, long ago. I tore away the collar. The broad white tissue of scars branded his back in a dozen places. There could be no mistake. They were burns, some years old.

Hearing the voices of the Branshaw servants approaching, I hurriedly rearranged his clothing over the scars and studied his features. With his black hair free about his face, the light mockery gone, and haggard evidences of pain limning the features I recognized from the portrait in the church, I wondered with a kind of horrid fascination, if I were looking at the Devil-Vicar who was dead these many years.

XVII

I stood in the dark and gloomy upper hall of the Branshaw house, just outside Marc's bedchamber, awaiting Dr. Lowther's summons. I stood under the forbidding eyes of all the Branshaw portraits, whose puritanical faces looked as though they were aware that the one who was called the heir to the Branshaws was an interloper after all, and not one of them. I could almost feel their animosity, their tight-lipped resentment against the man who called himself "Marc Branshaw" — and who might be dying at this very moment.

I had been standing in this spot for some time and, as it took the doctor two hours to arrive, I could see that it would shortly be dawn. This was a relief, for the winter sun might thaw the abnormally cold atmosphere of this house of illness and death.

I sent the housekeeper back to bed and Dilys was soothing the cook, who had gone into hysterics and had begun to see strange floating faces of dead Branshaws on the main staircase, plus other ghostly phenomena which she claimed would foretell the death of "Master Marc." She complained between sobs that "Master Marc would go the way of Miss Moyna." While Dilys explained carefully, and for the twentieth time, that the doctor was doing all he could (for we did not know in what condition Marc might be at this moment, or what his injuries were), I was sorely tempted to burst into hysterics myself.

I hinted to myself, during this long wait, that Marc might well be the man who had attacked me in the church and, almost as bad, the creature who had frightened me at Moyna's cottage. Could I really go on loving the man of the church darkness, the creature with those savage hands?

The thought of Marc's hands gave me pause. Surely, those fingers upon my throat, the terrible, powerful thumbs, could not belong to

Marc. . . . Could they? I tried to recall his hands, but I could not. I could not visualize anything except his own suffering, for, whoever he was, it did not in any way diminish my feeling for him. The horror was there, but as something apart from him. I was bitter against the impulse which made him commit these acts — if he had committed them — and against a fate which gave him so many attractions and then pursued him relentlessly with attempts to burn him alive, and to give him an illness that plagued him, and who knows what other sufferings that I was not even aware of?

And I will confess that the idea of my Marc and that incredible, fairy-tale face in the portrait being of the same blood and loving me, was so overwhelming that I didn't care if he were the Devil himself.

Dilys looked through the open door of Moyna Branshaw's room and said idly, as she gazed across the room and out the window, "Someone is up and about, over at the Owens'. That Miss Catherine, with her fire tricks, she's a sly one. Always trying to make up to the master. Playing he's the Devil-Vicar. As if Master Marc wasn't just as nice as that Other One."

Poor Catherine. What would happen if she found out that the lover of her portrait was truly alive, so near her?

More important, however, was the attitude which would be taken by Dr. Lowther. It was his response that I awaited with such trepidation.

When Marc still had not come to consciousness half an hour after the big Branshaw servant got him to his room, I knew I must send for the doctor in spite of Marc's plea for secrecy. I was determined, if the doctor made threats, to get Marc safely out of Maidenmoor before any action of a legal nature could be taken.

When Dilys mentioned the Devil-Vicar, I felt a strong compulsion to talk about him, and at the same time I was terrified for fear some tone in my voice, some casual glance or other little sign of awareness would give away Marc's secret.

"Did you know the Devil-Vicar?" I asked.

"Saw him once or twice, mum. But I remember him and Miss Moyna. They used to laugh — Miss Moyna did — and after a time, the Devil-Vicar would laugh too, at how they fooled the village. But he was much younger than Miss Moyna — twelve years, I'm told — and when he came, very serious. Sometimes he frightened the congregation when he preached of sin and the Devil and Gytrashes and all. It was terrible. After . . . the thing happened to him, we began to say he talked terrible and frightening because he was talking of his own sins. Do you think so, mum?"

"I'm sure I don't know," I said.

"It makes not matter, though. We felt dreadful to know he'd died in such a way. When Miss Moyna showed Miss Catherine and some of the others a miniature that her son had sent her — that would be just afore her death — we all was taken by surprise, and pleased, too. He looked so like the poor Devil-Vicar."

"And what did you think of Miss Moyna's husband, Dilys?"

"I tell you straight out, mum. Master Josiah, Miss Moyna's husband, was never one to make you take a fancy to him. Miser he was, and mean. Slapped Miss Moyna more than once, he did. Small wonder, a year after he died, Miss Moyna fell in love with the young Reverend when he come to Maidenmoor."

"Were there any others, before the Devil-Vicar?"

Dilys smiled. "None you might mention. She was very fond of young Master Marc and he come first with her. Such a sickly little boy he was! Miss Moyna did flirt a bit, that she did and no mistake. And then, even when she was in love with the Devil-Vicar there was others — the young curates that served the Devil-Vicar, lanky, awkward things as they was, that she smiled at and perhaps kissed once or twice in fun. But she was that way, and freer to misbehave after she'd took her boy to France for him to get well. That was just before she returned and met the Reverend Morgan."

I burned with a bitter jealousy against the dead charmer, Moyna. It was she and not Catherine who was my real rival.

Dilys had left the door to Moyna's room open. Without interest, I studied the whitewashed crossbeams that made the high-ceilinged room seem so much lower. Then I glanced beyond the beams and out the window, to the green rolling flesh of the moorland. I hated the moors and resolved that whatever Dr. Lowther did, I, at least, would not let another disaster befall Marc like the one that cost him those terrible scars.

The bedchamber door made a scraping sound as it opened, and Dr. Lowther motioned me to come in. I did so, looking quickly at the bed and noting that Marc appeared asleep and comfortable. At least, the lines of pain in his face had been erased, which was my greatest relief.

"He will do nicely now, I think," said Dr. Lowther. "A bit of laudanum. Just the thing for such emergencies. As you will observe, I've stripped off his burned clothing and gotten him snug in his own night things."

I said, "Thank you." He had not mentioned the scars. Was it possible he would answer all my prayers and continue to play the innocent?

He rolled down his sleeves and I helped him into his heavy riding coat. The task took an interminable time, for I was in dreadful suspense. I asked finally:

"Will he recover?"

"From this injury? I see no reason to doubt it. The wounds from the fire are superficial. Nasty blow at the base of the skull, but that's all gone by. Only time will tell if there's damage within. Those . . . old scars are curious."

So it must come. I felt my knees weaken and leaned back against the little table beside Marc's bed, pretending a firmness I was far from feeling.

"I know. I saw the scars when he collapsed."

"Just so. The scars of a very serious burning. Ma'am, are you aware of the appalling episode in this village some fifteen or sixteen years ago? A mass hysteria directed against a foolish young man who had committed sacrilege in his holy office?"

I nodded, and to spare him further explanations, I said calmly, "Can he be Ewen Morgan? I don't know. But he isn't guilty of the things that are happening here, whatever you may think. I know him. He may be ill — I don't deny it — but he wouldn't do those things. He wouldn't kill . . ." I felt my throat automatically.

Dr. Lowther smiled, a little smile at human trust. "How easily we are convinced by love! Believe me, Miss Wicklow, I hope you're right. Several villagers during the past year have asked me if it was possible that this man could be the same as the one who died sixteen years ago —"

"But the bones that were discovered when the ashes of the parsonage were sifted," I put in, hoping to lead him off.

"My dear lady, the parsonage was built on a part of the old graveyard. What else but bones would be found if one looked? At any rate, when I was asked, I could not be sure, until now. But I should not think those scars he bears are sixteen years old, if that means anything. They seem scarcely more than a year old — at the most, two years."

He paused, considering.

"I believe it is, in part, the very fear that he *is* the same man, which has kept the villagers from laying hands to him and accusing him a second time. They didn't intend that murder sixteen years ago. When it was committed, they held themselves responsible. Now, in a sense, they are defending this man, hoping he will prove his innocence. Whether they regard him as the Devil-Vicar's ghost returned, or as that creature's natural son, they're giving him this chance, in order to sponge out that other, involuntary murder they thought they had committed. But the moment is at hand when there will be a reckoning."

"What action do you intend to take?"

He took up his valise, choosing his words carefully.

"None, for a day or so, until he's up and on his feet. I doubt if, in his present state, we need concern ourselves with such matters. Send for me if he shows any decisive change."

"What — sort of change?" I asked, thinking, with a sense of increasing darkness that this was what I had been afraid of all along.

His face lightened. He very nearly smiled.

"No. Not the kind you're apparently fearing. No sudden attempted violence. On the other hand, I join the village in suspecting that someone would like us to believe in his guilt."

"That thought never occurred to me," I said indignantly.

"I understand. But let me know immediately if you note any change in his manner, or any undue

297

activity." He took my hand and I curtseyed to him. He turned away, hesitated.

"Miss Wicklow, I share your hope in the innocence of your friend, possibly because I can imagine his physical sufferings years ago, if, in truth, he is the late Devil-Vicar. But I must remind you again that he is a fraud, and that we still don't know what he's done with the real Marc Branshaw."

My face froze into a parody of politeness.

"It was quite unnecessary for you to remind me. Good day."

He smiled gently.

"There, there. Probably a very simple explanation. You had best get some sleep."

I sent Dilys to usher him out, while I pushed the table away and took up my place in a chair beside Marc's bed.

I sat there wondering how this would all end, and if we would ever discover the truth of the recent happenings. At least Dr. Lowther was withholding action.

What had become of the original Marc Branshaw?

The room was bitter cold. I wished I might light a fire in the fireplace, but I didn't dare because the noise would almost certainly disturb Marc. He was breathing quietly, as though his sleep were natural and not induced by the sleeping potion that the doctor had given him.

I don't know how much time had passed when I was aroused from a half-doze to hear the frantic

298

barking of the Branshaw dogs somewhere on the grounds, together with noisy shouts and screams of fury. I could not mistake the voice of the Branshaw groom, crying fiercely:

"Ay, my pretties! Worry him! The nasty outcomer! Set your teeth to him. That's my pretties!"

I looked over at Marc to see if the noise disturbed him, and got a severe shock to see him staring at me, his eyes luminous and wide, glazed by the drug.

I said softly, "It's just the dogs. Go to sleep."

A moment later I knew that he didn't understand. He was still under the influence of the laudanum. I closed my eyes so I should not be aware of that puzzled, confused stare. Then he whispered a name:

"Moyna?"

I felt sick at this blow, but said nothing.

Either the drug or some other calming influence overcame him, and to my intense relief, he closed his eyes and was still.

Outside, the quarrel over the dogs went on hotter than ever. I was too tense to remain quiet, and got up and went out into the hall and called to Dilys. She had brought a chair into the hall and was curled up in it, asleep, when I reached her.

"What on earth is that noise out on the moors, Dilys?"

She listened, yawning widely and smothering it with a mumbled apology.

"One of the villagers from Upshed, mum. They always take the crossing inside the Branshaw bounds. We don't stand for that, and set the dogs to them." She listened pleasurably. "Dogs caught this one, ay. Fair savaging him, they are."

"Well, tell the groom to stop the dogs, at once. They may do serious harm to the man."

The noise, the uproar and curses mingled to disturb us even here in the hall, but did not bother Dilys.

"I should hope they do hurt, mum. Everybody knows you can't cross another man's fields. Not in this Riding, you can't. That's what them stone bounds is for. Property's sacred, like church, it is."

"So is human life," I said.

"Now you sound like Mister Marc," she sighed. "He always says we're savages." Reluctantly, she went to carry out my orders.

I returned to Marc's room, and resumed my vigil, wishing the dawn would hasten, bringing with it a little sunlight to this benighted country.

Before I knew it, it was morning, and I was being awakened by Marc's voice, speaking to me from his bed. As I opened my eyes, I saw his hand outstretched to me. I took it and smiled at him.

"How much better you look!" I said, "You have color again." I added jokingly, "I believe you will live."

"I intend to," he told me. His hand was healthily warm on mine. "How long have you been here?"

"During the night," I explained, hoping to keep from him the knowledge that the doctor had been to see him, against his explicit orders.

"You? Alone?"

I did not reply. I didn't like to lie to him.

He raised the covers, regarded his body under the coverlet, and observed that he was in night clothing. His eyes sought mine and, when I looked away elaborately, he laughed at me, and said in his sardonic humor:

"Dear little love, I hope you're not always going to be so shy of my person. How did you manage? With your eyes closed?"

It sounded strange and embarrassing to be called "little love," and the rest. It made me aware of him in a way that was unfamiliar but tantalizing, and I was ashamed to admit it. I made a motion to get up.

"Where are you going?"

"I thought you might want a glass of water. Or something."

"Please." He could be very persuasive when he set himself to it. "Come and sit down, there's a dear. If you are the only one who attended me, then I take it you have some questions."

I sat down again. This sounded hopeful. Perhaps there were answers ready. I would accept any. But in order to let him think they did not matter, I said offhandedly, "Later. When you're more yourself."

"Never felt more myself. Ask as many questions as you like. I don't promise to answer," he added, still in excellent humor. "But that need not prevent your asking."

"Well then" — I turned and faced him — "I have two questions. Number One: What does Moyna Branshaw mean to you now? And, Two: What became of the real Marc Branshaw?"

"One," he repeated precisely, mimicking me. "Moyna was the first woman I allowed to come into my life, and she came very shortly after my mother died. When I was hard upon ten years old."

"But — but —" I stuttered, more confused than ever. "Ten years old?"

He grinned. "You see, I met Moyna at a sanatorium in Southern France where my brother had placed me, at great expense to himself, hoping for a cure of what was called when I was a child — a 'pthisis of the lungs.' And it was to this sanatorium that Moyna Branshaw came, with her boy, Marc Branshaw, for the same purpose. I was luckier than Marc. The poor lad died, very shortly before Moyna was murdered by this accursed village."

"Your brother, the one who placed you in the sanatorium —"

"Was the one this village called 'The Devil-Vicar.' Though he was a kind of Dark Angel to this sickly brat whose life he saved. I owe everything to Ewen. I grew up obsessed with the idea of avenging his death when I was well, but Moyna would not have it so. She felt that her own son's sickness, the long, long death in life that poor Marc lived until his real death two years ago — all these were, to her, a sign that God was punishing her for what she called the 'seduction of his vicar'."

"When did you decide upon the vengeance after all?" I was beginning to see new and more murky terrors behind the old one. Was his vengeance the thing that had caused these crimes at Maidenmoor?

"When Moyna began to feel that Ewen's death had not been an accident caused by mob violence, but something planned, by a vicious intelligence still abroad in Maidenmoor. We discussed her suspicions by letter. This was at the time young Marc was dying. I had recovered some years before — six years ago, more or less — and gone to Paris, but I returned to be with Marc when he died. The end was sudden. Moyna had no time to make the journey. There was a fire at the sanatorium while I was visiting the lad. I got him out very nearly unscathed. But the exertion was too much for him and he was dead before I recovered from my burns. When they told me, I knew at last the full of Ewen's sufferings before his own death. And I swore an oath to Ewen, and to Moyna, that I should return and find the evil creature whose mind conceived his death. Then, Moyna died."

I put my hand over my mouth. Yet the words came out:

"She was murdered by this — what you call evil intelligence."

"Precisely. I never doubted it, once I heard of her death."

"Who is this monster?"

He paused, then said thoughtfully, "I was very close. So very close before this happened, I cannot be quite sure — yet."

I said nothing. He watched me.

"What are you staring at?"

"Your hand."

He looked at it. His understanding was quick. "You're wondering about the hand that attacked you in St. Anthony's, aren't you?"

I nodded.

He considered his hand, turning it over, then finally held it out for me to examine. "But I couldn't have done that thing for you."

"Of course not," I agreed quickly, and added after a pause, "Why?"

"Because, my darling, I too have wanted to murder you on occasion — such as the time you slammed the door on my hand, and the following day when you gave these poor knuckles such a wrench that I still feel the twinge. And once or twice during the last few days. For instance, your charming taunt that we should both marry the Owens and thus become brother and sister. Delicate thought, that."

I had to smile.

"But you see," he went on teasingly, doubtless to get off the subject of Moyna, "every time I murdered you in my daydreams, I found myself making love to you at the same time. It's a more difficult feat than an innocent like you might suspect. But I'm up to it."

I felt sure he was.

"Apparently such a double pleasure never occurred to your friend the other night. Perhaps he didn't hate you enough. Couldn't have been me, you see." His reasoning was perfectly logical, for him. "Unless, of course — our attacker was a female." He studied me. "Your brows are knit unbecomingly, darling. You will make wrinkles. What troubles you still?"

"Why did you come here as Moyna's son? Why not as yourself?"

"My dear child" — by his voice he plainly thought me idiotic — "Come spying about as Padric Morgan? Do you think the creature I search for would not know at once and destroy any evidence I might hope to find? It was Moyna's idea, in the beginning, when word came of her son's death. She had a notion that it would be safer, for what we had planned, if I came as her son. And then she . . . died. And I knew it was murder! I knew the monstrous intelligence that brought Ewen to his death had found Moyna out."

"Did she leave her estate to you or to Marc?"

He smiled. "No, my skeptical darling, I have not stolen Marc's estate. The whole of it shall go to her Glasgow relations when I've done with my work here. But it seemed simpler to come and assume charge of the Branshaw place while I had my work to do."

"Moyna!" I said, hard put to restrain my jealousy. "Even as a child, you must have loved her as your brother did."

He smiled, the dear smile that had so often won me in the past. "You are like Moyna in so many ways, Anne. Did you know that? Not in looks, but in ways that I love; and yet, you're so much warmer, closer. I understand you as neither I, nor I am sure, my brother, ever understood Moyna." He was running his forefingers absently along my palm as he spoke, but he was thinking back to a time I could not know. "Moyna never allowed anyone to share a deep emotion with her. Perhaps she had none, except for her son. It's different with you. You don't hide your deepest passions. Your quick likes and dislikes, your furious cutting angers, your jealousy — these are things I understand, for I too am like that."

His searching eyes read in me my doubts and fears and interpreted them correctly. He said in a quiet voice that made me suddenly aware how tired he must be after his ordeal, "Look at me, Anne. The rest are part of the background canvas; only you remain."

"How can that be? In so short a time."

He said in a tender, teasing way, pretending a gaiety that was a shadow of itself, "I know you better than you think. I've guessed your every emotion. I'm good at it, you know. I've played on those emotions shamelessly." He added, suddenly humble, "I kept hoping you would need me, as I need you. You will now know how much."

Watching me, he had become less certain. I wondered at it, but noticed the growing intensity in his face, his manner, and especially his voice as he studied me. He was beginning to show the extent of his illness, as though the tight rein of his determination had loosed and he could not pretend any longer. I should never have put him through the strain of this cross-questioning.

His voice wavered. "Or has my story changed all that? Its ugliness repulses you. Does it?" He shook my hand painfully in his insistence. "Well, tell me! Does it?"

I was thinking, "All this is very well. But doesn't it prove him guilty of the horrible crimes here? Who had a better motive? A motive he has confessed to me." Yet there it was. I suspected him of hideous things, and loved him still.

"How do you know Moyna Branshaw was murdered? How can you be sure?"

Against my quick gesture to stop him, he sat up in bed, leaning toward me in his intense conviction. The effort must have cost him considerable pain, but I don't think he consciously noticed it.

"Someone removed the cover of stones and stout planks from the bog. Someone wanted Moyna dead. It was a dark, glowering day when the accident occurred. How easy to murder her so! And what murderer more convenient than Catherine? Or so I thought."

"But why Catherine?"

"Because she was one of Moyna's 'victims.' Moyna was always writing to me of her little amusements. She taunted Catherine about her absurd interest in the portrait in the Vicar's study. Moyna painted that portrait years ago, when she was teasing my brother about his dour, romantic look, as she called it. It was meant as a joke, she said, and she never finished it. Two or three years ago the MacDonnachies saw it in Moyna's house and asked for it, as a curiosity. A sinner to preach about, I fancy."

Tiredly, he rubbed the back of his neck and winced at the healing burns. I started to get up, but he reached out and held me.

"No. Don't leave me. Let me tell you the rest. I began my investigation with drunken old Will Grimlett, the creature who put the torch to Ewen's parsonage sixteen years ago. He was always prowling on the moors and might have seen something. He was so terrified of me when he first saw me last year that it took all the powers of persuasion in the village to convince him I wasn't my brother's ghost. . . . And then he was killed. Killed in such a way and at such a time that everything pointed to me; that is, to the Devil-Vicar. A ghostly killer, out for revenge, you see. With Abbie, it was the same. I very nearly had her ready to confess to me at one time. I used my resemblance to my brother deliberately. I hoped to start gossip, to frighten them all into thinking I was something unreal, ghostly. But every time I have nearly had the evidence in my hands, this monster — man or woman — has forestalled me. It's someone close, someone who knows, even before I do, what my steps will be."

"Yes, but which of them?"

"A mask," he murmured in a puzzled way. "Someone in the village is wearing a mask."

When I asked him nothing further, he said with a hesitation that was unlike him, "You keep putting it aside, Anne. Would it have made a difference if I had lied to you about my motives in coming here, about my masquerade as Moyna's dead son?" His voice broke as he demanded, in a way that twisted my heart, *"Why don't you answer me?"*

Dilys' voice came to us from the doorway, and I started, drawing away from "Marc," as I should always think of him.

"Mum, might I see you a minute?"

I got up, hearing Marc's desperate attempt at lightness. "Anne, this is a poor way to start our life together. You aren't very biddable."

But I wanted to ask myself what my emotions were, exactly. It is true that I was still suspicious, yet I knew that deep within me it did not sway my still holding doubts as to his innocence of the crimes; feelings as it should have done. I had a strong inclination to look back and give Marc a sign which would assure him that nothing between us had changed.

It was preposterous that I should have turned

from him just when he needed me most, but there was a bit of Moyna in me, after all. I thought it would do him no harm to be in doubt for a few minutes.

"It seems I must get up and play the host or lose you entirely, Anne," he began again. "Don't go. I've a feeling. Don't —"

I ignored him. It was a moment I would afterward have given my life to amend, and the opportunity was gone in the time it took to close the door behind me and step into the hall.

XVIII

The hall was stale and damp after the long night. With the lamps turned out, I could scarcely make my way, except by the faint, death-gray light that comes with the dawn.

"I think he means it, mum," said Dilys. "He's getting up."

"Nonsense," I said. "He isn't as strong as he imagines he is. He'll soon change his mind. Well, Dilys, what is it?"

"It's Miss Catherine. Cook and me carried her up to Miss Moyna's room. Huggins — that's the groom, mum — he brought up that chair she moves about in."

I was bewildered. "But why Miss Moyna's room?"

"Fair puckers me. But she says it's that important, you wouldn't believe!"

I went into Moyna's white bedchamber, which was pervaded by early morning sunlight, and found Catherine sitting in her chair beside one of the large bedposts, doing a curious thing. She was trying to pry the head of the post out of its socket. She did not seem the least discomposed at sight of me.

"Anne, how is he?"

"Going on very well," I said stiffly.

She looked relieved. "I prayed so. I sent Nettie over several times in the night but there was no news. You know, of course, that the whole village is aware you spent the night here."

"Really?" The thought amused me in some perverse way. "Shall I then be burned as a Devil-Vicaress?"

She smiled but did not cease her odd occupation with the bedpost. "Dilys" — she turned to the girl — "you may go, dear."

Looking affronted, Dilys glanced at me and, upon my sign of agreement, she curtseyed and closed the door, leaving us alone in Moyna's room. Catherine waited significantly until this act was completed.

"He saved my life," she explain to me then. "And it was my fault. I was so stupid, trying to trap him." Her big hazel eyes grew rounder at the memory of last night's danger. "I wanted so desperately to prove he was Ewen Morgan. I only succeeded in proving he was not." Suddenly, the head of the bedpost came off in her fingers and she said with a flourish, "Behold, how simple!

Look in this post. I'll swear it's hollow. It's going to prove Marc's innocence or guilt. I think it will be his innocence. Moyna herself may name our murderer."

I did as she bade me, and found, as I had begun to suspect, several tight rolls of paper, neatly bound in ribbons and slipped down the cylindrical hollow of the post. I drew them out.

"You see," said Catherine. "I believe it was I who gave the murderer the method of killing Will Grimlett and Abbie."

I looked at her, only half believing her. She appeared so calm to be confessing such a monstrous thing. Seeing my disbelief, she smiled, that sad little self-deprecating smile I was afraid of.

"I was so bitter when Marc would not love me. You must try to understand my feelings. It was then I began to write that awful novel. It gave me some outlet for my injured pride, and the trampling of my feelings. Someone read it, and even suggested ideas for Marc's guilt, as a joke — and later suggested those wretched fire tricks with which I tortured Marc. Someone I knew! As recently as last night, after the fire, we discussed it again. I asked questions. I was very careful, quite unsuspected. After that conversation I began to add up the little things — the attack on you, the dog, who was the weapon I suggested in my novel. I should have known before, but I couldn't bring myself to admit it.

"At dawn, I recalled something Moyna once

said — that her bedposts could tell whole volumes to the gossips of Maidenmoor. I used to think she meant something indelicate. But this morning I thought at last I understood the allusion. Moyna's journals. Somewhere in those pages she might have recorded the reasons which made it necessary for her to be killed."

My fingers were shaking. I took the little rolls of paper and tossed them into her lap.

"Take some," she told me. "Glance over them. We may find the name I'm searching for. Read me anything that mentions a name — any name. I'll do the same with these."

"Whom do you suspect?" I asked, hardly daring to hear the answer.

She shrugged, getting quickly to the beribboned cylinders.

"If I'm right, you will see all too soon. Perhaps I shall make a novel of it." Her fingers went on unrolling the tight pages as she added words I found fully as ominous as she intended them. "Anne, the truth is so horrible, so unimaginable, that even I, knowing all the facts, could not believe it. If I told what I know, I should not be believed. I'm trusting to Moyna to give my word the weight it will need."

I shuddered, as much at her dreadful calm as at the horrors she drew for me. There was a feeling of unreality in this room that had belonged to the dead woman whose spirit refused to die. The bright winter sunlight was harsh. It did not belong here. It cast everything it touched

313

into a sharp, ugly relief.

In my hands were many finely written sheets and it took some little time to separate them into dates and subjects. A number of items, which amounted to mere one-and-two lines of amusing comment about local citizens, culminated in several pertinent paragraphs which I read aloud to Catherine:

August, 1832 —

Home now a fortnight. Must return to my poor little boy next week. Fortunately, the latest word of him is reassuring. Here in Maidenmoor there is some excitement.

The new vicar is that incredibly handsome young man I met at the French Sanatorium, when I was placing little Marc. I remember thinking what a curious thing, to see so presentable a male in the collar of that stuffy profession. But his devotion to that sick young brother of his was rather touching, and eminently suitable to one of the Cloth.

August 7, 1832 —

The new vicar thunders about sin, not in the least aware of what sins his dark eyes and his other charm are planting in the minds of his parishioners. Absurd young man, and, somehow, endearing in his very ignorance of this effect. Was it pure coincidence he was assigned the perpetual curacy of this village? If it were not he who directed the assignment, can it be Heaven who assigned him, or the Devil, perhaps? We shall see.

August 9, 1832 —
There has never been a man in my life since Josiah died. My life is empty, and then I think of little Marc's illness. Is my loneliness and need of love a payment to me for producing a sick child? I am thinking of a man now, daily, hourly, as do many other stupid village women. But I cannot help myself. I am determined to have him. Whom do I mean but our dark-eyed friend, Ewen Morgan, at the chancel rail? I am even glad that my little Marc is away, with Ewen's young brother, for it gives us an added bond. Though in any case I shouldn't like my boy to see what I am about to do.

"Good heavens!" exclaimed Catherine. "She was frank, even then."
I would not admit it, for worlds that in her place, I too would have been hard put to resist the temptation of that new vicar.
"Pray go on," said Catherine eagerly. "If Josiah Branshaw were not dead, what a perfect suspect he would make!"
I read on:

September —
What delightful moments in the Wind-Rock! I wonder if he dreamed what I had in

315

mind when I suggested that innocent lunch and stroll, to discuss "theological matters." I must return to France next week to visit my little boy. Still, the infrequent letters say he is going on as well as can be expected. But, oh! One more week of love! That is all I ask to last me all the long years to come.

. . . .

Ewen wants me to marry him. What nonsense! Where there is nine years between us!

At the cottage with him again. Tried to tell him to beware of certain cohorts, and the long, lank one, the dun-colored donkey, for example, and the people in the village. How that lank one tries to imitate him — walk like my love, stand like him, and what a farce! He has so little charm, so ungainly, so tall, lacking in every grace. He even makes an attempt to win me. I encourage him as a joke. It will possibly make Ewen jealous. He only laughs at him now. I have trained Ewen too well, I fear.

. . . .

How the village tingles with gossip! It may destroy Ewen's career but he was never meant for this. Meanwhile, the tales of Gytrashes, and of Ewen turning into a Devil on dark nights, serves to give us privacy. They think he can command savage dogs because he very wisely wore the coat belonging to the late Heaton Moresby yesterday, when Heaton's dog was savaging a trespasser. It was the scent

316

of his dead master in the coat that soothed the dog. We said nothing. It was amusing to see the gullible faces of the villagers. They will accuse Ewen of having supernatural powers soon. What a joke!

. . . .

Tales are spreading absurdly. Ewen is truly a devil, they say. He casts a spell upon the animals and also upon the women hereabouts, they say. No one knows better than I that he has been true to me. Still, this is no part of the tale we have spread. Who wishes Ewen destroyed? There are one or two women in the village who seem so calm, so capable! Yet I have observed the looks they cast at Ewen, and him so unaware of them. I would not put the gossip beyond them, either of them.

I will go to France, to my little boy soon, but I have not definitely made my plans yet. Ewen would do well in France, as an artist, for example. But I cannot marry him. He does not realize, but I do.

. . . .

Who is our enemy? Someone who loves Ewen and is jealous of me? Someone who wants me and is jealous of him? Or a religious fanatic, caught over from those scenes of horror a quarter of a century ago. . . . I wonder.

. . . .

Our unknown enemy incited some of the fanatics to put a torch to the parsonage. Word was brought to me. I was sure Ewen would escape. But again our enemy forestalled us.

The creature came upon Ewen while he was at his desk, preparing the sermon for to-morrow, and struck him across the head. So it is gossiped in the village. And then, with the parsonage set afire and burnt to the ground — Oh, my love . . . my love. . . .

Catherine and I sat silent, considering what we had learned.

"Does it help at all?" I asked.

"I hate her," said Catherine. "It was her fault. If she hadn't done that to Ewen Morgan in the first place, there would have been no enemies, no envious admiring men who might turn dangerous, no gossiping, eager women. . . . I hate her!"

I told myself that I agreed with Catherine, but some part of Moyna's conduct seemed understandable. I found myself hating her less. "What else?" asked Catherine. "Very little that is pertinent in this roll. No. Stay! Here are two, some months later. In the winter."

Will God forgive me? Does it atone for Ewen's death if the Branshaw money cures Ewen Morgan's young brother? The boy shall stay in that sanatorium side by side with my little Marc, until both are cured. Does this atone, Oh Devilish God?

. . . .

Curious reversion to tragic days! Rumors

abroad that young Abbie Hinchley saw the person who struck Ewen down, and that she is frightened and will not talk. She believes if she does a Gytrash will eat her up. Bitter irony, that a fright created by me should thwart me now in finding that monster who made my love suffer so —

Catherine took up the roll in her hands and spread it so that the edges would not curl so badly. A frown ruffled her smooth, broad forehead.

"No proof there, but something in one of these pages, I think, that fits her previous remarks. It was written the summer before she died. What do you think of it?"

I am troubled by suspicions of a familiar face — Something in the manner, the shifting eyes, a hint now and then, a ludicrous imitation of the Ewen Morgan who is gone so long ago. I do not trust that one, nor ever did in Ewen's day. I should, but I do not. . . . Padric shall know of it. I must write him soon.

"But who is this 'Padric'?" asked Catherine, puzzled.

I did not answer, not knowing how much of his story my Marc wished her to know.

"Well, well, no matter," she said impatiently. "Read more."

I cleared my throat, tried to keep all emotion

out, and so read the rest of the scribbled page:

Once more I shall play my little game. A choice collection of silly victims: a jealous woman or two, jealous or imitative men who were, perhaps, the butt of ridicule in the old days. One of them tried to murder Ewen long ago. One of them spread our silly lies about Gytrashes and made them worse until the fire came. If this one I now suspect is innocent, then why the mask? And such a mask! Preposterous. Ah! But if guilty! I shall intimate that I have guessed his ugly secret. Dangerous, intoxicating game! If I cannot have that which I surrendered long ago, then I shall make a few others suffer, too. . . .

Catherine tapped the paper on her chair. At the same time, Dilys opened the door and peered in to catch my eye. Catherine paid no attention to her. She was thinking over the lines she had heard, and said to me finally:

"I see the pattern. The how and the why. That stupid woman! She deserved her fate. But no matter. The guilty must be punished. . . . What is it, Dilys? You are interrupting, I think."

"Miss Anne, there's someone below to see you, asking after Mister Marc. Would you be so kind as to speak with her?"

"Who is it?"" asked Catherine so quickly I was startled.

"Lady from London, mum. The one with all

the frills. She says Reverend and Missus is picking herbs for Mister Marc's bedchamber and will be by presently. Miss Keegan too, and other villagers, maybe. That means tea for a large party, mum." This she addressed to me. "And Mister Marc will be that cross, you may well think!"

Catherine made a swift, harsh gesture that surprised both Dilys and me.

"Don't let anyone come up. You hear me! Not anyone!"

I said, "Naturally not," and went out with Dilys to take care of this new problem. This was one more distinction between the satisfying indifference of a large city like London, and the hospitable, neighborly nuisance of the countryside. I was ashamed of my resentment, but there it was. I was exceedingly anxious to participate in any of the discoveries Catherine would make in the voluminous pages which she was about to unravel.

In order to brace up Cook, who had doctored her concern for Marc by the application of large quantities of spirits, I went down to the kitchen first, and helped Dilys prepare a tea tray. By the time I reached the drawing room, I could see that I need not have hurried. Mrs. Fothergay was examining every item of decoration that she could lay hands to, judging the quality, the worth and, I daresay, what it would have meant to her if she had succeeded in capturing its owner as the next Mr. Fothergay.

"My dear Anne, how very odd to see you here, but so handy. I always say, we must sacrifice ourselves to busy tongues if we are to do the necessary work. How is the dear boy, by the way? Has he asked for me?"

She ran a gloved finger over the mantel, studied the dust on the tip of the pink forefinger and sighed. I could not feel that I was responsible for the dust in a bachelor's house, but from her sidelong glance at me, it was evident she so regarded me.

"He is much better, I believe. Just badly shaken, and with some rather painful burns," I explained. "May I help you to tea?"

"Tea? At this hour? It is scarcely breakfast time. Still, I daresay the dear boy would want me to behave as though nothing had happened. Chin up, you know. The MacDonnachies will be along presently. Dear me. The tea is weak. I must say, this house certainly needs a mistress."

I was relieved to see the graying head of Mrs. MacDonnachie pop up under the drawing room windows, as she waved a streaming bonnet and a brave but pathetic little bundle of weeds at us, and then came around to the door to be let in.

"Do have them prepared, dear Miss Anne, in boiling water. Just on the boil, mind. Not a tisane. Dear, no. Ah, there, Cadmon. Have you had any success? Let me have yours too."

The Reverend MacDonnachie, puffing from his exertions, arrived from another quarter of the fields, rolling his eyes heavenward at the whole idea of herbs, and presented me with his handful. I thanked them both and took the dejected objects into the kitchen, where I consoled Dilys with the news that she might toss them out as soon as the guests were gone.

We were just entering the drawing room from the reception hall when a sound from upstairs, slight but nerveracking, caused us to pause and glance at each other uneasily.

"What a curious sound! Like a — a gasp!" whispered Mrs. MacDonnachie, looking up the stairs wonderingly.

Her husband, who was not in the best of moods, said, "If it were a gasp, especially a human one, you would not be likely to hear it this far away, m'love. More like an outcry of surprise, I should have said."

I was thinking of Marc, and the possibility that he had come out into the hall and perhaps been taken by one of those attacks the doctor had warned me of, so I was already on the stairs, hurrying up to find out what had happened. At the head of the stairs I stopped, shaken by the illusion I saw at the further end of the upper hall which was wreathed in mingled shadows and light from the open door of Moyna's room.

Standing in the doorway of that room, and facing me the length of the hall was the Devil-Vicar. The apparition was separated from me only by the weird, shifting pattern of the sunlight and shade which seemed to veer backward and forward in pendulum fashion as I stared at him. I saw the dark robes, the lustrous black hair, the same terrible, melancholy eyes looking enormous against the gray pallor of his face. A shaft of sunlight crossed his figure and the dreadful illusion was shattered, but not the panic that had been instilled by it.

The black habit that had misled me was nothing more than a dark dressing robe, whose hem just escaped the floor and blended into the shadows behind Marc, to produce that startling image. Wordless, he held out his arms to me. How far distant he was! I went to him, trembling with the foreknowledge that something was terribly wrong. The journey of a few seconds seemed forever, through twisting light and dark, elongated shade, piercing sunlit pools, and always ahead of me that one lengthening shadow swaying like a pendulum across Marc's face.

When I reached his outstretched arms, he drew me to him. He put his hands in my hair, taking handfuls and crushing the strands between his fingers as he began to kiss me. I was torn by stark, unreasoning terror, for I knew instinctively there was a purpose — perhaps mad, but logical — in this. His fingers were cold as marble but his pale lips had a peculiar, disturbing warmth. He kissed me on the lips and the cheek and the brow, and then I heard his almost incoherent voice at my ear, trying to lull my brain with his tender persuasiveness.

"I — came to look for you. That is all. And then I saw it. Let them think what they will. . . .

It's a lie. . . . You know it's a lie, don't you, darling?"

"I know," I repeated obediently, trying to conceal the strain of fear for him that obsessed me. "What has happened?"

The pendulum shadow came between us when I stared up at his white face, and I became aware for the first time that the shadow had cut off part of the light from Moyna's bedchamber. Almost afraid to look, I gazed slowly into the room behind me. The shadow began with the length of rope fashioned in a noose, slung over a crossbeam, and from that noose a body hung, twisting slowly, the carefully coifed brown hair tangled and loose as a harridan's, the hands clawed, the feet helpless, dragging. One shoe had come off. The foot, in its white cotton stocking, barely touched the floor.

I could not bear to look at the face.

But I recognized Catherine Owen's sturdy, pitiful, slightly bundled body. The sight of it obliterated every thought in my mind except the all-pervasive one:

Marc must be gotten away before the others found him here. I could not even ask him why he had done it. I must pretend to believe him.

But why poor Catherine?

Thinking this in despair, I made a slight movement in his arms, hoping to make him aware of his peril, but his grip tightened upon me, and I knew he thought I was about to desert him.

Our senses were assaulted by the chilling

shriek of Mrs. Fothergay, who had come up behind me and stood staring, with her mouth open.

The Vicar, hard on her heels, took one look at the hanging figure, then had the presence of mind to rush past us into the room, saying, "I may not be too late. Help me, someone."

But it was too late. I looked for the first time at the head, twisted cruelly to one side by the knotted rope, and the face. . . .

It was too late.

XIX

Mrs. MacDonnachie and Bedelia Fothergay stood in the drawing room, drinking fresh-brewed tea and exchanging hushed and horrified whispers which were interrupted guiltily when I came into the room. "Have they taken her away?" Mrs. Fothergay asked. "Dear me! What an appalling misfortune! And in his own house, too. I wonder where he found the rope so quickly. But I suppose murderers have such things secreted for . . . later use."

Mrs. MacDonnachie patted me furtively on the sleeve.

"Did you insist that he — lie down? Whatever happens, he must be himself, so that he may answer the charges. It will be hours before anyone reaches the Hall. The rest will do him good." She nodded complacently at Mrs. Fothergay. "He was not himself, you see. It is not a — what you call capital offense unless it can be proved that he knew what he was about."

"Small difference," put in Mrs. Fothergay in her irritatingly shrill voice. "He always hated the poor child. Never could see why, myself. Heavens! What a fate I escaped!"

At this, even Mrs. MacDonnachie's innocent features twisted a little and she gave me a side-glance. I did not care, either for the misplaced advice of the Vicar's wife, or the nasty and absurd comments of Bedelia Fothergay. For the past hour I had been desperately considering every alternative. Somehow, he must be gotten away, if the charge was to be murder. If, however, it could be proved that he was mad, then there would be some hope. I knew very little about these things, but I knew my Marc would come to himself one day, in the light and loving care, and that could only be accomplished if he were not tried as a sane man.

The Vicar had taken care of Catherine's body, a horror that haunted us women. I had only to see that Marc went back to his bedchamber, and then leave one of the servants on guard in the hall, to let us know if he stirred from his room.

About noon, Mrs. Fothergay remembered that she had not dined yet, and proceeded to walk back to the village in the company of the house-keeper, who promised to guide her clear of all bogs and unsafe moorland. As she left the Hall, she passed the Reverend MacDonnachie coming back. His huge figure burst into the drawing room like a wind from the moorland. All his red beard and his hair stood on end.

"What a business! Can't find her brother. He's over in Teignford buying new boots, I understand. Poor creature. Well, she'll rest in St. Anthony's, of course. I've old Jonas Weir, the sexton, an excellent cabinet maker, busy at the coffin."

"Don't, my love," his wife murmured. "It makes it all seem so — real."

The Vicar glanced up at the ceiling and, by intimation, at the floor above.

"It is real, m'dear. And it poses a very pretty problem. Are we to surrender that young man as a common murderer?"

"But — what else is possible?" she murmured plaintively, eager to be persuaded.

I thought I caught an edge of hope in his voice.

"Have you some idea, sir?"

"Several, m'dear." He sat down, puffing, and opened his frock coat and waistcoat. He considered his boots for a few moments while we stared at him. I was aware that my heart had nearly stopped beating as I waited for that one small word of hope from him.

"Miss Anne, tell me exactly. What did Marc say to you when he agreed to go back to bed? He would say nothing to me beyond drinking that foul draught I poured him. The merest hint of laudanum. Great specific, you know. But he ignored me as though I were a spectre he could look through. Damned near dropped the glass between my hands."

I remembered Marc's silence as we left that hall upstairs and went into his room. He had said then, "I'm so tired, I can't think clearly. There is an answer. It's obvious, and yet I'm too tired to see it." Then, as I put his hands to my lips to indicate to him that he was not alone in this horror, he took me by the shoulders and studied my face. With a dear, gentle expression in his eyes, he gazed at me. "I trust you with my life, Anne. More than my life — my sanity."

When the drug finally overcame him and he lay down, I ran my fingers quickly over the robe he had flung across the foot of the bed, but I found no scraps of paper from Moyna's journals, nor had there been any remaining in Moyna's room. What could he have done with them in so short a time?

When he spoke to me of sanity, I was sure this indicated his knowledge of his own condition. It would make it easier to persuade him to any course I suggested. But I did not want the Vicar to know he had admitted anything.

"He said nothing, sir," I replied to the Vicar now. "Just that he was tired."

"I should rather think so," the Vicar muttered. "He'd had a strenuous half hour, I should say."

"Cadmon!" cried his wife, putting her handkerchief to her mouth.

He ignored his wife's interjection but after a glance at my face, rigid with sick horror, he apologized.

"Beg pardon, ma'am. Didn't mean any offense. But to get back to our problem . . . I have several theories. Number one. I do not believe, for a minute, that a young man named Marc Branshaw murdered that poor girl and those others, in cold blood, for the pure pleasure of it. Let us suppose he is, as I have often suspected, our old friend, the Devil-Vicar."

"My dear, you must be joking," his wife exclaimed. "Young Reverend Morgan died years and years ago."

"Hmph. That remains to be seen. How he escaped from the fire is no concern of mine. He was injured in that fire, I don't doubt. Let us say he received a brain injury. That makes easier what I have in mind. He returned last year when Moyna died. Last straw, don't you see? Final blow from these fiends in Maidenmoor. He has systematically murdered all those closely connected with the fire. Abbie, the girl who saw him lying in that house and did not call for help. Old Grimlett who started the fire . . ."

"But poor Catherine was not even in Maidenmoor in those days, love."

"True. But Catherine found out his identity. She came over this morning to taunt him with, let us say, something he betrayed in the fire last night. She had to die. Mad, utterly mad. And they don't hang mad men. They lock them up. He is saved."

It was so near the truth that it terrified me. If it would save Marc's life, I might consent that it should be known. But if it would not! The risk was too great.

"What do you say, Miss Anne? Shall we try for a confession from him that he is actually the Devil-Vicar? It may well save his life."

"How would you go about it?" I asked.

The Vicar shrugged his great shoulders. "I have one or two ideas. Been playing with them all morning."

"One might search him for scars from that other fire," Mrs. MacDonnachie murmured, and then turned pink with embarrassment. "That is, you might, dear."

"Crude. Very crude," snorted the Vicar. "We must make him admit his identity. A trick. I might reveal to him certain information that he would use as the Devil-Vicar, for example — information that would make him want to tear my throat out. He would reveal himself transparently."

"No, please," I put in quickly. "Nothing that will excite him. The doctor said no excitement."

"Just a few questions, nothing too alarming. I might pretend to have been one of his old enemies back in the days when he was Ewen Morgan and I was his curate. My love, think back. It must be someone with whom he was acquainted sixteen years ago, someone who might have wished him ill. I shall claim that man's complaints are mine. We'll see what sparks we draw."

Mrs. MacDonnachie wriggled in her chair and then leaned forward triumphantly.

"He had another curate before you — the one

who held the office while I was still in Maiden-moor. Of course, you came just before I left for Scarborough that September. But there had been some nasty, jealous remarks involving the other curate."

"Yes, yes. But of what sort? What type? It must be someone whose crime and omissions he might conceivably lay to me. We are not dealing with a fool, you know."

"There was the other curate, dear, a friendly little creature with a snub nose."

"Now, do I look like a little man with a snub nose?"

"No, dear. How careless of me! But dear Marc, I mean — if he truly is the Reverend Morgan, might be confused enough to put that curate's delinquencies at your door. I know, while I was in Scarborough with my family that autumn, Lottie Sandbower wrote that it was absurd to see some of the villagers trying to do things as the Reverend Morgan did them. One of them a pink-haired silly creature, she said, tried to kiss Moyna Branshaw, hoping to make her forget the young vicar. I suspect he was frightfully jealous of the Reverend Morgan. But Cadmon, I don't think . . . After all, Lottie told me so little about that pink-haired creature. Who was he?"

I thought of Moyna's journal. She had feared the same person Mrs. MacDonnachie described. Was that person still in the village, and had Moyna been killed because she guessed the identity?

Meanwhile, the Reverend MacDonnachie happily schemed to enact his part.

"Just the man! Yes. Kissing Moyna. Of course. Any other peculiarities about this fellow?"

"Well, there was an unpleasantness at Communion about someone, Lottie said. The poor fellow was so clumsy the Reverend Morgan called him an ass before the entire church. Some unkind folk laughed, I understand. But then, dear Reverend Morgan was very cross that day. Lottie says he was preaching on" — she lowered her gentle voice — "sacred and profane love."

Her husband smiled. "Remarkably apt theme. And as for the 'ass,' my name lends itself to 'donkey' rather neatly. Let's see what we can make of that. But about the sacred and profane love —"

"It was a request from certain members of the congregation. You see, a movement was on foot to expel him, and they hoped to use this sermon as evidence, Miss Wicklow. But you remember, Cadmon."

"And did they use the sermon as evidence?" I asked.

"Dear me, no. He preached that to prevent adultery and profane love one must provide love, respect and understanding in a marriage. There was not a dry eye in the church that day — among the ladies present."

"I can vouch for that," said the Vicar.

The whole conversation was confusing to me. I hardly knew what he was talking about and

333

even less what his object was, but it disturbed me that he should settle on that pink-haired man, whose jealousy and eager imitation of Ewen Morgan had been noted even by Moyna Branshaw in her journal. She had thought him dangerous.

"I don't think I follow your reasoning. I wish you wouldn't play tricks on Marc. He's far from well."

"You will admit, Miss Anne, it's better that we find a plausible insanity in him than find him well and healthy. As Marc Branshaw he is in far greater danger of the rope than as Ewen Morgan, badly injured and obviously unbalanced. What do you say?"

"I — I don't want to be present."

He raised his hands at my idiocy.

"But then, where are our witnesses? Of course, you must be present. Out of sight, if you will. We might —"

Dilys called to me from the staircase and hurried on into the drawing room.

"Mister Marc sent me, mum. Sir." She curtseyed to each of us in turn. "He says he's a right to be heard. He's that set upon coming down!" She looked indignantly at us. There was no doubt in her mind of Marc's innocence. I blessed her for her confidence in him.

"Quick!" The Reverend MacDonnachie pushed me to the archway separating the drawing room from the darkened and long unused dining parlor. "You can see from here, and I'll maneuver him so that he can't see you. You too, m'love. Must seem to be speaking to him alone." He rubbed his hands together and said with great self-satisfaction. "We'll save that boy yet."

I did not like it. I was pushed and pulled this way and that, tormented by my fears. I thought of Marc coming to this inquisition, this shoddy pretense which might throw him clear off his head so that even he might suppose he was the Devil-Vicar. Now I wished I had been more vigorous in my refusal to permit this scene.

I heard Marc's light, swift footstep on the main staircase, and my heart thundered in my breast as I prayed for him. Then he came into the drawing room — I was tremendously proud of him. He had dressed and looked almost his old self — a trifle pale, perhaps, but self-possessed and calm.

"Before you say anything," the Vicar began, "let me assure you that you are with a friend. An old friend, I might add." Nonetheless, in spite of his seeming confidence, I saw him raise one of the teacups to his lips, then put it down shakily.

Marc raised an eyebrow. "Old friend? I don't think I follow you. How long is it since I returned from France?"

"Well, my lad . . . Pardon. I persist in calling you that when, God knows, I have been aware of your true age for sixteen years."

Marc retained his cool indifference before this odd beginning. He remained standing in one place, however, almost as though turned to stone.

"You're being cryptic for some reason, I suppose."

"As between fellow delvers in the same soil — sacred soil, that is — don't you think you had better rely upon that identity and save your life?"

"I don't know what you're talking about."

The Vicar heaved a great sigh. I could not help thinking "bravo" to Marc for standing firm.

"My dear Reverend Morgan —"

"What did you call me? You must be mad. He died sixteen years ago."

The Vicar took a turn about the room, passing close to us, and giving us a faint nod of confidence as he did so.

"He'll manage, dear," whispered his wife to me. "He's very clever, Cadmon is."

"No, my dear Ewen Morgan," the Vicar was saying, "he did not die sixteen years ago, though I thought so until the late Abbie Hinchley recognized me and asked me for money. Imagine! Asked a vicar for money! A good fright served her much better."

Mrs. MacDonnachie pinched me. "That was a clever remark. I told you Cadmon would do it."

Marc walked to the leaded windows and stared out over the green expanse of the moors. His back was to us and I wondered what he was thinking.

"Then it would be you who are the murderer, not this Ewen Morgan, even if I were he."

"Between ourselves," agreed the Vicar jovially, as one will agree to anything to humor a madman, "your deduction may be correct."

The Vicar, however, was a trifle upset by Marc's lack of response to his careful statements, and he ventured after a few moments of silence, "I'm afraid you must prepare yourself for the worst, my friend. Miss Anne had the doctor to see you. . . ."

It got its reaction from Marc, who swung about and faced him, blazing angry.

"That," he said deliberately, "is a stupid lie. Anne would be the last person to betray me to a prying doctor."

I winced at this dagger thrust, for I had betrayed him.

But it was too late, in any case. Perhaps the belief that he was the Devil-Vicar, insane and avenging, would save Marc. That was my only hope.

The Vicar shrugged.

"As you choose, sir, but I should think even your addled wits would tell you that you will do better in a court of law as yourself — since your identity is bound to come out — than as a creature who no longer exists. And he doesn't exist, you know. Marc Branshaw died two years ago, in a sanatorium in France."

The Vicar's wife and I gazed at each other in amazement — I at his discovery, she at the cleverness of her husband.

"Oh, yes," the Vicar went on. "I checked that, as soon as I saw the miniature of you that Moyna carried."

Marc stared at him, reaching absently for the back of a chair, to give him support as these facts came gradually and terribly to his consciousness.

"Who are you? Or rather — who were you, in the old days?" Marc's hand brushed against the teacup the Vicar had relinquished, and we heard the faint crack of his knuckles upon the china.

"Answer me!"

His command made the Vicar's wife shudder. She clutched me in her terror, but I was more concerned for Marc than for any possible danger to her husband.

"Dear boy, have you no recollection of that 'clumsy ass' your old curate, with the pink hair? Remember the Communion when you said poor oafish MacDonnachie should be called 'Mac-Donkey'? How that stung, dear boy! How that stung and festered, when I'd been prepared to like and admire and copy you, learn to be a gentleman, like you."

Marc slapped the back of the chair with his open palm. His eyes were burning.

"I knew you had been a curate but I never placed you. You must have been thin. And that beard of yours. You wore no beard then. . . . That is the mask Moyna was seeking."

Desperately, I saw that the Vicar was leading him to the very edge of insanity by confusing him so that what Moyna had confided to Marc of her suspicions now must surely make him believe he truly was Ewen Morgan.

The Vicar paused, no doubt to think up more

frightening fables. "Precisely. Thought you'd guess. I've put on weight, physical and spiritual. I learned from you after all, even acceded to your dignities. But then, you were really too young for them, weren't you?"

I could not help wondering at the fabulous talent the vicar had for improvising.

He went on, obviously proud of his gift. "Used a few of your tricks with the ladies. . . . Always admired you frightfully, old chap. You should not have used me so contemptuously, for I could have been your veritable slave."

Marc made a face of revulsion and bowed his head, studying the grain of the table and thinking, I've no doubt, of those days of his brother's life which the Vicar brought back to him now in all their pain and culminating horror. He reached for the cold tea and drank it down absently, not looking at the vicar.

I prayed that this charade would end soon, so that I might be of some comfort to Marc. He raised his head finally and stared at the Vicar, who was scratching his red beard and apparently reflecting that he might have gone too far in his make-believe.

"If you are the one responsible for those lies and other horrors, then was it you who incited them to that talk of my — of my being a devil and my habitat fit only for burning?"

"Dear boy, you know that was begun by you and Moyna. Remember? I merely helped it along. Moyna would have none of me. . . . Exquisite creature she was. I've never forgotten her, you know. Even years later, when she began to be puzzled about me, to make foolish hints, I remembered the hold her beauty had upon me."

Mrs. MacDonnachie clutched my arm, but gave me a watery, sad smile, as she whispered, "He is so clever, Cadmon is. But I wish he couldn't talk about Moyna. There were so few men she could not have had for the taking."

Marc was beginning to add up these terrible disclosures now. I saw that all hope of his remaining calm was gone. I saw the mounting fury, the dark color coming into his face as he challenged the Vicar:

"And she recognized you, so you killed her. Then you had to kill Abbie because — because —"

"Tiresome girl, Abbie," said the Vicar, after too long a pause. He had plainly not expected to play a mass-murderer. He began to invent rapidly, almost, I suspected, as though he enjoyed his role. "She was no longer afraid of me. When you returned and she fell in love with you, she told me it was over. She was going to confess to you what she knew about the burning. Well, my dear boy, what could I do? It was Will Grimlett and Moyna all over."

"Three murders!" Marc exclaimed. "And all carefully planned to be put at my door. All that Devil-Vicar cape and robe nonsense, everything so that it would appear I had committed them."

More for our benefit than Marc's, the Vicar remarked smugly, "Deucedly clever, don't you think? Of course, I always wanted to be Ewen Morgan, anyway."

Marc leaned across the table. He was in a killing rage.

"But one more . . . You've forgotten to describe that. One more you must tell me about."

He had taken the Vicar unawares. His invention flagged and he turned away from Marc, glancing in our direction, though he could not see us. I wondered if he were looking for help. Marc seemed about to spring at him.

"Ewen Morgan's murder! You haven't described how you crept up to him in the parsonage that day and struck him. . . ." Marc rubbed the back of his neck, where the fresh burns must still have been tormenting him. "You haven't described what it must have been like for you to know he was lying in that room — perhaps dead, perhaps not —" He moved forward and the Vicar backed away almost involuntarily, his small, jovial eyes wide with fear at what he had unleashed.

"Don't be a fool, Morgan. I was only play-acting for your sake! Don't —"

"Do you know what it is to die like that?" cried Marc.

This must have been how Marc looked, I thought, when he killed Catherine and the others — this terrible, dark-eyed fury, these passionate lips I remembered so well, twisted with pain and hate.

"Let me tell you, my dear, good Vicar — if that's what you are, and not a demon out of hell! I know what it is to be conscious and in a fire. I know what it is to find myself burning to death! I stank of the odor of burning flesh. My own flesh! I struggled. How long I struggled under that debris! I prayed for death to release me, but it would not come. Not even unconsciousness, for the agony was too unbearable. I was to endure it all, to be witness to the final consumption of my own body!"

It was done. I was sick with pain for him. He had begun to confuse his brother's death with his own sufferings in the sanatorium fire two years ago.

Marc's fingers curled into his palms uncontrollably as he reached for the Vicar, who barely eluded him. "You filthy, unnatural beast! I'll kill you! *This time I will kill you!*"

As I rushed into the room to stop him, he turned, hearing my footsteps. His face went suddenly white and he whispered:

"Anne — don't let . . ." He wavered. I saw that he was very near to collapse. As both the Vicar and I reached out to ease his fall, I saw his eyes close, and he dropped to the floor unconscious.

We knelt beside him, I frantically putting my hand to his face, pushing away a strand of black hair to find his forehead cold with icy sweat. The Vicar had put his hand inside Marc's jacket and upon his heart.

"Oh, Cadmon, what have we done?" his wife

murmured tearfully, standing over us.

"Hush!" said her husband. "Get me some brandy. Good God! I didn't know he was so ill."

I was rubbing his cold hands frantically. "What is wrong with him?" I asked, not taking my eyes off Marc's chill white face.

"Must be a heart attack," said the Vicar. "My fault. I take responsibility for it. I'm to blame. But I didn't know there was any question of a bad heart. Where is that dratted woman with the brandy?"

Mrs. MacDonnachie returned almost at once with a decanter.

"Cadmon, dear," she ventured as her husband tried to force a few drops between Marc's colorless lips, "he nearly killed you."

I closed my eyes, thanking God that at least Marc had been spared that crime.

Mrs. MacDonnachie was standing over us, staring at Marc.

"My dear, are you sure he isn't —"

The Vicar said, "Be still, woman!" and felt Marc's heart again. He waited too long to withdraw his hand. I raised my eyes to his across Marc's body.

"Well?"

The Vicar touched my hand — a gentle, brushing stroke for such a huge hand, and it spoke plainer than words.

"He's gone."

I was numbed. I didn't feel the least surprise. I went on rubbing Marc's hands absently, one at a time, between my own fingers.

After awhile, someone came behind me and lifted me up, and I went obediently where I was taken.

"She didn't sleep all night," said Dilys' voice.

I said, "Don't let them do anything to him until the doctor has been and gone. We must be sure."

"Later," said the Vicar's comforting voice. "First, drink this good, strong tea."

"There are so many things to do. To take care of."

"Drink, ma'am," said Dilys. "This will take care of all of them."

Dilys got me into bed and I looked around curiously. It was a lovely, happy room. I couldn't ever remember one that was more beautiful — all white, even the crossbeams. But the tea had made me dizzy, for I fancied the knob on one of the bedposts was set on crooked, and it bothered me.

There were things I had to do, but I wasn't sure what they were. It was all confused.

Presently I slept.

XX

During the late afternoon I awoke to see the Vicar praying at the foot of my bed. He looked up at me as I moved. His odd pose confused me momentarily. I was not used to seeing him at his more Christian duties. He looked tense and strained as he attempted to soothe me.

"There, there. Don't be alarmed. You shall rest again after I've gone. But — we must work quickly."

"I don't understand. Quickly about what?" I asked, still vague.

"Sir Gareth has returned, my child."

This meant nothing to me beyond a certain shared sympathy with him in his grief at the loss of his sister.

"I am sorry for him," I said. "He loved her very much."

"Yes, my child. Unfortunately."

I began to sense the root of his tension.

"Why? What has he done?"

"Can you not guess?" asked the Reverend MacDonnachie sadly. "Whom has he always blamed for his sister's sufferings? And now, his passion for revenge can burn itself out only on the body of that poor devil who —"

I sat up in bed, trembling.

"You can't mean that! Sir Gareth is a civilized man. He cannot hate the dead."

"Dear Miss Anne, surely you know that men under strong passion of love or hate are not civilized. Already, he is stirring up the same violent feelings that caused the near-tragedy sixteen years ago. He will not allow Marc to be buried in consecrated ground. He talks madly of burning Marc's body. . . ."

"No, no," I cried. "Marc always hated fire!"

He nodded.

"It depends upon time, my dear, and upon you. If we act quickly, he is saved from — whatever they intend."

"Upon me? What must I do?"

He took a paper from under his coat and offered it to me.

"It was all I could think of. It will serve, providing the work is done quickly tonight."

I could not focus my eyes upon it for a moment. Then I understood:

It is by my wish and with my approval that my beloved affianced, known to me as Marc Branshaw, should be buried without ceremony and for the public good, at once, upon this night. I sign this, in my bitter despair, to attest that what is done and has been done by the Vicar and sexton of this church is done by the order of the unhappy, Anne Wicklow.

Why must he make it so unbearably hurting, to pour out my feelings in this way, upon a public document: "unhappy Anne," "bitter despair". . . almost the words of a suicidal mind. Perhaps they were true descriptions of my present state of unhappiness, but certainly I was not suicidal, nor ever had been. To read my unhappiness paraded in a legal document was almost more than could be borne.

"No!" I cried. "Not so soon." The pain struck me with sudden, poignant force. . . . "I shall never see him again. Never."

"Dear child," the Reverend MacDonnachie murmured, "It is over. You must make up your mind to that, and look about you for a new life. Dr. Lowther has come and gone. It's upon his recommendation I am acting. He suggests that with all this tension building up in the village, by morning we may not be able to perform the burial."

The thought of the desecration of Marc's body, with the weapon which he had always dreaded, was enough to make me yield. The Vicar reached for his pen and offered it to me. Fumbling with it, trailing ink over the paper, I signed my name. I felt too weak to do more, and he took the pen and paper from me, placed his hand tenderly on my head, and I sank back upon the pillows, closing my eyes to this last horror, that Marc could not even be decently buried. He must go to his grave still as the murderous Devil-Vicar.

"God keep you safe," the Vicar said, and presently I heard the door close behind him and I was alone again.

I turned my face away from the door and began to weep.

Lengthening shadows of afternoon dissolved into the gray twilight of the North Country. Outside the windows I could see the long, endless march of the moors. They had won. By tomorrow their green tendrils would have captured Marc, just as I feared all along that they would.

Presently, small, twinkling lights appeared here and there in the distant farms, and I thought of those people I had come to know, yet whose secret hearts I had apparently not fathomed. At this moment they were planning the desecration of the body of a dead man. I lay in Moyna's bed and contemplated the village lights. I was beginning to react from the numbness of the afternoon, and the daze of what must have been a drug in the tea I drank. Now, the pain came and it made me want to scream at my loss, and at Marc's sufferings, which had all come to nothing but death.

I had known him such a sort time, I could not understand why his loss was like the loss of half my life. But so it was.

The room was quite dark when I heard the latch of the door move, and Dilys came in with a tray on which were the tea things as well as fresh-baked parkin and a pink china oil lamp.

"I've orders, mum. You're to eat and drink. You do look dreadful and no mistake. Please. Mum, don't be so unhappy. Reverend says he fears for your life. But you ain't that kind, to take your life, now are you, mum? You take that nasty laudanum indeed! What rubbishy nonsense he talked!"

She was talking rubbish herself and I didn't understand her in the least, especially about the laudanum. Why should I take laudanum? Pain is something that must be borne, not blotted out falsely by such methods. What would my mother and father have thought of me in such a state to join them?

"Is there any word from the village, about the violence, I mean?"

Dilys shivered. "Fair gives me the bumps to think of it the way the Reverend tells it. How could they touch poor dear Mister Marc? Like housekeeper and I says when the Reverend asks us for a shroud. Housekeeper made up one from Mister Marc's best sheets. But she couldn't bear to touch poor young sir. No more could I, so the Vicar alone put him into the shroud."

I cringed from hearing the details, but I could not protest. It seemed to me that if I spoke I should cry out, for the pain and anguish in my throat were suffocating me.

She sighed and went out again, leaving the tray.

The Branshaw dogs began to bark, first in the distance, then closer to the house, and I remembered the old superstition that they barked at a death. In my mind's eye I saw Marc lying in his makeshift coffin, with no one by him, no one to care for him. I had to be with him in that hour.

To take my mind off the terrors of the night, and to give me strength — for I intended to be present when Marc was buried — I reached for the tea and poured some into the cup. It was exceedingly bitter. I was about to take another sip when the door opened again, with so much caution my heart beat fast and I was half prepared for some new horror.

It was Mrs. Fothergay, wearing appropriate black, with some astonishing red frills. She came in and sat on the foot of Moyna's bed.

"Dear Anne, what a ghastly time you've had of it! But you mustn't think about it any more."

She made me so nervous, especially with her gloved hand patting my body under the coverlet, that I sat the teacup down with a clatter and tried to calm myself, to speak civilly.

"He wasn't the monster they thought he was," I said abruptly. "He'd been through so much, and he didn't know that he committed those crimes. I'm sure he didn't know. . . ."

She interrupted me by grating her shoe upon something at the foot of the bed and stooped to retrieve it.

"Dear me! A vial. Perfume?" She put the slim little bottle to her nose and sniffed. "No. Medicine of some kind, I should imagine. My late husband, the dear colonel, used to keep laudanum in a vial like this."

I had the notion that something terribly important had been said — yet my brain was so tired, and my eyes not focussing, so I could not concentrate. I took the vial and examined it. Why would laudanum be found in this room? Dilys had mentioned something about the Vicar's fear that I would take my life. Something about laudanum, but it had all been nonsense. Yet how came this vial to be just where I might have dropped it, if I had taken the poison?

My suspicion was confirmed by Bedelia

Fothergay's dramatic exclamation of horror:

"Dear Anne, don't tell me you've taken the wretched stuff! But you must not. Indeed, you must not. You have your whole life before you. What was that young man? A fraud. A murderer thrice over. And then, think of that poor Owen girl hanging — why — right there from that beam!" We both looked at the beam and then away quickly. "I tell you, I shall never forget it," she went on. "No, he is better dead, Anne. Believe me. Although," she added, "you are going to be stubborn about it. Just like Gareth. Now, tell me, dear, did you take it or not? We shall have to do something at once if —"

"No. I did not," I said quickly. "And I don't know why the Vicar has been going about telling such stories. But he was sitting just where you are now, and if anyone dropped that laudanum, he did!" Then I remembered the most important part of her ramblings. "But you've seen Gareth Owen! Surely, you can persuade him that this terrible business he's stirring up will only make the whole thing more monstrous. It will not bring back Catherine. You must stop him."

She looked at me with blank incomprehension. I felt inclined to slap her carefully powdered face.

"What are you saying, dear Anne? Why should Gareth stir up the people against Marc? He only arrived home from Teignford during the hour. Nettie told him of Catherine's death and gave him Catherine's last note. He's most anxious to talk to you. That's why I am here now — to speak to you on his behalf. But really! Stirring up mobs! That is not Gareth, I assure you."

I struggled to get out of bed, and whether it was that or her words, I was almost too dazed to comprehend these disclosures. Outside the window a dog howled mournfully, which set my teeth on edge, as I tried to banish everything but the essential fact.

"Am I to understand that Gareth Owen has not been in the village all afternoon stirring up people to — to burn Marc?"

Mrs. Fothergay looked as though I had said something utterly mad.

"Good heavens, Anne! Are you quite well?"

"Oh, God! The infamy of it! How wrong we've been, from the first! It was the Devil-Vicar, right enough. But we had the wrong vicar." I was reaching for my shoes when there was a rattle at the door and Sir Gareth came bolting in. He looked red and hot and kept putting his finger into the tight stock around his neck, to relieve the pressure, but he was a blessing to see.

"My dear Miss Anne, you must excuse this inexcusable intrusion. But ma'am, there is my poor little Cathy — foully done to death — over in St. Anthony's, and somewhere her murderer walks at large!" He took my hands and shook them both. "Dear Anne, we suffer our loss together. Can you help me, then, to find her murderer?"

"I think I can," I told him, while Mrs. Fothergay stared at us both. "You don't believe that it was Marc?"

"This note of Catherine's" — he waved a paper before me briskly — "puts that quite out of the question. Read it. And then tell me to whom she refers. I swear I'll have him done to death if it's the last thing I do!"

Hardly daring to believe this disclosure which, while saving Marc's reputation, was too late to save his life, I read the following:

Dearest Garrie:

I know, that Marc Branshaw is not Ewen Morgan. If he had been, he could not have saved my life in that fire last night. But whether he is or is not has nothing to do with the horrors we have witnessed here recently.

Who advised me to use such dangerous methods, which could lead, as last night, to a real fire? Who desired that I should drive Marc out of his mind, even kill him? Let me say, it was my dearest and closest confidant. We were drawn together because he too, or so I thought, had an unrequited love. He had always liked the attentions of women, and whether he loved them or merely, as I suspect, had a passionate and ridiculous desire to be thought of as the Devil-Vicar's successor in every respect, I know Moyna accused him of some crime and was trying to prove it. I did not know that crime was the murder of Ewen Morgan. At the time, I thought Moyna heartless. All my sympathy went to my friend. "This dun-colored beast," she used to call him. When Marc repulsed me and behaved as though he suspected me of the murder of Moyna I was bitter, and wrote my absurd novel. I did not suspect that my reader, my critic and friend, would use the very methods I outlined to kill Will Grimlett and Abbie. He even suggested I let Marc read the book, as my revenge, he said. But I see it was to divide suspicion, for my friend must have followed my book exactly — keeping the dog savage by starvation and cruelty, and then turning it loose upon his victims who were, perhaps, already stunned.

His position, his faithful, if short-sighted wife, his good nature and popularity — everything about my dear friend — made it impossible to suspect him. Until tonight. Shock and near-death stimulate the mind. Moyna Branshaw's journals should give us some sort of proof, for she was the first to penetrate that jovial, warm-hearted mask of his. I believe I know where those journals are.

Well, Garrie, if you arrive home before I return from the Hall this morning, join me there. I think we owe Marc an apology, and the village the truth about the monster it is harboring. Your loving Catherine.

"What does it all mean?" Sir Gareth demanded, as he stalked up and down the bedchamber, his heavy cloak swinging against the bedpost as he walked. "Who is this friend? She has so many. Obviously, he had committed the final atrocity. I must know his name!"

There were so many things that fitted now. The dun-colored creature Jamie had seen on the moor was Moyna's dun-colored beast. Of course, Moyna had to die. Not only had she suspected him long ago when she warned Ewen Morgan of the danger from "that creature who imitates and follows you in everything," but she made the mistake of hinting her suspicions, and of laughing and jeering at him as Ewen Morgan had. "The Reverend MacDonkey" was not a figment of Cadmon MacDonnachie's witty imagination. Ewen Morgan had called him that. And Moyna, that other jeering one, had to die, as Ewen Morgan had died. Our dun-colored beast was very proud in spite of his ridiculous exterior.

Poor Jamie told the truth when he said the dun-colored beast had turned into the Devil-Vicar. How easy to imagine, in the distant night, that a hunking, red-bearded man was a Gytrash, and what more natural than that this man should wear the vestments of the vicar he wished to be like, as well as the vestments of his own position! It served to throw suspicion on Ewen Morgan and, by inference, on the supposed Marc Branshaw.

Catherine's murder, besides being the most horrible, was the most ingenious. I remembered how, too late, that when Mrs. MacDonnachie arrived at the Branshaw door this morning she had looked around and called: "Ah! There you are," indicating that she and her husband had been separated on their search for those absurd herbs to help Marc. I never doubted now that the Vicar used his search for herbs to find and kill Catheerine. Small wonder he was breathless and puff- ing, when he came to join his wife at the front door!

The supreme irony came when the good Cadmon MacDonnachie confessed the ghastly truth in the presence of two witnesses, and yet only Marc Branshaw, his victim, recognized it. The Vicar, knowing Marc's condition, had chosen one sure weapon and had driven Marc to his death deliberately. He had murdered Marc while we looked on.

Why not murder me next, since he must know that sooner or later I would wonder at the intimate knowledge he revealed in his confession to Marc?

I remembered the odd things that had transpired since this afternoon — the talk of my committing suicide, the laudanum vial where the Vicar could so easily have dropped it. Even the bitter tea which he could have dosed when Dilys was busy.

I rang for Dilys. Sir Gareth and Mrs. Fothergay watched me with great puzzlement, the lady interrupting my thoughts several times to inquire if I were quite well. But Sir Gareth's quickly outthrust arm, to silence her, showed that he at least trusted me.

When Dilys came, staring belligerently at Sir Gareth, I explained to her quickly, "Sir Gareth is not an enemy. He is on our side. Now, do you have a particularly vicious dog on the premises?"

"Indeed, mum. There's Bruno. Took a big, nasty bite out of my ankle only last month, he did."

"Well then," I told her, "Take that tea out and tell groom to see that this Bruno drinks it. And — Dilys — !"

She turned with the tray in hand.

"Send someone to fetch Dr. Lowther."

"Dr. Lowther, mum?" Dilys stared at me. "But Dr. Lowther's been tight-bound to Upshed all day, so he has. Typhus real bad there, they do say."

I began to feel that we had not even begun to plumb the dreadful iniquity of the Reverend MacDonnachie.

"He was not here at all?"

"Not this day, mum — not since you sent for him last night and he came and went. Vicar said it weren't necessary, that he'd cared for the dead before this."

"My God, Miss Anne!" exclaimed Sir Gareth. "What are you suggesting?"

"Tell me what the Vicar said about my committing suicide, Dilys."

"He said he'd caught you with a laudanum vial and you'd tried to keep him from seeing it. Then he said he couldn't take it from you, but I was to beware."

I motioned her to go away with the tea tray. I turned to Sir Gareth. I felt the supreme bitterness of my own responsibility in all that had happened. Why should I have let the man's cloth stay my suspicions? I had allowed the Vicar to murder Marc and even abetted him.

"He wanted me to die as well as Marc. I heard his confession today."

"You can't mean it! Not that fat old friendly chap with the beard?" The baronet travelled back in his mind, remembering, I daresay, all the times he had seen his sister and the Vicar with their heads together, talking, planning. . . . There could be no question but that Catherine's "trusted friend and confidant" had been Cadmon MacDonnachie. No wonder she could not believe that the two killed on the moors had died at the hands of a dog deliberately driven savage by starvation and mistreatment. As in her novel, the dog had been but an instrument. To admit so much to herself, would have made Catherine, though without intention, an accessory to the murders.

"But I don't understand," Mrs. Fothergay put in plaintively. "If Marc is dead, why should the Reverend MacDonnachie act in secrecy and in such a hurry?"

I startled the poor woman by the frenzy which her comment aroused in me.

"Dear, dear Mrs. Fothergay — there can be

only one of two reasons. Either Marc did not die of a heart attack, or — *he is not dead!*"

Sir Gareth started forward at my words, but then relaxed.

"That cannot be, Miss Anne. Think: MacDonnachie would be burying the fellow alive. Even the Vicar of Holy Church needs permission for such a burial as he contemplates — someone upon whom the onus of guilt will fall."

"He found one," I said bluntly, as I hastened to get out of bed. "I signed permission. It may not be legal, for I am not Marc's wife, but it could serve the Reverend MacDonnachie if any questions arose. And in that note I also confessed, almost in so many words, that I was unhappy enough to make an end of my own life. Oh, he thought of everything, did the good Vicar."

"But consider," Sir Gareth said. "So long a time has passed. If he were poisoned, then he's done for. If it were a heart attack —"

"You don't understand. The only thing Marc drank, from the time I left him in his room to the time he died, was a small cup of cold tea in the drawing room. That may have contained laudanum. The Vicar placed the cup on the table in such a way, as I see now, where Marc could not miss it. I doubt if such a small dose, and in tea, would kill a man. So, if Marc is only drugged, then we may yet save him. Oh, do hurry, Sir Gareth!"

"Ma'am," he protested, stalking beside me as I ran out into the hall, "you don't even know that it was laudanum. It might have been the heart attack."

"Well then, we shall know. But if Marc is dead, why was the Vicar in so much of a hurry to tell those lies about you and about Marc's quick burial being the doctor's suggestion? He would have nothing to fear, even if Marc had died of laudanum poisoning; the Doctor prescribed that earlier. The Vicar had only to fear discovery that Marc was not *yet* dead."

I dared not believe it, and yet, inside me, I felt an almost frightening lift of spirits. To be so close to saving Marc, surely God would not let him die now. . . .

Mrs. Fothergay, who had taken Sir Gareth's arm, murmured softly, "One must bear in mind that so long a time has passed, we are certain to find him dead. The coffin will have been sealed, the grave covered over."

"Oh, I agree," said the baronet, puffing hard as he hurried after me down the broad main stairs. "It will be impossible to reach the poor devil in time. Buried alive! God, what a fate!"

I was remembering that a coffin had to be made for Catherine, and that country coffins were notoriously simple. A few pegs here and there and the thing was done. My greatest fear was that the coffin had already been overlaid with earth. There was no escape from that.

Sir Gareth's gig and the mare, pawing uneasily at the sound of the dogs howling, waited outside the gate. As we got into the gig, the Branshaw groom ran up to us.

"Mum, Dilys say ye want that dog to be put down. And down he is, mum."

"What?" cried Sir Gareth. "You mean the damned stuff was poisoned after all?"

The groom looked to me. "It was what ye wanted, no?"

"Yes," I said. "It was what I wanted to discover. Is the dog dead yet?"

"Not yet but as good as may be. Painless though. It will just go off into a sleep."

"We've not a minute to lose," shouted Sir Gareth. "Stand away from the mare's head, you there."

I had never thought I should say, "thank God" for that stolid, dependable Gareth Owen, but I said so now.

XXI

In spite of all that I had learned in the last hour, when we entered the village of Maidenmoor, at the top of the long steep curve of Main Street, I was prepared for disturbances among the villagers, and screams for the burning of the Devil-Vicar. I found instead solitude, and the deep, uneasy peace of night in a massive graveyard. All the shutters in town were bolted, as though against a common enemy. Occasionally a lone man — in the heavy black that was almost a uniform of the countryside — strode through the street, his face shadowed by the beak of his cap, the eyes staring downward at his feet.

The ancient stone church of St. Anthony's loomed up in the direct path of moonlight, and I got out of the gig without assistance and ran across the cobblestones to the entrance. The main portals were open. As soon as I entered, I made out one coffin behind the chancel at the far end of the nave, with candles at head and foot.

With Sir Gareth hard behind me, I went down the aisle, hoping against hope that I should see Marc's dear face when the coffin lid was removed. The lid itself had been left ajar. Sir Gareth moved it and we saw his sister's form, not yet in its shroud, but lying there in the candlelight as though she were alive. Only the telltale marks on her throat, and a certain forced set and rigidity about the mouth, told the true story.

Sir Gareth whispered softly:

"She was so when I saw her an hour ago. Almost as if she slept. My poor little Cathie."

I turned away, sick with disappointment and a presentiment of disaster. Could they have buried him so soon?

Sir Gareth saw my terrible dilemma.

"I'll look back of the altar. There's a storeroom. You go by the door in the south wall. They can't escape us both. Give me a hail if you see the grave-diggers or the coffin."

I made my way through the family pews to the south door but it was locked as before. Then I saw the Vicar's office close by. A single candle burned and no one was in the room. Possibly there would be keys in his desk.

I fumbled at the desk, raised the lid and felt for anything I might use to prize open the south door. Suddenly, my glance wavered from the desk to something resting on the floor, beside the desk. It was the marvelous portrait of the Devil-Vicar that had raised such havoc in the village. Across its surface were long, ugly scratches and tears, as if done by a blunted knife. Only the eyes remained as they had been before, terrible in their poignant bitterness.

It was the face of Ewen Morgan but so very like my Marc as well. I touched the portrait gently with one finger, tracing the ugly cuts and rips in the canvas as my other hand sought through the litter of papers on the desk for the keys to the south door.

"What a pity!" said an unctuous voice behind me. "But I do think I have sought inspiration long enough from that portrait, don't you? And now I'm a little tired of it."

I had not been quick enough. I knew before I turned to meet him, that it was Reverend Mac-Donnachie. Even though Gareth was within shouting distance, I felt the fearful revulsion this monster aroused in me, but I managed to speak politely enough.

"Have you stopped trying to be like him, sir? Now that all those who loved him are gone, all those who could testify to his innocence?"

"Dear me, dear me," he said, stepping into the

room. He moved very lightly and fast for a man of his bulk, suddenly rather like a horrid caricature of Marc's light tread. "I take it you did not drink the tea. What a shame. . . . You were ripe for suicide."

"Where is he?" I demanded, speaking loudly, aware that my voice carried in the great hollow confines of the church. "What have you done with him?"

He scratched his beard and shrugged.

"Too late. Just about . . . I should say . . . fifteen minutes too late."

I shuddered and reached behind me for a weapon, anything that might hurt this gross, dun-colored Gytrash.

"He wasn't dead. You knew that." If he would only agree with me, I should know there was, or had been, a little hope. He agreed smugly.

"But he will be by now, I think. There was so little time, my dear, in that drawing room, with you and my saintly Emily watching. Just enough laudanum in the tea cup to keep him quiet while the essentials were attended to. Once he was in the coffin it would make no difference if he came to consciousness. By that time it would just be a matter of . . . waiting. Yes. I think we may assume he is dead by now. I am sorry I had to destroy that portrait. I felt the urge come upon me quite suddenly. My dear" — he moved toward me slowly, putting his pudgy great hands out for my understanding. Upon me his touch had the same repulsive horror as an adder's fangs. I watched the moist little smile on his thick lips. "I am his match at last. I shall prove it — that is," he corrected himself, "I *have* proved it — tonight. That is all I have wanted for sixteen years — to be regarded as he was, to be what the young devil was when I was first assigned to this curacy. How I envied him everything! And how contemptuous he was of me — the clumsy, skinny curate with the pink hair! Well, that's all changed, my dear. It seems I laugh last. But you know about that don't you? I wondered if you guessed today during my catechism of the fascinating Reverend Morgan."

Waiting for Sir Gareth and expecting him momentarily, I watched the Vicar approach me. He had said something that gave me a flicker of hope, his words — "I shall prove that" — and then the curious change of tense: "I *have* proved that — tonight."

Did he mean the thing was not yet done?

"You do not congratulate me, my dear, yet I think I managed that tattling Owen girl rather neatly. I guessed, of course, last night, what she would be up to this morning, and followed her."

"And your wife?"

"Dear Emily, she is the perfect life partner — never asks questions. If I went around the back of the Branshaw house seeking herbs, what could be more natural? Admirable creature, Emily."

He raised his hands. At once I recognized the cruel, flat thumbs which had almost snuffed my life out a few nights ago in this same church.

How could I ever have mistaken them for Marc's hands?

I taunted him with cold fury: "If you strangle me here and now, it would be rather hard to explain, don't you think?"

"Hardly, my child. You will be found to have taken laudanum, poor unhappy wretch that you are. And your body will be artistically arranged upon the grave of your monstrous lover. . . . It is not the first time we have met like this, you know. Remember the night at Moyna's cottage? I always tried to make sure Morgan was there alone before the Devil-Vicar made an appearance. But when you called out 'Who are you?' how relieved I was! I hated to kill you."

"You were not so relieved that night here in the church," I reminded him, imagining I heard Sir Gareth's booted steps out in the nave.

My back arched against the desk to avoid his hands, and my fingers groped for the nearest object. As he reached for me, I swung the object in my hand across his face. It was the candle.

He screamed and his fingers instinctively grabbed handfuls of his beard. I swung the burning candle once more and as the flame leaped at his face I cried, "Where is he? What have you done with him?" He shrieked again, like an animal, and I felt nothing but a violent and savage joy. I was remembering Ewen Morgan and those terrible moments in the burning parsonage.

"Branshaw plot! But you're too late! Give me

that candle, you little fiend!"

This time he was able to snatch the candle from me. It rolled on the floor and I eluded him just as Gareth Owen appeared in the doorway. I ran past Gareth, not looking back. I left the moaning, cursing MacDonnachie to the tender mercies of the baronet. The last thing I heard was the Vicar's indignant scream, "But I'm burned! The witch burned my face. Look at me! No!" And then more screams. I shut my ears to them and hurried to the north gate.

I pushed open the gate and saw the old, wizened sexton and Frederick Niles, with an audience of several silent villagers, all watching the work of the two grave-diggers.

They looked in dismay upon me, with my rumpled dress, my hair blown wild by the night air and by my struggle with the Vicar, and my very odd manner.

"Stop it! He may not be dead. You don't understand!" I cried to them. Even as I ordered them to stop, one of the grave-diggers let drop a heavy clod of earth and I heard it strike, not on the coffin as I had hoped, but on the earth that had gone before. The grave was very shallow, probably because they had been ordered to hurry.

"I told them so. I told them," sobbed a small voice from the darkness beneath Moyna Branshaw's great stone. It was Jamie. He had been huddled there, under the protective and gentle hand of the curate, and at my voice came out in a gingerly way. Recognizing me, he ran to me and buried his face against my bosom. "He ain't dead. Say he ain't dead. Not my Marc — truest friend I ever had."

The young curate said to me gently, "I know your feelings, ma'am, and I appreciate them. But do you think it right to encourage the boy? Dr. Lowther pronounced Mr. Branshaw dead."

I ignored this. "Don't cry, Jamie," I whispered. "They will raise the coffin. They must. I order them to."

The sexton frowned at me, while the grave-diggers halted in their work and rubbed their hands. I could smell the wet, rich earth around us. I shall never smell that odor again without thinking of death.

"Is it Miss Wicklow, ma'am?" asked the sexton. "He's dead, believe me. Dr. Lowther says so."

"How do you know?" I demanded, beginning to lose control of myself in this dreadful moment. As the moonlight appeared suddenly from under a cloud, the great gray statue that hovered near the Branshaw plot began to cast its slanting shade over us. It seemed to me, in my over-wrought state, like the shadow of death waiting to snatch Marc from me. "Did the Vicar tell you Marc was dead? He lied!"

"Reverend said Mr. Marc was dead. Said Mister Marc was to be buried quick-like, so there'd be no trouble. Said you'd ordered it, what's more."

"Stay!" the Reverend Niles put in, startling us all, as he stared at me intently. "What do you mean, Miss Wicklow? I protested the indecent haste of this whole business. Do you mean that Dr. Lowther did not examine Mr. Branshaw? That the permission from him was forged?"

God be thanked for this man, I thought. He took the matter out of my hands.

"Open the coffin," he ordered the grave-diggers. "Do as the lady says."

The varied shadows of the tombstones gathered slowly, marching inexorably upon us, lengthening under the brightness of the moon. Every second added to Marc's peril — if, indeed, it were not too late already.

"Best oblige the Reverend Niles," muttered a rough man in the gathering crowd. Others took up the demand. The grave-diggers thrust me aside and shuffled behind the great Branshaw statue. I stared in stupefaction.

"What is it? I thought the coffin was in the ground."

"No, no," said the Reverend Niles hastily. "Not yet. But even so, we cannot do more than hope. Inside the coffin so long —"

"I know. Open the coffin!"

The grave-diggers dragged a rough hewn coffin into the moonlight. I noticed frantically that the box was not airtight, but revealed space here and there, where the boards joined imperfectly, or between the pegs that had been driven in around the top. I tore at them with my bare fingers, breaking nails, feeling none of the pain, nothing but my desperate hope. Vaguely, I heard the old sexton crying, almost dropping the lamp he carried: "Don't listen to her. She's mad. Vicar says she's mad."

"Nonsense," the Reverend Niles cut in at once. "She's as sane as you and I. Proceed."

By this time several passersby had gathered, among them Mrs. Fothergay, and lamps were being lighted in the Yorkish Lion Inn. Mrs. Fothergay's tongue was not idle. There was a whispering among the watchers that Marc was innocent as they suspected, and I heard the Reverend MacDonnachie's name repeated.

Miss Rose hurried through the graveyard.

"So here you are, Jamie-boy. Do you know I have been near frantic about you, love?"

Jamie looked up at her, his face tear-stained and older than I recalled.

"I had to be with Marc, up to when they put him away."

"Open the coffin!" the curate ordered the grave-diggers a second time.

This time they drew back and finally the Reverend Niles himself took the spade from one of the men and, as I continued to tear at the slivered boards, he began to pry off the lid while Mrs. Fothergay uttered a shocked gasp. Seeing that the curate and I were in earnest, several men in the crowd came forward and, with their bare hands like myself, did the screeching, tearing job of removing the coffin lid. Everyone moved forward to look into the coffin. We saw the shrouded figure, and a superstitious moan went up through the group as they backed off, slowly, step by step.

I ripped the threads of the shroud, and revealed at last Marc's face and then his body, just as I had seen him during his furious encounter with the Reverend MacDonnachie in the drawing room of Branshaw Hall. The Vicar must have been in a great hurry when he arranged Marc, for the black hair was dishevelled and the collar of his jacket twisted. These small items made him seem doubly dear to me. Gently, fearfully, I brushed back his hair and rearranged his collar.

Someone screamed. Under the bright moonlight his face looked unbearably white and fixed as marble. The curate studied him in what I saw to be growing discouragement.

A woman murmured with the dreadful finality of a requiem: "How peaceful he looks!"

I told myself that he had looked peaceful last night under the influence of the laudanum. Perhaps this might still be the case. I touched Marc's cheek and knew that if he were truly dead it had only been in the past hour, for in spite of his marble look he had none of the rigidity of a corpse. From the tortured sleep of the drug, his close confinement must have produced this coma. The easing of the lines of suffering in his face relieved me of one of my many horrors — that he had awakened in his coffin, and realized his fate. There was still hope. I began to rub one of his hands frantically as I saw the curate doing on his other side. All the while I was staring at his form for any slight sign of life. He was so cold, so very cold! But Marc had grown accustomed to colder temperatures than the rest of us. It would not be the first time his flesh seemed chilly to me.

The Reverend Niles looked up at Rose Keegan.

"If you please, fetch a mirror to apply to his lips. We must try every test. And fetch hot cloths, steaming. They may be of some help in restoring the action of the blood."

She went away at once.

Jamie knelt at the other side of his friend and called softly, as if he expected to entice Marc back. There was a terrible, aching hope in the child's face that kept me at this vain work, for I began to feel the lifeless chill of Marc's fingers creeping into mine.

I had come to the end of my shallow residue of hope. I bent over his hands and wept. The Reverend Niles put one hand upon my shoulder to give me comfort, and others came up, offering their wordless sympathy, but I did not know one touch from another.

Suddenly, there was a stir in the silent group of onlookers, and Jamie, raising his head, caught his breath. At the same instant I became aware of a slight, almost infinitesimal contraction of the muscles in the cold fingers under my hands.

My mind only half registered this movement and I remember thinking with despair that it was the last muscular spasm before the fingers stiffened in death. Then Jamie whispered in religious awe:

"His eyes, ma'am! His eyes!"

The Reverend Niles' voice murmured joyously, "God be praised."

My own eyes travelled slowly, unbelieving, over Marc's still form to his face. His eyes, luminous in the full moonlight, were open wide, and gazing at me. His pallid lips moved as he tried to speak. In the absolute silence of the northern night, we all waited for that word, and what he whispered was, "Anne. . . ."

I leaned over and kissed him and rested my warm cheek against his cold one. I was too overcome even to thank God for this miracle, but the people of Maidenmoor, and especially the good curate Niles, did so for me. They had proven their devotion and friendship in these last few minutes, and were saying all that was in my heart. I looked up at the curate, just for an instant. The Church was in good hands at last. The people of Maidenmoor could thank God for that as well. When my gaze returned quickly to the coffin, Marc had managed a faint semblance of a grin.

"Help me, darling. . . . I was never one for narrow beds."

His words were repeated through the crowd and presently they were all laughing their relief that Marc Branshaw had come back from the dead as flippant as ever.

Rose Keegan made her way through the crowd with steaming cloths but had to set them down to keep her eager, happy nephew from climbing all over his resurrected friend.

Marc's hand sought mine as he said, "I dreamed you came to me."

Yet I had nearly failed him. I blessed his dear confidence in me. I should never fail him again, as long as he lived.

He could not see the crowd around him which was beyond his range of vision, but he sensed their presence and flashed me one of those warm but willful smiles by which he always got his way.

"Anne?"

"Yes, darling."

"I want to be alone with you. Can't we go home?"

"Where is home?" I asked, not caring, so long as he was with me.

With an effort he raised his fingers and touched my lips as he answered softly:

"Wherever you are, love."

"How very odd!" exclaimed Jamie as his aunt finally lifted him off Marc by the scruff of his neck. "He called her *love*, like she be a Yorkshire lad."

About the Author

Virginia Coffman was born in San Francisco, California, and spent most of her childhood in Long Beach. She attended the University of California at Berkeley and in her spare time wrote book and movie reviews for the *Oakland Tribune* and did some acting.

Her family moved to Hollywood, where Miss Coffman gave up thoughts of a stage career and decided to concentrate on writing. She was associated with several major motion picture studios and worked on forty-six screenplays and teleplays.

The author has travelled widely throughout Europe and Hawaii and now makes her home in Reno, Nevada.